PRAISE FOR *THE BLOCKCHAIN SYNDICATE*

"A high-stakes poker game with America in the balance. Bach's thrillers race like Tom Clancy's, and Tamika Smith is as cunning and determined as Jack Ryan."

—**ROBERT DUGONI,** *New York Times* best-selling author of The Tracy Crosswhite Series

"Robbie Bach is a civic leader, technology developer, institution builder, and futurist, but more than anything, he is a storyteller. In *The Blockchain Syndicate*, Robbie—and his avatar Tamika Smith—race to prevent global financial chaos. It is a story of old school espionage and new age cyber-crime. As always in a Bach thriller, democracy hangs in the balance."

—**JASON GRUMET,** CEO, American Clean Power Association; founder, Bipartisan Policy Center

"*The Blockchain Syndicate* is a nonstop thriller filled with rich characters, turnstile plot twists, and powerful human emotions. But it also highlights an existential threat to our country. The budget deficit and the financial risks it poses are a real and present danger to America's future. Tamika Smith is more than just a U.S. senator and a thriller heroine. She represents the leadership we need to end the financial roulette game we are playing."

—**RON CHRISTIE,** former Special Assistant to President George W. Bush; Adjunct Professor, McCourt School of Public Policy, Georgetown University

"Bach's firsthand knowledge of business, politics, and technology explodes across every page, delivering a suspenseful and chillingly plausible thriller that mirrors today's headlines. It's fiction, but barely."

—**CARRIE SCHWAB-POMERANTZ,** Corporate Director

"Be careful! If you pick up this book, you will not be able to put it down."

—**J. LAWRENCE GRAHAM,** author of *Charlotte's War* and *The Hidden Front Line*

"*The Blockchain Syndicate* is fiction, but it's fiction with a purpose. It captures real-world headlines with a frightening fiscal message that resonates even today in the halls of Congress. Bach weaves his technological acumen into a five-star political thriller. Senator Tamika Smith fights a sinister organization that tries to destroy US democracy by creating a financial apocalypse. Her sacrifices to save loved ones and her country kept me fully engaged up to the surprising climax."

—**G. WILLIAM HOAGLAND,** SVP, Bipartisan Policy Center; former U.S. Senate Budget Committee Staff Director; former U.S. Senate Majority Leader, Budget and Appropriations Director

"In an increasingly divided nation, great leaders are called to sustain our democracy. Bach's heroine, Tamika Smith, is one of those leaders. In *The Blockchain Syndicate*, she demonstrates the resilience, principles, and courage required to fight the opportunists that want to tear our country apart for their own advantage. Bach takes us on a rollercoaster ride that is uncomfortably close to reality, demonstrating that there has never been a more crucial time for us to come together."

—**STEVEN OLIKARA,** President and CEO, Bridge Entertainment Labs; Senior Fellow at the Schwarzenegger Institute for State and Global Policy; founder of Future Caucus

ALSO BY ROBBIE BACH

The Wilkes Insurrection: A Contemporary Thriller
Xbox Revisited: A Game Plan for Corporate and Civic Renewal

THE BLOCKCHAIN SYNDICATE

A Contemporary Thriller

ROBBIE BACH

GREENLEAF
BOOK GROUP PRESS

This book is a work of fiction. Names, characters, businesses, organizations, places, events, and incidents are either a product of the author's imagination or are used fictitiously. Any resemblance to actual persons, living or dead, events, or locales is entirely coincidental.

Published by Greenleaf Book Group Press
Austin, Texas
www.gbgpress.com

Distributed by Greenleaf Book Group

For ordering information or special discounts for bulk purchases, please contact Greenleaf Book Group at PO Box 91869, Austin, TX 78709, 512.891.6100.

Design and composition by Greenleaf Book Group
Cover design by Greenleaf Book Group and Adrian Morgan
Cover images used under license from ©AdobeStock.com

Publisher's Cataloging-in-Publication data is available.

Print ISBN: 979-8-88645-400-0

eBook ISBN: 979-8-88645-401-7

To offset the number of trees consumed in the printing of our books, Greenleaf donates a portion of the proceeds from each printing to the Arbor Day Foundation. Greenleaf Book Group has replaced over 50,000 trees since 2007.

Printed in the United States of America on acid-free paper

25 26 27 28 29 30 31 32 10 9 8 7 6 5 4 3 2 1

First Edition

To Roscoe
A friend and companion for life

PROLOGUE

A SPECIAL DELIVERY

In the end, the actual job was easy. When he'd first read the instructions, his reaction had been, "No way in hell I can do that." And now he was doing it. Without a hitch.

What had begun as a simple act of defiance, the proverbial "stick it to the man" moment, had become a mission. An opportunity to change what was wrong in America.

His America.

The nondescript black van was unlocked with the keys in the visor, per the instructions. He followed the directions to the loading dock, carefully adhering to the timing of his trip. 3:45 a.m. wasn't an easy hour for him, but perhaps that was the point. He checked the security cameras as he parked, satisfied they were turned off. As were the exterior floodlights, leaving the parking area inky black in darkness.

Promises kept.

Pulling the metal cart out of the van, popping up its legs, loading the goods, and then rolling the cart up the ramp was really a job for two people. The damn thing was heavy—like moving a football blocking dummy uphill. He almost dumped the cargo as it came over the lip of the shipping ramp but managed to wrestle it back into position.

He laughed quietly to himself. "No harm, no foul, huh."

But better to keep things clean and neat. There was important evidence to preserve, after all.

He checked the luminous dial on his fitness watch to make sure he was still on schedule. Although he didn't know all the details, he assumed there were one or more guards on duty, and the timing was designed to miss them on their rounds. He was worried about darkness, but once his eyes adjusted, there was plenty of ambient light seeping through exterior windows and doors.

Thirty seconds to the elevator. Up two levels.

Down the hall to the right. Wait two minutes before proceeding.

Two more lefts, and he was in position.

Then came the only part of the mission that had scared him. He'd worn special shoes to reduce noise on the polished marble floor, and oiled the wheels and joints on the cart to make sure they didn't rattle or squeak. Out of the darkness to the right, he saw a flashlight sweeping across the room, a circle of yellow reflecting off the walls, creating echoes of illumination. He held his breath and subconsciously sucked in his stomach, as if that would make him harder to see. The light moved away down an adjacent hallway.

More promises kept.

After a few deep breaths, he began the walk out into the cavernous rotunda, wide open and exposed, and put the package on display.

But this wasn't just a Federal Express drop-and-run delivery.

There were very specific requirements for the presentation. A flag draped in a particular manner. Flowers and plants arranged just so. Battery-powered lights deployed to create just the right atmosphere. And a typed note placed so that nobody could miss it.

The moon shone down through the upper windows of the rotunda, creating shadows and shimmering light as it bounced off the beams he'd just arranged. He had no idea who had come up with this macabre display and didn't really care. He just wanted to get in, get the job done, and get out undetected.

He checked his watch again to verify the timing. Spot-on.

He pulled a photo from his pocket that showed how the scene should look. He checked everything to make sure he'd done it right. Then he realized he'd almost forgotten the most important item. He pulled back a white sheet, tucked it in on either side of the box, and then lifted open the top half of the container.

All he got in return was a blank stare.

He wasn't the squeamish type, but shivers ran up and down his spine as her bronze skin reflected in the light and her beautiful eyes bored through him accusingly. The deed had been done by someone else, but he was the delivery boy.

And now a United States senator was on display in a state capitol rotunda.

He didn't have any insight into the grand plan, but he was sure of one thing.

There were other rotundas just like this one.

And they each had a special delivery.

PART I

PLAN FOR A PLAN

So let it rock, let it roll
Let the Bible Belt come and save my soul
Holdin' on to sixteen as long as you can
Changes come around real soon
Make us women and men

—John Mellencamp

CHAPTER 1

OPENING GAMBIT

Aragon High School was built in the early '60s during the explosive growth of the San Francisco suburbs, and its eucalyptus tree-lined entry made it seem more like a community college than one of seven schools in the San Mateo Union School District. The campus included two baseball fields, a football stadium, a track, eight tennis courts, two gyms, a theater, and an outdoor courtyard with swimming pools.

And, of course, classrooms.

For Phoenix Humboldt, Aragon was a sanctuary from a home that had been divided by divorce. Her parents, Johnny and Margaret Humboldt, had separated and subsequently divorced during her freshman year in high school. While they remained friends, her father had moved to Seattle when his startup company was bought out, while her mom remained in San Mateo. The good news was that everyone, including her younger brother, Nathan, had adapted to the logistical arrangements. The bad news was that she felt like she'd lost her home base. FaceTiming with her dad and seeing him on weekends and holidays just wasn't enough. And while Phoenix loved her mom, she recognized she had plenty on her own plate.

Phoenix needed to discover her path forward on her own.

Aragon might seem like a strange place for her to find home. It was a large high school with almost 1,800 students and an ethnic makeup that was evenly split between Latino, Asian, and white students. For her first few months, the crowds of kids seemed huge to her, and it took weeks to find her way around campus with confidence. It was often loud, always in motion, and never boring.

But that was what Phoenix loved about the place. The diversity was energizing, the public school vibe refreshing, and the sense that you never knew what could happen next was the special sauce. She'd found a core group of friends, started running cross-country, and joined the debate team. By now it felt comfortable, like a nicely worn-in pair of jeans.

January 3, 2023, was the first day back at school after the holiday break, and Phoenix was enjoying some cool sunshine in the courtyard next to the swimming pools. She sat on a wooden bench at the top of a large sloping lawn that was surrounded by an elliptical walkway. Trees provided some shade on the northern side of the circle, but the southern side had another grassy area bathed in sunlight. The brightness and shadows were dancing with each other, and the glistening dew added some sparkle.

It was second period—technically a study hall for her—so she was relaxing with a few other students from her English class, pretending to read Eugene O'Neill's *The Iceman Cometh*. The storyline, writing style, and dramatic weariness were depressing, and her mind wandered back to a much more pleasant holiday break.

She and her brother had spent Christmas with her mom's family in Connecticut. She found her grandparents a bit stuffy—I mean who would have thought that her mom was an *Ashworth*? The house had grounds, wings, and riding stables, all nestled into five acres of land surrounded by a stone wall that must have been built a century earlier. Great presents, good food, and love at an appropriate distance.

All fine, but not much joy.

Then they'd flown directly to Seattle to spend New Year's with her father, and the difference was difficult to ignore. Johnny was now in a serious relationship with an Air Force vet and congressional leader, of all things. He'd met Senator Tamika Smith when she'd rescued him from a plane crash at Offutt Air Force Base in Nebraska almost four years ago. They'd reconnected when he moved to Seattle, and the relationship had grown from there. Phoenix struggled emotionally with her father being in love with someone other than her mom—somehow it felt like betrayal. But at the same time, she looked up to Tamika as something of a mentor.

And she was a badass, right?

The Purple Heart decoration was scary but cool. Serving in the US Senate also commanded respect, for sure. But Phoenix was mostly attracted by Tamika's general character. Striking up a conversation or asking Tamika questions she wouldn't dare broach with her parents was easy and natural, and she was also learning from Tamika's civic convictions. Although just in high school, Phoenix was having to grow up quickly because of the divorce, and she was already exploring her own sense of purpose. Seeing past her mom's and dad's role as parents was tough—but with Tamika, the concept of purpose was on display almost every day.

The New Year's Eve party at Tamika's home was an opportunity for Phoenix to be an adult in a protected environment. She'd been to some Aragon parties where there were alcohol and drugs, but she'd always felt the need to stay in control. Now in front of Johnny and Tamika and their friends, she took the liberty of exploring a few cocktails and working the crowd, even joining a conversation on the current federal debt ceiling debate with some of Tamika's Senate staff. Nobody at the party seemed to care. In fact, they treated her like everyone else in the room. Another opportunity for Phoenix to be more of an adult. That included the headache the next morning and the gentle laughter from her dad and Tamika.

The reverie brought a smile as she reread a paragraph from O'Neill for the third time.

"Vanessa, why are we wasting time on this *Iceman* thing? Reading a play makes no sense to begin with, and this one is so confusing and depressing."

Her good friend Vanessa Nathanson was sitting at the other end of the bench and responded with a dour look. "I can't believe you're still trying to read it. I went straight to the SparkNotes."

Bam, bam, bam!

What the hell was that?

Gunfire?

Phoenix instinctively dropped to her knees, crawled under the bench, and tried to process the rasping, rat-a-tat sound of a rifle coming from somewhere above and to her left. She heard the cracking of wood as bullets shattered bench boards and peppered the concrete walkway to her right. She felt Vanessa huddled next to her and could sense her fear.

"Holy shit!" she cried as another round of shots rang out. She tried to roll even tighter into a ball as the bullets continued to ricochet across the courtyard.

Play dead, she thought.

"Just stay down," she whispered to Vanessa as calmly as she could.

Phoenix heard yelling and screaming echoing across the patio area as students ran for cover. Reflexively checking herself to make sure she was OK, she saw flashes from the shooter's muzzle on the school's flat roof.

He was firing down into the courtyard.

"Get down!" she yelled at some other friends huddling across the walkway.

The pelting sound of bullets moved farther to her left, and she saw her classmates dive for cover. The gunfire seemed to encircle them, pinning them to the ground.

In the back of her head, Phoenix heard a voice demanding, *What would Tamika do?*

And then she jumped up to sprint to her friends.

She almost got there.

CHAPTER 2
SOUR NOTES

"From now on, you'll do exactly what I tell you to do."

Enough! That was the first thought that went through Tamika Smith's head as she read the last line of the email—prefaced by an expletive that was both automatic and unnecessary. She had been through enough over the past three years, and this shitty new email missive only added depth to the pit that constantly seemed to swallow her up.

Her mood matched the early morning chill in her Senate office on the north side of the venerable Russell Building. Unlike many of her Senate colleagues, she'd come into the office on January 3 to get a jump start on the new year. The sun was hidden behind lead-dark clouds as snow fell in the gloom. The glow from her computer monitor illuminated the angry scowl on her face. This turn of events was not the hoped-for New Year's resolution she'd imagined. With a grueling reelection campaign behind her and a solid victory ensuring six more years in the Senate, Tamika needed a reset. She had never been very good at self-reflection but had enjoyed the holiday break. She'd spent time with her extended family and recharged her batteries for the challenges ahead.

The email drained the proverbial juice in one fell swoop.

She forced herself up from her beech-colored mortise-and-tenon desk, walked over to a minifridge built into her matching office credenza, and pulled out a sparkling water. She was too disciplined to think about anything stronger, in spite of the situation. Looking out at the thin sheet of fresh snow enveloping the streets and the lit Christmas wreath hung above

Union Station, she recalled family Christmas gatherings with her father, General Frank Smith. Her current mood reminded her of his annual reading of Dickens's *A Christmas Carol.* She felt a bit like Jacob Marley being visited by the ghosts of the past, present, and future.

Her Christmas Past dream was nothing like that of Ebenezer Scrooge's, but she'd definitely had her share of Bob Cratchit moments. Her mother had died of cancer when she was in high school, and her brother was killed in the 9/11 attack at the Pentagon. As a mixed-race woman in the Air Force, she'd suffered her share of racist, misogynist slings and arrows, along with the PTSD that came with three tours in Iraq and Afghanistan. And then there was that horrific night at the hands of a captain at Maxwell Air Force Base that she still tried to bury deep in her subconscious, despite her therapist's best advice.

Her Christmas Present reverie was more balanced. Leading the rescue of 162 passengers after the bombing of a commercial jetliner had brought her national acclaim. Seemingly overnight, she'd gone from being a government policy staffer and Air Force combat search and rescue reservist to an elected US senator from the state of Washington. In the in-between space, she'd found a soulmate, cofounded a political movement called the Lincoln Coalition, helped catch and kill the anarchist Ford Wilkes, and lost a beloved mentor. Highs and lows, love and mourning, redemption and regret.

Life.

And now this email. She had to face a Christmas Yet to Come. With heavy steps, she returned to her desk and reread the message from someone that sent both fear and anguish through her soul. How could it be from Captain Derrick Tomlinson? She'd watched that asshole die.

> "Purple Heart my ass. I know the real story of what happened in Afghanistan. From now on, you'll do exactly what I tell you to do."

"Impossible," she said out loud.

Apparently, her Jacob Marley wasn't dead after all.

"Shit." She slammed the laptop closed, opened her office door, and banged it shut.

• • • • •

The door slam caused her entire staff to jump in unison. Tamika absorbed the shocked looks on their faces and tried to make light of it.

"Shit . . . sorry. Didn't mean to crush the door. I've already had too much coffee."

She noticed the nervous laughs and realized she needed to get them back to business.

"Who's got the briefing for the caucus meeting?"

She led a small group of staffers into her conference room. An oval table that matched the beech furniture in her office dominated the room with just enough space for six chairs on rollers to fit without banging the walls. The area had no windows but was painted a pleasing shade of olive green—an attempt to bring the outdoors, where Tamika loved to run, into her desk-chained life. The walls were covered with pictures from Tamika's service in the military and her first years in office. The centerpiece was a photo of her rescuing a survivor from a ditch at Offutt Air Force Base. It was Johnny Humboldt, now the love of her life.

Tamika was the flag bearer for the Lincoln Coalition caucus—a collection of Democrats and Republicans who believed in focusing on solutions to problems rather than using them for political advantage. As they entered 2023, she knew bipartisan policy was going to get tougher in the new Congress, in particular as members were already thinking about the 2024 presidential election year. New leadership in the House added to the uncertainty. The meeting that morning was about the House Select Committee to Investigate the January 6 Attack on the United States Capitol. Their final report had come out just before the holiday break.

"Ronald Stumper is at it again," began Lisel Orr, the senior legislative advisor for the coalition.

"What BS is he spreading today?" Tamika loathed Stumper but didn't take him overly seriously given the right-wing conspiratorial nature of his views.

"I queued it up on the screen so you could see for yourself. I think we should pay more attention to him. He's trending on Twitter." Orr had over twenty years of experience on the hill and was clearly concerned about Stumper's activities, as well as the general tenor of the new Congress.

Stumper's pompous face appeared on the screen, surrounded by a gaggle of reporters, complete with microphones, Klieg lights, and video cameras in the entrance hall of the Russell Building. Senator Ronald Stumper was seventy-one years old and looked every year of it. He had thinning white hair swept across his head in a comb-over designed to cover up a large bald spot. Red veins hinted at a deep affection for alcohol. But his voice was strong and clear.

"This report just confirms that the socialist Democrats in the House are on a witch hunt—an imaginative effort to paint facts into different colors. We know the truth. The so-called attack on January sixth was nothing more than a group of citizens exercising their Constitutional right to protest a corrupt and rigged election." He held his arms open as if offering something virtuous to God and then closed them in front of him like a prayer.

Tamika whistled. "Well, you gotta give him credit. He's got balls. They say that video doesn't lie—but apparently he doesn't know that."

Orr jumped in. "Senator, with respect, people are listening to him and taking him seriously. I've been following the social media commentary and it's frightening. He's running Trump's playbook and doing it quite effectively."

Tamika ran the video again. "Maybe I've underestimated him because most of what he says seems so absurd. But I guess what I think doesn't matter. If folks are listening to him, he's a problem. Let's not take any chances. Figure out how to get me in front of some journalists on this. With people like him, you have to knock them down early before they get any momentum."

"What's the message?"

"I want to flatten his ass."

CHAPTER 3

ACTIVE SHOOTER

Shit. I'm late.

Margaret Humboldt rushed through the front doors of her startup, Fifth Year, and saw the team waiting for her in the glassed-in conference room across the large office space. She felt the beaded sweat on her forehead and slowed her pace as she crossed the concrete floor of the refurbished industrial building in South San Francisco that had once been a tooling factory. She navigated the desks and workspaces that were arranged in long lines of tables between six-inch square steel beams that ran through the facility. Teams worked across from each other and next to each other, as needed. Even though they'd been able to continue expansion while working remotely during COVID, Margaret believed that culture and teamwork required presence. Everyone was in the workspace Tuesday through Thursday at a minimum.

At five foot seven with natural blonde hair and a well-toned figure, Margaret was a striking woman with an impressive resume. A Harvard graduate and Teach For America alumna, she had spent almost fifteen years focused on her family. She'd supported her ex-husband Johnny's intense drive for success in the startup world, raised two kids, and volunteered locally. It had been a relatively quiet, comfortable time. But simply existing ultimately was not enough for Margaret. She wanted to pursue her love for education and change the trajectory of those who faced challenges early in their lives. When she and Johnny realized they had grown apart emotionally, she knew it was time to resurrect her ambitions.

Freed from the supportive wife role, she'd founded Fifth Year, an apprentice training school where instruction was done online and through mixed reality technology. The program was designed to help kids who didn't need a four-year college education to build skills for a living wage career. Starting an organization from scratch had taken perseverance, concentration, and dedication she hadn't even known she possessed. And it also made her realize why her husband had been so laser-focused on his own startup dream. The divorce had felt like a failure at first, and sometimes late at night when she couldn't sleep, she worried she'd cut the cord with Johnny too soon.

Yes, she missed his adventurous spirit and was a little hurt that he'd found a new love so quickly. She worried about the challenges the divorce brought to her children, Phoenix and Nathan, who were going through the growing pains of puberty. And the pangs of loneliness were sometimes difficult to push aside. But then she came to the office and felt the energy and joy from the new opportunities she faced. She witnessed the life-changing achievements of Fifth Year students. She secretly basked in the warmth of personal success.

She knew their decision had been difficult to make but the right one. In the cold light of day, she and Johnny were both better off as friends.

Now as she regained her composure, she braced herself for another round of strategic planning with her team. The board of directors of Fifth Year had just met in December and approved the 2023 annual budget for the eight-city program. As CEO, her job was to allocate resources and ensure that the money was focused on their key priorities for the coming year.

She pushed the conference room doors open.

It was showtime.

"Margaret, we've completed the opportunity map for expansion and need to make some trade-offs." Her chief financial officer, Michele Delman, launched right in as Margaret sat down at the head of the table and placed her phone next to her. When you arrive late, you have to be ready to go.

"Atlanta, Miami, Boston, and Chicago all meet our entry criteria. We've got good corporate sponsorship across the board, and each of the city governments have lobbied for our services." Delman used her mouse to highlight some key financial projections as she said this. "We can scale our operations to serve all of them—the beauty of our online business model—but graduate placement opportunities are better in Atlanta and Boston."

"You know how much I hate to say no but running students through the program that we can't place in the community is a waste of resources. Let's focus on Atlanta and Boston for now."

"What do you want to say to Miami and Chicago?"

Margaret paused for a moment. How do you call someone who has basically put together a self-funding opportunity to serve thousands of in-need youth and tell them no? "Leave those calls to me. I'll enlist Shea to help us build a bridge for next fall for those markets." Shea Roscovitch led the foundation that provided seed money to Fifth Year as they entered new cities. The Roscovitches had been involved from the beginning, and Shea was almost family at this stage.

Margaret's phone tremored on the table in front of her, and she felt the twitch of her smart watch indicating that a new text message had come in. She consciously tried to ignore the interruption, but the phone and watch continued an avalanche of vibrations.

Sighing, she picked up the phone.

"Oh my God!" she shouted. Then she sprinted from the room.

• • • • •

Some eight hundred miles away, Johnny Humboldt was working from a different conference room with a view of Seattle's Pioneer Square. He, too, was facing challenging decisions.

In his previous life, Johnny had been the business and strategy leader for Cybernoptics, a fledgling company in the mixed reality tech market. Rising to the role of CEO, he'd sold the company to Facebook as they acquired assets to support their shift to the metaverse. While Johnny had helped with the transition, he didn't really understand Facebook's strategy or agree with the Meta rebranding. His pending divorce had also made it difficult to focus on his career. So he'd left Meta as soon as the merger contract allowed and become a free agent.

In the midst of these transitions, Johnny found himself unexpectedly reentering the dating scene. Whenever he thought about it, he laughed.

He'd scheduled a thank-you dinner with Tamika Smith, the recently retired Air Force major who a year earlier had saved his life by pulling him from a ditch after a Boeing 757 crash. An enjoyable night out turned into a romance, and Johnny never had to enter the world of swiping left and computer-generated dates.

Rescued, indeed.

He ultimately joined Tamika's campaign team as she ran to fill a vacated US Senate seat for Washington State. With her victory and subsequent reelection to a full six-year term, he'd officially joined her team as her de facto chief of staff. The new year found him working with the senior staff members evaluating strategic options for the coming legislative sessions, in particular in light of the Lincoln Coalition's agenda.

"What's your view of the House under the Republicans?" Johnny addressed the question to Mark Cavanagh, a political strategist who specialized in the House of Representatives.

"Well, it's definitely not going to be your typical conference. There are rifts between the traditionalists and the Freedom Caucus, to say nothing of the growing schism that runs along Trumpian lines. Holding that group together is going to be very complicated, especially since they only have a slim majority in the chamber. Defections on specific issues will make passing legislation more difficult."

Johnny jumped in. "So that's the crack we need to widen. There've been bipartisan gangs in the Senate for some time—maybe we can go issue by issue and create the same effect in the House?"

"Maybe," responded Lisel Orr with a look of doubt from her Zoom-boxed image, "but roving alliances are more difficult in the House because everyone is always running for reelection. People are more careful about stepping out of line to avoid getting pressured in their next primary."

"Still . . . seems like there is something there we can work with," mulled Johnny.

The door suddenly burst open, startling them all.

"How about a—" Cavanagh began.

"What is it, Stephanie?" Johnny interrupted, seeing the dread on her face.

Johnny's longtime assistant, Stephanie Ramirez, grabbed his computer, which was projecting the Zoom call on the flat panel screen on the wall opposite the window. She jumped over to Facebook and brought up some video. It was shaky cam footage of a large courtyard and pool. She hit the volume button.

A loud staccato *bam*, *bam*, *bam* cascaded and echoed across the brick-walled room.

Johnny froze as he saw a figure sprinting across a grassy area and diving toward some other people. The camera zoomed in erratically, and he thought he saw blood.

He definitely recognized his daughter, Phoenix.

• • • • •

Back in her office, Tamika made a conscious decision to disregard the morning's threatening email. She knew that Captain Derrick Tomlinson was dead. She'd seen his downed bird under attack by the Taliban and watched as an Apache helicopter lit up the whole area in fire and brimstone.

Besides, as a final act of contrition for choices she'd made, she'd visited his grave in Arlington National Cemetery. She knew he was a rapist bastard, but he'd served his country.

She was getting ready to prepare for a Senate Finance Committee meeting when a new email popped into her personal inbox.

The ghost of Derrick Tomlinson. Again.

> "I'm sure you think you can ignore me. But if you care about the future of your new family, you'll reply appropriately. Soon you'll know what I'm capable of. Don't fuck with me."

Who was this jerk?

Her cell phone buzzed.

It was Johnny.

CHAPTER 4

THE HOT ZONE

The triple emergency tone from his radio ended his break.

San Mateo Police Sergeant Marc Sagmoen dumped his coffee cup into the recycle bin and ran to his car, listening intently to the radio.

"All available units, active shooter reported at Aragon High School. See the school resource officer at the Alameda-Woodland entrance. Air is now closed for emergency traffic only."

"One Bravo 12, I'm two blocks out." Sagmoen hit the siren and whipped into a U-turn, heading back down Alameda de Las Pulgas. He was an Aragon graduate and knew the SRO well. Bruce Cohen had been his PONY League baseball coach.

"One Bravo 12, go to channel 9 for the incident commander."

Sagmoen flipped to the frequency. "Sagmoen for Commander Arpin."

"Arpin here. I'm ten minutes out. You own the site until I get there. You know the drill. Keep things locked down until we can assess the risks. Dispatch reports that the shooter is on the south roof firing into the courtyard. Proceed with caution."

"Roger that."

The San Mateo Police Department had done regular active shooter drills, and Sagmoen was well trained. Unfortunately, he knew that didn't mean shit. Every situation was different, and Aragon was a huge high school with an awkward layout that would be tough to secure. He was in charge until Commander Alejandro Arpin was on scene. Whatever he did would likely be second-guessed.

That was how this worked.

He spun hard into the school entry going down the street the wrong way. He turned the car to the left to block the road and put the vehicle between him and the shooter's reported location. The wail of other emergency vehicles in the distance rang in his ears as he cracked his door—this would be a full-blown circus in a few minutes. His job was to make sure there was some organization to the chaos.

Conscious of exposing himself in the open, he ran under a covered walkway to the entrance doorway just as Cohen came sprinting down the stairs.

"Damn glad you're here" was his greeting. Sagmoen knew Cohen well enough to note the distressed, angry look in his eyes.

Cohen continued, "The asshole was firing from the solar panel area on the south side. I've gone through that side of the school and locked the doors to the roof from the inside. If he's still up there, he's trapped. Classrooms are locked down. No shots inside the school."

"What about the courtyard?"

Cohen lowered his head, now with a look of anguish. "As best I can tell, there are about ten students pinned down beyond the pools. The rest managed to get into the trees to the north."

Sagmoen went into command mode. "I assume you have all external doors locked down." It was a statement, not a question. "I don't want anyone in or out of the building just yet. We need to figure out if our sniper is still on-site and active."

"What about the students in the courtyard? We know at least one of them has been hit and is bleeding badly. We gotta get in there and fast."

"Negative, Bruce." Sagmoen understood the desire to act but also knew the protocol backward and forward. "We're going to take a beat to assess the situation. If the shooter is still active, he's going to pick off any EMT folks. We also don't know if there's a partner or if the perp is roaming someplace else in the school."

"So what the hell *can* we do?" Cohen clearly wanted action, and Sagmoen knew how to channel his energy.

"I need you back inside. Door-to-door search in the other wings. The cavalry will follow you in as they arrive."

"I'm on it."

"Watch your six, Bruce."

Other units had now pulled up, including two SWAT trucks. First responders piled out, gathering equipment and looking for direction. Since he was still the senior officer on-site, Sagmoen started issuing orders.

"I want a coordinated breach through the entrance here at the gym, through the southeast entrance, and through the west entrance by the main office. We're going two by two door-to-door to make sure there are no perps and no casualties. Nobody comes out until we give the all clear. The SRO has already begun the search in the north wing. Heads on a swivel. Go!"

He paused to think about what he was missing. "OK, I need a UAS up immediately. I want to know if there's anyone up on the roof or in the courtyard." Drones—or unmanned aerial systems—were now standard issue for many units and were easy to deploy quickly.

As SWAT Commander Arpin rolled up, Sagmoen was on the radio to the California Highway Patrol to coordinate a search with their helicopter units. He was also setting up a perimeter to deal with the press and neighborhood crowds. "I want units on the west side of the school. That's a residential area, and people need to shelter in place until we know what we're dealing with."

Sagmoen then provided his report to Jandro Arpin. "Commander, we've got units going classroom to classroom with the SRO. Should have a drone view in a couple of seconds. Likely some wounded in the courtyard hot zone. Need to get help to them ASAP."

"Great work, Sergeant. Get a team ready to escort EMTs when we get the all clear from the drone. I'll take command until the captain or chief gets here."

Arpin started harnessing the quickly responding units. "Officer Black, I want your sharpshooters with sight lines on the roof and upper windows. Coordinate with the drone operators." He continued in rapid-fire succession. "Butters, I need you managing our ingress point; we need to track everyone going in and out—SMPD, sheriffs, state patrol, EMTs. Keep it to essential personnel for now."

Relieved of direct command, Sagmoen grabbed three other officers with bulletproof vests and moved the recently arrived EMT team through the gymnasium to get as close to the courtyard as possible. He could hear screaming voices from the grassy knoll.

"Jesus, she's bleeding like crazy. Where the fuck is everyone? Help! Help! Oh shit, I think she might be dying."

His radio finally told him what he needed to know.

"Command Center, roof is all clear. No sign of the shooter. Some climbing gear on the south side."

Sagmoen heard Arpin's response. "Sagmoen, clear for EMT escort."

The sergeant was ready. "Our hot zone has a warm path. I've got point. EMTs next. Garcia, Molloy, Reed—cover the rear. All eyes back on the school and the roof. Let's go."

They half ran, half shuffled as a group around the pool up the little rise in the grass, following the sound of the calls for help. The four officers searched the school roof and windows looking for threats, AR-15s moving up and down in sweeping motions. They reached two students leaning over a third, using their shirts to stop the bleeding. A blonde-haired teen was ashen white and only semiconscious. And there was blood everywhere.

He'd seen gunshot wounds before, but Sagmoen turned away.

He had a daughter too.

CHAPTER 5

AN UNHAPPY NEW YEAR

Paranoia was a prerequisite for intelligence work, and FBI Deputy Director Jerry "JJ" Jessup's anxiety meter was approaching the red zone.

Jessup was in his spartan office at the FBI reading through incident reports and intelligence updates from across his sprawling team. As the second-in-command at the FBI he was responsible for all domestic and foreign investigative activities, which afforded him tremendous influence at the expense of enormous headaches. Right now, he was getting more of the latter.

He and his teams were tracking a noticeable uptick in the number of nonlethal crimes. Bribery, extortion, fraud, identity theft—all major felonies and all showing a surge over the last two months. At first, he'd chalked it up to a side effect of the end of the pandemic. But he'd learned the hard way to avoid that trap. If there was a pattern he could identify or an enemy he could see and name, that would indicate some areas for investigation.

Grabbing his third cup of coffee and pivoting from his vintage Air Force–issue wooden desk to face the window, he leaned back in a military green reclining desk chair to continue reading the first report from a task force on the crimes. The summary left him more worried: "The striking red thread tying many of these crimes together is their lack of ownership."

Now what the hell does that mean? Crimes are owned by criminals.

"During interrogations, our suspects talk about a 'grand plan.' But when we press, they don't know anything about the plot or who is leading it. And the online chatter keeps referencing a great mission but with no details."

Shit. So this is some felony QAnon thing? Another jihadist-led group? Something new?

That's just perfect. Déjà vu.

It had taken Jessup eighteen months, thousands of man hours, and some amount of luck to expose Ford Wilkes, an anarchist who had killed thousands in six separate attacks. In the end, Jessup had tracked him to Arlington National Cemetery and killed him in a shootout. His methods might have been questionable, but results mattered. Largely because he took down the top of the FBI's Most Wanted List, he'd been promoted to deputy director. As a former colonel in the Air Force with significant intelligence training, he understood both the value of service and the burdens that commitment brought. His time belonged to the job, sometimes more than to his family.

Jessup knew that in spades.

His phone interrupted his reading. *Damn*, he thought. *All I want is just a few minutes of quiet.*

Annoyed, he answered the phone with a bark. "What?"

"Good to talk with you too," came the response. He immediately recognized the voice of Senator Tamika Smith. When he was a colonel in the Air Force, she had worked for him. Now the tables were turned.

"Apologies, Senator," he said with a bit more respect. "Not many people have my direct line. Happy New Year. I can see you're back to work earlier than most people on Capitol Hill."

"Colonel—I don't have any time for friendly chatter. We've got a serious problem."

He could feel the tension coming through the telephone line. If Tamika Smith was riled up, Jessup knew he needed to focus. "Tell me more, Senator."

"Have you been watching the news from California?" Now he could sense sadness . . . or was that fear?

"Yeah. I hate seeing another one of these school shootings. Makes me sick. There're just too many guns on the streets and no real control. That isn't our jurisdiction, but our local team will support the San Mateo authorities."

"Aragon is where Phoenix Humboldt goes to school." He could hear uncharacteristic emotion in Tamika's voice.

JJ had to pause for a moment to connect *Humboldt* with Tamika. Of course, Johnny Humboldt was her boyfriend. "Oh God, I had no idea, Senator. What have you heard?"

Tamika's voice cracked further. "I still don't have any good information—just some shaky cam video that might be her in the line of fire." She skipped several beats. "And that's only part of the reason I called."

JJ changed approaches. "Come on, Tamika, spit it out. What are you not telling me?"

In a nerve-filled voice, she read him both emails.

"Who the hell is Derrick Tomlinson?" Jessup had been Tamika's commanding officer at Offutt Air Force Base, but they'd never served together in Iraq or Afghanistan.

"He was Captain Tomlinson when I met him as a lieutenant at Maxwell. We had one very bad date."

Jessup could hear the mix of anger and sarcasm but still couldn't make any sense of the conversation. "So this is about . . ." He hesitated, not knowing what to say.

"The next time I saw him, he was firing a machine gun in a downed Pave Hawk in Afghanistan. I rescued his copilot." Another pause. "Left Tomlinson there to die."

Jessup was furiously trying to read between the lines. "You were wounded, right? Purple Heart? And you chose to rescue the other guy—"

Tamika cut in. "Tomlinson raped me."

Jessup was stunned. He knew Tamika's military record well, and there was nothing about a rape. The new data put everything in a very different light. He decided to go slowly.

"And you're sure he died in the Pave Hawk?"

"A hundred percent," she said emphatically.

He blew out a deep breath. "Jesus. Somebody's accusing you of leaving him behind? Blackmailing a war hero and United States senator?"

Silence on the line.

"And now the high school attack makes you think they're going after your boyfriend's kid to apply pressure?"

"Welcome to my world, Colonel."

Deputy Director Jerry Jessup paused for a moment, evaluating a number of factors, including his own objectivity.

And then he made up his mind.

"Meet me at Reagan in an hour. We're going to California."

CHAPTER 6

IN TRANSIT

"Come on, come on, come on" was all she could yell as she slammed her hands on the steering wheel. The other words she used didn't seem to speed up the traffic either. She needed to get to her Phoenix and she needed to get there now.

The Bayshore Freeway was jammed because of an accident near the airport—Highway 101 had been poorly designed and was always a mess—and Margaret knew that side streets were a maze of traffic lights and uncertainty. Her Porsche Cayenne SUV had plenty of muscle and maneuverability but no place to go. Where the hell was Johnny?

"What are they saying? Have you heard from Phoenix?" she demanded, finally reaching him.

"I just get voicemail when I call Phoenix. And the media keeps repeating the same facts," replied Johnny. "Shots fired on the campus. Lockdown in San Mateo. They're keeping the news folks away from the high school. Lots of video of police cars, flashing lights, SWAT teams."

"What about . . . casualties?"

There was a brief but noticeable pause on the line. "Nothing confirmed. But it happened less than an hour ago. Probably too early to know."

"What are you not telling me, Johnny? I know you know something." They'd been married for almost twenty years. She could tell from a waffling tone in his voice when he was holding back.

"Mags—there's some video online . . . it's not easy to tell . . . but Phoenix might have been in the line of fire."

"Noooo." She clicked off the line.

Then she swerved into the median and accelerated up the freeway, her mind racing faster than the SUV. The end of her marriage, the isolation in the pandemic, raising her kids with Johnny in Seattle—all of that was difficult. But she couldn't imagine life without one of her children. If she lost Phoenix, it would be the end.

Shit! She slammed on the brakes to avoid another car veering into the median. She wasn't the only one in a hurry.

Margaret felt the tears rolling down her cheeks, and her vision blurred for a moment. She wiped her eyes with her blouse and regripped the steering wheel.

"Pull yourself together," she said to nobody in particular. "Siri, call Johnny's cell."

"Mags, you OK?"

"Sorry. I don't know why I hung up. Nearly crashed the car."

"I know. I'm going crazy here too. I'm just heading down to Sea-Tac. I'll get on the next flight and be there as fast as I can."

Silence.

"Look, the video is super unclear—maybe it wasn't Phoenix. And even if it was, she could be fine. We've just got to stay positive. Say prayers—and hope."

"Oh Jesus, Johnny. I forgot about Nathan! Have you heard from him?"

"He must be in lockdown. If he's on his phone, he knows."

"I'm just getting off the freeway. Let me call him. I'll text you with any news."

"Love you, Mags."

It was the way he'd ended hundreds of calls during their marriage. Absentmindedly but still caring. Maybe there was still a bit of emotion there.

But she knew it didn't change anything.

• • • • •

The shooting was bringing back horrific memories. Thoughts that therapy could treat but never eliminate. Tamika was a bundle of nerves—an unusual state for someone so used to being in command.

She watched impatiently as Jessup pored through early action reports, facing her in leather bucket seats separated by a pull-out table. Jessup's senior position at the FBI gave him access to a Gulfstream G550, but getting from DC to San Francisco was still a six-hour proposition.

"Shit, JJ, what do you know? This is killing me." It came out angrier than she intended, but she only sort of cared.

"I get it, Senator, but there's nothing we can do from here. The local authorities have locked down the scene, they're gathering the forensics, and they're interviewing everyone in sight. I've sent an agent to the school. We'll know more soon." He raised his glasses, rubbed his eyes, and went back to his laptop. He was an imposing figure, tall with jet-black hair and a full mustache. She wondered how he stayed in such great shape given the pressures of his job.

"How many hit?" She could barely look at him as she asked the question.

He locked eyes with her. "Well, that's the miracle of the day. So far, looks like only one person was wounded. She was sent to the hospital."

She. Oh God.

"Damn it, do you have a name or not?" This time the anger felt justified. Tamika gave him a "don't fuck with me" stare.

He got the message. "Look, I'd tell you if I knew something. Higginbottom is the agent in charge. You know you can trust him. He's going to call us in about fifteen minutes."

Agent Franklin Higginbottom had protected her during the Wilkes anarchist attacks, saving her life not once but twice. But she couldn't calm down until she was sure Phoenix was safe. Tamika stared out the window, searching the cloud layer below for some solace, any solace, but didn't find any silver linings. Although she and Johnny had never discussed it explicitly, it was unlikely she would have kids of her own. That meant Johnny's children were her adopted family, and she would protect them just like her parents had protected her.

Not one more loss, she vowed, hands curling into fists. She'd had too many losses in her life already to bear another. But what would Johnny's kids think if they heard what she'd done in Afghanistan?

As if he was reading her mind, Jessup said bluntly, "Let's talk about the other situation. Your supposedly dead extortionist."

"What's there to know? He raped me. I let him die in a godforsaken place. Now he's haunting me in email. I think that covers it, right?" Hatred, shame, and confusion were all coming through. Sarcasm, too.

Jessup gave her a sour look. "Christ, you came to me for help, and these two things look like they're connected. Let's put the pity party aside and work the situation."

She felt the stinging rebuke and knew he was right, but Tamika wanted to get one thing straight. "Look, the dude is dead. I saw the downed bird he was in get lit up by an Apache—nobody survives that. There's no room in this story for ghosts."

Jessup gave her an appraising look, closed his laptop, and leaned in. "OK, let's go with that. If . . . wait, what was his name?"

"Tomlinson. Captain Derrick Tomlinson."

"If Captain Dickhead is dead, then who's sending you these emails? Did you ever report the rape?"

"No. That just wasn't something a woman in the military could do in 2001."

He looked at her sympathetically, which was worse somehow. As if he knew it—Jessup could always read a room fast—he fired off another question.

"How about the action report from Afghanistan?"

It had been twenty years—Tamika took a moment to think. "My report didn't have any names in it. I was sent out to rescue pilots from a downed Pave Hawk. No reason for me to know who was on it. I didn't know Tomlinson was the pilot until I dove into the Pave. He was firing the fifty cal at some Taliban moving in on them. I don't even think he knew it was me."

JJ seemed to absorb that bit of psychology carefully. "What about the copilot that survived? He must have written a report. Did you know him? Could he have known about the rape?"

Known that I left the pilot there to die?

"I suppose. Tomlinson would have been the type to brag." She let that sit between the two of them—that for a certain type of alpha guy, rape was a braggable offense. "But the copilot didn't even remember the firefight or our extraction. He showed up at my medal presentation acting like I'd saved his life."

"Well, you did."

Maybe. But Tamika knew she'd chosen between the man who was still alive and fighting and the one who was half dead. Her training told her she'd made the wrong choice, even if it had saved the guy's life. And she knew she'd left Tomlinson there to die.

"If it's not in your report and it's not in his report, where the hell did it come from? Who else have you told?"

"Deputy Director Jessup?" A secure video feed interrupted their conversation.

"Agent Higginbottom, what's your sit-rep?" Tamika recognized Higginbottom—wavy brown hair, average height, and built like the middle linebacker he'd been in college. He was sitting at a table in what appeared to be a gymnasium. She could see people rushing around in the background.

"The usual jurisdictional chaos, but things are getting under control. San Mateo PD thinks this is theirs, but they also want our help. When you land, we'll have a better picture of what went on."

"Anything on the victims?" Jessup gave Tamika a sideways glance.

"Just one, and she was sent to the hospital. Haven't gotten an update on her condition, but the EMTs said she'd lost a lot of blood."

"Higgs, I need a name." Jessup put his hand over Tamika's.

Higginbottom looked very uncomfortable, as if he wanted to hold back.

No, no, no, Tamika screamed to herself.

"We know her, sir. It's Phoenix Humboldt."

CHAPTER 7

FIRST RESPONSES

God, I'm going to die.

Pain, everywhere. Blood, tanging in her mouth. Phoenix couldn't speak, she couldn't move, she couldn't feel.

Then the sounds of someone screaming. "Help! Help! Oh shit, I think she might be dying."

Someone moving her onto what must have been her back. A needle prick. Mask over her nose and mouth. A fireman? And why was he yelling at her? *Why can't I hear him?*

Fog began to roll in. Phoenix heard the words "We're losing . . ."

• • • • •

Screech!

Margaret hit the brakes hard at a phalanx of barricades, jamming her forward into her seat belt harness. The roads around the high school were blocked off. In her urgency to get to Phoenix, she'd set aside the small issue of a full neighborhood lockdown. All she could see was a sea of colors, a daylight Fourth of July display of flashing lights from cars and trucks of all shapes and sizes.

She stuck her head out the window and yelled, "My daughter is in there! I need to get to her."

"Sorry, ma'am," came a bossy but polite response from a stout uniformed policeman. "We're still securing the area. You can park in the upper lot and wait. As we clear students, they'll be escorted there."

"Hell you say. I'm not waiting in some parking lot. I need to be with my baby." Mama bear was ready to rumble. She got out of the SUV, leaving the engine running, and tried to push the officer aside.

The police officer held Margaret firmly by the shoulders. "Ma'am, you've got to calm down. I can't let you—"

"Calm down?" she screeched. "I will fucking calm down when I'm holding my daughter." And with that she shoved the officer hard to the right and bolted past the barricade.

That generated an immediate response. Two other officers, hearing the commotion, moved over to block Margaret's path to the Aragon High School entrance.

"Lady, you're not going any farther." This matter-of-fact statement came from an officer who was a foot taller than Margaret and twice the weight. He was in full body armor, complete with an assault rifle, bully stick, and what looked like a mace canister.

"Don't make me use any of this," he said with an edge in his voice.

She was stuck. And with that, an eternally strong woman broke, tears cascading down her face, her sobbing ringing loudly across the approach to the school.

"So I'm just supposed to go sit in a parking lot and wait?" Margaret could barely get it out between sobs. The officers didn't seem to have a good answer for that, just painful vice grips on her arms as they led her back to her car like she was the perp.

The holding pen with other parents was even worse. Cars weren't parked so much as they were abandoned. Even before Margaret got out of her SUV, she was scanning the lot looking for someone she knew. Anyone. Parents were huddled in little circles peering over barriers in the direction of the school. Conversations were hushed, with the occasional outburst punctuating the air.

And then there was no noise at all.

An eerie, quiet hush.

What the hell? Margaret glanced wildly around.

Everyone's attention was on her. Everyone.

Had they heard her yelling with the police? Were they wondering why it took her so long to get there?

What?

Finally, a face she recognized. Margaret rushed over just as Louise Allen, one of the mothers from Phoenix's friend group, raced to her.

"Louise, what do you know? Why is everyone looking at me?"

"Thank God, you're here. They left ten minutes ago."

"What did I miss? Who left?"

"The ambulance—" And then recognition crossed her face. "Oh God, you don't know."

"Don't know what?"

"They just took Phoenix to the hospital."

• • • • •

"Honey, can you hear me?"

The fog was still there but so was a very bright light flicking across Phoenix's face. A spiraling howl of noise. She tried to reply but couldn't get the words out.

What seemed like an hour passed as the haze swirled around her. More light at her feet. She was moving.

"Seventeen-year-old female. Two gunshot wounds, in the arm and lower abdomen. Pulse thready. She's in shock. In and out."

Shock? Of course I'm in shock. I'm dying.

Lots of faces. But they faded to black.

• • • • •

Margaret had been here before.

The linoleum tile that amplified the noise. The waiting area filled with anxiety outside the emergency room. Nurses and doctors crisscrossing the hallway, moving quietly but with singular purpose.

Where the hell was Phoenix?

And was she OK?

An orderly pushed a patient on a gurney, and Margaret did a double take. Phoenix? Before she could check, they disappeared through doors on the other side of the hallway. Nobody noticed the middle-aged woman with her head down and tears welling in the corners of her eyes. Johnny had survived the airplane crash at Offutt Air Force Base—but what if Phoenix didn't?

The crush of silence. The crush of waiting.

Whenever Margaret's mind was cluttered, confused, or conflicted, she would turn to her journal to write out her thoughts, stream-of-consciousness style. That wasn't possible, so she turned to the one source of strength that was always available, no matter what she'd done or what was going on in her life.

Dear God, I know I've been silent for a while—forgive me. But right now I need your help. Phoenix is in surgery—she needs all your love. And the doctors and nurses need your guidance, skill, and wisdom. And I just need the calming presence of your spirit to know that I can get through to the other side.

She paused there, allowing the thoughts and words to come to her.

Why are there so many bad people? Bombers, shooters, terrorists. Why is there so much violence and anger? Why is the world spiraling downward into a pool of hatred? Why does this keep happening to me and the ones I love? I can feel the evil infecting me. I'm afraid of the things that cross my mind. Afraid of what I might do. I love my daughter so much—I'd do anything to save her. How am I supposed to forgive those who trespass against us?

And with those words she realized the real meaning in the prayer. If you would do *anything* in revenge, forgiveness was the toughest test. Translating that from her head to her heart was not a place she could go just yet.

So she waited. For something. For someone.

She knew they were divorced and that they had both moved on. But that didn't change the fact that he was Phoenix's father.

She needed Johnny.

CHAPTER 8
THE GUARDIAN

Bryce Roscovitch was a technical prodigy.

But even this maestro of the computer keyboard was having trouble keeping up with the breaking events and the flood of new information. The attack in California was only a few hours old, and he was already following a host of threads that needed investigation. Proof that when shit hits the fan, it goes everywhere.

Bryce never knew what to call his work area. *Office* certainly wasn't right—that sounded far too corporate and legitimate for his activities—but *cubicle* or *workspace* didn't fit either. He liked the sound of *lair*, but he knew that was a bit too flamboyant since he hardly had a mask or cape or alter ego in the real world. The term that probably fit best was *man cave*, although Bryce's form of escape was more from the world as a whole than from any particular family obligations. Instead of a big TV with chairs, couches, and a bar, his cave was dominated by four large computer monitors, matching tower CPUs, and the elaborate networking configuration required to protect his security business.

He paced behind his customized ergonomic chair, looking back toward the cinder block walls and black-curtained windows that enclosed the basement. He nudged aside a portable whiteboard and took a Diet Coke from the minifridge while stretching his neck and back to relieve some pent-up stress.

Bryce was an internet entrepreneur, but he required no VC funding, no board of directors, and no investor oversight. The dark web dispensed with those niceties as unnecessary constraints in a world awash in opportunities and profit. Bryce had launched his startup business by supplying goods and services to those in need of items that were not readily available in official markets. Put more bluntly, he traded in contraband and activities that were in the gray area. And because of his extreme technical skills, Bryce was great at what he did.

And no matter what others might think about what he did, he was his own judge. He was, he knew, the best.

It was true that two years ago, he'd supplied explosive material to the anarchist who killed thousands of people during what became known as the Wilkes Insurrection. And one of the victims had been Bryce's own father, Charles Roscovitch. The pain and shock of his culpability—especially since he'd been estranged from his dad—moved Bryce to track down the perpetrator and covertly help the FBI eliminate the threat. Permanently.

Even now, though his corrective actions saved thousands of lives, his sense of redemption was incomplete. His self-worth was still a tangled mess of making a living the best way he knew how and using his talents to make things "right." He'd gone from being completely agnostic about who he worked with to being highly selective about each opportunity. And the principles involved in making those judgments could only be reconciled in Bryce's head. He loved fantasy adventure books and identified with both Robert Louis Stevenson's Captain Flint and the legendary Robin Hood.

A pirate guardian angel.

The complex mélange made decision-making messy.

Right now, he was on the side of the angels. His father had made billions through an electronics company he'd founded, and now his mother, Shea Roscovitch, was investing that money in causes she thought were important to the future of the country. That included Margaret Humboldt's Fifth Year initiative as well as Tamika Smith's Lincoln Coalition. As penance for previous sins, Bryce had become the unacknowledged and self-proclaimed digital watchdog for both families. He had a phalanx of AI bots and algorithms deployed to monitor their physical, financial, and technical safety. And in the past two weeks, all sorts of alarm bells had been ringing.

First, there had been a flurry of suspicious activity in Tamika's email accounts. Someone was sending messages to her private email while hiding the IP source and related servers. Although phishing, malware, and other social engineering efforts were common on most consumer email platforms, IP masking was a higher art form. At first, Bryce avoided reading the actual messages—he now had an increased sense of decorum, especially with his own family—but as the efforts continued, he was compelled to dive in.

"Jesus," he said to himself. "What the hell did she do in Afghanistan? I thought she was a hero." He pulled his hands away from the keyboard to ponder the possibilities.

"I don't know, Bryce, but you certainly know a lot about blackmail, and she has someone digging in." He had a bad habit of talking to himself in the third person—but it helped him sort through knotty problems.

Then the shooting at Aragon sent him into overdrive. He'd never met Phoenix Humboldt, but he'd seen her on security video and tracked her progress from middle school into high school. Keeping a teen safe in today's digital world was complicated, both because they were more active and because they were more digitally savvy.

He put his computing power to work on the Facebook video of the shooting. "A little advanced facial recognition should do the trick. Zoom in, enhance, process." He narrated the entire sequence. He did a bit more digging on the video and didn't like the results.

"Fuck," he said. It was definitely Phoenix.

Bang. He hit the table with both fists in frustration. The keyboards and monitors bounced. "Hit twice and bleeding badly" was the latest report. Things like this weren't supposed to happen on his watch. After all, he was guarding over all of them. He was responsible for their safety. There could be no redemption if he failed in his penance. And Bryce hated failure.

As his heart rate settled, he admitted that he could do all the analysis he wanted, but there was no way for him to help Phoenix right now. That was up to the doctors and nurses. He switched over to the San Mateo police frequencies to monitor their response. Then he sat back and stared at his screens, searching for an answer.

After about sixty seconds of nothing, he grabbed a pad of paper and jotted some notes down—an old-school habit Bryce had maintained despite his technical prowess. The shooting raised a whole set of questions, each with a branching series of concerns:

1. FBI and local police?

Bryce knew he could hack into law enforcement databases way easier than they would like. More information would be coming soon, and he needed to know everything they knew.

2. Shooter? Location?

It seemed the perp had gotten away from the scene—but Bryce didn't think anyone could hide from him for very long. There was no such thing as being off Bryce Roscovitch's grid.

3. Phoenix status?

He could get the information on her physical health from the EMT data or the hospital but had limited tools to ensure her safety once she was there. He'd have to find another way to support the police on that front.

4. Connections…

Here Bryce set down the pen, unsure what to jot down—but he didn't believe in coincidences. Even if he couldn't see a direct line between the blackmail and the shooting, it could hardly be accidental that Tamika Smith and the Humboldts were once again involved in trouble at the same time.

His brain told him he was doing everything he could. But all his senses were tingling. A nagging sense of helplessness made him pay attention to the unwritten warning signs. This was bigger than just a blackmail scheme.

"Come on, Bryce, you've got to dig in," he said. Now he was Bryce the tech-savvy superhero again, ready to lend the cops a hand. They were always a few steps behind.

An AI bot from one of his tracing systems dinged, indicating that something unexpected had happened. It was a tracker he had on Johnny Humboldt's activity.

"Oh shit" was all he could say. Johnny was headed the wrong way. And with the wrong people.

CHAPTER 9

CRIME SCENES

In his heart, he knew it was Phoenix.

Johnny Humboldt exited from Alaska Airlines Flight 1178 in San Francisco's Terminal 2. For once, his thoughts on the flight had not been dominated by potential turbulence or mechanical problems. He'd left his fear of flying behind when he boarded the plane. Instead of the usual email cleanup or watching a TV series during the flight, he'd stared out the window, thinking only of Phoenix.

In his mind, he was trying to convince himself that the figure running across the courtyard—the one that was wounded and bleeding—wasn't his daughter. But the way she ran, the bobbing of her hair, the slashing of her arms—he recognized all of them from her time running track. It was as if she were sprinting down the straightaway for the lean at the finish line, but instead she was sliding to cover her classmates.

He didn't want to accept the truth.

Freed from the physical and emotional confines of the plane, he hurried down the terminal passageway, determined to get to his baby as quickly as possible. The airport was filling up with passengers getting ready to make the end-of-the-day trip to wherever they called home. They were rushing down the recently remodeled concourse, occasionally ducking into one of the many boutique shops and fast-food outlets along the way. Johnny was laser-focused on the exit but felt like a salmon struggling upstream as he navigated his way out.

A text from Margaret confirmed his worst fears.

San Mateo Medical Center. In surgery.

He sent a quick text to Tamika telling her he'd landed and was headed to the hospital. He promised to call when he knew more. He veered to the right to clear the security area. As he walked through the double set of glass doors that freed him into the wild, he was greeted immediately by an attractive red-haired woman in a dark blue pantsuit and maroon scarf.

"Mr. Humboldt?" She looked Johnny up and down and seemed to be comparing him to a photo on her phone.

"Yes, that's me," Johnny confirmed. The woman flashed an ID embedded into a leather wallet.

"My name is Special Agent Blakely Owens." The voice was confident and commanding. "Please follow me."

Johnny paused for just a flicker to ask, "Where are we going? I'm in a hurry to be with my daughter. She was hurt at her school." He realized how weak that sounded, but saying she'd been shot by a terrorist seemed a bit over the top. He found himself following the agent through the crowd, as if tied by a cord.

"Believe me, I know all about your daughter. Deputy Director Jessup sent me here to escort you to the hospital directly."

Damn, thought Johnny. *Jessup again.* He was really on his game to be involved already and offering help.

"How'd you know the flight I was on?" He knew it was a lame question as soon as it came out of his mouth, but he just couldn't get over the surprise greeting party.

"We're the FBI, sir." Agent Owens flashed a smile. "Just follow me down the escalator. Our car is right out front."

Johnny went along with her down the moving stairs, past the baggage claim area, and out through the sliding glass doors. It was a bit dark under the overpass of the roadway above, but a black SUV was parked in front of the terminal, waiting. Agent Owens opened the rear side door for Johnny, then ran around the back of the car to hop in beside him. She offered him a bottle of water for the journey. After taking a big sip, Johnny saw a much larger man in the driver's seat.

"Let's roll," said Owens with a hint of a grin at Johnny. "We have a schedule to keep."

• • • • •

Deputy Director Jerry Jessup and Senator Tamika Smith arrived at Aragon High School at dusk. The kaleidoscope of lights, a beehive's worth of uniformed activity, and the Klieg spots from what seemed like every news service in the country had turned a thriving high school into a disorganized carnival.

"What more do we know, Higgs?" Jessup quickly scanned the chaos, recognizing that there was more order than met the eye. Law enforcement was at work.

He'd been in regular communication with Special Agent Franklin Higginbottom as his team worked with the local police to scour and catalog the scene. A command center was set up in the main gymnasium, and Higginbottom met them at the door. They walked in between foldout tables filling up with computers, TV monitors, printers, and other equipment. Extension cords, surge protectors, and additional electronics gear were strung like spaghetti across the gym floor. They found some privacy in a PE instructor's office.

Higginbottom got right to the point.

"Based on San Mateo PD's report, this wasn't a random shooting. This was well planned, carefully orchestrated, and precisely executed."

"Shit. A professional." Jessup glanced over at Tamika to assess her reaction. His gaze was met with a cold stare. Determination or shock? Probably a bit of both.

"Take us to the shooter's nest, before it gets too dark."

"Follow me." Higginbottom grabbed a flashlight and led them out of the gym.

They went down a wide corridor lined with lockers separated by classroom doors. The overhead lighting was on, casting some shadows across the hallway. They went up a back stairwell for several flights and pushed through a metal fire exit door at the top. They emerged onto an asphalt-and-gravel roof pockmarked with ventilation ducts, exhaust pipes, air-conditioning units, and two other door areas. The latter looked like little huts on the flat canvas of the roof. Shadows from the setting sun added hidden figures that seemed ready to jump out and shoot. After a reflexive pause to secure the area, Higginbottom led them over to the edge of the south building roof, which was covered with solar panels.

"He shot from right here." He turned on the flashlight to expose the area. "You can see how the dirt and grime have been disturbed. We also found a shell casing he missed when he policed his brass. It bounced under a solar panel. We'll get ballistics and forensics to look at that more closely. Looks like he was using a HK417 with .308 Winchester ammunition—plenty of firepower. He had a stock rest here on the parapet—you can see the marks—and a perfect view of the whole courtyard."

Jessup leaned over the edge of the roof, peering into the quickly darkening grassy area below. A herd of police were sweeping the turf and the sidewalks, marking spots with little numbered triangle signs, indicating places where shots had hit home. Powerful stadium lights were being set up in preparation for a long night of bag-and-tag work.

"That's high-end military-grade equipment. How many rounds?" Jessup's level of anxiety was rising as the circumstances became more clear. He noted that Tamika was intently staring down, likely processing the implications.

Higginbottom responded, "We think he got off about sixty shots, but we'll know more as the team finishes the canvass."

Tamika jumped in. "That's a lot of ordnance. How many targets were in the courtyard?" She sounded like she was back in the military.

"Again, we're still piecing that together, but we've interviewed twenty-seven students so far who were in the area and saw the shooting."

"How'd he exfil?" Jessup was wondering how the shooter had managed to get away undetected, but Tamika had beaten him to the question.

"Well, that's the creative part," Higginbottom said. "Take a look at this."

He led them all the way across the roof, zigzagging through a cornfield of solar panels to the far edge of the building. A series of ropes were attached by carabiner to the base of a power unit.

"He rappelled down the side?" Jessup felt a certain amount of admiration. He pointed farther south. "Once he was on the ground, he could jog through those trees."

"That's what we're thinking. That's Woodland Drive—from there he could wander back through the neighborhood side streets or jump on to Alameda de Las Pulgas. That's practically a superhighway to anywhere."

"What about school security footage?" Tamika again.

"Yeah . . . well . . . the security system was shut down for exactly fifteen minutes on each side of the shooting. The tech nerds tell me it was hacked from an outside IP address and the timing was down to the second."

Jessup turned to Tamika. "On the plane, I was thinking this was a targeted hit." His mind was still working the Tamika blackmail discussion and the threat to Phoenix. "But he'd have used a different weapon and only fired a few times. This looks more like a mass shooting. Except it was executed by a professional with significant support."

He gave Tamika a meaningful look. "You thinking what I'm thinking?"

Tamika grimaced. "Yeah. How the hell did he miss?"

CHAPTER 10

A VALLEY STARTUP

Web 3.0.

It was a buzzworthy phrase that meant various things to different people. For some it was a clarion call for independence from big tech and the dominance of established internet platforms. For others, it was a way to disintermediate the central institutions that provide structure and order to the economy. When integrated with blockchain technology and artificial intelligence, Web 3.0 was the inevitable future and the next pathway to fame and wealth. In the rarefied air of Silicon Valley and its venture capital hallways, if you wanted to be the next Elon Musk or Marc Andreessen, you were either building a Web 3.0 service or providing the underlying AI technology to bring it to life.

Lee Bowen was already a highly successful venture capitalist, having worked for multiple Silicon Valley funds before forming his own investment company. Unlike some in the Valley, Bowen didn't pretend he understood the deepest parts of the technical specifications. Instead, he specialized in financial structures, valuations, and deal-making. His business partner, Ely Basof, was the computer science and engineering expert. Basof was a hardcore programmer with a deep resume in product creation and development leadership. When Bowen and Basof were considering an investment, they each had their spheres of excellence, making them a strong team.

The two venture capitalists had met during one of Bowen's early successful investments—a company that made Basof rich as one of the cofounders and netted Bowen a 7x return. When they agreed to join forces, they joked that they were the "killer Bs" in the Valley and named their firm B^2 Ventures. Like many in the VC business, Bowen was driven by the capitalist urge to generate transformational wealth. But that's where his vision diverged from the norm.

For Bowen, wealth wasn't about racing high-end sailboats, funding endless nonprofits, meddling in politics, or firing rockets off into space. Since he was single, he didn't even have anyone with whom to share the money or collect on his eventual estate. People had doubted his skills every step of the way—he'd been labeled an average student in high school, struggled through Princeton as an undergrad, and got into the Wharton MBA program through his parents' influence. Even in the VC community he was just another guy. None of his teachers or peers saw what he knew: that he was exceptional. Leaving the comfort of his established VC firm to form B^2 was a big risk, but he knew he could never rise to the very top within the established community.

What Lee Bowen really cared about was winning—climbing the financial hill so that everyone in the Valley would look up at him and know he was the king. And he knew how people in the Valley measured success. Wealth accumulation was the only metric that mattered. For him, anything that got in the way of this objective needed to be set aside or destroyed. He had to prove himself worthy.

Yes, B^2 was a vehicle for continuing to build his financial empire, but he had a more bold and purposeful long-term mission. He needed to remove all the perceived obstacles that could get in the way of his financial crusade. And in his mind, government oversight and regulation was a seminal problem. With a personal portfolio in the hundreds of millions, and certain overseas investors chomping at the bit to achieve similar outcomes, his well-funded mission was to remove those obstacles so that he could accumulate even more money. Because that is what it took to win.

To win everything.

To that end, he'd recently launched a subversive, career-defining initiative. His organization had been steadily expanding its activities, mostly in what he categorized as harmless white-collar crimes. He had used these early missions as an opportunity to test his decision-making structure and iron out some of the bugs in the process. Since he'd never met or talked with any of his fellow syndicate members, creating a culture of discipline and execution was problematic.

But the early efforts had gone remarkably well, encouraging him to extend and expand his ambitions more quickly than expected. In startup terms, he'd gone from minimal viable product (called an MVP) to a full product launch, taking the risky step of skipping over many of the alpha and beta phases of development. Somewhat predictably, his first major operation had gone pear-shaped in a hurry, bringing the FBI into his orbit long before he was ready.

Holy shit, nobody was supposed to die!

His email gambits and the high school shooting had flushed Senator Tamika Smith and her lover, Johnny Humboldt, out into the open. That was right on plan, but he should have considered the potential for FBI involvement. Why had his contractor hit the girl? That wasn't part of the mission spec. If she died, the FBI would make sure someone paid.

Sitting in his stylish B^2 Ventures office, he tried to tamp down the anxiety by remembering what he'd already achieved. The teak furniture was always polished to a pleasant gleam. The tombstones—Lucite mementos from every deal he'd ever completed—covered the credenza to the left of his desk. He walked over to admire them and the pictures of famous people he'd met along the way. He knew it was vanity to collect the photos and display them, but he couldn't resist. They had meaning to him.

As he returned to his desk facing the peaceful panoramic view of San Francisco Bay, someone knocked on the door.

"Come," he said a bit brusquely, bristling at the interruption.

"Sorry to barge in, Lee." It was his executive assistant, Ellie.

"What is it?"

"There are two DocuSigns in your inbox that need attention today—Ely has already signed."

"I'll get to it." He immediately regretted the dismissive tone.

"Are you OK, Lee? Anything I can do to help?"

"No, no, sorry. I'm fine. Just a little tired." The last thing he wanted was Ellie or anyone else getting closer to his affairs.

"Let me know if you need anything . . ."

He faked a smile and nodded. "Will do."

Allowed to return to his unanticipated FBI problem, he couldn't stop the anger continuing to well up inside him—anger usually reserved for some subordinate who'd done something particularly stupid. Anger that came from his childhood. Anger he'd learned to camouflage on the outside but never actually conquered internally.

"Fucking hell," he said quietly, but with passion. He whipped his hand around and knocked two of the tombstones to the floor, cracking one in the process.

As if a release valve had sprung, he took a deep breath and then surprised himself with a belly laugh. That wasn't the first time he'd broken a little glass. While he didn't have anyone to yell at for the mistakes, it also meant that the three-letter authorities would hit a dead end too. He'd have to do what he always did when someone challenged or ignored him. Channel the anger.

What was it Robert Burns said about the best-laid plans of mice and men?

Bowen just needed to shift into a higher gear.

CHAPTER 11

IN THE WIND

Tamika's private phone rumbled in her coat pocket. A quick glance told her it was Margaret Humboldt calling. She stepped away from the group.

"Margaret, what's the news on Phoenix?" No salutation or introduction was necessary between them.

"Thank God you answered." Margaret's voice was hushed, but the anxiety was palpable. "She's still in surgery. I can't get any information here. I suppose you're back in DC, but I thought you might be able to break through the bureaucratic clutter."

"I'm actually in San Mateo. I flew out here with the FBI when we heard the news." In fact, she was back in the gymnasium watching the sound and the fury as police, first responders, school officials, and the Feds tried to bring order to the buzz of activity.

"The FBI? Was this a terrorist attack?" She could hear the anxiety in Margaret's voice, even some panic.

Tamika paused to consider her options. She and Margaret had a mostly friendly rapport despite Tamika's relationship with Johnny and his children. She wanted to be straight with her, but she couldn't go into the full story. She also didn't want her to worry that the shooting was more than it was—more than enough of a tragedy already for a mother.

No, she thought. *Just keep it simple for now.*

She went with a standard PR response that was mostly true. "They're here to help the San Mateo PD, Margaret. These shootings are always complicated, and the FBI has resources that can accelerate the investigation."

"Well, can they use some of those resources to find out how my daughter's doing? And while they're at it, can they manhunt the asshole who did this?"

Tamika smiled in spite of the situation. "I'm with you, Margaret. I'll see what I can do." She hesitated for a split second and then went ahead. "Can you have Johnny call me when he has a minute?" She hadn't heard from him since his short airport text.

"He's not here yet. I assumed his flight got delayed, or he didn't get my message about the hospital and went to the high school. I've tried to call him, but he must've left his phone in airplane mode or something stupid like that. You know how he is about flying."

Tamika paused for a split second. "I'm sure that's what's happened. Things are crazy here at the high school—and I doubt the police would let him through the perimeter. I'll track him down and get him over to you." Inside, her stomach started turning.

"Thanks, Tamika. And tell your FBI friends to get me some information!"

"Will do. Talk soon." She hung up and made her way back to the gymnasium command center and found Higginbottom talking by radio with the team collecting evidence in the courtyard.

"Agent Higginbottom?"

"Franklin is fine, Senator. What can I do for you?"

"Tamika works," she responded in kind. "Can you check and see if Johnny Humboldt has shown up at any of the perimeter checkpoints? He was flying down from Seattle, but his ex hasn't seen him at the hospital. He should have been there a while ago."

"Give me a sec and I'll find out." He turned away, picked up the radio, and broadcast a system-wide request for information on Johnny. She could see him nodding a few times as responses came in.

Tamika's stomach was now in full rumble mode. It wasn't like Johnny to go incommunicado—he hated being disconnected, and she'd never seen him use airplane mode. She knew his plane wasn't delayed, and he'd been to SFO hundreds of times, so he knew the drill.

Higginbottom returned. "Nobody has seen him, ma'am. Doesn't mean he hasn't been here. Things are still a bit hectic out there. What flight was he on?" He waved her over to a computer.

Tamika consulted her text stream with Johnny. "Alaska 1178—but I know it arrived safely—he sent me a message from the gate."

After a bit of keyboard whacking, Higginbottom responded, "No unusual police activity at SFO, and no traffic issues reported in the area."

Tamika didn't have to say it. She and Higginbottom just stared at each other.

Where the hell was Johnny?

• • • • •

Bryce Roscovitch knew part of the answer.

Instead of heading south from the airport toward San Mateo and the hospital, Johnny had gone in the opposite direction toward San Francisco. His AI system had detected the inconsistency, so Bryce backtracked to see what had happened. He hooked into airport security cameras and was able to follow Johnny all the way to the curb, with a red-haired woman and a black SUV. Naturally, no plates.

He followed the SUV using Cal Trans cameras on US 101 but eventually lost it in the San Francisco jumble. He went old school and pinged Johnny's phone for another fifteen minutes, which got him as far as the Golden Gate Bridge. Then the signal died. Either he'd ditched the phone or turned it off. Bridge cameras for a few more miles, and then the SUV exited the freeway headed east.

Where the hell's he going? That's wine country. And who's the redhead?

"You can't lose him, Bryce." Back to talking out loud. "You let Phoenix get shot. You can't let Johnny disappear."

His alter ego got right to the heart of things. "First things first. Is there any chance that Johnny is off on his own? Could he have been involved in any of this?"

"Johnny? He could be a bit self-centered, but there's no way he'd hurt his daughter or leave his new love behind."

The logic flow continued. "So that tells you that the redhead was up to no good. You just can't trust a redhead."

Politically incorrect, but it eased a bit of tension. "So . . . that means he's been . . . kidnapped? His daughter attacked so that he comes out in the open? Seems like he was already an easy target in Seattle, so why go through all the effort to smoke him out? Either way, he's clearly been taken."

Bryce began rapidly keyboarding his way across the Sonoma and Napa Valleys. There must be a destination there that made some sense. Maybe you could hide him in a wine cave or an abandoned vineyard, but it'd be easier to use a warehouse in South San Francisco.

His virtual friend struck the right chord. "The only reason to go there is for more privacy—to get away from the big city and all the security. Cameras are bad for kidnappers."

"OK, but where do you go next?"

Airports.

I'm an idiot, Bryce thought. Both Sonoma and Napa have private airports with way fewer people and less security. Big private jets flew in and out of there all the time.

Even if you're flying private, a flight plan has to be filed. Bryce dug into the data for both airports. After several queries, he found the answer in Napa. A Bombardier Global 8000 had just departed with a routing to Casablanca. The security footage from the airport made it clear that the redhead and a much bigger dude had lugged another passenger up the boarding ladder into the plane.

Bryce didn't know shit about private airplanes, but a quick internet search told him that the 8000 could take these creeps anywhere—and fast. This plane was a beast, and not cheap. Whoever had taken Johnny had the resources to do just about anything they wanted.

With a bit more research, he realized that the flight plan created more complexities. Every flight had to use the eAPIS system to file a manifest declaring all passengers with the Customs and Border Patrol. There also had to be an FBO (which stood for fixed base operator) to receive the flight at its destination and arrange for customs formalities. Finally, there was the actual flight plan. Any changes had to be coordinated with air traffic control, especially for flights going across the North Atlantic, where there were areas without full radar coverage.

Any deviations from the manifest, prescribed flight path, or radar checkpoints would lead to an immediate radio inquiry from the relevant air traffic control center. A lack of response or an unsatisfactory answer would lead to predetermined actions, including scrambling fighter jets. Ever since 9/11, the authorities tracked planes very closely and did not hesitate when something unusual took place. The kidnappers would need to avoid all these systems.

That brought Bryce back to the Bombardier flight with what looked like Johnny Humboldt on board. While the plane's path was now known, several critical questions remained.

Bryce pushed the keyboard and mouse away and tapped himself on the head as if to knock some sense into him.

"Who the hell has him? And why Morocco?"

CHAPTER 12

THE COMMAND CENTER

"So what the hell's going on?"

The anger in her voice was intentional, but Tamika Smith was losing control of her emotions. She was grateful that Jessup had jumped into the investigation and taken her with him to California. Now she'd seen the shooter's nest and the blood where Phoenix had been shot. The new love of her life was missing, and nobody knew if Phoenix was going to make it. Even Tamika, who was accustomed to incredibly stressful situations, was being pushed over the edge.

FBI Deputy Director Jerald Jessup's response didn't alleviate her symptoms.

"Right now, you know as much as we do. We have a bunch of data points but no real information. It's our job to step back and put the pieces together." His tone was neutral, as if they were having a chat at a dinner party. They were still in the command center in the gym, surrounded by a swirl of law enforcement people who were suddenly aware of the commotion.

"Step back? Really? That's your strategy?" If looks could kill.

"Senator—"

"Don't *Senator* me. You know damn well that 'stepping back' isn't going to wash. And if you expect me to sit and wait for you to figure things out—well, you know me well enough to realize how that's going to end."

Even Tamika thought she might have gone too far. With her experience in the military and the Senate, she could deal with personal attacks. But her love for Johnny was visceral, and Phoenix felt more and more like her daughter. The emotions were stronger than she'd expected.

JJ just glared at her, the red-faced anger rising quickly. Tamika knew she was making a public scene. Higginbottom watched from his computer table with a worried but bemused expression on his face. The entire command center had gone from the cacophony of a Turkish bazaar to the solemnity of a church service. Some pretended to look busy, while others froze in motion. All that was left was the background computer buzz and the apocalyptic glow of the screens.

Jessup broke the silence. "Come on, work with me a little. We've got data gathered from the courtyard and up on the roof. We don't have any video here, but we're doing a full screen on street cameras in the neighborhood. The computer nerds are trying to backtrace the lockout of the school security system. The neighborhood canvass will give us more. Somebody had to see the guy on the way in or out. We'll be on his ass soon."

Tamika did like Jessup and she respected him, but he still made her bristle. They had a history.

"Look, you and your agents need to follow your protocols and pursue your evidence. I get it. That's good investigative work that has to be done. But you know about the emails. Phoenix is in surgery. Johnny is missing in action. And I'll do whatever I have to do to protect my family. My entire family. So get on with your work and just make sure you stay the hell out of my way." She glared straight at him, no longer a subordinate, daring him to respond.

She wasn't exactly sure what she was trying to accomplish, but it sure was satisfying.

And with that she was gone.

• • • • •

"Get that smug look off your face," JJ said quietly, deflecting his anger with Tamika back at Higginbottom. To his credit, his lead agent responded quickly.

"Sir, we've analyzed the shooting pattern from the courtyard. I think you'll find this very interesting."

JJ walked over to a fifty-five-inch TV screen that was set up on a portable stand around what usually served as the free-throw line of the gym. Higginbottom brought up an overhead view of the courtyard.

"Each of these figures represents where the students were when the shooting began as best as we can determine. And the red dots indicate our estimate of where each round hit."

JJ looked at the images and quickly grasped the main points. "The guy was a professional. The pattern is almost a perfect semicircle. Like he was going back and forth, mowing the lawn with his shots."

"Exactly," Higginbottom said. "But they don't look like they're really directed at any of the people in the yard."

"Tell that to Phoenix Humboldt. Have we heard from the hospital?"

"Nothing yet. In surgery." He skipped a few beats to honor the seriousness of that situation before continuing. "But I don't think she was really a target."

"You'll have to explain that one to me. The paramedics told us she was unconscious and losing a lot of blood."

"See, that's the thing. I think she did something the shooter didn't expect." With that, he grabbed the computer mouse and traced a line from one bench to another across the courtyard. "In the middle of the shooting, she ran from this bench over here—which is just outside the line of fire—and crossed through the shooting pattern here to the other bench."

"And that's when you think she got hit." Jessup completed the thought for him.

"You bet. There's a small gap in the shot pattern right there. Why the hell was she running in the middle of a shooting?"

Jessup paused. "She was found close to some other students, right?"

"Yeah . . ." Realization spread across Higginbottom's face. "Holy shit. She ran and dove on top of them. You think she was trying to protect them?"

Jessup nodded his head. "Does that sound like someone else we know?" He tipped his head toward the doors. "I know a lot of heroes, thank God, but that can also get you killed."

"You gonna tell the mom?"

"Are you kidding? Not my job."

Then he added, with a bit of satisfaction, "But I'll tell our hero and let her decide."

CHAPTER 13

UPON FURTHER REVIEW

Based on the early flight data, the Global 8000 was indeed headed north into Canada, seemingly on the polar route to North Africa. There wasn't much Bryce could do about that at the moment other than track the plane's progress and see if Casablanca was actually the correct destination.

He returned his attention to the San Mateo PD and FBI investigations into the actual shooting. Hacking into their systems wasn't a huge issue for Bryce, but he had to be very careful not to overstay his welcome. It was easy to leave unintended digital footprints. He'd barely escaped from the FBI's investigation into the Wilkes Insurrection, and he didn't want to tempt fate twice. His background contained plenty of sins that the authorities would love to prosecute.

After reviewing the data, he had no issues with the FBI's conclusions—a single, professional shooter on the roof. The rope-assisted evacuation over the side was equally obvious. Watching the shaky cam video of Phoenix getting hit was heart-wrenching, but it didn't immediately lead to any obvious insights into the identity of the shooter or his motives. All of which left Bryce with three important areas for investigation.

First, he would dig into how the school security cameras were turned off. The locals and the Feds were on that trail too, but Bryce knew from experience he would be faster and get further. Turning off the cameras was not difficult to do technically, but masking your footprints was not easy. Bryce assumed he'd eventually be able to trace the activity to a source, but that work would take some serious computing power and time.

The more immediate task was to clean up the Facebook video that showed some brief glances of the shooter on the roof. He also started accessing neighborhood security cameras—the ubiquitous Ring, Nest, and other cameras that the police couldn't use without permission or probable cause. If the perp had gone through the neighborhood or headed straight back to Alameda de Las Pulgas, maybe Bryce could find a clean image. In both cases, the ultimate goal was to do some facial recognition to make an identification.

Bryce pulled himself out of his chair and grabbed a bag full of mixed nuts out of the cabinet. Leaning down, he grabbed yet another Diet Coke in preparation for what he knew was going to be a long session. The snacks were a nervous habit. The drink was a functional necessity.

Three hours later, around midnight in his office cave, he had the beginnings of a very interesting answer. The Facebook video never provided a clean facial view—just a shortish figure dressed in a black body suit and a hoodie. Interesting but not useful. The neighborhood cameras yielded better results. No images of someone in a hoodie going through the area. But there was someone in black leggings with a white sweatshirt and an oversized backpack walking casually down Woodland Drive just after the shooting.

The face, body, and gait looked familiar. Bryce pulled up some other video and did a quick double check. Well . . . damn. The FBI was looking for a man. That's what the profilers would tell you about shooters. But in this case, the profilers would be nowhere close.

Their shooter was a woman.

Turns out, the redheaded kidnapper was also talented with an assault rifle.

• • • • •

A deep breath. She let the tension out of her body and sank back into the seat.

She took off her red wig as the airplane cleared US airspace, climbing into Canada. This latest mission had been her first in the United States, and consistent with her perception of US security services, had gone off with only a small hitch. Wounding the girl was not ideal, but as long as she pulled through, no damage would be done. Besides, it was the dumb bitch's fault for trying to play hero. Who runs through a hail of live fire?

She looked over at her unconscious package, strapped into his seat with both a seat belt and a security restraint. The gag in his mouth seemed silly but was part of the job specification. Not that she cared, but he was easy on the eyes at over six feet tall with brown hair that was just beginning to show some signs of gray. She had no idea who he was or why he was important. Sometimes as an operative you had the flexibility to make in-the-field decisions. This was not one of those times. The instructions had been quite clear.

Take the target with as little public attention as possible. Extract immediately.

She'd done her job blindly, but successfully. Whatever the purpose, it had to be something significant. Taking a US citizen when they were in the motherland was one thing. Trumped-up charges could easily be brought, and justice would then move very slowly. Executing someone on foreign soil could also easily be accomplished using difficult-to-trace toxins and other means.

But kidnapping someone in the US and extracting them overseas? She smiled and let out a low whistle. She didn't understand how RallyAmerica worked, but she knew they had serious resources and no fear.

Finally, someone had the balls to fight back.

CHAPTER 14

FACING THE MUSIC

Tamika realized that leaving Jessup behind meant she had no wheels. Even though it was almost nine hours after the shooting, the traffic around Aragon High School was still a mess. It took her almost thirty minutes to get an Uber close enough to take her to the San Mateo Medical Center.

The delay forced Tamika to take a few deep breaths and clear her head. As she calmed down, the guilt began to seep in. She knew Jessup was only doing his job. Yelling at him certainly didn't help him figure out what had happened or get a lead on the perp. She'd been a high-maintenance distraction—perhaps a bit too much like a typical senator. She was pissed at herself.

Just as the Uber pulled up and she verified the plates, her phone rang. Jessup.

"You're not going to like this," he said before Tamika could even get out a greeting.

"Look . . . I'm sorry I was such a bitch back there." Tamika wanted to clear the air and relieve some of the guilt.

"I've been there too. And unfortunately, I have more weight for you to carry."

"Something happened to Phoenix?"

"No . . . still no word from the hospital. At this stage, I think that's good news. But I have more on the shooting."

"You've got a lead?"

"Stop and just listen for once. It looks like the shooter wasn't trying to hit anyone. His shooting arc was in between the students—intentionally."

"Then how did Phoenix get hit?"

"She ran to try and cover up some other students." Tamika could almost hear him pausing. She quickly realized why.

"She followed my example."

Jessup didn't reply.

"I'm at the hospital now. I'll tell Margaret." She disconnected the call, feeling the guilt wash over her.

God, Phoenix, what the hell were you thinking?

She knew shifting the blame to Phoenix wasn't fair. Tamika was still young enough to remember her own awkward high school years. A gifted athlete who was also a bit of a geek in the classroom, Tamika hadn't fit any of the typical high school cliques very well. Making multiple military-induced moves from city to city and losing her mother to cancer had made those years especially difficult. Her father had tried to help, but mostly it was her brother who got her through. The brother she'd lost on 9/11.

As she thought about Phoenix, she realized she was just trying to grow up—struggling to figure out what it meant to be an adult. The drinking at the New Year's party was one sign, but their conversations also showed a level of maturity that was advancing rapidly. With a busy mother and an absent father, she was searching for role models. And Tamika was part of filling that void.

She knew that Phoenix looked up to her as a big sister. They'd talked at some length about Tamika's tours in the Middle East. Never about that fateful day in Afghanistan—that was off limits—but there had been other rescues. Had she made them sound too glamorous? Did her dedication to serve come across as some heroic crusade? She had to face an agonizing thought.

Did I just get Phoenix killed?

As the Uber pulled up to the hospital, she had to address a collection of damning realities. Not only was Phoenix inside the hospital fighting for her life, but Margaret was sitting in some waiting room praying. Tamika was dating her ex-husband, and her influence on Margaret's daughter may have convinced Phoenix to make an ill-advised rescue attempt. To cap it off, she now had to tell Margaret about both Phoenix and Johnny.

Tamika couldn't go through the hospital's sliding glass doors.

She looked around as if she was in the Air Force assessing her tactical situation in the field. The hospital was a three-story brick affair with an emergency room semicircular drive and a typical glass overhang at the entrance to protect patients from the weather. There was a modest-sized parking lot in front, with small areas of trees planted on little islands of dirt and grass. Just another hospital in Tamika's long list of medical visits. Her mom . . . Johnny . . . and now Phoenix.

Why me?

She walked out into the parking lot and sat on the curb under a eucalyptus tree, its limbs shedding leaves on the surrounding ground. She pulled out her phone and tried Johnny one more time. Straight to voicemail. Her father was next on the speed dial list. She pressed the button.

"Hey, honey, how are you doing?"

"Hey, Daddy." She tried to sound upbeat but failed.

"You sound down. Tough day at the office?"

"Have you been watching the news?" She felt a jumble about to come out. "Phoenix goes to Aragon High School. She was the one wounded in the shooting. She's in the hospital and may not make it." A big exhale.

Silence on the line. Tamika waited for a moment and then just started crying. Through the sobs, all she could say was, "What's wrong with—"

"Nothing's wrong with you." She was used to General Smith's military tone, but the firmness shook her up a bit.

"But—"

"Take a deep breath, Tammy. I've been watching the coverage and didn't realize Phoenix was the victim. But I do know that whatever happened today can't possibly be your fault. Another crazy shithead opened fire at a high school. You can't bear the burden of human hatred."

Tamika could imagine him sitting in the living room of his three-bedroom bungalow just outside Olympia, Washington. There would be a fire going and the TV humming in the background. He'd have his glasses up on his forehead and a crystal rocks glass of whiskey on the side table. She came back to the hospital curb.

"But there's more to it than that, Dad. I'm being blackmailed and now Johnny is missing. Coincidences are piling up high, and they're all falling down on me."

"Whoa, whoa, whoa—let's back up the truck. You better tell me everything."

So she did. And as she did, it didn't even seem possible or real to her. She broke down crying again as she discussed what little she knew about Johnny's disappearance.

"And now you have to go into the hospital and talk to Margaret Humboldt and explain all of this?" When her father said it, reality returned.

"That about sums it up." She added *sucks* in her head.

The silent interlude meant he was swirling his drink in thought. "Tammy, I wish I could be there to give you a big hug. I didn't know you were in California. I'll fly down first thing tomorrow morning to help. I know how much Johnny and his kids mean to you. They are our only family."

"OK, but—"

"No buts, Tammy. I know you don't want to hear this, but you have to be the strong one right now. Margaret has nobody around her for support. She almost lost Johnny in the crash at Offutt, and now Phoenix is in the same situation. She's got Nathan to worry about, too. We can sort out your issues later—that's clearly a serious mess—but right now you have to help Margaret."

"How can I help her? She's going to hate me."

"If she does, so be it. She deserves to know the truth, and you're the only one she has right now." Tamika didn't have any response.

"Look, honey, I've lost men and women in the field and had to tell their spouses and loved ones that I was the one responsible for their safety. In life, when we lead, there are consequences, and we have to take accountability. I don't think you caused any of this, but even if Margaret thinks you did, you must be the one to tell her. Anything else is failure. A failure of character . . . and leadership."

Tamika felt the bitterness of the words but also recognized the truth. Sometimes right, sometimes wrong. But always accountable.

"Thank you, General." There was love, and then there was authority.

She hung up, walked across the parking lot, and went through the glass doors of the hospital to face the music.

CHAPTER 15
WORKING THE SCENE

Jessup knew his team would cover the basics of the investigation well. Evidence would get gathered, forensics processed, and a suspect profile created. The cooperation with the San Mateo PD had gone pretty well so far. They seemed to understand that the involvement of a United States senator shifted the jurisdictional grounds a bit. In any event, he had no desire to be in the limelight at this stage—he'd discovered through experience that the big stage had its pitfalls. So he'd agreed that the SMPD chief of police should do the late evening press briefing.

JJ stood quietly in the back of the crowd outside the high school as a middle-aged man, looking surprisingly fit for a desk officer, walked up to a podium that had been set up on the sidewalk near the school entrance. Large spotlights had been placed to illuminate the area, but they only seemed to add more shadows, misery, and gloom. The reporters stood in a jumble of semicircles facing the podium, seeping out into the entrance road and parking area. He'd seen this scene way too many times and felt the sickness in his stomach with each shooting. It was an epidemic that the country just didn't have the will to stop. *Responsible gun ownership, sure, but nobody needs assault rifles.*

"Hello, my name is Miguel Page and I'm the San Mateo chief of police. I want to start this briefing tonight by praising the work of our officers and first responders. They were on site quickly, secured the scene, and enabled us to evacuate students, teachers, and administrators safely. As difficult as all of this is to imagine in our community, it could have been much worse." He paused to allow that to sink in a bit.

Good for him, thought Jessup. *No bullshit. Just a simple acknowledgment and on to the facts.*

"With that said, I'll get right to what we know about today's tragic events. What we believe was a single male shooter gained access to the south roof area of the high school and fired over sixty rounds into the courtyard. Sadly, one of our students was hit multiple times and has been taken to San Mateo Medical Center where she's in surgery. We don't have an update on her condition yet but are praying for her recovery. Given the nature of the attack, we were fortunate that nobody else was hurt."

He paused to shift some papers on the podium. JJ hoped he stuck to the script carefully. They wanted to release just enough information to get some help from the community without tipping off the assailants to what they knew. Which honestly wasn't that much.

"The perpetrator rappelled down the back wall of the school and left the scene from that area. We don't know if anyone else was involved in the attack nor do we have any information on a possible motive. Naturally, we're pursuing all avenues in the investigation. We're asking residents around the high school to report anything suspicious they witnessed today, especially between the hours of 8 and 10 a.m. We've established a hotline and text center people can call or message with any information. The hotline and text number are 887-555-8436. All this information is available on our website. With that, I'll open it up to questions."

Wow. Perfect, thought Jessup. Maybe they'd get lucky with the neighborhood canvass. That said, like Tamika, he hated this part of an investigation. He was a man of action with military intelligence training. Grinding through a bunch of interviews, video, and ballistics information just wasn't his cup of tea. They were a bit short on leads at this point, and waiting for something to break frustrated him. He called Higginbottom over.

"Do we have any new information on the Humboldt situation?"

"Yeah, I was waiting to update you on that. We have him on video going through SFO and out into an SUV with a redheaded woman. You're not going to believe this, but she actually flashes a badge at him."

"And I'm sure neither us nor SMPD sent someone for him."

"How could we? We didn't even know he was coming. We're not exactly set up as a taxi service."

"Let me guess. No plates on the SUV, his cell phone isn't responding, and we have no idea where he is."

Agent Higginbottom didn't have a response for that.

"Shit." Jessup looked the other way, shaking his head. "Extortion emails. A shooting. And a kidnapping. One extended family. A US senator." He looked back at Higginbottom.

"Buckle up, Higgs. I think the road ahead is going to be long, dark, and bumpy."

CHAPTER 16

RALLYAMERICA

Lee Bowen sat in an office he'd rented specifically for his extracurricular venture. It was sparsely furnished with an IKEA wood laminate table, a laptop attached to a monitor, and a desk light. There was nothing on the walls, no furniture for guests, and no potted plants to add ambiance. No windows or receptionist. Just Bowen. He was never in the office for more than the few minutes necessary to complete a specific transaction. This venue was all about anonymity and security.

He'd left B² Ventures at 7 p.m. after watching the press conference on his phone. He was worried that there was still no report on the victim's prognosis, but it also didn't sound like the authorities were making much progress. Before plotting his next steps, Bowen took a conscious detour to review the milestones that had brought him to this historic moment.

When he was locked down during the COVID pandemic, Bowen had spent hours evaluating how he could take his budding wealth to the next level. In his mind, the problem with the American system was that it was regulated. Perhaps not well, but there were centralized institutions and government agencies designed to hold back what he thought of as the legitimate destiny of those who were the winners. He'd made a living maneuvering around the rules and regulations with creative financial structures. But there were limits to that type of work.

He wanted more.

In adolescence, his parents had demanded excellence from him. When he didn't deliver in their eyes, there were consequences that had seriously scarred him. But the wounds had proven to be a strong motivator. Failure was physically and emotionally painful. So now he needed more.

He also resented the idea that the Googles, Apples, Amazons, and Metas of the world controlled so much of the proverbial real estate. To achieve his goals, he needed a major disruption in how America governed itself. The old guard needed to be retired, the government-curated post–World War II order destroyed. With the state of American democracy already fragile, a tipping point of energy was needed to push it over the cataclysmic edge. He believed someone had to orchestrate this process and dictate the decisive instructions for the endgame. And he was convinced he was uniquely qualified for this herculean task.

He'd also persuaded a collection of international interests to support and add funding to his cause. They wanted similar levels of turbulence but for different reasons. They were in an existential fight with the United States for dominance in the world economy. They hated the idea that most of their assets had to be held in dollars and desperately wanted to end American meddling (their word) in their efforts to extend their economic and political power around the globe. Asia, Africa, and South America were all up for grabs—and his partners intended to take control. Turmoil in the United States would give them the opening they needed to achieve their goals.

As the startup environment came clear of the COVID cloud, he and his partner, Ely Basof, had strategized on how to raise their next fund. Ely had unintentionally paved the way for Bowen's own ambitions by explaining how Web 3.0 innovations, the accelerating AI revolution, and new business models created a next generation of VC opportunities. It had been a pivotal partnership meeting in Basof's office.

"If you're serious about being cutting edge, you need a high-security transaction system, one that can track records without anyone being able to trace back the origins of the information." Ely could get into preacher mode easily, Bowen remembered. And the preaching quickly led to a condescending attitude. Smart and insufferable. A necessary pain in the ass.

Bowen had nodded solemnly. "Of course, that only makes sense." Security and anonymity were his top concerns.

Getting up from his seat at the four-person oak conference table to the side of his desk, Ely continued. "Blockchain creates a distributed ledger that tracks everything without any individual being able to access the specific data. Everyone can see what is happening—there is a type of full transparency—but you have no way to trace who is involved."

Bowen loved that approach. But he also desperately needed to hide his syndicate of investors from the octopus arms of the traditional banking system. He followed Basof with his gaze, wondering if the guy would ever stand still. "So how do you keep the financial activities out of the public eye?"

His business partner laughed as if the answer were self-evident. "That's the practical side of cryptocurrency and NFTs. All the trading and speculation in the market around Bitcoin, Ethereum, and Tom Brady's latest digital poster make me laugh. Interesting, I suppose, but not the powerful part of the technology. Crypto and nonfungible tokens have incredible commercial potential if we can create more stability in the market."

That wasn't Bowen's problem. In his mind, less stability was better.

Basof wasn't done. He went to the whiteboard on the wall, erased some technical spec information, and began diagramming. "The other element here is generative AI. In most businesses, people are a huge expense, and their productivity has limits. AI tools can dramatically reduce the number of people companies need—or in PR-speak—make employees more productive. This is true for all workers, including programmers. The double whammy comes when the resulting products use other AI systems to create content, disrupt and automate existing industries, and propagate new business models. Less cost, faster innovation, more disruption, better decisions. A VC wet dream."

All Bowen could do was smile. Although not deeply technical, he had more product aptitude than he let on, so the fundamentals were clear in his mind, even if he thought Ely's diagram obfuscated the important points. For his purposes, he didn't need to understand the detailed bits and bytes of the tech or challenge Basof's opinions. He could already see some ways to tear into the fabric of the existing system. But there was one final piece that needed to fall into place.

"How does all of this get organized? It can't just magically come together and work, can it? All this technology seems so disconnected—and completely alien to the ways companies and organizations work. How do we convince our LPs to fund us?" He acted as if he was a bit lost in the conversation, knowing that would get the response he wanted.

Basof was back standing behind the conference table, cleaning his hands from whiteboard ink. "Yeah, that's a huge hurdle to overcome. Our limited partners are so used to the traditional top-down structured system that they can't think outside of that box. But I'm excited about a nascent Web 3.0 solution called a DAO, which stands for decentralized autonomous organization." Basof waved his hands to create the quotes around the name.

"Clearly nobody is doing any marketing for this stuff—these names couldn't possibly be worse." Bowen chuckled for effect.

"Not my department," Basof interjected as he moved over to his desk. "But DAOs can work. They're a way to form a collaborative group or business without any central administration or control. Trades and transactions can be recorded and managed using blockchain, smart contracts, and tokens to grant voting power to the Web 3.0 equivalent of shareholders."

"So someone could form a company, attract investors, pursue a project or mission, and distribute profits without anyone knowing each other?"

Basof smiled. "No pesky board of directors, no Delaware incorporation laws, no government oversight."

That got Bowen's attention.

"You mean the government isn't trying to control this?" His incredulity was genuine.

"That's an area where you probably know more than I do. But generally, they're having so much trouble dealing with yesterday's problems that they don't even see the blockchain and AI trains about to slam them down the track. Hell, they're still trying to figure out TikTok and how to manage social media." Ely actually cracked a smile with that.

In Bowen's mind, the painting he'd been crafting had shifted from a Jackson Pollock abstract piece into a Rembrandt portrait. He still needed to figure out the specific brush strokes to make it a reality, but the composition of the art was now clear. He thought it could be a financial masterpiece.

He and Basof had gone on to use their B^2 Ventures platform to raise a $2 billion fund from limited partners to invest in Web 3.0 and AI businesses. They'd already made ten investments and were competing for several other deals in one of the richest VC veins in history. Bowen had great confidence that together they would make millions, which would add to his personal war chest.

But for Lee Bowen and his investors, that was insufficient.

Not nearly enough.

Under a cloak of secrecy, he'd taken things a step further because he saw a unique opportunity to do more than just disrupt an industry or two. He latched on to Basof's ideas by creating a DAO cynically called RallyAmerica. But this DAO would invest in more than just companies or financial instruments. A specific group of overseas supporters were happy to provide additional resources when they saw the fullness of his new plan.

Bringing himself back to the IKEA-furnished office, Bowen logged in to the computer using one of his several aliases and prepared his next missive carefully. He typed the email message that would escalate the fight he'd begun and hit the send button.

Tamika Smith was only the beginning.

The chaos he was creating would be epic.

And there would be nobody to blame.

CHAPTER 17

GAME ON

Tamika found Margaret sitting on a plastic chair in the emergency room corridor. Medical personnel buzzed around her, moving quickly back and forth down the hallway and through the swinging double doors that said Authorized Personnel Only in red letters. The bright overhead fluorescent lights were in sharp contrast to her downcast expression. Margaret's head was lowered with her hands crossed in front of her. She was clearly worried, scared, and likely in prayer. Tamika sat down next to her quietly and put her arm around her shoulder. After a few moments, she broke the silence.

"Come on, Margaret. Let's go someplace we can talk."

"I don't want to leave. My baby is on the other side of those doors."

"I'll make sure they call us as soon as she's out of surgery. Sitting here isn't helping you or Phoenix." Tamika approached a nursing station and spoke in quiet tones with a man in nursing scrubs.

She then helped Margaret gather her coat and purse, and the two women walked down the hall, following directions to the cafeteria. Five turns and an escalator brought them to an open area with tables and chairs arranged around some fake potted plants. The floor was antiseptic tile, and the walls painted an off-white. The cafeteria serving area was closed, so a bank of vending machines was their only option. A few people dressed in scrubs were drinking coffee, others were chatting, and some read newspapers or checked their phones.

Tamika was starving, with FBI airplane food as her only sustenance during the day. But the best she could do was a Vendomatic ham and cheese with a Sprite chaser. She brought some tea for Margaret, hoping it might help calm her nerves a bit. There was more silence as she brought the food and drinks over to the table. Tamika didn't know how to start the difficult conversation.

Finally, Margaret looked at her and said, "I'm guessing that the silence means you haven't heard from Johnny."

"Oh, Margaret, it's worse than that, unfortunately."

"What do you mean, worse?"

"The FBI found video of him getting into an SUV with a woman pretending to be a law enforcement officer. They're still trying to track them, but it looks like he's been kidnapped."

Margaret covered her face with her hands. "Kidnapped? Why would someone kidnap Johnny, especially today? What could they possibly want with him?" The words came out as a baleful wail, causing heads to perk up around the room. More tears came.

Tamika looked down to dig deep. "We think all of this is connected."

"You mean the shooting and Johnny's disappearance? How?" A little quieter this time but still filled with anguish.

"I've been getting threatening emails over the past few weeks. It's possible the attacks are an escalation."

"You mean they tried to kill my baby to get your attention? And Johnny was some icing on the cake?" Tamika could feel a coldness spreading across the table. Margaret's anger-filled face was turning crimson.

She took a deep breath. "Not exactly. It looks like the shooter was only trying to scare people—but Phoenix ran to protect some students and got hit in the crossfire."

"Hang on—are you trying to blame Phoenix for getting shot? How dare you. She idolizes you. She—" Other people in the cafeteria were glancing toward them now.

Tamika took her voice lower with an added urgency. "Margaret, listen to me. I'm not blaming Phoenix for anything. All she did was try to help some classmates. Sounds just like what you or Johnny would want her to do."

She took the final step. "And yes, I worry she may have been emulating me."

"That's just as bad." Margaret clearly wasn't going to let her anger go. "It sounds like it's all your fault. If they're going after Phoenix and Johnny, they must want something from you. Who's going to protect me and Nathan? I don't want my family caught up in your bullshit political games."

Tamika soldiered on. *This isn't a fight I can win*, she thought. But she had to try.

"I don't think this is about DC politics. My congressional opponents don't have these types of resources. I think this is something much bigger. I don't know who they are or what they want, but I doubt I can give it to them."

"Well that's just beautiful," Margaret snapped, her voice thick with sarcasm. "I've tried to be very friendly about our little relationship situation. You and Johnny all cozy. Playing second mother to Phoenix and Nathan. For damn sure, I'm done with that." The slam of her hand on the table echoed across the room.

Before Tamika could say anything, Margaret stood up, tea sloshing from her cup. "Your world has crossed into mine and you've screwed it all up. Why are you here? I don't want or need your help. The best thing you can do now is stay the hell away from me and my family."

And with that, Margaret grabbed her bag and marched out of the cafeteria, muttering "what a bitch" as she left.

Tamika felt everyone's eyes on her. She tried to ignore them while she cleaned up the spilled tea, but there really wasn't any place to hide. After a few minutes she got up from the table, took the escalator up a floor, and walked out of the hospital into the cool air of the night. It was now past midnight. She was physically and emotionally spent.

And then she realized she didn't have any place to stay.

She pulled up her email, hopeful that her assistant had thought this through and gotten her a hotel room. She no longer had a "go bag" at the office like JJ clearly did. She'd have to figure out clothes and the rest as well.

With her email open, another message came in. Her friend Tomlinson was back.

"Shitty day, huh. You can't say I didn't warn you. Now we have Johnny and there's nothing

> you can do about it. You just have to say the word and we can unwind all of this. But you need to play ball. I own you."

So there it was. Out in the open. A United States senator was being threatened by forces unknown. She'd had her fill of crazy people trying to bring down the country. Was this about her official role in Washington, DC, or more about the Lincoln Coalition? Maybe it was another domestic terrorist? Could it be a Proud Boys–type conspiracy? But this group was too well funded and more organized than the alt-right had ever been. So who was left? A drug cartel? Some other foreign interest?

Whoever it was, they clearly didn't give a shit about who got hurt along the way. And that made them extremely dangerous. Losing her mom to cancer and her brother in the 9/11 attacks had ripped a wound in Tamika's soul. While time had provided some healing, the pain was never too far from the surface. And now the wound was open again, spreading like a wildfire within.

Her new family was threatened, and she had choices to make. Give in to them to rescue Johnny and maybe get these assholes out of her life. Or stand and fight, no matter the consequences.

Either way, it was game time, with someone else making the rules.

And she was going to have to play ball whether she liked it or not.

PART II
THE BEST MADE PLANS

I may not know it
But these are the moments
That I'm gonna remember most, yeah
Just gotta keep going
And I, I gotta be strong
Just keep pushing on, 'cause
There's always gonna be another mountain
I'm always gonna wanna make it move
Always gonna be an uphill battle
Sometimes I'm gonna have to lose
Ain't about how fast I get there
Ain't about what's waiting on the other side
It's the climb

—Jon Mabe, Jessi Alexander

CHAPTER 18

SONS AND FATHERS

Bryce Roscovitch was finally able to take a nap. The cot he had installed in the basement looked like army surplus issue, but his body somehow molded perfectly into the canvas stretched across two lengthwise poles. He wasn't sure whether he slept in the night or through the morning, but the three hours rest and two Diet Cokes recharged his batteries enough to continue his multi-threaded investigation.

As he suspected, the Bombardier 8000 hadn't gone to Morocco. At least, not yet. The "it's an Islamic al-Qaeda" head fake was quickly put in doubt. He'd negotiated his way past the ATC firewall and was receiving real-time feeds from their systems. The pilots had reported strong winds en route and were requesting a temporary stop in the Netherlands to refuel. Digging into the Dutch border control system, Bryce determined that the plane could stop there without passing through customs, refuel, and continue to another destination. Perhaps in Morocco. Perhaps elsewhere.

One of the 8000's selling points was that it could land on very short strips, which made finding its eventual destination more complicated, and he was nervous about trusting the ATC system, given the resources of his adversaries. Bryce concluded he needed to put some airport video hacking techniques to work. He had the total mileage range of the plane (possibly extended through refueling), a visual description of the aircraft, and a minimum airfield length of 2,500 feet. Using those parameters, it didn't take him too long to write a routine that would do the search for him and report any possible landings. Video searches were time-consuming and the land mass to cover was immense, but that's why he had his multi-PC tower rig along with plenty of cloud processing available.

Turning to other investigative angles, his facial recognition search for his female shooter/kidnapper hadn't generated any hits yet. Given Bryce's access to global criminal databases as well as domestic civil lists, a null response was highly unlikely. He went into exploratory mode.

"How does someone keep their photo out of US databases?"

"Don't be dense, Bryce," his alter ego immediately responded. "She's obviously not American and almost certainly hasn't been in the country before."

"OK, but I've also got access to US Customs data, and she doesn't show up there, either."

"That just means she entered the country illegally. And before you ask, the fact that she's not on Interpol lists means she's a clean asset. Likely not from a NATO country."

"Hmm . . . so you're thinking old school. Let's say Eastern Bloc—but that doesn't exist anymore. She certainly doesn't look Chinese, Iranian, or North Korean. We're talking Russian or perhaps Belarusian?"

"No guarantees, but that's the most likely result."

Bryce paused over that premise.

What the hell was a Russian spy doing shooting up a San Mateo high school?

• • • • •

General Frank Smith had taken the first flight from Seattle-Tacoma airport to San Francisco. A retired combat pilot in the Air Force, Smith was no stranger to life-changing tragedies. He'd lost his wife, Deirdre, much too early, and still regretted not being there as much for her as he should have been. Tours of duty were never timed with personal needs in mind. Losing his son, Alex, had been a second devastating blow. Alex had followed his father into the service, albeit in the Navy, and Smith blamed himself for his son being in the wrong place at the wrong time. He'd tried therapy, but that had proved to be a Band-Aid, not a solution.

As he walked through the SFO terminal, conscious that Johnny had walked the same path the evening before, General Smith was more than concerned about the only family he had left. He knew his daughter was deeply committed to the Lincoln Coalition's pursuit of practical, bipartisan solutions. He also knew that she was principled to a fault and very stubborn. He took the threats against her seriously—his training taught him that much—and he realized that she was unlikely to comply with extortionist demands. He also recognized that she loved Johnny, and he knew what that meant. His job, as father and confidant, was to help her navigate this rock out of a very hard place.

He followed the ridiculous walk-escalator-walk-train-walk-some-more route to the SFO rental car area and picked up a silver Toyota Corolla so he and Tamika could get around more easily. He then drove down the 101 freeway to the Holiday Inn in San Mateo that he'd arranged for Tamika the night before. The buffet breakfast area wasn't fancy, just a slightly cold selection of scrambled eggs, overcooked bacon, and sticky buns, but the room wasn't crowded either, so talking was easy.

"Hey, Daddy," Tamika greeted him with what felt like a fatigued hug as he approached her table.

"Tammy . . . I love you." He wanted to ask how she was doing, but that seemed ridiculous under the circumstances. "Did you get any sleep?" he added.

"You know how it is. I felt like I was back on duty in Afghanistan. You get as much as you can." His daughter was never fussy about her appearance, but the bedhead was particularly bad this morning, and she'd definitely slept in the only clothes she had. The emotional strain was written in the lines on her face.

"Any word on Johnny or Phoenix?" No point in beating around the bush with his daughter.

"I couldn't get any information myself—and I can't call Margaret at this point. JJ dropped me a text saying that Phoenix was out of the woods. Apparently, she lost a lot of blood but was extremely lucky that no major organs were hit." She looked away. "Nothing on Johnny."

"Phoenix is young—she'll bounce back quickly." General Smith said it with a manufactured conviction and consciously avoided the Johnny topic. "Sounds like you had the difficult conversation with Margaret."

"It went about how you would expect. She was already an emotional wreck."

"I know it doesn't seem that way now, but she'll realize this wasn't your fault. It's just going to take some time."

He could tell from Tamika's expression that she wasn't buying his line. It also occurred to him that she was thinking about something else entirely.

"Come on, Tammy, what's going on inside your head?"

"I got another email . . ." She slid her phone across the table to him.

"Shit" was all Frank Smith could come up with.

"What am I supposed to do? I don't care that much about what he'd say about me. Hell, some of it might be true. But I can't give in to this asshole, and I can't have him attacking my family."

The general knew the question was mostly rhetorical. As he'd suspected, his daughter was going to fight. There was no way she was going to let a bully push her around, regardless of the personal stakes. There wasn't much for him to say. The vibration of her phone with a new message made things easier.

"Well, Tammy, I think this might help."

He handed back the phone so she could read the text. She had to read it twice to process the information.

Where the hell is De Kooy Airfield? And why is the text coming from Shea Roscovitch?

• • • • •

The tail number made confirmation relatively easy. The Bombardier Global 8000 had touched down at an airport at the tip of the northern peninsula of the Netherlands. Bryce did a quick search on the town of Den Helder and realized that the name was appropriate. Aside from being the home port for the Dutch Navy, it was more of a provincial outpost and gateway to the Wadden Islands. Not much to report.

The Kingdom of the Netherlands (as it is formally called) only has about thirteen thousand square miles of land area and five international airports. Amsterdam Schiphol is one of the largest airports in Europe, but Rotterdam The Hague, Eindhoven, Maastricht Aachen, and Groningen also service international flights.

Bryce suspected that the perps landed at Den Helder's De Kooy Airfield to limit their visibility. He'd used airport surveillance cameras to confirm that they'd landed to refuel. The three passengers and two pilots had moved into the FBO's waiting area, although one of them was clearly being helped across the tarmac. Presumably they went in to use the facilities and perhaps grab a bite to eat. The stop lasted about thirty minutes before they reboarded, with the plane continuing on a new flight plan headed to Budapest.

So much for a jihad in Morocco.

While the Eastern European eye candy was interesting, Bryce didn't fall for the ruse. His AI system alerted him to two inconsistencies. First, there was no way the 8000 needed to be refueled if the eventual destination was Budapest. Weather data indicated that high-altitude winds had actually been helping the flight rather than hurting it. There was no need to refuel. Second, his system automatically ran facial recognition on the people who reboarded the plane. The pilots were the same. The three passengers were not.

Clearly a switch had been made, and the FBO likely had processed the plane without informing the customs authorities. Hence the landing at Den Helder rather than one of the commercial airports. Someone had been bought off—yet another sign that his adversaries were well-financed and connected. Bryce knew Johnny was someplace in the Netherlands. The question he faced was what to do with the information.

Notifying the FBI was certainly the correct course of action—and exactly the type of thing he couldn't do. First off, they didn't really know who he was, so credibility was an issue. More importantly, it was imperative that he stay off their radar screen. They would want more information on why he was tracking Johnny, how he got the information, and what else he was up to. Once that thread began to unravel, there was no limit to how much yarn could come undone. He had plenty to hide.

So as a good son, he contacted his mother, Shea Roscovitch. When his father was killed in the anarchist attack at the Lincoln Memorial, Bryce had come out of seclusion both to comfort his mother and to try to heal some of his own wounds. As part of that process, he'd established secure electronic communications with his family—including code names and burner phones that he periodically rotated out of service. He knew Shea thought the entire charade was silly, but she didn't fully understand some of Bryce's activities. It was better on multiple fronts if she knew only what was necessary.

"Sally, this is Billy."

He heard Shea hesitate on the other end of the line. "Hello, Billy . . . how . . . how are you doing?"

"I'm excellent, Sally. Don't worry about me. But I have some important news for you to pass on." He paused to make sure she was paying attention.

"Please write this down: He landed at De Kooy Airfield."

"Who landed? Decoy is a strange name for an airport. And who am I supposed to call?" It all came out at once, and clearly Shea was not tracking.

"It's two words, Sally. D-E, then K-O-O-Y. Please text Iceman. And only Iceman. Iceman will know what this means."

"Iceman . . . uhm . . . I got it." He certainly hoped so.

Shea continued, "Br—Billy, I saw the news."

"It's gonna be OK, Sally. I promise. I'm on it."

And he hung up.

CHAPTER 19

ONE STEP BACK

Jerry Jessup was scheduled to fly back to Washington, DC, the evening after the active shooting incident, leaving Higginbottom to continue the investigation locally. But before he left, he arranged a meeting with Senator Smith, and, as it turned out, with her father, the general. They met at the San Mateo Police Department in a nicely appointed—at least by police standards—conference room adjacent to the police chief's office. JJ practically had to close the door in Chief Page's face to exclude him from the meeting, but he really wanted Tamika one-to-one. Albeit with a father addendum.

"I hope you were able to get a bit of shut-eye last night," he said, starting off the conversation as he pulled shades down to cover the interior glass windows of the conference room. He intentionally went with an opening line that would hint at their shared military background.

"I'm doing OK, all things considered," came Tamika's crisp reply. "Allow me to introduce my father, General Frank Smith."

JJ nodded and extended his hand in greeting. "I know you by reputation, General, but I don't think our paths crossed in the service. Nice to finally meet you in person."

"Likewise—and let me add my thanks for the help you've provided Tammy over the years." General Frank Smith held out a chair for Tamika as they all sat down at the end of the conference table.

Tammy . . . that was a new one for Jessup.

"Well, I suppose Senator Smith and I have been looking out for each other." He gave Tamika a sideways grin to see what reaction that would get. He was shocked to see a corresponding smile. He knew the truth was that their relationship had been through some very difficult ups and downs. More shouts than laughter.

"The deputy director is being too nice," Tamika said, smiling. "Mostly, I've been my usual pain in the ass, and he's put up with me over the years."

While probably accurate, that comment really had Jessup's radar spinning in search of meaning. Where was the usual piss 'n' vinegar edge? The anger from the previous evening? Right about now, he expected her to be demanding that he find the shooter, chase down Johnny's captors, and lock up the extortionist.

JJ quickly regrouped. "I'm headed back to DC tonight, but before I leave, I wanted to give you an update on the investigation."

"Great," Tamika Smith replied with continued enthusiasm.

"The best news is that Phoenix Humboldt has been upgraded to serious condition. Her mother is with her, and the doctor is confident she'll make a full recovery. In fact, he even used the words 'quick recovery.' I have an FBI detail assigned to the Humboldt family until we understand the nature of the incidents better. Scary shit for anyone, much less a teenager."

"She's a tough nut, but I'll have to give her some advice on running away from bullets rather than toward them." Tamika said this with a chuckle, and her father joined in with a nervous laugh.

Jessup plowed ahead. "I wish I had better news on Johnny. We have a full team canvassing airport personnel to see what we can learn. We're also looking at traffic cams and other digital data to see if we can track him. No hard leads yet, but we're on it."

"I'm sure you're doing everything you can," came the canned response from Tamika.

"Hmmm . . ." Jessup was now completely flummoxed about where to go next. He'd come prepared to restrain a stubborn and headstrong former Air Force major. Now he was dealing with a seemingly calm and composed significant other of a man who had vanished.

"Well . . . we still need to talk about the extortionist, Senator."

"Tamika and I were discussing that this morning," the general interjected. "The only path forward is to work with the FBI and see if we can help you trace the emails. If that means going along with their demands for a bit, so be it."

"Let me know what you'd like me to do," Tamika added. "This is your area of expertise." Jessup continued to expect the snark but didn't find any.

He glanced from one Smith to the other, not sure exactly what to say. He'd have lost a bet in Vegas predicting their reactions. He stalled for time.

"That's great," he said, although somehow he didn't think it was. "Agent Higginbottom and I are formulating a response this afternoon. We'll come back to you with a plan. Tamika, can I give you a lift back to DC?"

She shook her head. "Actually, my dad's convinced me I need to step back a bit and regroup. All this bullshit is just coming at me too fast. I need to be off the grid to get my bearings. I'm going to our family cabin on the Olympic Peninsula west of Tacoma. No internet and shitty cell coverage there. That will give me a chance to breathe. Probably easier to reach me through my dad. He can get a message to me."

"Did you catch up with Mrs. Humboldt at the hospital?" JJ decided to pick at a possible sore spot to see if he could get a reaction.

Tamika let out a sigh. "I feel responsible for what happened, so I decided to tell her everything. You can imagine her reaction. I'm not going to be a conduit for information with Margaret. I'm not sure our relationship will ever recover." She started to rise from her seat, indicating that the meeting was coming to an end, at least for her.

Stumped by the perfectly human reaction, JJ admitted defeat and said what he thought was the truth. "We all know none of this was your fault. You can't take responsibility for every asshole that decides to do something shitty."

"That's exactly what I told her," the general interjected.

"General, can you give me your cell number and email so we can reach out with our plan?" JJ offered a notepad and pen.

"Of course." He scribbled the information on the paper. "And let me just thank you again for everything you're doing." Another shaking of hands.

JJ opened the door, allowing first Tamika and then General Smith to exit the room before walking them to the front door. They left the police station quickly. A perfunctory meeting completed.

Jessup wasn't stupid.

No way Tamika was going to regroup. A cabin in the woods with nothing to do? Not a chance. Jesus—another random particle bouncing around the atomic nucleus of this investigation. He'd have Higginbottom track her whereabouts. That was awkward, given her status as a senator. But nothing about this situation made any sense.

What did Senator Tamika Smith know that he didn't?

• • • • •

Tamika blew out a big breath of air as she and her father walked to their silver Corolla. "Do you think he bought the bit about you going to the Peninsula to recharge?" General Smith ventured.

"I certainly hope not—he's way too smart for that, and if he does any kind of research at all, he'll know the truth. In a way, I'm counting on that. Frankly, the stepping-back story is really a cover for my absence from DC. I have a few weeks until the Senate goes back into session, but people in the Beltway keep track of things."

She knew Jessup was serious about putting the full weight of the FBI into these investigations. He was a professional, well versed in the craft on all sides of the equation and dedicated to the law. Unfortunately, he didn't know what Tamika knew about Johnny's location. With the Humboldts receiving better protection than Tamika could possibly provide, she shifted her attention to more important issues.

While the situation with Margaret was complicated, they respected each other—at least they had in the past. Her relationship with Phoenix and Nathan was more difficult to describe. She certainly cared deeply for them and was devastated by the recent turn of events. And yet she knew they were not her kids—and she might never feel the love that comes with bringing children into the world. Reconciling that with her feelings for Johnny was a conundrum she wrestled with often. Now, with Johnny's kidnapping, the conflicting emotions brought a knot to her stomach.

She had to find Johnny.

She still struggled to express her feelings for him publicly—something he seemed to understand and accept. Johnny knew about the rape, he appreciated her sense of abandonment from the loss of her mother and brother, and he had a way of making her smile that made all the hurt fade to black. Never gone but safely stashed away. She loved Johnny for that.

There was also a deeper connection that she could not easily describe. How do you explain the electricity that runs through your body when you are with someone special? Can you articulate the feeling you get from a simple touch of the hand or a brush of the lips? What breaks down all her inhibitions and self-control when she is in his arms making love? And doing it in ways she'd never thought possible? The emotions cut deep to the core of her being.

That all left her with one mission.

She had to find Johnny.

Her father interrupted her thoughts. "You still here?"

"Sorry, you know where my head is."

"I assume you're returning with me to Seattle to keep up appearances?"

"Yeah. I'll check in with my team there to set the hook for everyone else. Then I'll head to the border and fly out of Vancouver."

"Jessup will definitely catch that trail if he looks."

"Exactly."

"Do you have any contacts in the Netherlands?" General Smith looked at her expectantly.

"None that I can activate without getting the State Department involved. US senators can't just walk into an embassy and ask for CIA assistance."

The general laughed. "I suppose not. Let me reach out through some of my Air Force contacts at NATO. I doubt anybody will pay much attention to me. We might be able to get you some quiet support."

"Daddy, you know I love him, right?"

"Of course. And I know what that means." He looked searchingly into her eyes.

"That's why we'll do whatever it takes."

CHAPTER 20

ONE STEP FORWARD

The light was bright but so was the smiling face. Her mom.

Phoenix tried to pull her head up, but that brought a dizzy feeling, so she just lay back into the pillow. She glanced around to take in her new surroundings. She wasn't in a room—just an area closed off by a giant screen pulled around her bed in a semicircle. She could hear the beeping of several machines that were just out of her view. An IV bag hung on a pole to her left, along with a bag that looked like blood. She was suddenly aware that wires and tubes were connected to her arms and chest. She felt a dull pain in her stomach and glanced down as best she could. All she could see was a hospital gown.

"Welcome back, young lady. You gave us a good scare."

"Hey, Mom," she whispered. "Where am I?"

"San Mateo hospital . . . in the intensive care unit."

Some foggy memories began to flood back in a jumble. Sitting in the courtyard. Gunshots. Eugene O'Neill. Vanessa. Running to her friends. Pain.

"Was anyone else hurt?" Phoenix could feel her heart rate increasing, and she tried to lift her body up again.

"Relax, Phoenix, everyone is fine. Including you. Just lie back and rest."

"Did they catch the guy?"

Her mother gave her what almost looked like an angry expression. "Is that really what's on your mind? You're not some crime fighter."

"What's wrong, Mom? I just want to know what happened." Phoenix's head was steadily clearing and tracking the conversation more fully.

"Well—what the hell were you thinking?" her mother demanded. "You're not supposed to run into the gunfire."

Phoenix paused to process that. "My friends were going to get hit. I just wanted to help them."

A little smile cracked through the anger on her mom's face. "Honey, I know." She looked away for a brief instant. "I know you were just trying to help. But you have to take care of yourself. I can't lose you."

As her mind crystalized even more, Phoenix began to understand. "I'm sorry, Mom. I know you've been through a lot. I just reacted."

"You aren't in search and rescue just yet. You're still my baby."

The reference to search and rescue seemed odd at first. But as Phoenix thought it through, she understood the meaning. She shifted the conversation.

"How bad was I hurt? I can't really feel too much."

Her mother seemed relieved at the change in direction. "I'm sure the doctor will come in soon now that you're awake. All they told me was that you were hit twice and lost a lot of blood. But they seemed optimistic."

As if on cue, the curtain was pulled back and a nurse and doctor walked in.

"Well, good to have you back, Phoenix. My name is Doctor Jenny Doucette. I had you in surgery for almost three hours. You are one lucky girl."

"Am I going to be OK?"

"Honestly, I haven't seen many cases like this, even during my time in the Army. You were hit twice in the torso, but neither bullet hit any organs. One went 'through and through,' as they say, and led to a great deal of blood loss. The other was more of a flesh wound. Once we stopped the bleeding, the rest was fairly straightforward."

"Thank God," her mom interjected.

"How long am I going to be in here?" Now that she was awake and fully conscious, Phoenix was already becoming antsy.

"One step at a time," Dr. Doucette said with a bit of a chuckle. "I'll take a look at your wounds, we'll get the dressings changed, and then move you up into the surgical ward. If all goes well, I'd guess a few days. But you need to take it easy for now."

She walked around the bed and pulled up Phoenix's gown. Phoenix could see her poking around a bit, although she couldn't sense the prodding.

"Why can't I feel very much?" she asked. She tried to move so she could see better.

"Just lie back, Phoenix. You're on some painkillers. You'll feel plenty as they wear off and we reduce the dosage."

"What about scarring?" her mom asked.

Dr. Doucette furrowed her brow. "Shouldn't be too bad." She abruptly turned to the nurse. "Antonio, the sutures look good to me. Could you change the dressing and make sure Phoenix is comfortable?"

"Of course, Doctor."

"Mrs. Humboldt, could I speak with you outside for a minute?"

As they went outside and the nurse attended to her chest and abdomen, Phoenix's mind switched gears. She was grateful for the doctor's great work and for the good prognosis. But even in her current state, she felt some pangs of frustration. The private conversation between the doctor and her mom only reminded her that they weren't treating her like an adult. She knew why her mom was being so protective, but she also realized she wasn't anyone's baby anymore. And the search-and-rescue comment was a clear reference to her relationship with Tamika. She was always tiptoeing around that subject. She'd have to figure out how to handle that.

She'd ask her dad for advice. He'd know what to do.

• • • • •

Margaret paused to collect her thoughts before she entered Phoenix's room the next afternoon.

Her daughter had been moved out of ICU onto the surgical ward for recovery. Friends had brought Nathan to the hospital. He was in with his sister now. Margaret was worried about him, but she could only deal with one problem at a time.

Dr. Doucette had been clear with her that Phoenix needed rest. And in particular, she needed some emotional support. The physical injuries would heal quickly, but there was no way to predict the mental anguish that could arise from a shooting. Margaret was still kicking herself for the question about scars. What a stupid thing to worry about under the circumstances. Now she had to face a much more pressing issue, and there was no way to avoid the subject or prevent the stress that would follow.

She tried to put a smile on her face and pushed through the door into Phoenix's room. Her daughter was sitting halfway up with the support of the bed and eating what looked like Jell-O. The tubes and wires were still attached, but there was less machinery and fewer beeps and buzzes.

"Great to see your appetite is returning," Margaret said with a forced laugh.

"I'm just glad they got me into a regular room. That curtain closet was creepy."

"Believe me, I've seen way too much of hospitals, and the ICU is the worst. Always something crazy going on. You'll be more comfortable here and can get some rest." Margaret was avoiding the elephant in the room as long as she could.

Nathan cut in, "Are you feeling better? I can't believe you got shot." Margaret was glad to hear him expressing himself, especially with some concern for his sister.

Phoenix screwed up her brow and looked up and down at her body as if performing a twenty-point safety check. "My head is perfectly clear, which is great. There's more stomach pain, but they told me they're weaning me off some of the painkillers."

"You look like Dad did when his plane crashed," Nathan said. Then he smiled sheepishly. "OK, maybe not that bad, but there sure are a lot of tubes and wires."

"Just let us know if it gets too bad. They can adjust the meds based on what you're feeling." Margaret appreciated Nathan's curiosity but didn't want Phoenix to focus too much on the medical issues.

"Honestly, Mom, I'd rather they just stopped the drugs altogether. I want to feel my body again." Her daughter had Johnny's impatience—and there was the rub.

"Go easy, Phoenix. You'll be back to yourself before you know it." Margaret wasn't sure where to go next, dreading the inevitable conversation. "Your friends have been calling and texting me nonstop. They're really glad to hear you're OK."

"Where's my phone, Mom? I want to call Dad."

And the elephant arrived.

Still, Margaret delayed. "I have to go down to the front desk to claim your clothes and other things. I'll do that in a minute."

"Is Dad coming down? Can I borrow your phone to call him?"

"You can use mine, Sis." Nathan was trying to be helpful.

"Phoenix . . . Nathan . . . God, I don't know how to tell you this."

"What? Is Dad not coming?"

"No, Phoenix, he's not coming. In fact, we don't even know where he is."

"What do you mean? He's just up in Seattle . . . or maybe in DC," Nathan interjected.

"Kids—you don't understand. He's . . . he's missing. The FBI thinks he's been kidnapped."

Margaret wasn't sure how to process Phoenix's and Nathan's expressions. Shock, surprise, anger, pain flashed across their faces. The sobbing and tears followed. When Phoenix finally spoke, it was the anger that won out.

"That's bullshit, Mom. Why'd you wait to tell us? You might not love him, but he's our father."

"Phoenix . . ." Margaret tried to reach down and hug her.

"Leave me the fuck alone, Mom." And with that, Phoenix buried her head in the pillow.

Nathan just put his head on the side of his sister's bed.

All Margaret could do was walk out.

CHAPTER 21

A THOUSAND WORDS

The only way to describe it was grisly.

Bryce was the first one to intercept the photograph, and it made his stomach turn. And after second and third looks, he went to the bathroom in his basement abode and threw up violently. Although he dealt with the underworld regularly, he wasn't frequently exposed to the more unseemly parts of the dark side. The deaths from the plane crash at Offutt Air Force Base had been horrifying in concept, but he'd never had to look at the mangled bodies. Even his father's murder had occurred from a certain distance—the horror obscured by physical and emotional rocks and rubble.

This was different.

He took his role as the digital guardian of the Roscovitch, Smith, and Humboldt clans seriously, and he hated to face failure. In this case, Johnny Humboldt's face screamed *failure*.

One eye was swollen shut.

His nose was bent at a twenty-five-degree angle.

He was a white man turned black-and-blue.

An arm and a leg skewed akimbo like a Gumby doll.

And a full spectrum of red bloodied the rest of his body.

Now with an empty stomach, Bryce began the difficult task of analyzing the email-delivery vehicle and the digital components of the photo.

His first question—whether Johnny was alive—was answered by the email.

Your lover is hanging by a thread. You have twenty-four hours before I make the last cut.

"Shit," said Bryce. "How can someone butcher another person and then wax metaphorical about it?"

As his sensibilities returned, so did his natural investigative curiosity. He talked himself through the process.

"Bryce, you've got to figure out where these emails are coming from. There has to be a digital trail you can follow."

"Yeah, duh. But it's not that easy. It's not like someone sent it with a postmark."

"OK, but you now have an IP address to chase for the security hack at the school. You have multiple emails to Tamika Smith's personal account. And you know they took him to Den Hell-fuck or wherever in the Netherlands."

Despite berating himself for not solving the IP riddle, he knew it would take hours of painstaking tracing to make meaningful progress. Answers would eventually be found, but only with a significant investment in time.

Tedium with no immediate gratification.

He turned to the photographic attachment itself. Digital productions were much easier to dissect, and Bryce had created some custom tools of his own to identify and authenticate various elements of a photo. He gladly set aside his squeamish stomach and went to work on the JPG image.

After two hours of serious digital gymnastics, he pulled away from the keyboard. No matter how good they were, everyone who doctored images left some residue behind—as if they were a painter with a unique, distinctive stroke. Even the new, more advanced AI-generated photos left trace evidence. Over time, Bryce had learned how to read these trails like a fingerprint and identify where the work had come from.

Unfortunately, he recognized this digital trail all too well.

And now he was really scared.

• • • • •

JJ's team saw the image shortly after Bryce. Tamika had given her father and JJ access to her personal email so they could track communications with the extortionists in real time. JJ's phone rang almost as soon as he got the notification from his team.

"Jessup here."

"JJ, it's Frank Smith." Titles had quickly become a luxury they could not afford.

"I know. I just saw the photo. Sick bastards."

"You know what they say a picture is worth . . . Do you think he's still alive?"

"No way to tell from the image, but the threat doesn't work if he's dead. We'll put the photo under the microscope so to speak and demand proof of life before we go any further."

"How should we respond? Now there's a deadline."

JJ noted the use of the plural for the response. "We'll draft something for Tamika to send—it'll include the proof-of-life demand and a willingness to engage. That should slow the timeline a bit."

"Do you want me to send that, or will you do it directly from her account?"

"Frank, I thought the agreement was you could reach the senator so she could respond. This needs to be in her voice, even if it's drafted by us."

"You know as well as I do that she's not available. We need to buy time." After a pause, Smith continued. "We need to buy *her* some time."

"Goddamn it, Frank, what's she up to?" JJ couldn't keep the frustration out of his voice.

"Come on, Colonel, what do you think?"

• • • • •

"Where the hell is she, Higgs?"

JJ's next call was to Higginbottom.

"She flew to Seattle, and I know from her cell records that she called and met with her team there. Since then, the phone's been dead."

"So you don't know where she's at?" Now his annoyance was out in the open.

Higginbottom's response reflected the attitude. "Actually, I know exactly where she is. She crossed the border on an Amtrak train of all things. Flew out of Vancouver a few hours ago. She's someplace over Greenland right now on the way to Amsterdam."

"Why the hell is she going there?"

"On that, I have no clue. That's as far as she's ticketed, but it could just be a transit stop. Schiphol is a giant European intersection."

"Has she logged into her email?"

"Not that I can tell. But her father may have contacted her."

"Your sit-rep is that I have a military-trained US senator, presumably in search of her boyfriend, running solo on foreign soil. And she was pissed *before* she saw a photo of her mutilated lover."

Jessup wasn't expecting a response from Higginbottom. "Higgs, we gotta know what's in Europe. And if it's in the Netherlands, we need to get some boots on the ground."

"Roger that. Oh yeah, what do you want me to tell Mrs. Humboldt? She's called me twice today to get updates on the investigation. Should I share the photo with her or just lie about it?"

JJ looked down, realizing how impossible the situation had become. He had no good answers.

"Shit," he said. How was he supposed to deal with this mess?

CHAPTER 22

MEANS AND ENDS

Senator Ronald Stumper sat at the dark-stained oak desk in his office in the Hart Building, the newest of the aging office buildings allocated to United States senators. Three credenzas and a bookshelf occupied the walls of the office flanking a window that looked out toward a parking lot and the Monocle Restaurant. Two wingback chairs faced his desk with a meeting table in one corner and two flags on poles in the other corner. Memorabilia and photos from more than thirty years in the Senate covered every available space in the office. The Senate wasn't back in session, so he was taking a relaxing morning to read the news while sipping on a cup of black drip coffee. Men from Texas didn't drink Starbucks.

Stumper was the senior senator from the Lone Star State, as well as one of the oldest legislators in the Senate. With that seniority came a meaningful amount of influence in a body that valued tenure as much or more than it did policy ideas or intellectual rigor. And Stumper didn't place much value on either ideas or rigor. He'd learned long ago that in politics, the key to survival was flexibility and reading the tea leaves. While he was a lifelong conservative, the exact meaning of that phrase had evolved over time. He'd often been called a Reagan Republican, but he'd recently realized that being part of a dying breed was no way to get reelected.

When Trump ran for president in 2016, Stumper supported Jeb Bush initially, believing that he had the experience and pedigree to lead Republicans to victory. He was surprised when Trump ran away with the nomination and won the subsequent election, believing that he was ill-suited to be the leader of the free world. But he also believed that those advising the president would keep him on the straight and level on important issues. That had turned out to be only partially true. As Stumper's own reelection campaign came into focus for 2020, he concluded that he either needed to be a MAGA believer or risk losing in the primary to a Trump-backed opponent.

He got in the clown car.

During that campaign, he'd burnished his credentials as a MAGA-leaning Republican by supporting Trump's claims of election fraud. His unwillingness to impeach Trump for his actions had further solidified his successful transformation from the old-school GOP into a modern MAGAnite. He found the whole process a bit demeaning, but he'd always believed the ends justified the means, and this change in loyalties was no different.

Turning the pages of *The Washington Post*, he noted the coverage of a school shooting in California. He read the angry calls for better gun control provisions. He had no patience for people who blamed the Second Amendment for mass shootings. The right to own a gun was at the foundation of his American narrative. He knew that the real issue was the crazy people themselves.

"Don't blame the tool, just the craftsman," he always said.

He also hated California and what he considered its prima donna government. Not only were they too liberal but the state government there seemed to think they could impose stricter laws on individuals and businesses than the rest of the country. The effect was that to sell goods in California, companies had to live up to the state's standards everywhere. The extra costs to businesses were passed on to consumers across the country. Why should he have to pay for stupid California regulations?

"If their law enforcement was better, they wouldn't have these problems," he said to the picture window as he looked out over the DC landscape.

Then he noticed a photo of FBI agents at the scene of the shooting and recognized his fellow senator Tamika Smith in the shot. They'd butted heads during her short time in the Senate, and he knew that was going to continue.

"What the hell is she doing there?"

He made a note to find out.

Switching publications, he also enjoyed *The Economist* editorial page's update on the raging inflation problem and the risks associated with the rapidly rising federal deficit. Fiscal policy was one area where he'd not sacrificed to Donald Trump's altar. He'd voted against Trump's $1.5 trillion tax cut legislation in 2017, believing it wasn't necessary to drive the economy and would only increase the debt. This was one of his few bright-line issues, and he'd been proven right, as the editorial pointed out.

The Tax Cut and Jobs Act of 2017 was a mixed blessing. It simplified the tax code by eliminating or limiting a number of special deductions and exemptions, and provided an influx of cash into the economy, both from reduced taxes and money repatriated from overseas on a tax-free basis. The corporate tax cut also increased profits. However, given that it came during a continuing economic expansion, the tax changes did not lead to increased investment and contributed to the inflation we are now experiencing. In addition, the short-term economic spike it generated came at the expense of a dramatically increased budget deficit. Overall, the tax cuts helped those with money but increased income inequality across the country.

Now with a Democrat in the White House, Stumper had even more reasons to complain about out-of-control federal spending. The Biden administration had forced through almost $1.9 trillion of additional COVID spending with the American Rescue Act. Beyond his knee-jerk rejection to a Democrat spending bill, Stumper viewed this spending as totally unnecessary and irresponsible. In hindsight, the inflationary results had proven him right.

Both the Trump and Biden bills were passed on a partisan basis using a legislative procedure called reconciliation, which avoided the usual need to get 60 percent of the Senate to move forward on a bill. Stumper knew that the national deficit was quickly approaching the statutory limit and that there would be an effort to raise the debt ceiling before the so-called X date when the government could no longer borrow money. Partisan reconciliation was unlikely to save either side this time.

With the federal debt approaching the legislative prescribed ceiling, a showdown is looming. Facing the dual threats of an inflationary dumpster fire and an uncontrolled budget deficit

> spiral, Congress has tied itself up in knots. The only easy answer is to raise the debt ceiling so that the government can continue borrowing money. But another kick of the can down the road is a short-term panacea. It doesn't constrain spending, nor does it help in the fight against inflation.
>
> There are only two ways to go—cut spending or raise taxes. Neither of these are popular nor likely outcomes. According to the Lincoln Coalition, a bipartisan group that has introduced multiple pieces of legislation to return to fiscal responsibility, a targeted combination of increased taxes, better tax collection by the IRS, and specific cuts in ineffective legacy government programs are a good starting point. The group argues that the only long-term solution is to tackle the triple crown of budget behemoths—health care, defense, and Social Security.
>
> Since Congress is unwilling or unable to address those third rail issues, a day of financial reckoning is fast approaching. Given the current distrust and divisions between Republicans and Democrats—not to mention fractures within each party—it's difficult to envision a productive path forward. The US economy has long been a beacon for the rest of the world and demonstrative proof that capitalism works better than any other economic system. The house of cards that American politicians have built is about to bring that all down on top of its citizens. And it will be the average person who will suffer the most.

Screw the Lincoln Coalition and their pack of compromising pansies, Stumper thought. They believed that governing was about finding common ground. That crock of shit went out with landline phones, as far as Stumper was concerned. Governing was about protecting the pieces of the pie that were important to you and the people who funded your campaigns. This fight wasn't about leadership—it was about power and survival. Sometimes you had to draw a line in the sand and fight.

The article reminded him to get the wheels in motion for serious strategy discussions on painting that line permanently. He picked up his cell phone.

"Dyer, you in the office yet?" John Dyer was his chief of staff and primary gofer.

"I'm just walking into the building, Senator. What can I do for you?"

"I want us to be ready for the debt ceiling debates coming up."

"Any information you'd like in particular?"

"No information. I want an endgame."

"An endgame, sir?"

"Dyer, the debt ceiling is not going to be raised." He clicked off.

He looked at the US and Texas flags in the corner, contemplating what they meant to him. He thought about the reaction he'd get from senators like Tamika Smith when he pushed his agenda.

"Fuck 'em."

CHAPTER 23

ONGOING INVESTIGATION

The key questions were *why*—and *why now*?

Jessup knew that investigations ran into difficulties because of a lack of evidence. For his team, the current problem was exactly the inverse. They had a surplus of evidence and numerous trails to follow. The deputy director of the FBI should have been happy with the abundance, but JJ was both perplexed and nervous. The volume of criminal activity made it difficult to see through the murky mist, and in the absence of clarity, his team was chasing everything at once. The Tamika Smith factor added to his mosh pit of issues.

While none of the fraud, extortion, and bribery cases would have been meaningful enough to make his desk individually, the sheer volume of activity was problematic. And then there was the attack at the San Mateo high school, which created all kinds of crazy possibilities. Was this connected to the rash of crime that was spreading like a computer virus across the country? It was clearly related to the threats against Senator Smith, but the nature of the attack was a radical escalation. The capper was the Humboldt kidnapping on the same day as the shooting. Coincidence? Jessup didn't think so.

"Higginbottom here, sir." The voice from the secure video channel startled JJ a bit as he sat in his DC office fresh from a long flight home. *Stale* probably would have been a better word.

"Did you have a chance to evaluate the material I sent you last night?" Jessup had decided to read Higginbottom into the broader investigation.

He needed his agent on-site in the Bay Area to have the full background, so he knew what questions to ask and where to look.

"Yes, sir. With the exception of the shooting and kidnapping, it's not clear if any of these things are connected."

"Agreed. So we have to attack each piece, recognizing that it might all fit into the same puzzle. Or not." The expression on Higginbottom's face told him all he needed to know.

"I assume I'm still focusing on the attack and kidnapping here, right?" The field agent held up a fat folder that was presumably filled with evidence from the scene of the shooting.

"Roger that, but I'm going to keep you copied on the rest of the work we're doing here in DC. I have a small army tracing the money involved in all these schemes. There has to be a trail we can follow somewhere. And we can't afford to miss any connections."

"Understood. How did the call go with Mrs. Humboldt?" Jessup had agreed to follow up with Margaret.

"About like you'd expect. The good news is her daughter is recovering quickly, giving her some peace of mind. But she's remarkably loyal to her ex-husband and is worried about the mental health of her kids."

"That all sounds natural to me."

"Sure. But what I left out was the expletive-laced harangue directed at me, you, and the rest of the FBI. She clearly doesn't think we're doing enough."

There wasn't much for Higginbottom to say. "Comes with the territory, I guess."

"She told me that her kids could do a better job than we are."

As he disconnected the call, he let out a deep breath.

Maybe not her kids, but a US senator is going to try.

• • • • •

Phoenix listened intently to the conversation between her mom and the FBI.

She and her mom were sitting in her hospital room waiting for the doctor to come for what she hoped would be a final checkup. The wounds were healing normally and the pain was manageable, which should enable her to go home. She was still pissed about the way she found out about her dad's kidnapping but had concluded that her mom had more than enough on her plate. With her body on the mend, Phoenix's mind was running a million miles an hour. She desperately wanted to hear the full FBI conversation.

"What do you mean you have a photo of him but you don't know where he is?" Despite what she'd said to her mom initially, Phoenix knew that the divorce hadn't wiped out the years of marriage and the deep caring that came with it.

"Well, send me the picture. Maybe there's some way I can help."

Pause.

"What do you mean you can't do that?" Another break. "Of course I know it's an investigation. And I'm part of it! If there's a ransom demand, I'll pay it."

More words from the other end of the line, and then her mom lost it. "Don't be an ass. Just because we're divorced doesn't mean I'm not family. I'm the mother of his children for Christ's sake. And oh, by the way, my daughter was shot by some fucking terrorist that you still haven't tracked down. My kids could do a better job."

Her mom mouthed *blah, blah, blah* as she listened to more talking on the phone. "Fine. I'll do that." She hit the red button to end the call.

"Asshole."

"Who was that? What did he say? Is Dad all right? Do they know where he is?" The questions were accompanied by a range of hand gestures. Phoenix was still connected to some monitors but could move around her hospital environment more easily now. Her rush of questions was partly a rising sense of anxiety and partly anger at her inability to help her dad.

"That was the deputy director of the FBI. I guess he didn't trust his local people to shut us out. Apparently they have a photo from the kidnappers of your dad, but they won't show it to us. He didn't mention a ransom demand—but what the hell else would they want with your father? The director made a bunch of excuses, but I'm not buying it. Something else is going on."

"Give me a hug, Mom. It'll be OK. You know Dad's a fighter. He'll find a way out."

Margaret slumped into her arms. Phoenix had the strange sensation of a child comforting an adult. She wasn't sure if she was supporting her mom or just trying to make herself feel better. Probably a bit of both.

But her deeper thoughts weren't on her growing young adulthood. And she really wasn't looking to comfort or be comforted. What she really wanted was action. Someone needed to find her father.

And she knew where to start.

CHAPTER 24

THE NEW WAR

Nastya Andropov had been born in Berezniki on the banks of the Kama River at the base of the Ural Mountains. It was a nondescript mining town that was well past its prime, if such a thing had ever existed. When a potash plant is your claim to fame and the centerpiece of your economy, it's time to move on.

And that's exactly what Andropov had done, moving to Moscow at the age of eighteen. Her goal was to build a life there that reflected the original glory of her family name in the old Soviet Union. Her father had told her stories about her grandfather, Yuri Andropov. He had been the Soviet ambassador to Hungary and put down the 1956 Hungarian Uprising. He was also chairman of the KGB. He ascended to the role of general secretary of the Communist Party, making him the leader of the Soviet Union. She felt shame when she thought about it. He only served for fifteen months before he died amid Soviet decline.

Seven years later, the USSR collapsed, and with it her family's status in the country.

Once in Moscow, she wrangled an introduction to the Federal Security Service, commonly known as the FSB. This successor to the KGB was quickly gaining a reputation as being as repressive as its predecessor. Fluent in six languages and deadly with a gun, Andropov had risen in the ranks as a field agent. In Cold War terms, she was a spy. She'd undertaken a number of missions across Europe, including several terminations. Driven by her hatred for what the West had done to the Russian motherland, she had no qualms about her work. She wanted a return to past glory. That goal was all that mattered.

There were two schools of thought when establishing a permanent base for clandestine activity. The first was to find someplace remote where the authorities weren't experienced and where nobody was expecting a spy to show up in their midst. The trade-off was that among a small population, it was difficult to stay anonymous. The alternative was a big city, with efficient and convenient transportation, a larger population, and more transient visitors. But with the ability to blend in came more experienced police.

She preferred to hide in plain sight.

She'd established her home base in the Netherlands five years earlier on the island of Texel. This outpost was the first of the Wadden Islands covering the northern entrance to what used to be the Zuiderzee—the sea lane for shipping in the Dutch Golden Age of the seventeenth century. The building of the Afsluitdijk (the "closing dike") converted much of the Zuiderzee into an inland freshwater lake now called the IJsselmeer. This engineering achievement effectively cut off the Wadden Islands from the heart of Dutch commerce, forcing Texel to convert itself into a tourist and farming community. Rural and isolated, Texel fit her needs perfectly.

The most difficult part of her original assignment to the Netherlands was learning Dutch. She'd taken up German at an early age, and while the languages had some common origins, she needed to be very careful to expunge much of her German thinking. The Dutch were proud of their independent heritage and had a bad history with the Germans. If she was going to blend in as a single Dutch woman, her language, attitudes, and habits had to match. Her cottage in De Cocksdorp at the northern tip of the island near a large lighthouse had the requisite flower garden and was kept immaculately in good Dutch tradition.

To cover any remaining linguistic mistakes she made, her backstory included a family history of Georgian ancestors. In the last few years of World War II, the Nazis had conscripted Georgian soldiers to supervise the Dutch on Texel. At the very end of the war, the Georgians revolted and a battle with the Nazis raged on the island for several weeks after the official German surrender to the Allies. Almost 1,500 people were killed, leaving the Georgians with a mixed reputation with local Dutch families.

Her faked ancestry both made some language mistakes permissible, as well as isolated her a bit from some older locals. The fewer people coming for tea and a chat, the better.

Completing the daily double—a shooting and a kidnapping on US soil—had required careful planning, but the risk had also been reduced by using fewer resources. The exfil out of the country was a bit dicey, but if anyone was tracking them, there were several dead ends to follow. Now her American friend was hidden, awaiting developments in the US, and she was safely ensconced in her cottage with a winter storm swirling around her. Texel was nice in the summer, but the North Sea knew how to unleash some fierce storms, and she'd be happy to ride this one out.

She logged into the RallyAmerica Discord account to monitor activities. She'd always been a user of the Russian app Telegram, but her US handler had introduced her to the American Discord tool, which was uncomfortable at first. Drafting off someone else's plan without any detailed knowledge of the endgame added to her unease. Agents are control freaks, and Nastya was no different. But her instructions were quite clear:

> **The RallyAmerica DAO is focused on destabilizing the US government and economy. While your mission may ultimately diverge, for the time being, you should allow RallyAmerica to do its work. Pick and choose missions that are offered so that you can exercise some level of control in pivotal areas. For the rest, just observe and track. Patience will bring an opening to pursue our silent war more aggressively.**

She hated being passive and patient. She'd watched the earliest efforts at blackmail, fraud, and identity theft and sat on the sidelines given the simplistic nature of the operations. She didn't think much of the way these missions were pursued. She knew the American expression was "bush league." But when the opportunity at the high school came on the radar screen, she and her handler jumped in with both feet. This mission both suited her skill set and required a level of professionalism and precision that they couldn't trust to other DAO freelancers. Letting the blockchain-run organization meander a bit was fine, but ultimately it had to be successful.

Returning to the RallyAmerica communications on Discord, she noted the continued efforts to leverage Senator Tamika Smith. Andropov had done a profile of Smith herself and reviewed the FSB dossier as well. In both cases, her conclusion was that Smith was likely to do the opposite of what the DAO wanted. Instead of giving in to their demands, she was more likely to work with the FBI as she had in the past.

Or worse, Smith might go rogue.

Andropov looked out the window toward the beach through the mist and gloom, as if expecting a landing by foreign agents. The thought of facing a US military officer was more intriguing than it was fearful. At five foot eleven with an athletic build, Smith looked closer to thirty than forty and was a physically imposing opponent. But Nastya Andropov was a cold-blooded professional who had taken down bigger, more powerful men. What chance did a government bureaucrat have against her? She glanced at her tabby cat, Sonny, who was sauntering across the windowsill.

"Don't worry, boy. If she comes for me, I'll take her out."

CHAPTER 25

CHECKS AND BALANCES

Lee Bowen didn't really believe in vacations. Sitting on the beach just wasn't his idea of relaxation, and he wasn't much for skiing, hiking, scuba diving, or golf. His recreation was his financial passion, and vacations generally didn't help you make more money. So while his trip to the Four Seasons in Maui had been marketed to others as a Christmas holiday trip, it was really an opportunity to work on his grand project without the prying eyes of his partner Ely Basof and other B^2 employees.

With the genesis of his plan, he had spent a great deal of time analyzing what had happened during the January 6 attack on the US Capitol. He'd never thought something like that could happen in the United States, but once it did, his eyes were opened to many possibilities. If a disorganized mob of poorly trained conspiracy theorists could storm the Capitol and come very close to shutting down the government, he realized someone with a bit of brains and resources could go so much further.

At first he'd thought that the political parties would join hands, or at least work together, to condemn the attack and take steps to make sure it would never happen again. At a minimum, he thought a bipartisan committee would be formed that would make recommendations that might or might not be followed. Much like what happened after the 9/11 attacks.

But over time, he realized that the normal political calculus had changed in fundamental ways. One plus one no longer equaled two. In fact, there were very few pluses to be found. The Democrats, perhaps out of self-interest but certainly out of frustration, decided to use the insurrection for their own political gain. Fearing their own voters, the Republicans decided to either look to the future or litigate the past by whitewashing the entire event. Trump, for his part, went into full denial mode, claiming he won the election, that the criminal investigations were all part of a grand witch hunt, and that the insurrectionists were just peaceful protestors.

As this political maneuvering was progressing, Bowen had slowly put together his DAO plan, gathering investors, creating the basic technical platform, and establishing a structure that enabled him to control RallyAmerica without others knowing he was doing it. While Bowen's technical skills were nothing like his VC partner's deep computer science knowledge, he knew the right places to research the DAO process.

Ultimately, he started the development using a tool called Metamask. The account he created there would become his blockchain ID, his Ethereum cryptocurrency wallet, and his voting signature for the DAO. He laughed as he saved the twelve recovery words required should he somehow lose his Metamask password. He saved all this information in his password vault, hopeful to avoid the horror stories he'd heard from people who got locked out of their accounts permanently.

Next, he built the actual DAO with another site, Aragon.org. This tool used a step-by-step process to create the code required for the DAO, enabling Bowen to establish the structure without any programming skills. He connected the RallyAmerica DAO to his Metamask wallet and to a Discord channel he'd created for DAO-related communications. Aragon required a purpose for the DAO, which he inscribed as "to invest and support companies that are committed to American democracy." While this reflected some of his natural cynicism, it also served as a camouflaging statement that would protect both his investors and his own activities.

The final phase of the DAO creation revolved around governance. Since there would be no board of directors, specific rules needed to be embedded in the code that defined RallyAmerica. Bowen chose to have voting based on ownership percentages, knowing that this was something he could control. Instead of shares, blockchain organizations use digital tokens as their proof of ownership. He gave the RallyAmerica tokens the appropriate name of *rallycoin* with a token symbol of RCN. He also decided that any proposal for action needed 60 percent approval to be enacted and set a high minimum threshold for voting participation to make sure no surprise proposals were approved by only a few token holders. The Aragon.org tool published the RallyAmerica smart contract to the blockchain and the DAO was ready for action.

Bowen had immediately begun initiating and approving proposals that targeted business, political, and community leaders with tactics that ranged from social media harassment to extortion threats to false flag campaigns. While some of these efforts had been strategically targeted, most of this early work proved that his system worked and escalated the noise level in the US social ecosystem. Creating general anxiety was a good place to start. And a great place to stress test the process.

All this work was built on his evaluation of the January 6 fallout. He surmised that there were people in both parties who understood what had happened and the longer-term risks to democracy that had been exposed, but they didn't seem to have the power to get anything done. See Liz Cheney. Ask Adam Schiff. For himself, Bowen wasn't deep into politics, taking more of a libertarian attitude toward most issues. His primary focus was the government's overreach and regulation that prevented him from doing what was clearly in his best interest. Making more money.

Winning.

As he began his campaign of unrest and civic disruption, he realized there were others working to stop him, even if they didn't know it yet. The Maui Christmas trip was a personal retreat to figure out how to deal with his competitors, and at the very top of his list was Tamika Smith and the Lincoln Coalition. Their form of rational discourse, detailed negotiations, careful policy work, and thoughtful compromise was anathema to his need for chaos and social disruption.

Looking out the window at the waves breaking on the shore, he decided to watch the Washington senator's speech again—the one she'd given on the floor of the Senate after the House Select Committee to Investigate the January 6 Attack on the United States Capitol (now that was a mouthful) released its final report in December of 2022. Bowen cast the video onto the room's large-screen TV, lay back on the bed against the headrest, and absorbed the senator's style and message.

Regardless of your political point of view, what happened on January sixth was an affront to our democratic system. We can all disagree on the various levels of free speech and civil protests that are an important part of our freedoms. But what happened on 1/6 leaves no room for debate. The halls of our government were violently breached, government leaders were threatened, and law enforcement officers were murdered. These are incontestable facts, reinforced by video evidence and the experiences of many of you in this very chamber.

The Select Committee has also highlighted related attempts to overturn the election, including proposing alternative electors, pressuring secretaries of state and other election officials, spreading misinformation about election fraud, and encouraging the vice president to not certify the verified votes of the Electoral College.

Bowen nodded passively as Senator Smith paused dramatically for effect. He knew instinctively that she was a significant enemy—a potential roadblock to his carefully orchestrated plans. But he was also a businessperson who had seen real leadership before, and he had to respect the way she was pursuing her craft. All the more reason to study her carefully and remove the obstacle before it was firmly anchored.

I know that some of you would rather not face the reality of January sixth. It is an inconvenient truth that our country came very close to a governmental meltdown. A democracy China Syndrome that could have led to mass chaos and the third world equivalent of a bloodless coup. I'm certain you don't want to hear that because you're afraid to oppose the forces within our institutions and your own party that were behind these traitorous actions.

There are others who want to use the tragedy of January sixth as a political tool to castigate and label others as the "fascist right." If enough people can be convinced that the "others" are to blame, your own interests will be served. This is just another form of disinformation and manipulation that doesn't belong in our democratic society.

In the end, it was the rule of law that saved us. The vice president followed the law on January sixth by certifying a legitimate election—and we should be exceptionally grateful for that. Courts at every level have heard and rejected arguments related to claims of election fraud, vote tampering, and rules violations. They also have enforced the law by steadily trying, convicting, and sentencing insurrectionists to real jail time.

I and my Lincoln Coalition compatriots will fight for that rule of law to provide the checks on power abuse that are far too common in our partisan politics.

With that, Lee Bowen felt a double-barreled jolt of electricity run through him. First, it was clearer than ever that the country had come very close to melting down in the aftermath of the last election. The House had impeached President Trump with limited Republican support, and the Senate had refused to convict him, falling several members short of the sixty-seven votes required. Given all that the House Select Committee had chronicled, and the legal indictments that seemed in the offing, it was stunning that no action had been taken. With a little push from Vice President Pence or a random ruling from a judge, the peaceful transition of power could have been disrupted. For Bowen, that near miss had smelled like a venture capital opportunity.

After Smith's speech, he'd been equally certain that Senator Tamika Smith and her Lincoln Coalition were a serious problem. She was a born leader, articulate, and principled—not attributes in long supply on Capitol Hill. He'd already done the background work and digital digging to develop material he could use against the senator. If she could be fully neutralized, the Lincoln Coalition would become a paper tiger.

Step one was firing off the first email salvo to Smith's personal account. Then he'd go after additional pivotal senators to create another opportunity to topple the government. This time, the effort wouldn't come up short—and he'd be ready to monetize the chaos.

The Senate, after all, controlled the financial keys to a very valuable kingdom.

CHAPTER 26

BELOW SEA LEVEL

She had to find Johnny.

As Tamika walked down the center aisle of Schiphol Airport's Pier E, she used the moving walkway to accelerate her pace, taking in the sights and sounds of a United Nations of people and languages. Aside from her military brat travels and her own service in the Middle East, she'd never vacationed much outside the US. Now she found herself in the midst of everyone else's business trips and tourist journeys. It would have felt invigorating except for the tragic and dangerous nature of her journey. Instead of feeling positively energized, she was numb to what was going on around her.

While she was in flight, the general had texted the photo of Johnny and the attached message to her burner cell phone. She'd gone to the restroom to steady herself. Her memory was emblazoned with any number of horrible images of injury and death: between her three tours and the crash at Offutt, gruesome was a regular companion. But this was Johnny. This was the person she knew she loved.

Her Johnny.

While the message indicated he was still alive and there were some suspicions that the photo was doctored, she could not imagine the pain he was going through. The tears turned to anger, and the anger morphed into determination. By the time she returned to her seat, she was composed and committed to whatever it would take to kill the people responsible.

She blocked out the terminal's hubbub and rushing chaos to focus on her own mission. She'd gone old school in her travel preparations, packing one of her military duffel bags that was now slung over her shoulders like a backpack. She wore a baseball cap with her hair tied up in a single ponytail hanging out the back, an old sweatshirt from some bygone track meet she'd competed in, and a pair of faded jeans. Her attire was part of the "don't be a senator" mission parameters, but it also fit her general personality—comfortable, active, performance oriented, and unpretentious.

She had no choice but to go through customs, so she knew the US authorities, including JJ and the FBI, would pick up her trail. She was hopeful that nobody else cared enough about her trip to track her, but the school shooting and kidnapping reminded her that with the stakes so high, she should be careful.

Schiphol Airport, one of the busiest international airports in the world, had originally been built as a World War I airfield in a marshy area southwest of Amsterdam. Now it served as a transit hub between Europe, the Middle East, and Africa, with ongoing service to North and South America. It was the perfect place to enter Europe and hope to lose whoever was tracking her. And while the Netherlands was a small country as haystacks go, it was plenty large enough to make the search difficult.

She stopped at an ATM to add to her pool of euros. She then went to the NS train kiosk and used a credit card to purchase a round-trip ticket to Maastricht, a city deep in the south of the country as far away from her real destination as possible. She wasn't convinced this would fool anyone, but the ticket would have enough cash value to get her to Johnny's last known location.

She walked across the teeming main airport entry atrium and found the escalator entrance to the train station located below. She tapped her ticket on the entry reader, stepped on the escalator, and rode the flat metallic carpet down to platform 3. Fifteen minutes later she was on the Sprinter train to Zaandam, where she would make a ten-minute transfer to the much faster Intercity train going north. Finally settled into an upper-level seat at the back of a second-class car, she watched the low, lush Dutch farmland flash by out her window.

On the flight over she'd read up on Dutch history and the economy, wondering why they'd taken Johnny there. She already knew that over a quarter of the land was below sea level and the country was among the most densely populated in Europe. And yet it was the world's second largest exporter of food and agricultural products and home to a significant number of European and global companies. Perhaps the most relevant Dutch attributes for her current circumstance were a history of social tolerance and a common transit point for all of Europe. Indeed, she suspected that there was much activity that transpired beneath the surface of the canals, tourist sites, and wind turbines that belied the beauty and peacefulness of the landscape. She shuddered as she revisited the image of Johnny's bloodied face and twisted body.

Nobody would believe that that could happen here.

As the train jarred to a stop, Tamika realized she'd nodded off to sleep. "Good thing my stop was the end of the line," she said quietly to herself. She picked up her duffel bag from the overhead rack, exited through the sliding door at the rear of the car, stepped down to the exterior door, and walked out onto the platform.

She was greeted by Dutch drizzle, a steady breeze, and forty degrees. *Seattle weather*, she thought. Despite herself, she smiled. It reminded her of recent walks she'd taken with her father. Even as he moved into retirement, she was still leaning on him for support and guidance.

She looked up and down the platform to find some shelter but had to walk fifty yards to the station house to her left, where she tapped out at the exit reader and glanced across a small plaza. She found the building she was looking for and checked in to the Hotel Wienerhof. "Eclectically mediocre" was a good description, but that suited the duffel bag–carrying Tamika just fine. She plopped down in her white paneled room with a single bed, small bathroom, and tiny plastic walled shower and took several deep breaths.

Now she had to wait.

• • • • •

The next morning, as she sat in the spartan hotel breakfast area, she looked up from her coffee to see a middle-aged man walk in through the side door. She pulled the photo up on her phone that her dad had sent and knew it was a match. Jan Lugtenberg greeted her with a big smile and three kisses on her cheeks. Tamika was taken aback at first but relaxed a bit as he introduced himself.

"My apologies if that was a bit too much for you—I suppose the greeting is typically Dutch and more than most Americans are used to. Welcome to the Netherlands, Senator Smith."

"All good," Tamika replied with an effort at a smile. "And Tamika will be fine. I'm just a bit tired and a little out of my element. I should be the one thanking you for agreeing to help me."

"I've lived in Den Helder most of my adult life—stayed after serving in the Dutch Navy. Always happy to show off the town and help a fellow service member at the same time."

General Smith had used his military contacts to provide Tamika with a guide. She wasn't sure how much her father had told him, but Lugtenberg fit the bill. A big man, though still fit, with graying temples and thinning black hair, he spoke excellent English and obviously knew the area. He was dressed in jeans and a gray raincoat with a hood, and she noted the hint of a thick sweater underneath. He was prepared for the elements.

"I'm not exactly sure where to start," Tamika began. "A friend of mine flew into De Kooy Airfield on a private charter. He was supposed to stay in touch during his trip, but I haven't heard anything from him since he landed." The cover story was transparently thin, but she didn't want to divulge too much information.

"Must be some kind of friend. We don't see many international private charters here—pricy to jump across the pond, and when people do, they're usually headed to Amsterdam. Why was he coming to Den Helder?"

"That's a great question—I guess I just assumed it was less busy than Amsterdam. He mentioned something about wanting to sail, so maybe this was his jumping-off point?"

"Could be, although I don't think I'd want to be out on the North Sea in January." He hesitated, as if there was something else he wanted to say.

Tamika cut in to shift the conversation. "Would it be possible to go to the FBO at De Kooy and see if anyone saw him or talked with him?"

"Of course, of course. My car is just out back. The airport is mostly used by helicopters servicing the offshore oil and gas fields and wind turbines, but there's a fixed base operator there for private planes."

The trip to the airport was uneventful and equally unfruitful. The agent at the FBO had no record of a transatlantic private flight landing on January 4, nor did he recognize the photograph of Johnny. When asked if there was a way to view aircraft landing records, he said that would require police or court approval.

As they left the airport, Lugtenberg turned right—a move that looped them back around the airport a second time.

"Where are we going?" Tamika asked a bit nervously.

"What are you not telling me, Tamika? I saw the FBO clerk watch us as we left and then make a phone call."

"What are you talking about?"

"Have you noticed that the same car has been following us since we left the hotel? And just now, as I took us back through the airport, it continued after us."

Tamika popped down the cosmetic mirror on the passenger side so she could look behind the car without being obvious. A small black SUV was matching their speed about three hundred yards behind them. "Are you sure?"

"Maybe your dad didn't tell you. I do security for a living. Someone is following us. Or more accurately, you."

CHAPTER 27

CRACKS IN THE PLAN

Lee Bowen knew he should wipe the self-satisfied, shit-eating grin off his face, but he couldn't help himself as he reread the email. He'd assumed that Senator Tamika Smith would be the last brick to fall into place. With her written capitulation, she'd been the first.

> "I need to know that Johnny Humboldt is alive and that you'll release him if I do what you want. And the rest of my extended family comes off your hit list. Just tell me what it will take."

While he could imagine her writing the words, he was a bit stunned at the completeness of his victory. "Huh," he said to no one in particular. "I guess she put up a good front but was soft in the end." Clearly, the photo had done its magic.

He could prove that Humboldt was alive, but he damned sure wasn't going to release him or take the pressure off her family until she played her role in making his plan a success. That said, he knew from experience that once someone asked for the terms, they'd already given up.

He decided to let her stew a bit before replying, but he did send a Discord message to get an audio recording of Johnny reading a current headline from a newspaper to prove that he was still among the living. Given the circumstances and the nature of the blackmail, a picture was out of the question. But he needed to be prepared with the proof so that Smith would live up to her end of the bargain.

Taking the leader of the Lincoln Coalition off the table might influence a few others, but Bowen needed to be sure. He'd targeted three other fiscal moderates in the Senate, knowing that he needed to control their votes to create the chaos he craved. A certain junior senator from Missouri was susceptible to a relatively basic honey trap scheme. Bowen was reviewing several DAO proposals he'd received and hoped to close on that investment in the next week or so.

He'd issued additional DAO proposals for the other Senate targets, but so far had not received anything that looked manageable or likely to succeed. If only he could have been working the House of Representatives. That organization had so many loose cannons and people with shaky morals that generating influence would have been relatively easy. But the House was likely going to go his way without much pushing. The Republican Speaker of the House owed his leadership position to the Freedom Caucus. He was certain to serve their needs or pay the price of their wrath. Either one was just fine for Lee Bowen.

The Senate, however, was entirely another matter. While it was also highly partisan, members had six-year terms, which gave them a bit more independence. It also seemed to hold its members to a higher standard of behavior—or maybe the voters were more careful with their votes for statewide roles. Either way, the Senate's filibuster rules effectively required sixty votes to pass most legislation, leading to either gridlock or horse trading depending on the issue. To succeed, he needed to own the Senate—with an evenly split Senate, that meant influencing the swing votes.

He yelled across the office, "Ely, you ready for lunch? 'Cause I'm buying." The Smith capitulation had put him a huge step closer to his ultimate goal.

He could smell the scent of victory in the air.

• • • • •

"*Belachelijk*," she said in Dutch.

Nastya Andropov was reading the latest RallyAmerica update on Discord and noted that the Tamika Smith operation was marked as *complete*. Did they really think she would fold like that?

"Total bullshit," she emphasized to Sonny the cat. "Whoever's running the DAO may be clever, but they don't know jack about intelligence operations."

She loved using American slang to show off her proficiency in the language.

"Nothing in Smith's dossier indicates she'll cave that easily—in fact, I'd bet Putin's dacha outside Moscow she'll never give in. This one will die before she sacrifices her principles. Just like us, right, Sonny?"

And Andropov knew something that she had not reported to the DAO. Senator Smith was right across the channel in Den Helder searching for her lost lover. Nothing suspicious happened in the north of the Netherlands without Andropov knowing about it. Her sphere of influence was subtle but very wide—all the better to protect herself. Because self-preservation was necessary to serve the ultimate objective.

Mother Russia.

She knew that many in Putin's inner circle and those in the broader oligarchy were focused on themselves—their perceived status, their organizational power, and their personal wealth. Sure, they cloaked themselves in a veneer of patriotism, but when real decisions had to be made, their true motivations won out. Putin himself was a bit more complicated. He seemed to believe in a true, rebuilt Russia, but at the same time was clearly the leader of the grift.

Andropov had decided long ago to distance herself from this cabal. Her family's history in the USSR ran deep and true. She believed in communism as the ideal state, and while the Soviet Union had been flawed, those flaws were human in origin. She'd been raised to support the communist mission, and nobody was going to dissuade her from that goal.

She and her America-based handler had agreed from the beginning that the DAO was just a tool and that they would not be bound by any of its rules or requirements. Personally, she'd rather ignore RallyAmerica completely and pursue their objectives directly. But she wasn't in charge. So for now, she would ignore the online self-congratulations and focus her attention on what to do about the senator.

She walked outside to sweep the sidewalk and prune some of her flowers. She had to keep up appearances, after all—especially in a Dutch town, where the neighbors all knew each other. Her role in the FSB may have been the only kept secret in the town of De Cocksdorp. Her neighbor, Janneke, gave her the Dutch "hoy, hoy" with a wave as she walked past the front of her property. Andropov gave her the required wave in return.

As she tidied up, she considered three options for dealing with the growing threat.

Of course, she could just choose to monitor the situation for now. Smith was nowhere close to finding Humboldt and really had no clues at this point. She didn't have much intelligence support on the ground and wasn't trained in this kind of work in any event. Where was she going to go next now that the airport had proven to be a dead end?

Perhaps that was the wisest choice, but Andropov wasn't one to sit around and wait for the action to come to her. It might be smarter to persuade Smith to look elsewhere. The misdirection would have to be convincing—she knew Lugtenberg reasonably well, and he was no fool. But perhaps she could convince the Westerners that the Netherlands was just a transit point, and Johnny Humboldt was already much farther east. The airplane flight plan had already planted that seed. It might not end the search, but it would move it away from the immediate area. Let Smith burn herself out in Budapest. By the time she figured it out, it would be too late.

Of course, there was a more aggressive alternative that made her smile.

Andropov could just take Smith out.

CHAPTER 28

STEPPING OUT

"You and I both know I have to get back to school." Words Phoenix had never thought she would say.

Six days had passed since the shooting. Six days since her father had been kidnapped. Six days in which the FBI had done nothing to find him or bring him home. Physically, Phoenix's recovery was proceeding at a rapid pace. She still had stitches with a heavy bandage across her stomach, but she was completely off the pain meds. She could walk comfortably, although she didn't quite feel ready to break into a track-and-field training run. Dr. Doucette had told her to protect her chest area from any bumps or bruises.

"Not yet," her mother said, shaking her head. "I'm still not even sure *I* should go into work."

Her mom's rejection just increased her emotional unrest. Phoenix was determined not to let her mother hover over her. She could take care of herself.

"Come on, Mom. You've seen me around the house. I'm fine. My friends say school is filled with police officers—it's probably the safest place I could go." She could sense her mom hesitating.

"Look, you need to get back to work," Phoenix pressed. "I've heard you on the Zoom calls with your team. They need you in the office to keep things moving. I promise I'll call or text you between every class. We both need a regular routine to stay sane."

Under the circumstances, there was nothing regular or routine about life in the Humboldt household. Her mom was totally on edge now that Phoenix was out of the hospital and back home; Nathan was more of a fourteen-year-old mess than usual. The family therapist was going to be busy over the coming months. Friends had been calling and sending messages offering to help, but as far as Phoenix was concerned, their efforts would not actually be helpful. She'd decided to just put them off—social niceties didn't seem very important at the moment.

Phoenix decided to turn off all her social media accounts. There had been too many posts in the past week saying "you're a hero"—which were just embarrassing. And then there were the "what were you thinking, you stupid bitch" comments, which were unsettling to say the least. The memes and TikTok videos ranged from hilarious to evil and made her think for the first time that maybe her social status wasn't as important as she'd thought.

When you've been shot and faced the reality of dying, life seemed significantly more precious than a clever social media post.

She hadn't really taken the time to reflect on what had happened and what she'd done. The shooting itself was another reminder that even her bubble-wrapped world was a dangerous place. She'd been slightly injured at the Lincoln Memorial bombing during the Wilkes affair and had watched as Charles Roscovitch died at the scene. Now that sad day seemed like a faint memory, as events at the high school were much more visceral. Running to cover up her classmates was just one of those instinctive reactions she couldn't explain. Maybe it *was* stupid, but she didn't regret doing it. She was discovering a part of herself she didn't know existed. It was energizing and a bit frightening at the same time.

She played back through the event frame by frame. The sun on her face, the sound of gunfire from the roof. The smell of the grass as she curled up to avoid the first shots. The moment she started her run. What had made her do it?

She paused and the answer came to her. *What would Tamika do?*

That question still hung in the air and was even more relevant now that her father was in danger.

The next morning, her mom finally relented and commuted to work, leaving Phoenix at home alone. As she watched her mom's car drive off, she returned to the kitchen to plot her next steps. No chance she was going to school. She had a mission, had thought through options, and would do anything to get the ball rolling.

First up was a visit to the basement, which wasn't her favorite place. Dark, damp, and creepy, it had terrorized her when she was young. Now she just thought it was foul and gross. But what it did have was a backpack her parents had bought her for a summer camp in the Sierras. Just big enough for her purposes without weighing her down.

Next up was a visit to her mom's desk just off the kitchen. The nook was where Phoenix had watched her mom sit late into the evening catching up on email, organizing the family's life, and completing her school volunteer work. There was a drawer with some files that collected the important Humboldt papers—birth certificates, Social Security cards, and the like. Phoenix quickly found what she was looking for in her designated file.

So much for the easy stuff. Now she had to make the call that would require some finesse and guile . . . and she felt bad about that. Nevertheless, she picked up her phone and selected the right number.

"Hey, Auntie Shea, it's Phoenix calling." Shea Roscovitch was certainly not her real aunt, but that distinction had long been lost given how close the families had become. Her mind went back to Charles's death at the Lincoln Memorial.

"Phoenix, my love, what are you doing on the phone? Shouldn't you be resting? Dear Lord, that whole thing must have been so horrible. I try to forget my own experiences."

"I'm doing fine, Auntie—the doctor says I was lucky, and I'm feeling pretty good already. I suppose it was scary at first, but I'm at home now and will be back at school soon." The thought of going back to school terrified her much more than the prospects of her current plan. But she was too ashamed to tell anyone that, especially since most of her friends now thought she was so brave. Maybe if she could talk with Tamika . . .

"I just want you to know how proud we are of you. Thinking of your friends first . . . I don't know if I could have done that." Then realizing Phoenix was dealing with more than just the attack, Shea gave her the entrée she needed. "Honey, have you heard anything from the FBI about your father? I should have asked that first."

Phoenix winced as her five-foot-six-inch frame bumped into the corner of the kitchen counter. Dr. Doucette had been right: That hurt. "Actually, that's why I'm calling, Auntie. I know the FBI is doing everything they can, but so far, they haven't been able to tell us anything. Mom is going crazy, and Nathan is really struggling. My calls to Tamika are going straight to voicemail."

"Good grief, you poor girl. How can I help?"

Phoenix bit her lip. How could she say it delicately? She needed Shea's help but didn't want to drag her through the whole tragic event and the loss of her husband. Phoenix had heard some vague references at the dinner table but wasn't sure exactly what they meant—but she had a hunch. The only way to find out was to dig around and see what turned up.

"I met Bryce after the memorial service for Uncle Charles, and you mentioned to me that he had helped save us." She let that hang in the air, wondering if Shea would take the bait. When she didn't, Phoenix went one step further. "I just thought . . . maybe he might . . . I don't know, somehow be able to help now?"

The silence on the line wasn't a good sign.

Finally, Shea cleared her throat and spoke. "Dear . . . Bryce doesn't really have anything to do with this. And I don't hear from him as much as I'd like. Is there some other way I can help?"

A deep breath as she sat on the counter stool. "Auntie, I can't just sit here and watch everything and everyone around me go sideways. I need to do *something*. I've been attacked twice now. I'm not going to wait around for the third time to be the charm. I'm counting on you to help."

Another long silence. Phoenix wanted to jump in and push even harder but decided to just let Shea stew with her own thoughts. Lately she'd learned that holding back was a useful way to manipulate adults when she really needed something.

Her patience paid dividends. "Phoenix, sweetie. Don't do anything until you hear from me. I'll see what I can do."

After she hung up she felt a bit guilty about twisting Shea's arm, but not for long. She had a mission to accomplish and wasn't going to let a guilty conscience get in the way. And Phoenix knew more guilt was coming.

She sat down at her mom's desk, found a pad of paper, and wrote a note:

Dear Mom,

I don't quite know where to begin. I know you and Dad have worked really hard to protect Nathan and me during the divorce and to help us feel like everything is normal. But we all know that nothing is normal right now. Dad nearly died . . . then the divorce . . . and now he's been kidnapped. We don't know where he is, if he's alive, or if we'll ever see him again. I'm seventeen years old, and I've survived two terrorist attacks. Definitely not normal. Normal left the building a long time ago, as Daddy would say.

I can't go back to high school and pretend like nothing happened. I just don't see getting excited about Friday night games, a chemistry test, prom, or weekend parties. And I can't wait for the FBI to get its act together and tell us what's going on. I know you need to be here to take care of Nathan, so that means I have to do something. I have to, Mom.

I love you to the moon and back. You and Dad always said you were preparing us for life in the real world—well, this is as real as it gets. That's why I need to go. I'm doing it for all of us. I have no idea what's going to happen or even where I'm going, but I've learned a lot from Tamika. Try not to worry about me. I know I can take care of myself.

One way or the other, I'm going to find my dad.

I love you,

Phoenix

She put the note into her backpack for safekeeping, hoping that somehow Shea would come through for her.

Either way, she meant what she said.

She was going to find her dad.

CHAPTER 29

BITS AND BYTES

Good God, what does she want me to do?

Bryce Roscovitch was rereading the code-name-filled email exchange he'd just had with his mother. The only good news was that she'd somehow managed to use the encrypted email process correctly.

From: Sally
Sent: Monday, January 9, 2023 11:21 a.m.
To: Billy
Subject: SOS

I just got off the phone with Fawkes. She is bound and determined to head out on her own to search for Elon. I know that's foolish and makes no sense, but there's really nobody to stop her. She relies a great deal on Iceman for advice and guidance, and Iceman isn't responding. So Fawkes is going to go looking . . . but she doesn't know where to start.

I know you're doing everything you can to help Iceman find Elon. Do you have anything new you can share with Fawkes?

With love,
Sally

At first, Bryce just had to laugh at the email. He could see his mother sitting at her desk in the living room, first struggling to create the encrypted message envelope and then trying to craft the email. He was sure that despite what he'd told her, she had a cheat sheet with all the code names on it. What was the point if someone could just find the sheet? And how did Fawkes know to ask for his help? That was a problem for a whole set of reasons. Being part of the family and staying hidden was increasingly untenable.

Once he let the exasperation pass, he got up from his chair and paced around his cave office. He'd barely been outside for almost a week; had all four of his machines processing video, audio, and digital data; and was digging in for the long haul. He'd ordered a big pile of food and drinks and picked them up at the local grocery store, paying with cash. He wasn't going to starve, but that didn't provide any easy answers for Shea's email.

The whole premise was ridiculous. The FBI was digging everyplace they could—and while they were not always brilliant, they had tremendous resources, experience, and actual authority. He'd given Tamika (a.k.a. *Iceman*) an initial starting point because he knew she had military experience. And based on what he saw from the FBI's activities, they knew roughly what she was doing and weren't actively trying to stop her.

But *Fawkes*? Shit, Phoenix was seventeen, had no training or expertise, and no visible means of support. Giving her any information or assistance was completely irresponsible, and he knew it. He was equally sure that Shea realized this as well. And yet she'd still asked for his help, effectively transferring the moral dilemma from herself to Bryce. Subconsciously, his mother knew that his standards were a bit lower than hers.

He talked to himself as he marched back and forth. "Even if I wanted to help, I don't really have that much to share. Sure, I can send her to the Netherlands, but what good would that do? She'd have even less chance of success than Tamika."

The self-generated response was a bit obvious. "Well, either way, you need to make more progress on your search. If you can't find any trace of Johnny or the shooter, it won't matter where you send Tamika or Phoenix."

He accepted the next step, even if he didn't like it. He tiptoed into and out of the FBI's internal systems with some care—but he understood their security protocols well and knew how to avoid detection. Now he had to do something he was less excited about.

It was time to penetrate the FSB.

And he knew that might not end well.

• • • • •

Jerald Jessup was an old-school spook.

He believed in boots-on-the-ground intelligence, physical evidence-gathering, agent dossiers, and contingency planning. He was post–Cold War but well before the cyber era. Now faced with a lack of progress in his various investigations (and he had too many going on to keep track), he realized something had to give.

In each of the cases of blackmail, fraud, or extortion under investigation, the MOs were never the same. Different techniques, no matching physical evidence, and a seemingly random set of victims. The only thing they had in common was that the targets were wealthy and influential. In his thirty years of intelligence work, he'd never seen anything like it.

He'd watched the video of the suspect interrogations. The story was the same. They'd accepted some proposal on the dark web but knew next to nothing about the source of their instructions. The trails went hardcore cold, no matter how much pressure they put on the perps. JJ had come to believe that they actually didn't know who was running the show.

"Higgs, we need help." JJ had just finished a briefing with the director of the FBI and was in his sensitive compartmented information facility—what they called a SCIF. It was a specially designed room to prevent any digital or physical incursions. Higginbottom was still on scene in San Mateo, conferencing in from the FBI's local office equivalent security facility.

Higginbottom's face was some cross between shock and relief—an effect that made even JJ break into a small grin.

"I know, I know," JJ said. "When do I ever ask for help?" He paused to decide how to navigate this with his field agent. He needed focus from Higginbottom but also wanted his brain on the broader landscape. "Look, I need you to keep digging in the way that only the FBI can. Interviews, background checks, financial records, physical searches, and the rest. We need to pursue that aggressively so we can interrogate and prosecute any suspects. That's critical."

"Totally agree, Director. My team will stay on it."

"But we aren't making enough progress on the—shit, I don't even know what to call it—the digital side, I guess. These perps are getting instructions from someone, and the only way to generate this level of anonymity is through tech and the dark web."

"I wish I could help more there, Director, but I'm an ex-football player. Cyber was never my deal." He paused. "That said, I may have someone who can help."

"We've already roped in a bunch of our tech geeks—" JJ began.

"I know. And they're all fine. But you and I both sense this is going way deeper than our regular technoids can track."

"Hmmm." JJ looked away from the screen as if he was distracted by something in the room. Mostly, he was just trying to clear his head to think.

"Permission to speak freely, sir?"

"Go, Higgs. You know you can."

"Sir, we never did figure out what happened in the Wilkes attacks. You and I both suspected that most of the dirty work was done on the dark web. That was how Wilkes tricked us into thinking there was an Islamic terrorist involved. We even found some evidence that a white hat hacker intervened and helped divert the drone attacks."

"Right—believe me, I remember." JJ didn't want to disclose why he'd prematurely terminated that investigation. He'd taken some questionable shortcuts to take down Wilkes. He had no trouble justifying the end despite the means, but he wasn't sure everyone on Capitol Hill or in the courts would agree. And giving a firearm to a US senator to act as your backup probably was malpractice. He'd closed the investigation before they got a full picture of what had transpired.

Higginbottom continued to push. "Sir, the guy who found the white hat trail wasn't in the FBI. He's a freelancer we used to do some digging off the books. His background wouldn't pass muster, but he's deep in the hacker community and technically elite."

"What's his name?"

"Well, I don't actually know his name. Nobody does. That's sort of the point."

"Well, what the fuck do we call him?" JJ didn't have much patience for prima donnas.

"He goes by the name . . . well, he likes to be called *Mufasa*."

Great, JJ thought. *Our technical savior is a make-believe Lion King.*

CHAPTER 30

TAIL CHASING

Dumbass.

As soon as she accepted that she was being followed, Tamika knew she'd been a fool. What the hell had she expected? Everything that had happened so far had been sophisticated, coordinated, and perfectly executed. Did she think she was just going to jump on a commercial flight and avoid detection? Of course she was being followed.

"Look. I owe you an apology. This isn't about some friend lost on a sailing trip. It's way more complicated than that." She and Lugtenberg were still in the car driving back from the airport toward the Den Helder town center.

"I'm all ears," responded Lugtenberg. "You're my client. I think of it like being your doctor—I'm bound to keep your information private."

Tamika gave him a quick briefing on her hunt for Johnny. She left out the Afghanistan blackmail backstory but made it clear that the stakes were high.

"What do you want to do?" Lugtenberg asked after a brief pause. As his facial muscles relaxed, Tamika concluded he'd made some sort of decision. She sensed a growing trust. "I can try to lose him. There's enough traffic and side roads to disappear if we want."

Tamika knew that her next move needed to match the quality of the enemy, and that meant a step up from her previously naive attempts. "Is there a way for us to turn the tables on this guy?"

"What do you have in mind?"

"I want to corner him. I want to make him talk."

Lugtenberg gave her a sideways look. "Your dad warned me about you. Said you'd be stubborn and determined. He mentioned *reckless*."

"Yeah, well. Generals get soft. Easy to give commands when you're in a comfy chair and others are doing the work." *Reckless* was in the eye of the beholder.

"Hey look, I'm here to help. Just tell me what you want to do. Short of shooting the guy, I'm in." He cracked a grin as he said it.

"Let's play a little game of cat and mouse. See whether he'll go for the cheese. Drop me off at the hotel. Maybe he'll stay and wait for our next move." She fidgeted in her seat, feeling the anticipation of possible action.

"But you want me to circle back, right?" He squeezed his fingers together with his thumb in a claw-like gesture.

"Exactly." It was a classic pincer movement. Tamika hoped this guy was running solo.

They navigated back to the Wienerhof. When they pulled up, Tamika got out of the car, leaned into the window as if to dismiss the driver, and walked briskly into the hotel lobby. Just in case someone else might be there watching, she hustled up the stairs and down the hall to her room and went inside. Moving quickly to the window, she saw the tailing car pull down a side street. The hotel faced the train station and a bus and tram loading zone. There was no place to park in front. Likely he was headed for the parking lot in the back.

She pulled out her phone to send a text.

Parking behind the hotel?

The response was swift.

I've got him. Let's do this.

Tamika trotted back down the stairs and through the double doors at the back of the hotel lobby out into the overcast skies above Den Helder. She scanned the lot and easily found the car. She also saw Lugtenberg moving down the street to the north. The tail's eyes met Tamika's. With a quick glance in his rearview mirror, he knew his cover was blown. He grabbed the door handle, jumped out, and started running down a street on the south side.

"*Really*?" Tamika said, louder than she'd anticipated. She went into sprinter mode. He ran left down what turned out to be Gravenstraat. *Digging his own grave*, she thought. She cut the corner around a building like it was a curve at the top of a stretch run—and took him down with a flying tackle after about fifty yards. He struggled, but Tamika rolled him over on his stomach and straddled his back with her legs, both of his wrists pinned in front of her.

"Where the fuck do you think you're going?" There was no response except for some additional squirming.

At that moment Lugtenberg trotted up. "Well, I'm glad one of us can run." Tamika rolled the man on the ground partway over so they could see his face. He spit at her, just missing. She mashed the side of his face down onto the concrete. He was tall and slender with blond hair and a mustache.

"I don't recognize him," Lugtenberg intoned. "I know most of the talent around here—must be imported."

"Did he think he was going to outrun an NCAA champion? Let's get his ass back to the hotel."

"That might be a bit too public. I've got a better idea."

• • • • •

The boat shed turned out to be perfect for their purposes. It was a forty-by-fifty-foot industrial enclosure with big double doors on both sides. Two fluorescent fixtures provided enough light to get work done. A selection of nets and fishing equipment hung on pegs on one wall. The opposite wall included a workbench and a serious set of tools, along with two outboard motors up on engine racks. There was also a large sink with a metal table and a small white container next to it. The center of the shed was dominated by a roughly thirty-foot boat resting on a metal trailer.

"I keep my boat here during the winter—clean and freeze my fish during the summer. It's also great for maintenance work in the off-season." Tamika watched as Lugtenberg grabbed a broom and brushed some excess water into a drain.

She immediately realized he could also do some private people maintenance, when required. Clearly, taking someone to the woodshed had a slightly different meaning to the Dutch. Although their captive remained dutifully silent—the cloth gag in his mouth probably helped—it was clear that Lugtenberg was ready for business. "There are several ways to go from here, and none of them should involve a sitting United States senator. There's a pub on the dock down the road. If you tell them you're my friend, they'll get you a beer and some bitterballen or frites with mayonnaise. Not gourmet, but very filling."

"And what are you going to do? You barely even know what I'm looking for." She recalled his statement about doing anything up to shooting someone.

"I think it's a *who*, not a *what*. If this gozer has any information, you'll have it soon enough."

Reluctantly, Tamika succumbed both to his logic and his confidence, even if she didn't know what a gozer was. She stepped out through a crack in the double doors on the street side, closing them tightly behind her. After a short walk she was sitting on the pub's deck facing a strip of water heading out toward what appeared to be a large lake. The channel was lined with a series of industrial docks—one with a crane—and a hodgepodge of boat types. Some were up on blocks, but many were tied to pier posts, presumably ready for work. As promised, the food in the pub was no better than your average American tater tots and chicken wings, but the mayonnaise on the fries was a revelation. Tamika realized she was starving and ate two servings.

After almost an hour, she saw Lugtenberg trot down the road to join her on the pub deck. Tamika noticed a bit of blood on his shirt, which was now untucked with some sweat in the right places. The serious expression on his face matched his purposeful stride.

"Did you learn anything?" The question sounded pathetic and unnecessary, but he seemed to be waiting.

"He's a nobody—someone pulled him up from Amsterdam for the effort. I doubt he knows more than your name and the amount of money he would have been paid. But he did give me one important piece of information. He arrived at De Kooy about the time your friend's plane would have arrived. He saw a silver Mercedes G-Wagon leaving the FBO. Said it headed south."

"What the hell does that tell us?"

"Well . . . two things. First, you need to get some intel on G-Wagons headed south around that time. I assume you have someone who can help?"

"Of course," she said without hesitation. *When you lie, do it with conviction*, she told herself. She grabbed her phone as if the request would be that simple.

"OK, then. Get your information and get to the train station."

"Where am I going?"

"The only place south worth going."

Amsterdam.

CHAPTER 31

ENEMY MANEUVERS

What the hell had she expected? Hire a rookie and rookie results will follow.

Andropov had picked an operative on the dark web to follow Lugtenberg and Smith as they plowed around Den Helder. She had consciously selected someone with no possible connections to her past work or to the FSB's activities in the Netherlands. While protecting her own identity and mission was paramount, the consequences were sometimes painful. In this case, her contractor demonstrated why he wasn't on the FSB's active list. She'd watched some video from the Den Helder hotel's parking lot camera—the only thing that impressed her was Smith's speed and the flying tackle.

Note to self: Don't get in a chase with that woman.

She pulled back from her computer screen and stepped into the kitchen to grab a hot tea. She had picked up the Dutch tea habit and was now fully addicted. She found that sipping the warm drink helped her think. The truth was that her contractor, Joost Pruijmboom, didn't know anything useful, so the security risk was low. The real problem now was that she didn't have any active intel on Lugtenberg or Smith. She'd put a local snitch on the hotel and train station to see if she could pick up a trail. She had no idea where Smith would go. The trip to De Kooy was a dead end by design, so what clue could she follow?

More importantly, she'd lost the opportunity, at least for the moment, to take Smith out. She had another option in mind but was chafing at the constraints of the mission parameters. RallyAmerica would never approve her proposed action—and for logical reasons. Controlling Senator Smith was a shared goal, and right now, Smith had promised to play ball. RallyAmerica was counting on that pledge.

Andropov was certain Smith would never do what they wanted. Her incursion into the Netherlands demonstrated that she didn't have the personality or disposition to give in. She was stringing them along—probably with the help of the authorities in the US. The FBI was unlikely to negotiate with what was effectively a terrorist threat directed at a US senator, among other leaders. The whole DAO approach lacked commitment to the difficult actions that needed to be taken.

To be taken seriously, someone had to die.

Nastya Andropov knew just the person.

• • • • •

No fucking way.

Lee Bowen was totally committed to the disruption of the US government. And he was quite willing to go to extreme lengths to achieve that goal. As were his investors. But murder was a step too far—especially killing a retired general in the US military. At a practical level, he didn't think it was necessary. More importantly, even *he* was uncomfortable with the moral implications, to say nothing of the legal risks if he were somehow caught. RallyAmerica was not going there.

DAOs were completely blind entities. Bowen had no idea who had proposed the assassination and no way to figure it out beyond a screen name. Anonymity through blockchain was a double-edged sword. But it really didn't matter, because he controlled the majority voting in the DAO. There would be some noise as members debated the merits of the idea on Discord, but Bowen would vote "no" and that would end the debate.

While he opposed turning RallyAmerica into a murder-for-hire organization, Bowen knew that his operation had reached a tipping point. Clearly, it was time to shift from a random series of blackmails and extortions to a more directed approach. Action would speak louder than words—and perhaps that was the lesson to learn from the murder proposal in any event.

Bowen had been preparing for this moment ever since his strategy retreat to Maui, so the next step was clear. His activities hadn't just been experiments to determine whether the DAO structure could work. A few of the influence operations had been selected carefully so that they could be leveraged effectively. Now the time was here.

His new favorite Missouri senator was about to make a speech to the Business Roundtable. Historically conservative, this group was certainly not a proponent of extreme measures from either end of the political or economic spectrum.

This time, they weren't going to like what they heard.

• • • • •

Ely Basof truly loved the venture capital business. He enjoyed meeting with young entrepreneurs, reveled in the process of weeding out the winners from the charlatans, and loved the art of closing the deal. He certainly didn't believe in the idea of win-win. In his deals, he and his firm were the winners and everyone else was along for the ride. And the financial windfall he'd experienced was well beyond anything he'd originally thought possible. Despite his background and training, he'd become a committed capitalist.

That said, partnering with Lee Bowen in B^2 Ventures was not his favorite part of his assignment. Bowen was a great salesman and decent financial thinker, but coming from Basof, those weren't intended as compliments. In his mind, Bowen didn't have the technical chops to make the critical investment decisions. Basof also didn't think his partner knew how to *think big*—how to take outsized risks to achieve unicorn-type rewards.

When Bowen asked him to invest in a DAO, Basof was both surprised and impressed. His partner had made it sound like a straightforward financial investment in which members would vote on various business opportunities. Basof did not give up control to anyone, much less to a faceless, anonymous organization, so he had politely passed on the offer. Once RallyAmerica was established, he did the technical work to explore its governing documents—and he realized that Bowen was up to something far beyond investing money. The DAO was something closer to a criminal syndicate—albeit with anonymous leadership. Basof had immediately contacted his superiors, sensing an opportunity. He'd also invested a small amount of money in the DAO so he could easily track its activities.

He smiled at the idea that Bowen thought he could execute his grand plan behind Basof's back, but then again, Bowen didn't know about the resources Basof had at his fingertips. The initial moves looked like an out-of-the-box effort to pursue an aggressive and truly earth-shattering agenda. But now, as he watched each of Bowen's subsequent actions, he worried that the will to achieve greatness might not be there. As he'd always suspected, Bowen didn't have the heart or the courage to take revolutionary action.

He brought up Discord on the second of his three-screen setup in what he called his "workshop." In fact, it was a corner room in the basement of his Woodside home, which itself was up a dead-end road in a small, wooded canyon. The room had originally been open to the rest of the basement, but Basof had closed it off, doing the cinder block and cement work himself. Now it was hidden behind a false door. In addition to his computer and networking gear and self-contained air system, it was equipped with a high-end communications system that kept him in touch with his handlers.

Basof also smiled when he thought about RallyAmerica's assassination proposal, knowing immediately where it had come from. His compatriot was aggressive and unafraid to take the fight directly to the enemy. While it ran a bit counter to the operational parameters, he understood the logic and rationale. Deep down, he approved even if he knew it would be a nonstarter for Bowen.

Ely Basof would let his partner win this round. But the time was coming when he would reap what Bowen had sowed. He had a full FSB-collected dossier on Bowen and knew all about the childhood Bowen tried to hide. His B^2 colleague would never know what hit him. Because Bowen didn't know the pressure Basof could bring to bear. Didn't know that his business partner was actually serving another master. And the FSB never left hanging chads.

Lee Bowen would be left out to dry.

CHAPTER 32

STUCK IN THE MIDDLE

Bryce's head felt like it was about to explode.

In the world of computing, he was someone with exceptionally high bandwidth. But even he was feeling overwhelmed by the amount of data to evaluate and the points of the compass from which it was coming. He was also feeling isolated—an odd feeling for someone who was used to working alone—but what good was having information if he had no acceptable way to share it with the authorities? After wasting a bunch of time wringing his hands by pacing back and forth across the basement, he decided to go old school.

Bryce pulled a whiteboard he hadn't used in years out of a corner. Ink was dried on the board, a seemingly permanent reminder of a security hacking deal he'd done some five years earlier. After a good scrubbing with Clorox spray, he had a mostly clean surface. He found an extra box of dry-erase markers he'd never opened and began to outline his dilemma.

He started his highly nontechnical diagram by putting printed photos of Johnny and Phoenix Humboldt and Tamika Smith in the center. Nothing like being in the crosshairs of a giant conspiracy. His task was to find any common elements in the broader picture.

"First up is the school video trace. Someone shut those cameras down." He drew a crude schoolhouse with a lightning bolt line coming out of it connected to the sketch of a camera. "I need to review the IP trace results and see if it leads anywhere positive."

He went over to a keyboard and pulled the analysis up onto one of his screens. “Damn, this is like watching a Pong ball going back and forth across the TV. Whoever shut down the cameras routed the hack through about fifteen different server clusters.” Ultimately, he couldn’t trace it all the way back to its origin, but he studied the various server nodes along the way, thinking it might come in handy later.

“Next up is the De Kooy dead end. Johnny probably isn’t in Den Helder, so where did they take him? And why to the Netherlands?” He colored a little Dutch flag in the lower left corner of the whiteboard. “Shit, which order are the colors? French flag or Dutch flag . . . whatever.”

This time, instead of looking for a trace, he analyzed the outcome from an AI agent he’d created to search the De Kooy video. He’d asked the tool to evaluate ground transportation at the airport for the past three months and identify anything that was new or unusual. Bryce believed in human intelligence, but AI was quite useful for pattern matching.

“Ah . . . now that’s interesting. And the timing is about right.” He sent his AI assistant off on an additional video hunt that would reduce the size of the haystack he was searching. Even if this lead played out well—and he thought it might—he still had the problem of how to share the information and with whom. Sucked being a good guy with a very mixed past.

He moved on to the upper right corner of the whiteboard.

“Looks like our ginger is from the Eastern Bloc—probably Russia.” He used a magnet to put her picture on the board. “I’ve done the background work to prepare the FSB hack. Just need to get it over with and live with the outcome.” He’d have to wait to pursue this work. It required a certain level of concentration and precision that he could only do once his head was clear of the rest of the distractions.

Pausing again, he decided to put the FBI initials in the bottom right-hand corner. “They don’t seem to be making much progress, but maybe they’ve managed to trace the emails to Senator Smith.”

He pulled up another window and found what he was looking for. The email IP trace was equally as complicated as the high school video hack search. When Bryce dug into the details, he noticed that a meaningful number of the server nodes were the same. Someone had tried to cover their tracks but out of habit had fallen back on some nodes they used regularly. He could work with that.

"So what've I got?" Asking the question out loud reminded him how much more work was needed.

He had some credible information in the Netherlands but no way to communicate it. The traces were making progress, but all he'd accomplished so far was establishing that they were related. Not surprising. And then there was the FSB infiltration to pursue. Somehow, he kept postponing that one.

As he moved his hands across the board and drew some connecting lines, he knew he had to determine the who, what, where, and why of what was going on. Or at least have a good guess.

"If I don't figure this out, sooner or later, somebody's going to die."

• • • • •

Twelve hours later, he had some answers. And he didn't like what he'd discovered.

The FSB was a first-class intelligence agency, and their digital security was among the best in the world. Like most such organizations, even if you could break through the perimeter security, they compartmentalized information so that one piece of data was difficult to connect to another. Firewalls within the firewalls. Add a myriad of code names and the Russian language barrier and you had a tasty borscht. Other than that, it'd been an average hacking session for Bryce. His brain went sarcastic when he was tired.

He got up from his panel of screens and grabbed one of the ready-to-serve meals he'd ordered. Three minutes in the microwave and he had dinner. Except when he looked at the digital clock on one of his screens it said 0400. His stomach was paying no attention to military time. He chewed on the mediocre orange chicken with rice, not really acknowledging the bland taste. His head was back to sorting through the new information.

The red-haired woman was almost certainly an FSB agent. There wasn't much in the way of personal information, which wasn't all that surprising. But there was a code name executing several operations, and every signal pointed back to a particular asset: a female asset based in Europe, code named "Maaier." The name was an odd reference, but with a bit of language research, Bryce realized that with four vowels in a row, this was likely a Dutch word. It literally meant "Reaper." Well, at least there was no ambiguity.

Pieces were starting to fall into place, or at least the edges of the puzzle were close to completion. If he took the Dutch reference at face value, the Aragon High School shooter and Johnny Humboldt kidnapper was a Russian agent based someplace in the Netherlands. Hence the choice of De Kooy Airfield.

A ding from one of his computers indicated that another bot was complete with its search. It had tracked several Mercedes G-Wagons on the De Kooy video, which was highly unusual for a remote airfield next to a town nobody cared about. The AI engine had continued the search accessing Dutch public and private cameras ranging from police speed trap videos to wind turbine maintenance feeds to warehouse security recordings. Bryce had enough computing power (and code intelligence) to piece this together into a kaleidoscope of a probable travel itinerary. The G-Wagons were on a mission, and Bryce had a likely destination.

He paused to think about various people to notify, possible means of cloaking his identity, and a host of related personal risks and ethical dilemmas. He was aware of the growing sense of responsibility he felt and was weary of the internal conflict. High pressure situations were not his gig.

Fuck it, he thought. *I'll just send a text.*

CHAPTER 33

WHEELS IN MOTION

Margaret Humboldt came home from her second day back in the office. She knew that Nathan had soccer practice and his carpool would drop him off at 6:30. Phoenix had received her driver's license when she turned seventeen, which was a godsend. She could drive to school and, on this day, could take herself to her follow-up doctor's visit. That left Margaret with some time to enjoy some wine, organize dinner, and plan a seminormal evening. It had been a typical working Tuesday.

Until it wasn't.

She found an envelope on the kitchen table with "Mom" printed on the fold. She opened it and read it quietly, as if she were examining a grocery list or a note from the housekeeper. Her brain refused to process what she was reading. Nothing seemed to make any sense at all. Then she collapsed on the floor and began to cry. After the initial shock wave had passed, the tears turned to anger.

Goddamn it. She came into our lives, took control of my kids, and now they're following in her footsteps.

Pounding her fists against the base of the cabinets was a physical release but didn't seem to change the situation. She rose slowly from the kitchen floor, brushing at her clothes as if cleaning herself up would sort out her emotional mess. She grabbed a napkin to wipe her eyes and went to the refrigerator for the wine. She stopped partway through pulling out the cork and went to the liquor cabinet. Scotch seemed like a better alternative. Sitting down at the table on their deck with the view of the dusk-washed backyard, she sipped the alcohol, hoping to shock her brain into action.

Margaret had no idea what to do next. And who could she call? Johnny had always been her rock and protector, even after their divorce. Her parents had never endorsed the life she'd chosen, and they certainly wouldn't know what to do now. If Charles Roscovitch was still alive, she would have called him immediately. But Shea? She didn't know if she was up to the challenge either.

Finally, she decided to do what a rational, normal person would do. She pulled out a card and called the authorities.

• • • • •

"She did what?" Even though the volume on the secure video call was turned low, JJ's voice came through loud and clear. The man could certainly project.

Agent Franklin Higginbottom was again sitting in the mini-SCIF—in the back of the FBI's Silicon Valley office. He was sipping from a big cup of black coffee designed to keep his system running on three hours of sleep. The life of an FBI agent went through cycles of feverish work and calming lulls depending on the case load and the actions of a variety of idiots and sometimes a few cunning criminals. The current case—or set of cases—was pushing the activity thermometer into dangerous territory. Higginbottom was beat, and he knew that was when mistakes could be made.

"I'm still trying to track down the details," he replied to JJ. "Ms. Humboldt called me thirty minutes ago and read me a note from the daughter."

"The same kid who was just shot at the high school and hospitalized."

"Yeah—I know. You'd think that would be enough. The doctor sent her home with some restrictions, which she promptly ignored. Apparently, she doesn't think we're capable of finding her father, so she's going to do the work for us."

"Jesus Christ."

"Let's hope it doesn't end that way." Higginbottom hated being irreverent, but he was as frustrated as his boss. "You'd think people would let us do our job."

"There's a lot of that going around right now, Higgs. This whole *weaponization* thing has hurt our credibility even if we're doing the right things. Trust is difficult to earn but easy to lose." Higginbottom watched as JJ sat down with a more purposeful look on his face.

"All we can do is our jobs, and right now that means figuring out the bullshit that is going on and putting an end to it. If the Humboldt extended family wants to go rogue, there's not much we can do about that."

Higginbottom took the cue. "I've put a flag on Phoenix Humboldt's passport. We know she took a flight to Schiphol."

"How'd she pay for the flight?"

"Logged in to her mom's frequent flier account and used the authorized credit card from there."

"They all get an A for resourcefulness. The senator also went to Amsterdam . . . have we heard anything on that front?"

"Well, Schiphol is such a transit spot that it's tough to trace people after they land. She bought a train ticket for Maastricht using a credit card, which was either incredibly stupid or a decoy."

"Higgs, it's the latter for sure. We need more eyes and ears on this overseas. I know that's not our gig, and I certainly don't want the CIA in our hair, but I'll reach out to the embassy and see what resources we have available."

"Sir, Smith and Humboldt going there isn't the only reason the Netherlands is interesting."

"Shit, what else?"

"Remember our friend Mufasa?" He could tell by Jessup's expression that he was either pissed or bemused.

"Sure. What does the Lion King have to tell us?"

"Actually, quite a bit. He's certain that Johnny Humboldt was flown there on a private plane."

"They took him out of the country? Well, now we have an international incident on our hands. That means terrorists of all shapes and sizes. Anything specific in the Netherlands?"

"Unfortunately, no. But he did pass on one other piece of information. He thinks the FBI's been compromised. Actually, more than once."

"*What?* That's impossible." Then after a resigned pause: "Who and how?"

"The Russians. The trail leads back and forth across Europe, but his bet is Belarus."

"At least that's a trail and not that surprising. Anybody else stomping through our files?"

"You wouldn't believe me if I told you."

• • • • •

Nastya Andropov was not surprised by the negative DAO vote. She didn't think the group collectively had the will to take someone out. So now she was counting on her handler to make some progress to change their operational instructions. She needed more flexibility, and RallyAmerica was a frustrating obstacle. Destabilizing a government wasn't easy in the best of circumstances and in the current environment would require drastic actions to achieve the goal. In her opinion, the DAO had to go—and she'd made that clear to her superiors. But as a soldier, she would wait for more instructions.

In the interim, she also had to safeguard her newly acquired asset, as well as protect herself. She would not underestimate Tamika Smith as a threat. Her informants at the Wienerhof and the Den Helder train station had come up empty. And without current intelligence on Smith's whereabouts, she had to assume the worst. The mere possibility that Smith somehow knew about Andropov's Texel location or had decided to go to Amsterdam was sufficient motivation to take action.

She sent several secure messages to put the process in motion. Then she grabbed her go bag and car keys. She wasn't letting another group of incompetent contractors fuck this up.

If you wanted it done right, sometimes you had to do it yourself.

CHAPTER 34

BOXED IN

Johnny Humboldt heard the sounds of a truck firing up and machinery beginning to rumble. It was the first meaningful activity, outside of meal deliveries and a forced voice recording, since he'd been abducted ten days earlier. During that time he'd had almost zero human interaction. Certainly no positive contact. But also nothing aggressive or painful. Just . . . nothing.

As a result, he felt a real sense of deprivation. It was as if his captors had denied him some primal need without doing anything more than removing all electronics from his possession, including his watch. His ten days of confinement were more of a guess than a certainty—based on some occasional glimpses of sunlight and darkness as he was fed. The lighting was also regularly turned on and off as if to mark the passing of nighttime. Regardless of the precise number of days, he was suffering emotionally even if he was fine physically.

The original abduction had been a shock to his system. As soon as they used the short I-380 freeway and then turned north on I-280, he knew something was wrong. When he turned to the supposed FBI agent to ask where they were going, he felt a sharp prick in his left arm. Then nothing until he awoke to the jolting of an airplane going through some turbulence. The window blinds on the plane were all down, but he could tell that it was dark outside. Unless he'd been asleep for quite a long time, they were headed east into the night. He again went to ask the red-haired woman a question and realized he was gagged.

Eventually the plane began to descend, and his gag was augmented with a blindfold and bag over his head. He supposed they could have drugged him again, but he was probably easier to move if he could walk by himself. His sense of time wasn't great, but he guessed they'd traveled by car for two-plus hours after they'd landed. They helped him out of the car and held his arm while they walked several hundred yards, through a series of doors into his current home.

"We're going to take the bag and blindfold off and remove the gag—as long as you behave. Nobody can hear you, so yelling will be pointless and just lead to other forms of punishment. Understood?" The voice spoke English with a British accent, but one that was tinted with another language. Johnny was no expert, but it sounded Germanic or perhaps Nordic.

Johnny nodded, and the immediate source of sensory deprivation was eliminated. He glanced around at his surroundings. He was in a forty-by-eight-foot metal box, which he assumed was a shipping container. The ceiling was over seven feet high with one battery-powered light casting a pale stream of illumination across the barren interior. The guard holding the blindfold, gag, and bag was over six feet tall and built like a bouncer. Except he had a winter-style face mask on.

"Make yourself at home—you're going to be here for a while. The portaloo in the corner is for you. Don't stink it up 'cause I'm not cleaning it." And with that, he left through a steel door like something you'd see on a submarine. The bolt was turned shut from the outside after his captor left.

Aside from the toilet, the only other furnishing in the container was a futon complete with a pillow, sheet, and blanket. Johnny quickly realized the door was the only exit, and there were no obvious points of vulnerability. It was a well-constructed steel box. The walls were cool to the touch, but the area itself was a comfortable room temperature. There was the faint hint of salt water—not surprising, if the container had previously been on a ship. He didn't sense any movement at the moment, so he assumed he was on dry land near a body of water. Maybe a dock?

Over the next several days no one came. Food was delivered through a slot he hadn't noticed in the door, but that was his only external stimulus. The food delivery was accompanied by footsteps in both directions and a small whiff of salt air, but no other commentary or noise.

Johnny set about creating a daily routine of sorts just to keep himself occupied. He'd sleep for what he thought was six or seven hours while the lights were out, scratching a tick mark into the metal wall to keep track of the passing days. After eating the delivered breakfast, he'd walk two miles by marching around the edges of the container walls in squared-off circles, counting steps both to occupy his mind and ensure that he'd covered the required distance. After lunch, he'd exercise by doing what he remembered from Margaret's yoga moves in their home gym. His repertoire was limited, but at least it got the blood flowing. The rest of his routine involved mental gymnastics designed to pass the time.

Could he estimate the number of golf balls that would fit inside the container?

How many of the world's capitals could he name, at least semireliably?

How many countries were there in Europe? Africa? South America?

The days slowly, painfully passed. And the deprivation was a draining death.

The only brief interruption in the monotony involved his original guard entering the container with a newspaper and an iPhone.

"Read the headlines and the date. If you say anything else, we'll just delete it, knock some sense into you, and do it again."

Johnny had followed the instructions, figuring there was some sort of ransom attempt going on, but he couldn't imagine why they'd selected him. There was some money from his company's buyout, but not enough to justify this level of work. Could it be related to his work at Facebook? Seemed unlikely. What about his new role with Tamika? Maybe . . .

Whenever he allowed his brain to relax, his thoughts immediately went to Phoenix. Was she okay? Was she even alive? And anxiety about Tamika, Nathan, and even Margaret was not far behind. The overwhelming gloom would sweep over him when he let his guard down, and "depression" didn't begin to fully describe the depths of the pain. At first there were tears, but eventually those dried up into a smoldering frustration and anger that came and went without warning. In clear-headed moments, he also worried about them . . . what they must be thinking . . . how this must be affecting them.

Margaret and the kids had been through this once before when he was severely injured during the Offutt Air Force Base crash. The divorce had added to the fragility that must now have evolved into a real crisis. And while Tamika was strong, she had her own demons to manage. This would only add to the emotional burden. All of which made Johnny feel somehow responsible. He felt himself descending into a dark hole.

Shit, why am I such a burden to others? Everyone I touch is in pain.

Now the welcome sound of the trucks and equipment accelerated, accompanied by some shouts Johnny could hear but not understand. The sudden activity created a sense of excitement and anticipation for him, if for no other reason than it was a change. It pulled his mind out of the painful dark place. In fact, he had no idea if this was a good thing or a bad thing.

But most importantly, it was something.

• • • • •

Tamika and Jan Lugtenberg had discussed her options. They concluded that going back to the Den Helder train station would be a mistake. Someone was obviously trying to track her movements, and returning to the scene of the crime, so to speak, didn't make much sense.

Based on his advice, she did go back to Amsterdam via train, but picked up the only north–south train in Alkmaar. The station there was far enough removed from Den Helder to give her some comfort and also busy enough to enable her to hide in a commuting crowd. Sitting again in the upper deck of a second class car, she contemplated her next steps. She'd lied to Lugtenberg about having sources who could help her continue the hunt for Johnny in Amsterdam. Now the lie seemed stupid. He'd said goodbye, clearly assuming his job was done, leaving her alone down a blind alley.

She got off the train at Amsterdam Sloterdijk, preferring to avoid the probability that someone was waiting to pick up her trail at Amsterdam Central Station. From Sloterdijk she rented a bicycle from a local shop, slung her duffel bag up on her back, and blended into the Dutch commuting scene.

Her first few minutes in bike traffic were nearly catastrophic. Everyone else was riding at light speed and seemed to know exactly where they were going. She was the proverbial deer in the headlights hoping nobody would hit her. The incessant ringing of bike bells as people passed her was unnerving. Nevertheless, guided by Google Maps, it took her twenty-five minutes to arrive at the US consulate around the corner from the Rijksmuseum in the museum quarter.

The brick consulate building fit into the traditional architecture of the neighborhood but was surrounded by a modern, sturdy metal fence that projected out into the adjoining sidewalk. The main auto entrance had additional reinforced posts that would block any car trying to ram through the gates. The posts moved up and down to allow vehicles to enter once they'd been inspected. Tamika walked around the fence and found the pedestrian entrance housed in an angular glass structure attached to the original building. This addition created a security area to screen citizens while still protecting them from the frequent Dutch rain. Tamika thought the entire structure found the right balance between fitting into the area and providing security.

It wasn't every day that a US senator showed up metaphorically ringing the consulate doorbell, bicycle in hand, so the consulate general's schedule was suddenly clear for a meeting. Thirty minutes later Tamika was armed with contact information for the local authorities, some hotel options, and the promise of additional support if she managed to uncover any actionable information.

"Shit" was all she could say as she left. She wasn't sure what she'd expected, but in hindsight, the visit was probably not worth the risk of detection. She was no closer to figuring out where Johnny was being held, and the consul had no real influence to get help from the local police authorities.

The hotel list was at least useful—she found a boutique spot that also fit in the neighborhood's style, an older building with slanted walls and narrow staircases that had been updated with modern conveniences. She paid a bit extra in cash to avoid showing her passport and stowed her gear in a room that had a double bed, some seventeenth-century reprints of Dutch paintings, and a window looking out toward the Singelgracht canal.

An hour later, her burner phone pinged as she was riding her bike around the ring of the Museumplein trying to pretend she knew what she was doing. She stopped her bike in the middle of the lane, again generating a barrage of bell ringing. She nudged herself off the path to the side.

Only one person had that number, but the message wasn't coming from her father. How the hell did someone else know how to reach her?

And where the hell was Coenhaven?

CHAPTER 35

LINE OF FIRE

Coenhaven was a cyclone of inactivity. For an active industrial area, it was shockingly quiet. No boats came in or out of the docks, and Tamika saw only a few cars through her binoculars as they entered and exited along Coenhavenweg. After two days, there was no sign of Johnny and no new leads.

For her original reconnaissance, she'd ridden her bike around the rings of the Amsterdam canals and past Westerpark, one of the city's abundant green spaces. Entering an industrial zone near the harbor area, she marveled at several monstrous manufacturing and refuse recycling facilities and a pterodactyl series of wind turbines that continued centuries of Dutch windmill tradition. Traversing under a highway, she found a collection of warehouses surrounding several fingers of water that came in from the Amsterdam–North Sea canal, called Het IJ.

Coenhaven consisted of a long wharf and warehouse area on the left side of the inlet with a series of smaller piers crowded with containers and fenced-in areas at the base and on the right side of the haven or harbor. The piers formed a rough W-shaped area sticking out into the water. The sightlines down the main wharf weren't great, but since she wasn't sure which location was on her watch list, Tamika sought a location that would give her a good overview of the area.

Now she was sitting at the base of a road called Pier Azië in a car she'd rented with cash, managing a slightly obstructed view down the center wharf of the area. It wasn't ideal, but it was the best she could do without completely exposing herself. All of which raised the more important question: Why was she blindly following a single-word text from someone she couldn't identify?

The physical and mental exhaustion of solo around-the-clock surveillance was taking a toll. Again, she regretted parting ways with Lugtenberg, who almost certainly would have stayed to help. But at the same time, nobody had more at stake with Johnny's kidnapping than she did, and nobody would have followed such a flimsy lead for as long as she had.

Still the questions continued.

Maybe something happened when she'd stepped away to grab more food?

Maybe she'd dosed off at the wrong moment.

Or maybe Johnny was still in California.

On the third afternoon, as she was considering tossing in the towel, a cyclone blew in. It began with a large barge tying up at the docking area just off the canal in front of a warehouse on Pier Afrika. Through her binoculars, Tamika could see two men who clearly looked like stevedores. She also saw a slim, dark-haired woman wearing trim dress pants and a blue overcoat who seemed more like a business executive than a dockhand. She was clearly giving the orders, both to the boat operators and to someone on a radio.

Next up, a large bald man drove up in a truck, waddled over to the barge, and chatted with the boss woman. He then reversed course, parked, and climbed up into a crane rig next to the warehouse.

What the hell are they doing?

A low rumble grew steadily into a series of bangs and clatters as large doors on the side of the warehouse slid open. Refocusing the binoculars, Tamika could see a large container inside. And the crane was moving that way.

The wheels in Tamika's head started to move faster than the sliding doors.

What's in the container? Is this what the text message was about?

Then the realization hit her.

Even if she wasn't 100 percent sure what the mysterious text was trying to tell her, she couldn't take any chances. First, she called the number the consul had given her for the Korps Nationale Politie, commonly known as the Dutch National Police, connecting with a desk clerk who was directing calls.

"I'm reporting a kidnapping of an American citizen . . . ," Tamika began. The fact that she had no real evidence wasn't going to stop her.

"Please identify yourself," came the predictable response in perfect English.

Jesus. "I'm United States Senator Tamika Smith." She wasn't sure how or why that was going to help, but it was the first thing that came out. And it clearly threw the desk clerk off track.

"This line is reserved for legitimate reports of crimes in progress," he responded. "Fake calls are a crime."

"I'm not a crank caller, and this is not a fake crime. My boyfriend was kidnapped in the United States last week. Just check the news reports. His name is Johnny Humboldt."

After a meaningful pause. "Hmmm . . . I have a report here. What makes you think he's in the Netherlands?"

Tamika hung up. That was going nowhere fast. And the crane was lifting the container toward the barge. It would be loaded in a few minutes.

Out of desperation, she called the consul's private cell number and told him that she believed Johnny was being held in a warehouse in Coenhaven . . . and that someone was in the process of moving him.

This time she got a better reply.

"Senator Smith, the FBI sent me a priority communication this morning indicating they had evidence Mr. Humboldt is here."

So Jessup is on his game, Tamika thought. "So why are we talking on the phone?"

"The FBI message has no specific information about a location or how to proceed."

"Damn it, we don't have time for this. I'm in Coenhaven. Send the cavalry."

"Senator, it doesn't work—" He started to object but never got the chance to finish.

"Well, it damn well better. I don't want you to be the one to blame for him disappearing again."

And then she saw something that transformed her urgency into fear. "Dear God, I gotta go . . ."

Raising her binoculars, she confirmed what the naked eye was telling her.

"What the fuck!" she yelled out loud.

She dropped the field glasses and began to run.

• • • • •

Andropov didn't hesitate.

From her vantage point on the front of the barge, she recognized the woman moving down the dock road toward the ship.

Holy shit, what the hell is she doing here?

The FSB agent immediately whipped out the Glock 17 that was tucked into the back of her pants under her coat. She cursed herself for not having the silencer attached already. After all, she couldn't just shoot someone in broad daylight in Amsterdam and expect to get away with it.

She pulled a BANISH 45 silencer out of a shoulder bag and screwed it onto the muzzle of the pistol as the woman started yelling something. When Andropov raised the weapon to fire, she saw someone else running down the dock, but this time at top speed.

Now she smiled.

It had to happen eventually—might as well be now.

She shifted her attention to the woman she knew was US Senator Tamika Smith and squeezed the trigger. Just as she fired, the container was dropped on the barge, rocking the vessel sharply.

"*Chort vozmi!*" she cursed in Russian reflexively. Not even close. She heard sirens wailing in the distance. And her target was now within ten yards of the girl the assassin had almost killed at the high school.

Run or shoot?

She jumped from the barge to the pier.

"This time, I won't miss the bitch." And as Smith lunged to knock the younger woman out of the way, Nastya Andropov fired.

Both targets went down in a heap.

PART III

A CHANGE IN PLANS

The boots are worn, the days are long,
But still we march, forever strong.
Through dust and dawn, through fire and rain,
We hold the line, endure the strain.
We are the quiet in the storm,
The oath we swore, forever sworn.
No flags in hand, no fame or bands—
Just duty bound, the watch still stands.

—**Anonymous**

CHAPTER 36

AFTER ACTION REPORT

Commissaris Pieter Snijders whipped his Mercedes B-200 around the last corner and accelerated down Pier Afrika. It wasn't often he got a kidnapping-in-progress call, and unprecedented for the report to originate with the US consulate. He killed his siren, leaving the swirling light on as he slammed to a stop halfway down the concrete dock. He angled his car to put it between him and the end of the wharf. Jumping out while pulling his weapon, he peered over the roof, half expecting someone to shoot at him. Three other cars arrived ten seconds behind him.

"This is the National Police," he called out in Dutch, using the broadcast function of his radio. "We have you penned in. Come out with your hands up." He wasn't exactly sure what was going on, so this seemed like the best default approach.

No response.

He repeated the call, this time in both Dutch and English.

Still no response.

He looked across at the six other officers, their weapons trained down the dock, and gave them the appropriate hand signals for a two-by-two approach and search of the area. Four of his men carefully approached the warehouse doors, which were wide open, angling in from two different directions. He and the remaining officers searched a pickup truck and navigated around a crane. They got to the end of the dock without seeing anyone. Looking beyond the small harbor to the busy canal, he saw the usual boat and barge traffic that came with a commercial port area.

"The warehouse is clear," came the report from the search team. "And I mean completely empty. *Brandschoon.*"

"Shit. *Het zal wel een dwaalspoor zijn.*" A wild goose chase. Sometimes his job was just desk work—and then it could go from zero to sixty, and then back to zero again. "OK, this seems like a waste of time, but let's be sure there's nothing here. Start at the end of the pier and walk back toward the cars."

"What are we looking for, sir?" A good question.

"Anything that might tell us if there's been any activity here today. Supposedly, someone was kidnapped."

They spread out across the pier with about ten feet separating them and walked back as directed.

"Commissaris, I've got a shell casing here."

Snijders put on some latex gloves and bent down to pick up the shell that had wedged its way into a crack in the concrete. He lifted it up and put it to his nose before placing it in an evidence bag.

"Recently fired nine millimeter. Damn, what happened here?" He scanned the warehouse roofline. "Strange. No cameras." A quick pause. "OK, let's secure the area. This might be a crime scene."

"Sir . . ." The call came from the far side of the pier.

Snijders looked up and his worst fears were confirmed.

• • • • •

Nastya Andropov eased off on the accelerator and let out a breath. She slowed to the pace of traffic to avoid attracting any attention. Her mind, however, continued racing.

On the one hand, there was the inevitable adrenaline rush from taking out an enemy. It was perverted, but she had learned to accept it.

But what the hell had just happened?

Nothing that transpired at the warehouse made any sense. Nobody outside the FSB knew about the location. How had not *one* but *two* people found it so easily? She could perhaps believe that Tamika Smith had connections that might give her an advantage. After all, that was why Andropov had decided to move her captive in the first place. But the girl? The high school girl?

That was impossible.

Her immediate conclusion was that there was a leak in the FSB. And that scared the shit out of her.

She replayed the entire sequence in her mind.

She knew she should have been ready to shoot the minute she saw the girl. But the whole exercise was a precautionary measure, not something that would involve real risk. Or at least that was how she rationalized the mistake.

Nothing she could do about the first shot at Smith. Just unlucky timing. And she was certain she'd been her usual efficient self with the shots that followed. She'd seen them both go down.

She also applauded herself for the quick exit as soon as she heard the sirens coming. Getting the barge quickly into the canal had been key. Luckily, the container and crew were already on the ship, even if the cargo wasn't fully secured yet. There would be plenty of time to take care of that on the tame waters of the canal.

Her car had been prepared by the team and was already running on the back side of the building. She'd been able to drive away without the police seeing her. Now the authorities would have two bodies to clean up and nothing else for their trouble.

Still, something was nagging at her in the back of her mind. Maybe it was just the realization that there was a mole inside her vaunted organization. But as she thought about it, there was something else.

While pulled up at a stoplight, she pulled three shell casings out of her pocket. Somehow she'd had the wherewithal to grab them before running toward the car. She counted three in her hand. She went back through the sequence one more time.

Fuck. Four.

She had to assume they would find the last shell casing, a loose end she could not afford. Now there was only one way for the incident to be a complete dead end.

Johnny Humboldt had to go down with the ship.

CHAPTER 37

UP THE RIVER

The minute he'd uncovered the Coenhaven location, Bryce had hunted around for cameras to monitor the situation. He knew that Johnny Humboldt's captors would be faced with a difficult decision. Having on-site cameras increased their external security and early warning systems. It also minimized the number of personnel required to secure the site. But being connected digitally exposed them to hacking. In the end, they'd compromised. He found several cameras inside the warehouse but nothing externally.

He monitored the interior of the facility for three days, and he'd seen nothing in the warehouse except a shipping container located at the back of the area. Someone entered the building three times a day to deliver what looked like food. The door to the shipping container was located in a blind spot, likely by design, so Bryce wasn't able to see inside the enclosure. Nevertheless, the regularity of the food visits indicated that this was likely Johnny's prison cell.

Externally, Bryce was forced to access a camera across the canal that had a distant view of the dock area. The angle was terrible and the video was difficult to enhance, but he could see the same lack of activity that Tamika had observed. Still, his eyes, and more importantly, his computer systems, were focused on the location that mattered.

Bryce's original text message disclosing the Coenhaven location had been to Tamika Smith. While he hated sending something out in the open, he knew they were both using burner phones, so the risk was limited. And he assumed she was being careful about her communications, trusting the senator to keep the information to herself. That text had been the easy decision.

Surveillance was rarely exciting, and Bryce welcomed the fact that his computer systems could do the viewing for him. He continued working on a more detailed trace of the threatening emails sent to Tamika, hoping to narrow down the source location. For almost an entire day, he went back and forth between his tracing work and the video monitoring. Eventually he was noisily interrupted when his computing systems detected a flurry of activity on the dock. He immediately returned his attention to the live video feed, entranced as the crane moved into activity.

"Holy shit, they're going to move him. He's got to be in that container." Bryce wasn't sure if that was good or bad, but it certainly got him excited.

"Who can I call?" And with that, his excitement turned to panic. He realized that he was largely helpless as events unfolded. Even if he wanted to contact US authorities, there was nothing they could do. Certainly there was no reason or logic for the Dutch to listen to him. And any contact exposed him personally, which was a bridge too far.

"Jesus, Tamika, I hope you're there and paying attention." He ran his hands nervously through his long hair and rearranged the ponytail at the back.

Then he sat speechless and watched events unfold, seemingly in slow motion.

"No, no, no!" was all he could yell as he jumped up from his seat and ping-ponged around the basement from cot to whiteboard and back to the screen.

Silence.

He stared at the screen.

He fell back onto his cot and accepted what he hated to admit: The second text had been a mistake. Shea had put him in an impossible situation. He understood Phoenix's dedication and love for Johnny, even though he'd struggled with his own parental relationships. He also knew that the FBI wasn't making enough progress fast enough to track down Johnny. He wanted to reward her loyalty and her sheer chutzpah—secretly wishing he was that brave. But why had he thought that Phoenix had any hope of rescuing her father? Stupid.

What the hell was I thinking? Why did I tell the girl . . .

He'd let emotions get in the way. And now more blood was on his hands.

Then the voice in the back of his head kicked him in the ass. *Stop crying, you idiot. You can still help. You can track the rats as they jump ship.*

Or more precisely, he could track the barge—now with Johnny in the container. He immediately grabbed a keyboard and started checking the Amsterdam ship monitoring systems. He guessed that all major boat traffic on the North Sea Canal was monitored digitally, much like air traffic. He found the information on both the MarineTraffic and VesselFinder sites.

Now Bryce was in his element. Public traffic information was just that: public. He needed the private planned routing information that was supposedly protected. Within fifteen minutes he had burrowed his way into the canal management system to see what routes vessels had submitted to the service.

From the live video he was able to see the name on the barge, *de Pijp*. Going back to the ship traffic system, he couldn't find a route filed for the vessel. Moreover, he couldn't see the barge on either public digital tracking system. Clearly, the captain was running rogue and had turned off his transponder to avoid leaving a digital trail.

"Nice try, but that's not going to fool me." Bryce suspected that the entire path of the North Sea Canal was blanketed with video coverage. He could easily follow the barge to its likely destination on the open seas by jumping from camera to camera. The sun was getting low in the sky, but even under darkness, the boat would be difficult to miss.

Ten minutes passed.

"Why's he going east? Shouldn't he be headed west toward the North Sea?" But no, the barge was continuing east down the Het IJ extension of the North Sea Canal. Over the next two hours Bryce tracked (and recorded) the barge's passage past Amsterdam Central Station and around Java Island. A turn to the south and then southeast made the boat captain's intentions clear.

"He's going for the Rhine River," Bryce realized. He followed the route of the Amsterdam–Rhine Canal on his digital map and realized that the canal did indeed live up to its name. The barge would head down the canal from Amsterdam to Utrecht, traverse the Lek system, and connect with the Waal River. From there it was a straight shot to the Rhine and the center of Europe. Along the way were literally hundreds of places the barge could stop, discharge cargo, or take on additional people or supplies.

Bryce leaned back in his chair and stared up at the ceiling, rubbing his eyes.

In other words, Johnny might end up anywhere from Utrecht to Budapest.

• • • • •

The Amsterdam–Rhine Canal had been completed in 1952 after almost twenty years of intermittent construction and was expanded several times over the next thirty years. At forty-five miles long and almost one hundred yards wide, it runs roughly south-southeast from Amsterdam to the navigable waters of the Rhine River and is one of the most utilized artificial bodies of water in Western Europe. The barges that ply the waterway vary in size, but all feature long, flat decks with a taller control tower at one end that houses the navigation systems and pilot. The overall profile is kept low to enable passage beneath the many bridges.

To Bryce, the canal resembled a giant landing strip for boats, running in long, straight sections bordered by tall trees and bike paths on both sides. Based on his video surveillance, the barge traffic was steady, passing regularly under large bridges that had cameras and radar to manage traffic. He was able to use those digital devices to track the *de Pijp*, which was on the smaller side as river barges went. As it navigated past the town of Weesp in the deepening dark of night, it entered another straight portion of the canal that was less populated. Camera access slowly decreased until there were stretches where Bryce couldn't see the barge at all.

"What I wouldn't give for a drone or satellite coverage," he muttered at one point.

He picked the ship up again as it came near the tiny town of Nigtevecht. And for the first time, there was meaningful activity on board. Most importantly, every exterior light on the barge, including its required running lights, had been extinguished.

That can't be an accident.

The moon and other ambient light created enough visibility for Bryce to just make out the outlines of the ship, and he noted the crew moving around quickly. He consulted his map, but there wasn't a great place for them to dock or somehow put someone ashore. The canal was perfectly straight—so straight, in fact, that an autopilot could keep it on course easily. The barge went out of camera view just as things were getting interesting.

"Fuck."

His next visual opportunity would be about five miles north of the hamlet of Loenen aan de Vecht, where another bridge spanned the canal. He tapped into the camera feed there and waited. After forty-five minutes he saw the outline of the prow pushing water in a gentle wave, lights still off, slowly coming into view.

"What the hell?" His exclamation was louder than he intended, echoing across his basement cave.

The front of the barge was slowly dropping closer to water level. And then to his shock, it dipped under the water.

In less than a minute the barge was gone—taking Johnny Humboldt's container with it to a watery grave.

CHAPTER 38

PLAYING CATCH-UP

Lee Bowen knew he was a control freak.

In brief moments of self-reflection, he realized his need to be in charge was a function of his childhood. His parents, in particular his father, had pushed him constantly to perform and to perform well, no matter the activity or venue. The pressure was unrelenting and intense in sports, school, social settings, and more. And when Bowen had missed his father's high bar—which happened all too frequently—the consequences had not been pleasant. The physical wounds had healed, but the emotional scars still infected Bowen's psyche. Like a psychological boomerang, he'd grown to hate his father but internalized the need to win at all costs.

He'd also embraced the isolation that resulted from his own cutthroat attitude. Consequently, he appreciated the personal anonymity that the RallyAmerica DAO and associated blockchain tools brought to his venture. It was one of the technical ironies that he loved. Blockchain was not designed to hide activity—in fact, quite to the contrary. The whole point of blockchain was to create true transparency in an organization. It was a Web 3.0 response to those that felt traditional governance structures were too opaque and allowed leadership to avoid accountability. In the process, however, the lack of a central repository in the blockchain enabled people to hide their identities even if they couldn't camouflage their actions.

And that anonymity was what enabled Bowen to pressure others to do his bidding, often using questionable or outright illegal means. He could do it without exposing himself to any liability. Even if the FBI or some other authority eventually caught on to RallyAmerica itself—and he accepted that they might—if he was careful, they would have one hell of a time tracing anything back to him.

The flip side to the DAO structure was that it was a terrible command-and-control structure. The military would never, ever operate this way. Decisions required voting, individuals responsible for action were invisible to the rest of the group, and information and intelligence reporting were slow and often inaccurate. When everyone is in charge, nobody's in charge.

And at the moment, he knew he wasn't in charge.

"She did what?" he yelled into his computer. He was working from another of the WeWork offices he'd secretly rented to maximize his digital security. He had firewalls everywhere, but he'd worked with enough geeks to know that firewalls were meant to be breached. Physically distributed security was an added protection in his system. Given the current office vacancy rate, it was also exceptionally cheap.

Of course, there were a few others in the facility, and his yelling at his computer pulled a few heads up from their screens. He raised his hand in apology and gestured to the screen as if to say, "We all have to deal with idiots." That got a few knowing looks.

He returned to his screen and reread the Discord message.

> **Had to take action to secure our prize. The bitch was on our trail. Threat terminated and trail cut. All assets secured.**

He scratched his head, trying to figure out exactly what that meant. Some of these people spoke a completely different language. The code felt like a code. He understood the reference to the prize. Clearly, the agent had moved Johnny. "The bitch" was also pretty clear. He now realized he'd been naive to think Senator Smith would roll over so easily. She'd pursued a delaying action in response to his threats and then gone on the offensive. Bitch, indeed.

But what did "threat terminated" mean? Had she killed the senator? If she was dead, she would be useless to him. In fact, it was worse than that: They'd just replace her as a senator, and he'd have to start over with someone else. And the FBI would go completely ballistic in its attempts to track the perpetrators. RallyAmerica had not authorized termination. He'd just voted successfully against a similar scheme.

Finally, where was the asset? He'd been assured it was secure before. Why should he trust the information now? If he didn't know where the asset was or how to access it, how could he use it?

Goddamn it! All he had was a shitty post that he couldn't understand. No command. No control. A venture capital nightmare.

What he really needed was a throat to choke.

• • • • •

Unintended consequences.

Deputy Director Jerald Jessup read the field report on his dual twenty-five-inch monitors—the report on the left screen and the photos on the right. All he could think was, *What a clusterfuck.*

He'd known all along that Senator Tamika Smith wasn't going to leave the investigation alone. He'd tracked her to the Netherlands, uncertain exactly why she had chosen that destination, but equally sure that she was there with a purpose. Once he had the information from Mufasa—Jesus, he couldn't believe he was stuck relying on someone with such a stupid name—he'd informed the consulate that Johnny Humboldt was likely in Amsterdam or somewhere in the Netherlands. In short, he'd followed the book. He couldn't restrict Smith from traveling, he couldn't take unilateral action on foreign soil, and he didn't have anything close to a full picture of what was afoot.

Yet now he was stuck with the consequences. The Dutch National Police had contacted the consulate with a "shots fired" report at Coenhaven, and the consulate had contacted Jessup. Of course, he'd also gotten irate calls from underlings at the State Department and the CIA wondering why they weren't already in the loop.

What loop? There was no loop.

Just a cluster.

The only person who'd been reasonably helpful was the Dutch officer who was on-site. After a connection from the US consulate general, Commissaris Pieter Snijders had sent him the full report, including all the crime scene photography and ballistics evidence. Jessup wasn't sure his superiors would be happy with that, but that was one problem he didn't have to manage.

JJ shared his screen with Higginbottom as they evaluated the situation.

"What do you see, Higgs?"

"Well, clearly something was in the warehouse. No other reason for anyone to be on the dock. The doors are wide open, and you can see the dirt and dust marks where a container was stored." The agent used his touchpad to zoom in on a few of the photographs.

"Agreed. The consulate got a call from Smith saying that Humboldt was in a harbor area. She must have thought he was in the warehouse."

"Sir, if two plus two equals four, Johnny Humboldt was in the container, and she saw them moving him. She went in to stop them."

"OK . . . and she got shot for her trouble. Somehow the girl got in the way as well. What was she doing there? And how the hell did they both get there at the same time?"

Higginbottom gave him an empty look.

Neither one of them had any answers.

Jessup continued. "The police arrived less than five minutes later. According to their report, the girl was bleeding from the abdomen but kept screaming, 'They took my daddy, they took my daddy' over and over again. They had to sedate her before the ambulance took both of them to the hospital. Fortunately, I got them on a C-17 before there were any police interviews." Jessup didn't want the Dutch publicizing that a US senator had been shot at a crime scene. The CIA had at least agreed with that.

Agent Higginbottom jumped in with the important question. "So where the hell is the container? You can't just make something like that vanish."

They both said it at the same time.

"The canal."

CHAPTER 39

COMING HOME

Phoenix Humboldt checked out the interior of the mammoth military plane. She felt the desolate gray of the cargo hold seeping deeply into her body. A double line of metal boxes was stacked down the middle of the fuselage, lashed to the floor of the plane by huge cables. She couldn't see above or around the cargo, as it extended the full length and height of the plane, making the huge hold feel claustrophobic.

She was plopped in a harness seat that folded down from the left-hand side of the cabin. Obviously designed for function over form, the seat was impossibly uncomfortable, and every bounce reminded her that the stitches in her abdomen had popped and had to be re-stapled. With the slightest movement from the aircraft, her stomach throbbed. And with every bump, her aching heart reminded her that she'd failed. Her father was once again gone, and she would never be allowed back into the game to search for him. They would treat her like the child she'd shown them she was.

She felt a hand reach across from her right and gently touch her shoulder. Tamika had to stretch her right arm all the way across her body, as her left arm was bandaged and in a sling. Phoenix could see the scratches across her face and the bandage covering the stitches they'd placed in her chin. The bullet and the concrete dock had not treated her well.

"It'll be OK" were the first words Tamika said.

Phoenix didn't have the energy or desire to respond. She didn't believe the words, in any event. Nothing was ever going to be right again.

"Look, I know we didn't get him back, but your dad is alive. We know that now. If they wanted him dead, they wouldn't have moved him."

Phoenix saw a tight smile on Tamika's face. "But I fucked the whole thing up," she said. "I should have known you were there. All I did was get in the way and get you shot."

Tamika shook her head. "First, let's go easy on the language. I have the military as an excuse—you don't." This small rebuke was delivered with a real smile.

"Second, you were just trying to help your dad. Nobody, including me, can blame you for that. And while we're at it, I'm the one to blame. I should have called in the cavalry when I got the message about Coenhaven. If I'd called the FBI, my friends there would have figured out how to help."

"But—" Phoenix started to protest.

"No buts. I'm supposed to be the experienced, mature adult—and a veteran to boot. I knew better."

"How are we going to find my father?" For Phoenix, that was the only thing that mattered.

Tamika didn't respond right away, and that scared Phoenix. She'd always thought that her father's girlfriend had all the answers, and now it was clear she didn't.

Finally Tamika said, "Well . . . the simple fact is that I don't really have any idea. I know this. We need to rely on my friends at the FBI to figure it out. Whomever we're up against is well funded and professional. We can't rescue him on our own."

Well at least she's being honest, Phoenix thought. "How did you know where they were keeping my dad?"

"I should be asking you that question. What the hell were you doing in Amsterdam, much less at that warehouse?" The military tone shouldn't have surprised Phoenix, but it reminded her that Tamika was not just a friend.

Phoenix hesitated, not sure how much Tamika knew about Bryce. "I left on my own—Mom didn't know." That much was true.

"You didn't answer my question."

Phoenix fiddled with the straps on her seat belt. "I had some help." It was weak, but the best she could come up with.

Tamika gave her a sideways glance, clearly trying to read her face. "Hmmm. Did you get a text message from a number you didn't know?"

Phoenix jumped. *How does she know that?*

She gave in to the trust she felt. "I asked Shea for help from Bryce. And I used Mom's credit card to buy the flight to Amsterdam. I Ubered to the docks."

Tamika gave her a bemused look. "I'll remember not to underestimate your ingenuity. When we get home, we have to stop all the secrecy. We need all hands on deck to catch these . . . oh hell . . . these assholes." Tamika reached her hand out to touch Phoenix's shoulder again. The plane hit an air pocket and lurched downward.

Despite the resulting twinge of stomach pain, Phoenix couldn't hold back a bit of a grin. She knew now why her dad loved Tamika. And for the first time, she felt a tiny ray of hope that Tamika would get him back.

• • • • •

When the ramp on the plane came down at Joint Base Andrews in Maryland seven hours later, Tamika could see JJ waiting with the predictable black SUV. The fact that he was practically standing at attention did not bode well. Margaret Humboldt was also there, her scowling face visible from the plane. This was not going to be any fun at all.

"Go to your mom," Tamika whispered to Phoenix. She knew that their reunion was the most important next step.

Phoenix didn't need much urging. She ran down the rear ramp before it had even hit the tarmac. She threw her arms around her mom, both of them crying and yelling at the same time.

Deputy Director Jessup walked up purposefully as Tamika stepped carefully to the tarmac, still feeling the effects of her arm injury.

"You OK?" At least JJ's first words weren't to accuse her of being stupid.

"I'll recover, thanks. Second time that arm's been hit. Need to kick that habit."

"Well, you need to stop running into fire. And you need to let me do my job."

"Not here, OK?" Tamika gestured over to Margaret Humboldt and her daughter.

Jessup nodded and joined her in walking over to them. The tarmac was a flurry of activity as the crew moved in to unload the cargo and another C-17 taxied out toward the active runway.

"Mrs. Humboldt, I don't believe we've had the pleasure of meeting." JJ had to shout above the noise.

"Thank you for bringing my baby home," came the polite response.

"That was the easy part. Senator Smith is the one who saved her."

Tamika tried to contain her composure. While Jessup may have been factually correct, she was pretty sure Margaret was going to blame her for the whole episode.

Instead, Margaret just stared at her daughter, who was the one to break the awkward silence.

"That's right, Mom. She dove in front of me and rolled me to the ground. I think the bullet would've hit me." Tamika felt Phoenix touch the sling on her left arm, using it as a prop to prove her point.

The mother in Margaret came out. "And just what were you doing there in the first place, may I ask? You scared the shit out of me. How dare you run away. Did you think getting shot was going to help your father?"

"Mom—"

"She's right, Phoenix," Tamika interjected quickly. "Neither of us should have been there. We've agreed to let the professionals do their jobs from now on. Right?"

Phoenix gave her a serious-looking nod in return.

Tamika thought JJ was going to lose it, but he held it together.

He turned to Margaret. "Ma'am, we're continuing the search for Mr. Humboldt—please know we have our best people working on it. For now, our driver will take you to Reagan National for your flight back to California. I'll get a full report from Senator Smith. If it's OK, I may have some follow-up questions for Phoenix, but we can do that on video."

"Thank you very much for everything, Director," Margaret said. Tamika felt her "no thanks to you" gaze as Margaret continued with Jessup. "Zoom is fine. Just make sure you do it after school hours. This young lady is headed back to high school tomorrow."

Tamika smiled at the expression on Phoenix's face. "Give me a hug. You focus on school and helping your mom. I promise we'll get your father back."

"Hmmf." Jessup made some noise.

"Actually, the FBI will get him back," Tamika corrected with a smile.

• • • • •

An hour later, Tamika regretted her promise.

"What do you mean the container disappeared? You must have some way to track it. Satellites, drones, whatever." She and Jessup were in a briefing room at Andrews.

JJ's response wasn't reassuring. "Well, the military has those resources but not the FBI. And spying in an ally's backyard is frowned on by just about every other department in the government."

"Well, what do we do now?" She glared at him, wondering how they could lose something that conspicuous.

"My newfound friend at the Dutch National Police shared that they're searching for a barge named *de Pijp* that was seen leaving the area and headed east. So far, they've had no luck locating it, which, given the limited travel options, is a bit concerning."

"Don't they have an electronic way to track commercial ships?"

"These bastards are pros—they almost certainly turned off their transponders. Plus, it got dark shortly after the shooting. There's a lot of barge traffic on those canals."

Tamika paused, thinking through various options in her head. She suspected her guardian angel could find more information than the FBI, but she didn't want to violate his confidence. At the same time, running around on her own following up on secret leads had to end. Oh, by the way, she had to reemerge as a US senator soon.

"JJ—give me a day. I have a source that may have more information. I can't promise that I can share the data, but I'm going to try. We need every asset we have."

Jessup nodded with a slight smirk and turned away quickly. Tamika wasn't sure how to interpret that, but it made her worry for Bryce's safety.

Friends, enemies, and frenemies. Kind of like being in the Senate.

CHAPTER 40

JENGA MOVES

Lee Bowen thought he understood the US financial system.

Since World War II, the American economic model had dominated world markets. With all due respect to London and Tokyo, Wall Street was the center of the world's financial system, in theory allocating capital to the most promising ventures and winnowing out the losers. The Dow Jones Industrial Average, and more recently the S&P 500, were indexes used to measure the health of the world economy, with the US as the largest market.

The corollary to this American dominance was the central role of the US dollar as the world's primary reserve currency. Bowen had majored in economics at Princeton and studied financial markets during his MBA at Wharton, but it didn't take an advanced degree to understand the massive advantage the dollar provided the US government. Most countries could run a deficit for modest periods of time without facing serious economic risk. Of course, they could borrow on the open market, but investors didn't want to risk holding large amounts of non–dollar denominated assets. There were limits on what countries like France, Germany, the UK, and Japan could borrow without severe currency and economic risks. Within the EU, with a common currency, the constraints were even tighter. Of course, developing countries faced even more challenges, frequently accessing and then defaulting on IMF and World Bank loans.

What fascinated Bowen was the US government's ability to avoid most of these restrictions. Because countries and investors wanted to own US dollar-denominated assets—and because there was an unspoken belief that these securities were the safest in the market—the US government could run massive deficits and finance the shortfall by selling treasury securities that most treated as if they were cash. Nobody believed the US would default on its debts, or at least nobody wanted to acknowledge the possibility.

Even Bowen was boggled by the numbers. Total US debt was over $30 trillion. It cost $800 billion each year to pay interest on that debt, a shocking 14 percent of federal spending and rising. The alternatives to more borrowing were not easy. Cutting spending was deeply unpopular, especially given that over 50 percent of funding was tied up in Medicare, Medicaid, and Social Security. The defense budget, which accounted for another 13 percent of the total, was also difficult to cut for political reasons. Nobody who wanted to get reelected loved raising taxes, and many even argued that reducing taxes was the best way to stimulate growth. In short, it was a political quagmire.

Sitting in his Silicon Valley office at B² Ventures, Bowen read through the text of Senator Jonathan Hawkins's recent speech to the Business Roundtable. Hawkins had done exactly as he'd been instructed, effectively shifting his views from a budget moderate to a deficit hawk.

> **The time has come for us to rein in government spending. This is just simple kitchen table economics. We are spending dramatically more than we earn, so we have to cut back. On current course and speed, we are hurtling to financial Armageddon. Everything should be on the table, including eliminating entire areas like the Department of Energy, the Department of Education, and the IRS. Government giveaway programs that allow people to leech off of hardworking Americans must be cut. We should stop acting like the world's policemen and should reduce our spending to defend Europe and Asia. The time has come for us to focus on home.**

It wasn't an earth-shattering event—just another political speech in front of a relatively conservative business audience. The ideas were not all mainstream, at least not yet, but they reflected what the far right had been saying for some time. What was significant was the meaningful change in position this implied for Hawkins. While he wasn't a well-known or prominent senator, he was a reliable moderate in the Senate that leadership could count on for key economic votes.

No longer.

Bowen had now confirmed that Tamika Smith had survived the attack in Amsterdam, but he still had no clarity on the whereabouts of Johhny Humboldt. The entire plan was designed to deliver specific results in the Senate, and he needed to determine whether Smith could still be turned. He was working on other senators, but she was the linchpin.

And the important votes were coming up. The US was closing in on its self-inflicted debt ceiling rules. If Bowen could orchestrate a government default, it would be a first step in bringing down the worldwide hegemony of the US economy. And if cracks started to appear and the building started to teeter . . . well, Lee Bowen could almost hear the Jenga blocks falling to the ground.

And he was betting everything on the mayhem that would follow.

• • • • •

Nastya Andropov had had enough.

"Jesus, at this pace, we'll never get there. What's the American expression . . . *watching paint dry*."

She was talking by secure connection with her handler in the United States. They'd both read the Business Roundtable speech, unimpressed with the progress. His reply mollified her a bit. "You know I agree with you. He doesn't have the balls to make the tough decisions we need."

"Does Moscow agree with you?" While a committed communist, Andropov was a regime skeptic. She'd seen too much bureaucracy and grift to buy in to the current leadership even if she appreciated Putin's focus on Mother Russia.

"Right now, I can't get any clear answers from Moscow. The *special military operation* in Ukraine has paralyzed everyone. Do you believe that shit? We can't control a two-bit former stage actor."

Nastya understood the desire to reclaim the Ukraine as part of the

Russian empire, but her concerns about Moscow went far deeper. The FSB was as corrupt as any agency.

"Mischa, I think we have a leak someplace in the FSB." She did not know the identity of her handler beyond his cover name, and their communications were voice only.

"Maaier, what are you talking about? Only three people know about our work, and they are all at the very top. A leak is not possible." Nastya didn't know if he knew her real identity, but she was accustomed to the alias.

"Then how did they know Humboldt was at Coenhaven? How did Smith and the girl both show up there? We have a security problem."

The response back was not what she wanted to hear. "Maybe the problem is with you. Shooting the girl was sloppy to begin with, and somehow they traced your exfil to the Netherlands. I told you we should have taken him further east immediately—and away from your base."

She could feel her face beginning to flush along with the anger. "Well, if we'd done that, they'd have recovered him already. We're lucky I was paying attention and close by. I'm the only reason we're still in the game."

"But you missed the senator."

That stung. She could imagine his death stare, daring her to continue challenging his authority.

She broke the standoff. "Either way, we have to turn up the pressure. And fancy speeches aren't going to cut it."

"On this we agree," her handler replied. "The hackers are working on it. They say they are close."

"I still think my way would be better." She was a field agent being held back by paper pushers.

"Your time will come. And together, we'll bring all of them down."

CHAPTER 41

SOURCES

Bryce Roscovitch jumped at the buzz of one of his several burner phones. He could count on one hand the number of times any of his phones had rung. After several buzzing rings, he picked it up and answered tentatively. "Hello?"

"I don't think we've been formally introduced."

Bryce immediately recognized the voice and froze.

He hung up.

He knew he'd opened a can of worms with his texting to Phoenix and Tamika, and now the problem was coming back at him. He was exposed, and he hated it. He glanced around his basement cave, hoping for someone to save him. The gloom and darkness brought no comfort.

The phone buzzed again.

He just stared at it as if that would make it shut off. Eventually it did.

And then it buzzed again.

He knew she would be persistent . . . that was her nature. He took a deep breath and answered.

"Why are you calling this number? You know the risks for me as well as anyone."

The voice was scathing. "If you were less worried about protecting yourself and more worried about saving Johnny, we'd already have him back home." Bryce could feel the anger vibrating through the phone. She was probably someone he shouldn't piss off.

"Well . . . ," he began but didn't really know where to go. "You know

I've tried to help. I've been watching over my family . . . which is sort of your family now."

"But Bryce, what good has that done anyone?"

He cringed at the use of his name on the line. And then at the rebuke.

"Look, you have to understand—"

"No, actually, I don't. Johnny is fighting for his life, Phoenix and I have both been shot, and God knows what's coming next. We need your help, and we need it now."

Bryce took a deep breath. "What do you want?"

"The FBI is trying to find Johnny, but you seem to have access to information they don't have."

"Which is why even this call is very dangerous for me. I don't exactly have a permission slip for what I do. And remember, they might be watching you, too."

"Do you really think I'm under surveillance? Can you imagine what would happen if the FBI spied on a US senator?"

"Actually, I wasn't thinking about the FBI. There are others . . ."

After a long pause. "I guess that's just a risk we're both going to have to take. They've already tried to kill me once."

Bryce repeated his question. "How can I help?"

"What do you know about the barge that took Johnny away from the warehouse?"

Now Bryce was really stuck. There was no good answer to that question.

Tamika continued. "Look, I know you don't want to expose yourself to—"

Bryce jumped in. "The barge is at the bottom of the Amsterdam–Rhine Canal."

Silence on the line.

"Tamika?"

"I'm here. What canal? Was the container on the barge when it . . . sank?"

Bryce saw a bit of a way out. "Well, that's the interesting thing. I don't think it sank."

"What do you mean by that? If it's at the bottom of a canal, it sank."

"Actually, I don't think so. I'm nearly certain it was run aground intentionally. I've enhanced the video and watched it frame by frame. It looks like several seacocks were left wide open and water just flowed in. The barge was autopiloted to the side of the canal to keep it out of the shipping lane. It just slowly went under. I don't think the crew was on the barge when it went down."

"But what about Johnny?" Bryce could hear the sad, lonely panic. There was no way for him to avoid the uncomfortable truth.

"It makes no sense for them to kill him," he told her. "But the container was still on the barge. That's all I know."

• • • • •

Tamika turned off the burner phone and shoved it in her pocket. She'd gone out to the Senate Park to make the call. Now her first instinct was to run. That's what she always did. She sprinted back to her Senate office in the Russell Building, trying to clear her head. She bolted past her staff and asked them not to disturb her, trying hard not to slam the door in the process. She failed.

She plopped down in her desk chair, trying to catch her breath. She agreed with Bryce that killing Johnny would be illogical. But the evidence said that Johnny had drowned in the container. Was he really gone?

Her life had been filled with too many deaths. Losing her mother had been difficult, but the cancer inevitable. Her brother's murder by terrorists had filled her with anger and rage. She'd eventually had her revenge and lived with the resulting PTSD every day. But this was different . . . Johnny was her love—something more fundamental that cut to the core of her soul. If Johnny was indeed dead, she knew she'd never recover.

Survival meant holding on to some sliver of hope. It was all she had.

She knew that her torn heart didn't change the reality of the situation. Johnny had been kidnapped to leverage her, and when she'd defied the perps, they'd shifted gears. And her experience told her that terrorists weren't always logical. All she could do was get Bryce's information to the right people to determine whether Johnny was still in the container. She placed the call and Jessup answered.

"What do you know?" was his greeting.

Tamika took a deep breath and tried to stay professional. "I know where the barge is, and I think Johnny might be . . . dead."

"How could you possibly know where the barge is? And how can they blackmail you if he's dead?"

Tamika said nothing.

"Oh shit, Major. I'm so sorry. That just came out . . . wrong. I'm an ass."

Yes, you are, she thought.

Out loud, she said, "I understand, JJ. In fact, after an initial cry, I had the same thoughts you did. Just in a different order."

In a quiet, calm voice, Jessup tried again. "Tell me what you know."

Tamika passed on the information Bryce had given her, including the exact location of the barge.

"I'll follow up with the Dutch authorities. Should be easy for them to confirm the barge's location. But it will take them time to dive on the wreck and check on the container."

"I appreciate that" was all Tamika could manage. One way or another, she'd know.

Jessup continued, "You know I'm praying for him . . . I've been here a few too many times before."

"We both know how that works." Tamika had prayed for every soldier she'd rescued—and knew the pain when some didn't make it.

Jessup had one last thought. "I won't ask where you got this information—I know you won't tell me. But I'm going to figure it out eventually."

Tamika took a deep breath and revealed her source. She hated betraying Bryce, but her love for Johnny was what mattered the most.

"And you better not do shit against him until we catch these bastards."

CHAPTER 42

ON THE RUN

Bryce paced between the refrigerator and his computing towers, going psychologically from cold to hot and back to cold again.

His life had shifted from a solitary existence in a dark room lit by computer screens to a sudden burst of personal interactions. Johnny Humboldt, his daughter Phoenix, and Tamika Smith were all people he'd tracked digitally since the original Wilkes attacks almost four years ago. But now he was getting to know them as people. For Bryce, that was a problem.

He'd always justified his dark web work by telling himself that someone else would do it if he didn't. He might as well profit from the opportunity. When Ford Wilkes had killed thousands of people using explosives provided by Bryce, that veil of deception had fallen away. He'd conveniently replaced it with the idea that he would protect his extended family and vet his clients more fully.

Deep down, he knew this was also total bullshit. The fact of the matter was that he was great at what he did, and he wanted to keep doing it. He felt the guilt and yearned for forgiveness, but didn't want to sacrifice his sheltered existence. Tamika had called him out. Now he had to face the music. And he only knew one way out.

Catch the bastards.

He went back to his whiteboard.

"Well, the traces on the original email threats to Smith and the high school video feed overlap. In fact, the FBI believes that several threats to other officials have used a similar trail."

His alter ego cut in. "Hey, idiot, there's obviously someone pushing the buttons on all of this—a central organizing group."

"OK, so someone is orchestrating this activity. You think this is part of some plan—some conspiracy? What do they want to accomplish?"

"Let's assume they're Russians . . . now what could the Russians possibly want to do to the United States?" The self-inflicted sarcasm cut deeply.

"OK, so their goal is to interfere with elections, co-opt leaders, or destabilize the government."

"Could be all of the above."

"Who in the United States would want to support the Russians?"

"You've got to go deeper on those traces. You need the actual locations."

Bryce did another lap between the refrigerator and his desk, returning with a feeling of determination.

He was up to the challenge. "And," he said aloud, "I'm gonna need more heat-and-serve meals."

• • • • •

Phoenix hated her English class. Studying dead playwrights from the twentieth century was a drag, and Eugene O'Neill was at the top of her list. Who ever heard of writing a four-act play that chronicled a single day in the life of some random family? Addiction, failed dreams, a broken family—why would she want to read about such a depressing situation? *The Iceman Cometh* should have been called *The Boredom Goeth*. She put the play down and picked up her phone.

The screen indicated it was 11:30 at night, and her bedroom was lit by a single lamp on her nightstand. Shadows danced around her, reflecting off the drawn paneled curtains covering the window behind her desk. Some clothes were strewn on the floor where she'd dumped them over an hour ago. She was already in her flannel pajamas and had been reading the last part of O'Neill's opus in an attempt to fall asleep. But even blowhard O'Neill was failing her. All she could think about was her father.

She knew that chasing after him had been foolish, and she blamed herself for interfering with Tamika's efforts to rescue him. She should have left things to the professionals. But the anguish she felt was deep, and sitting around doing school busywork wasn't going to cut it. She grabbed her laptop from under the nightstand and pulled up her digital diary, a habit she'd inherited from her mother. If she couldn't rescue her dad, she'd at least try to keep him company.

Dad,

First, I hope you're OK. Mom doesn't know it, but I saw the picture they sent. They told Mom it's probably a fake, but she doesn't trust the FBI anymore. Either way, I can't imagine what you're going through. I'm so sorry I screwed up. We were so close, and I got in the way. You always tell me to trust my instincts, to take control of a situation if I can. I guess this one was beyond my reach.

I pray that you feel the love coming your way. No matter what's happened, I know Mom still cares for you too. I know she's been praying for you, writing frantically in her journal, and pestering the police every day. Nathan doesn't say too much, but he misses you and is thinking about you every minute. And Tamika's doing everything she can. She says she's going to leave it up to the FBI, but I don't believe that for a second.

I want to do more to help, but right now I've been put in the high school penalty box. I hope you know how much I miss you. Our late-night conversations, our runs through the neighborhood, even you pestering me about my homework. You and Mom always said that faith and family are all that matter. Now I know exactly what you meant.

I need a big hug and a good-night kiss from you.

I love you,
Phoenix

She let out a deep breath, knowing that nothing had changed. But now she felt a little calmer. Just imagining he could somehow read the words she'd written helped at least a little bit.

Still not ready to go to sleep, she read back through the journal entry and hit on a solution to her restlessness.

Her mom would kill her, but she had to go for a run.

• • • • •

Working through the night was the same as working through the day for Bryce. He just kept going until he had some answers.

He'd narrowed the digital footprints down to four locations, which surprisingly were all in the Palo Alto area. The attack on the high school video cameras had been executed from a location on Concar Drive in San Mateo. That made sense. The emails to Tamika had originated in two different locations, both in San Jose. One at the Riverpark Tower and the other on Santa Clara Street. One other location showed up on the traces—at Park Boulevard in Palo Alto. What were the Russians doing running around Silicon Valley?

"OK, so we have a team of people using different WeWork locations as touchdown points." Bryce went to the whiteboard and noted the locations.

His alter ego jumped in. "Well . . . each of those facilities has a bunch of different customers. Could be anyone."

Bryce thought about that for a minute. He then checked to see if any of the offices were registered under the same name. Not surprisingly, the answer came back in the negative.

"Well, shit. One person had to pay for each of these offices. When in doubt, follow the money."

After two hours of a combination of manual and AI-assisted searches, he hit pay dirt.

"Got you!" he yelled in triumph.

At that precise moment, all four of his systems started to ring alarms.

The alarms could only mean one thing.

"Oh, fuck."

He had to leave immediately.

CHAPTER 43

DISCOVERIES

"Empty? You're sure?"

It was three days after he'd heard from Tamika Smith, and Jessup was on a decidedly unsecure phone line with Commissaris Pieter Snijders of the Dutch National Police. They'd found the barge down in thirty-five feet of water, just outside the main shipping channel in the Amsterdam–Rhine Canal. He knew that without Tamika's information the barge would have gone unnoticed for who knows how long. Apparently, that stretch of the canal wasn't exactly a prime fishing spot.

"I assure you, Deputy Director, that the container lashed down on the barge was empty. It looks like someone *was* there—there's a WC and a cot—but no body."

Jessup punched the air with his fist. This was the first piece of good news in the entire case.

"Was the door to the container open?" Jessup wondered if somehow Johnny had escaped.

"No—it took a blowtorch to get it open."

"What are you going to do with the barge? Any chance there are any forensics?"

"It'll be a navigation hazard, so it needs to be raised. Of course we'll do some analysis once it's up, but I wouldn't hold out much hope on DNA or anything like that. It's been in the canal for several days and the water isn't exactly pure. Besides, it's going to take several weeks to raise it."

Jessup's mind was going a hundred miles an hour. Humboldt was likely alive. But how? Where was he? Who had him? Why fake his death? The questions just didn't end, and nothing was adding up.

"What about the crew? I assume there were no bodies on the ship?"

"Correct. We're doing some background work to identify the ownership of the barge. Maybe that'll get us to a crew list. We'll keep digging. I'll keep you informed, as a courtesy, of course."

"Many thanks, Commissaris. I appreciate you going the extra mile on this. I'll share what I can from our side if I think it's connected."

"Roger that."

Jessup hung up the phone but wasn't sure what to do next. Obviously, this shifted the scope of their investigation, and he needed to discuss that with Higginbottom. But there also was the matter of what to tell Senator Smith and the Humboldt family—and when—and Jessup had no idea how he was going to do it.

Higginbottom first. He went to the SCIF and connected with his field agent in the FBI's Silicon Valley office.

"Higgs, you're not going to believe this."

"Actually, I think I will, Director."

Jessup paused for a moment, enjoying the dramatic effect. "Johnny Humboldt wasn't in the container."

"No shit! So how did he get out?"

Jessup went one step further. "Look, we don't even know if he was ever in the container. Remember, nobody ever saw him during the shootout. And we have no way to verify the original source of the information."

"But Senator Smith and Phoenix Humboldt were shot at for a reason, right?"

Jessup thought about that. "Fair enough. Let's assume for the moment that he was being held at the warehouse. Where the hell did he go and how did he get there? And who took him?"

"Maybe they took him off the barge at some point before they sank it?" Higginbottom proposed.

"Or maybe he was never on the barge at all. What a great decoy that would make. Put the container on the barge, send it down the river, and sink it. By the time everyone figures it out, you're long gone with Humboldt in tow."

"So they took him away by car or truck while the barge went down the river?"

"That's what I would've done," Jessup said. "The barge was always too risky as a holding point. Too easy to discover and pull over. Once you're on the boat, there's no place to go."

Except down, he thought.

"OK . . . ," began Higginbottom slowly. "What are you going to tell . . . everyone?" Jessup understood the reference to the extended Humboldt family.

"Let me handle that." Jessup knew Tamika thought Johnny was probably dead, and the rest of his family still assumed he was missing. He'd have to square that up soon.

Jessup pressed on with another urgent topic. "What do you hear from Mufasa?"

"I'm glad you asked," Higginbottom said. "He's found our man. Not far from you in Virginia."

"We have an actual location? I thought the guy was better than that."

"We do—should I organize a field team to bring him in?"

Jessup looked back at Higginbottom across the video connection. "No, just send me the information." He ignored the second quizzical glance he got in return. He hated keeping Higginbottom at arm's length, but these were delicate issues.

He wanted to deal with all of them in his own way.

CHAPTER 44

LIST OF TRAITORS

Dutch efficiency.

The FSB agent, code named Maaier, the Reaper, pushed back from her computer screen in her converted office. Originally a second bedroom, her workspace was under a window with a view of a garden in the back of the house. And from there out to the waters of the Wadden Sea. For most people this would have been an idyllic place to work. For Nastya Andropov, it was quiet and isolated and that was all that mattered.

Her own safety was why she was pissed at the Dutch. How did they find the barge so quickly? The whole point of the ruse was to buy time so she could resettle her prized possession. Now the Dutch, and likely the FBI, knew that Johnny Humboldt was not dead after all, and probably was never on the barge. They would intensify their efforts to find him . . . and that put her at more risk.

As she thought about it more, she couldn't figure out how the Dutch had found the barge at all. The canal was a big, wide stretch of water that ran for over seventy kilometers. Somehow, they'd found the needle in that haystack. They were good, but not that good. She came back to her FSB leak theory. A tip to the Dutch police would explain everything. Who had known about the plan?

First up was the crew she'd hired to steal and operate the barge. They'd never planned to keep Johnny in the warehouse permanently. Moving him down the Rhine and then by truck to the east was always a possibility. It had just been a question of timing. The guards in the warehouse were part of a larger crew she had on standby—and when it became necessary to move Humboldt sooner, she'd activated the full team quickly.

The idea to pull Humboldt from the container and sink the ship had been her snap decision. The crew thought the prisoner was in the container, and they certainly knew where they sank the boat. One of them could have squealed. But that implied that they'd been caught, and she already had confirmation that they were well on their way back to Hungary.

So it was unlikely the crew had betrayed her.

Next up on her list was someone within the FSB in Moscow. The idea that the Americans or someone else within NATO had a spy in the FSB did not surprise her. Russia had their own spies across Europe and the United States. That was just how the game was played. Mischa had said he wasn't getting any attention from his superiors in Moscow, and he claimed that only a few very senior people knew about their mission. She couldn't rule out that one of them had a mistress or had spoken out of turn in a meeting, but the recency of the boat decision again made this unlikely.

That only left one option: Mischa himself.

Why would Mischa want to jeopardize her identity or the mission?

A handler like Mischa had to have the ultimate trust of his agents. Anything he did that ran afoul of that principle was both counterproductive and dangerous. He had been quite tough on her during their last conversation, basically accusing her of screwing up. Now he'd be justifiably upset about the barge discovery. Was he setting her up to take the fall if they failed?

Then an even worse thought occurred to her. Maybe Mischa had been turned? Or if he hadn't been turned, maybe he'd just been co-opted by the conveniences of a capitalistic society. She understood that the temptations for an agent in the US were frequent and great. From their conversations, she knew his reasons for entering the FSB were not as pure as hers. And she could tell he was enjoying his assignment in the US. Given what was going on in Russia, who could blame him for falling prey to something or someone?

She understood there was no resolution to this conundrum. But she also knew that paranoia was the first defense for any field agent. The current situation went far beyond suspicions. She was sure someone was betraying her.

When she found them, they would pay.

• • • • •

"What's our play?"

Ely Basof had already expressed his anger at the barge discovery. He knew Andropov's reputation was exceptional, and he'd thought the original call to sink the ship was sound. Now it looked foolish. He'd made sure she knew that.

Andropov's reply was quick and sure. "You know as well as I do that we still have two important cards. We have Humboldt, and now that they know he's alive, there's still an option to pressure Tamika Smith."

"But you already know she's not going to play ball." Basof was getting impatient.

"That's certainly true for a traditional-style blackmail sting. But you're forgetting about the daughter. If the daughter knows about the blackmail, there's no way for Smith to refuse."

Basof paused and thought for a moment. "You're suggesting that the next threatening note doesn't go to Smith."

"Correct. It goes to the girl."

Basof respected the creativity. "I like it. How soon can you execute it?"

"I need a day or two to put things in place. My security antenna is way up. I want to deliver the communication in a way that absolutely cannot be traced."

"OK. Do it. I assume our second play is in my court." Basof tapped his fingers on the desk as he gazed back at the brick walls of his Woodside enclave.

"Mischa, tell those assholes to hurry up," Andropov said tersely.

"What can I say; they're Belarusians."

CHAPTER 45

AN OFFER

Culpeper, Virginia.

How could a historic Virginia town be the home of a notorious hacker? On Friday morning, before making the ninety-minute drive, Jessup had read through the Culpeper Wikipedia article. Founded in 1759, the town was surveyed by George Washington, of all people. Given its location, it was also a crossroads for both armies during the Civil War. As JJ pulled up to the address on Asher Street, he thought that the idea of a civil war in America didn't seem so far-fetched.

He drove a block past the address and strolled down the street, casually glancing from side to side as if he were on an afternoon walk. The house at 211 Asher was entirely unremarkable at first glance: a small-town ranch house built in the 1950s. The house was registered to Jim Jones. The deputy director wondered if that was just a generic name or a rude joke. A short driveway led to a garage that was likely too narrow for two of today's SUVs. Small portico over the front door, a maple tree in the front yard.

But Jessup wasn't your average afternoon retiree getting his daily exercise. He saw the night vision cameras discreetly hidden, peeking out from under the gutters. Motion sensors in the bushes across the front of the lot. High-intensity floodlights under the eaves. Nobody was sneaking up on this guy without warning.

None of the security really bothered JJ. He was almost certain that his hacker had evacuated. The likelihood that Mufasa had tracked Bryce back to a specific address without being detected was very low. Besides, Jessup had come in peace—or at least to negotiate a truce. If he triggered an alarm and flushed his target out, all the better.

On his second pass, he walked up to the front door and rang the bell. He heard the ring echo through a seemingly empty house. After thirty seconds without a response, he pulled out a lock pick set and went to work on the front door. He was grateful and a bit surprised it wasn't a digital lock, but maybe that would have attracted more attention than it was worth.

After about a minute of fiddling with what turned out to be a complicated tumbler set, Jessup opened the door and walked into a small, musty hallway. He moved around the main floor through the living room, kitchen, and two modest-sized bedrooms with a connecting bathroom. The furniture was straight out of IKEA and didn't seem to have been used much. Dust had accumulated in places, and the refrigerator held next to nothing. No cars in the garage . . . in fact it was perfectly empty.

Am I in the right place?

Then he found a door in the back hall and knew Mufasa was on his game. This time he found the digital door he'd expected the first time, and the door itself was new and made from steel rather than wood. No way he was getting beyond that barrier. He jiggled the knob in passing and was surprised when it gave way. Not sure how to process that, he decided not to look a gift horse in the mouth and crossed the threshold.

More accurately, he went down a long flight of steps into what was once a basement. Now it looked more like a NASA control room. He noted the four computer towers with corresponding dual monitors, special cooling equipment, and network wiring. Once he looked beyond all the gear, he saw an army cot, a refrigerator, and a microwave.

Shit, the guy must live down here.

He moved off the bottom step and swung around to the computer area. Everything was powered down, so not much for Jessup to evaluate about the setup other than to note that it was impressive. Then he saw an out-of-place whiteboard, and he felt his heart begin to race. He traced the lines on the board with his fingers and realized that his hacker had been ahead of the FBI at every step. And he'd made even more progress that they didn't know about.

Sitting down in the high-tech chair in front of the computer monitors, he spun around slowly, taking in the full room. After a minute of simply absorbing the whole scene, he stood up and added a couple of nodes to the diagram on the whiteboard, including a note at the bottom.

Well, now I've officially gone over the line.

Then in a loud voice he said, "If you're as smart as I think you are, you've been watching me since I walked down the street. I'm not here to bring you in or arrest you. I know that's my duty, but there are more important things that need attention right now. You hold the keys to helping me save lives. And that's all that matters. Come home and get back to work. If I found you, others will follow. I can protect you."

A quick beat. "I know you have my number. Call me."

CHAPTER 46

BACK ON THE HILL

"How can people be so shortsighted?" It was Friday afternoon, and Tamika Smith was back at work. After a day recovering from the jet lag, she had returned to her office to face an entirely different set of obstacles. She had only just begun to process Johnny's probable death and knew from experience that there was no timetable for that. She couldn't imagine replacing the gaping hole in her life, much less the sorrow in her heart. She also couldn't fathom what Margaret, Phoenix, and Nathan would feel once they found out.

General Smith had told her to take a leave of absence. Her therapist had told her something similar. But she didn't think meditating in the woods was going to help her, nor was talking it out in some sessions on a couch going to accomplish anything either. She made the choice to dive in to her work, as she'd done many times before. Today's issue was the looming budgetary crisis.

But jumping back in turned out to be easier said than done. Ordinarily, she'd be meeting with Johnny as her chief of staff to help her think through the latest set of legislative issues. Johnny's job was to act as a sounding board for her thinking, to challenge her when he thought she was wrong, and to translate her decisions into action with the team. Now she was without his judgment and missing his ability to drive the team forward. In his absence, she was meeting with her senior policy leaders in their conference room in the Russell Building.

Not surprisingly, it just wasn't the same.

"It's a crazy situation," began Mark Cavanagh. "The GOP has a narrow majority in the House. If McCarthy can carry a vote to win the speakership—and that's a big *if*—he's going to have to make some promises to the far-right wing. And the Freedom Caucus folks have decided that the deficit matters again. Oh—and they want to impeach Biden."

Another staffer cut in. "When their guy was in the White House, they were happy to cut taxes and drive up the debt, but now . . ."

"I know, I know," Tamika interjected. "Neither party can control themselves. One side cuts taxes and wants to get rid of the IRS, and the other hasn't seen a program they don't want to fund."

Cavanagh picked up the narrative. "And now we're coming up against the debt ceiling and the Freedomites are demanding concessions to raise it. Here's the latest from Stumper."

He clicked a link on his tablet and cast it onto the big screen. The camera was cut in tight on Stumper's face, the red veins seeming to pop out of his cheeks. As he raised his voice, pieces of phlegm could be seen coming out of his mouth like the first waves of lava in a volcanic eruption.

> **Enough is more than enough. We can't just keep spending as if there are no limits to our resources. The deficit is not only an economic problem, but it's become a national security issue as well. Socialist spending is killing our economy and exposing us to the whims of investors from around the globe, including China. I am making my last stand here. I will vote against raising the debt limit unless I see a 2024 budget that has 15 percent less spending than in 2023.**

"Does he realize it's politically and practically impossible to cut fifteen percent from the budget in one year? If you take him literally, he wants a default. How can he think that will help?" Tamika rarely raised her voice, but she was on edge. From the faces around the table, her team could feel her pain.

She continued, but with a quieter intensity. "A default would be the financial apocalypse. Massive market volatility, currency devaluation, rating downgrades, skyrocketing borrowing costs, and more. If the world loses confidence in the dollar and US Treasuries, the entire world economic network will collapse." She threw her hands up in the air to register her disgust.

Cavanagh replied, "I think this is a negotiating tool—a threat to get everyone's attention. He's an ass, but he's been around long enough to understand the consequences."

"I hope you're right. It would be chaos." Tamika didn't even want to think about that.

An aide knocked on the door.

"Come." It was her military response.

"Senator, Deputy Director Jessup is on the line. He says it's urgent."

"I'll take it in my office. Excuse me, folks—Mark, keep this going—we need a response to this for me and for the Lincoln Coalition more generally."

With that, she walked quickly into her office through a side door, closing it behind her carefully. She hustled around her desk, put on her headset, and picked up the call.

"Smith here." She could feel her pulse quickening.

"Jessup. Are you alone?"

"Affirmative. On my headset in my office."

"Take a seat. I don't know exactly what to say or in what order."

"Out with it, JJ." Tamika could feel the impatience rising as her chest began to tighten. The guillotine blade was about to fall.

"The Dutch found the barge and opened the container."

She could feel her heart about to explode.

"And?"

"Johnny wasn't in it."

Silence was all she had. Deep down she'd had a sliver of hope, but she'd refused to allow it any oxygen. Now, she knew she should be elated . . . and she was. But she was also just emotionally exhausted. Going from sixty to zero and then back to sixty again was more than she could manage.

"Tamika? You good? This is positive news, OK?"

"I know, JJ. It's the best news. But I just don't know what to feel, think, or do anymore. I'm spent."

She could imagine Jessup sitting in his office, trying desperately to act as a confidant and counselor. Not so much.

"Look, Tamika, you know I can't help you there. I really wish I could. What I can do is bring him back."

"I get it. I understand. How can I help?"

"You've already provided a big breakthrough."

"How's that?"

"I think I've got a connection to your source."

Tamika panicked. "I thought I told you not to go after him."

"Relax, I'm not going to bring him in. I want to . . . partner with him."

"And he's agreed to help you?"

"Not yet—but I don't think he has much choice at this stage. Especially if he's serious about helping his friends. And I'm going to believe that's his goal until proven otherwise."

"If he contacts me, I'll kick him your way."

"Good . . . but unfortunately, there's more to consider."

Tamika paused to think. "Oh shit, have you called the Humboldts yet?"

"Don't worry; I've handled that already. Call went about like this one. First, I had to tell them about the barge and then explain that Johnny wasn't on it. They are thankful but drained."

"What then?"

"The enemy knows we've found the barge, and I'm confident they still have Johnny."

Of course, she thought. The nightmare was still there.

"Which means they're going to come back after me."

"Time to suit up, Major," Jessup told her. "You're going to have some tough choices to make."

CHAPTER 47

TRUST BUT VERIFY

"Now that's more like it!"

Lee Bowen whispered to himself from a WeWork cubicle in Riverpark Tower in San Jose.

He read the RallyAmerica proposal with great interest. It was from the same source that had proposed the murder-for-hire scheme, but this idea was much more in alignment with the venture capitalist's views on how to pressure others. He still didn't have full clarity on Johnny Humboldt's location, although he knew he was alive and useful as bait in a fishing expedition.

Deep down, he also felt a sense of unease as his plan moved into a new phase. He'd always been the one in control of the action—the ideas, the selection process, the timing—everything. He now realized that as he'd escalated into more dangerous efforts, he wasn't in the driver's seat. He guessed it was the way a general must feel in the heat of a battle. In the final analysis, combat decisions were made at the front, not by the people sitting in chairs looking at a map. That realization aside, the unease was deep-seated and would not dissipate.

He probably should have figured out this control issue earlier. He knew that the very nature of a DAO provided both transparency on the one hand and insulation and secrecy on the other. Even though he controlled the votes, he could not micromanage the people doing the actual work. Clearly, RallyAmerica had attracted some seasoned professional criminals, and they were equally accustomed to driving their own strategies and making their own decisions.

In the venture business, he'd learned to listen to his gut when making investment choices. Picking early-stage companies involved some science, but there was also a great deal of art involved. More than once, he'd backed out of an investment because it just didn't *feel right*. RallyAmerica was headed down that path, but in this case, there was no way for him to back away. And if he wanted to achieve his goals—and the financial windfall was sizable—this was his only vehicle.

To satisfy himself, he reread the proposal to ensure that the parameters of the engagement were clear and that there were limits on what could transpire. Then, he cast his deciding votes in favor of the proposal and went back to the other questions that were vexing him.

He had two major challenges on his radar. First, when the time came to push the country over the edge, he needed someone in position to take the final step. This wasn't as simple as leveraging a moderate political leader to make a certain immoderate speech. He needed someone who was already far out on the tail of the bell curve willing to take radical action. His dark web research was yielding an interesting opportunity.

The second issue was a bit more obvious. If you think everything is going to go to shit, where do you put your money?

• • • • •

Bryce Roscovitch was dealing with his own sense of unease.

The minute he'd sent the unencrypted text messages, he knew he was exposed. The subsequent evacuation from his Culpeper home had been sudden but orderly. He had prepared extensively for just such an eventuality, recognizing that with his profession came certain unavoidable risks. There was no good way for him to wipe clean his own DNA or other forensics from the cave. He'd never bothered to wear gloves while he was there, and it would have taken too long to go through the entire house. To his knowledge, neither his DNA nor his fingerprints were on record—and he had done his own search on that front—so the authorities or his competitors would gain nothing from having that information.

As his last act before leaving the house, he ran a program that wiped clean all his machines and reformatted the hard drives. Doing this completely required some careful programming, but he was confident that nobody could piece any information back together from the local storage units. His data was all stored on secure servers that were off-site. He'd detected no intrusion into this private cloud—at least not yet—so his core business tools were still available.

He kept a go bag packed with clothing and other essentials, and he had a car stored in a local garage ready for his departure. The car was titled to a fictitious character (one Brian Ceremsak) and registered in another state as an additional precaution. He'd even gone to the trouble of mapping a route to the garage that had enough camera gaps that someone couldn't trace him to that location. He wasn't a cloak-and-dagger operator at heart, but he knew how to find people. Working in reverse enabled him to hide better than most.

The move to his secondary location was now complete. He had a duplicate setup to his original office, although his internet bandwidth was a bit reduced given the remote mountain location. He had connected to his secure servers and reinitiated several of the digital searches that were underway when the alarms went off. He was particularly interested in the financial search he'd begun to track the money behind the office rentals. His initial exuberance had been tempered by a tangled web of partnerships and shell companies that were making it difficult to get to a real owner.

No matter. The search could continue from his new location.

His progress was inevitably interrupted by the expected intrusion alerts from his 211 Asher Street location. First the cameras, then the motion sensors, and then the key lock on the front door. He was particularly proud of that last one, because it looked like a normal lock but sent him information as soon as a key or any other device was inserted.

He watched Deputy Director Jerry Jessup's entire visit, sitting quietly in his new chair. At first, he was offended that someone had found his cave and was walking around it with impunity. He had seen Jessup at his father's memorial service, but they had never met. He knew from his own digital sleuthing that Jessup had shut down the inquiry into the Wilkes drone attack before it could involve Bryce. He was sure it had been done for the deputy director's own selfish reasons, but Bryce relaxed a bit as Jessup began to speak.

As Jessup made his offer, Bryce had only one thought.

Opportunity or trap?

CHAPTER 48

BATTLE LINES DRAWN

Nastya Andropov now had three balls in the air.

For some that would be intimidating or stress-inducing, but for the Russian agent, it was her preferred state. It meant she had several paths to pursue, and in her line of business, optionality was a luxury.

First up, she had to put the wheels in motion to leverage the Johnny Humboldt asset. She wasn't going to trust RallyAmerica with a single bit of the implementation. This performance was now hers to produce, and she was going to do it all personally. That brought certain risks—but working through others on this assignment had only brought problems. And if there was an FSB leak, all the more reason to compartmentalize all of the work in the confines of her Texel operation.

She crafted the message that would be sent, trying to use phrases and style elements that were similar to those in the original Tamika Smith blackmail notices. The basics were straightforward, but she had to remember that there were several audiences for the communication. Obviously, there was the daughter, where the goal was shock and emotion. That wasn't complicated. But the message was really intended for Smith and her lackeys at the FBI. Since they would ultimately decide on a response, she needed to be crystal clear about her demands. Given the dynamic state of US politics, that wasn't an easy task.

Next, Andropov needed to deal with US Senator Tamika Smith. Nastya was pissed that she'd only wounded her in Amsterdam and missed the daughter entirely. She rationalized that it had been a surprise attack, and the target was moving quickly across her field of fire from forty yards away. Not an easy shot, even for a professional. She revisited the entire sequence in her mind over and over again. Each time, she reached the same conclusion.

You fucking missed.

So now it was personal. Smith was a trained fighter who had distinguished herself on the battlefield. Her military training made her an enemy combatant and fair game in the war, even if the record showed she was a glorified stretcher carrier. Andropov would take her out as a point of honor—and if that supported the broader plan, all the better. But if it didn't, Smith would still die.

The final ball she was juggling was internal to her team. Her issues with RallyAmerica were all about strategy and execution, and efforts were in motion to eliminate that dependency. The bigger problem was that she feared the entire mission was compromised, either by a mole or by Mischa himself. This possibility put her on a figurative island with nobody to trust internally. Her only choice was to avoid sharing information with her handler. She could manage that up to a point, but Mischa wasn't stupid. He'd played this game all his life and survived to tell the tale. He was more dangerous than Smith or the FBI.

Andropov smiled.

Despite the dangers, this was why she was a spy. The intrigues, risks, and traps were all part of an elaborate game that didn't really have any rules. And despite her recent mistakes, she was one of the best in the world at this, and Nastya Andropov found deep pleasure in her successes. The fact that it served her beloved Mother Russia and could vindicate her grandfather made it that much better. She would take down the American capitalist system, kill an enemy, and expose any FSB traitors.

A triple play for her country.

And some redemption for her uncharacteristic missteps.

• • • • •

Major Tamika Smith, US Air Force (retired), was making battle plans of her own.

From the moment Jessup issued his warning, she knew he was right. No matter how she viewed it, this was about her role in the US Senate, and the threats were not going to stop. Jessup had told her about the rise in blackmail, extortion, and intimidation in the business world. Presumably this was spreading to the political arena. Someone was trying to manipulate her for political gain, with the stakes much higher than some financial payoff. Tamika was self-aware enough to know that she was now a big fish in the Senate with the Lincoln Coalition as a major source of influence. As she went, so would others.

Without Johnny's advice and counsel, she turned to her father to prepare for the inevitable attacks. He'd flown to DC from Seattle as soon as she'd called. They met in her apartment in Arlington.

As a senator, she could have afforded a larger place in DC proper, but she wasn't willing to give up her one-bedroom perch across the river. She loved the view over Arlington National Cemetery and the outlook on the Pentagon—two places that had significant meaning for her and her family. Visits to her brother's burial site at the 9/11 Memorial in the cemetery were a regular part of her routine.

"You want something to drink?" Tamika asked. Her father walked over to appreciate the view out the window after giving her a long, tight hug.

"Just some water would be great. Any chance you have a sandwich or something?"

Tamika checked the fridge. "Two slices of pizza?" She was no culinary expert, and her work usually meant rubber chicken affairs for dinner.

"That'll work. Not much to eat on the flight, and my food clock is messed up with the time change." Despite his advancing age, he still held the upright posture and solid physique of a military professional. Tamika had learned from his workout regime.

After warming the pizza in the microwave, Tamika brought the plate, two glasses of water, and some potato salad to the coffee table by the couch. She had to move some dirty dishes off the table and put them in the sink. "Sorry—I haven't been home much lately." Her father chuckled.

"When have you ever stayed in one place?"

"Difficult to do as an Air Force brat" was her quick response.

"Touché."

Tamika watched as her father dug into the pizza. She didn't really know where to begin. Based on his silence, it didn't feel like he knew what to say either. They sat in their own worlds, nibbling on the food and sipping on their water. Both seemingly waiting for the elephant in the room to stand up and trash the furniture.

The general finally took the dive. "I don't know what to say, Tammy. I know how much you love Johnny, so this whole situation is just . . . impossible."

With a long, drawn-out exhale she said, "I can't put it into words either, Daddy. He's such an important part of my life. The kidnapping was awful and the photo scary, but at least I knew he was alive. In a way, the trip to Amsterdam was cathartic. I was doing something to find him, and I came so close to getting him back."

She took a drink from her water to hide the tears she could feel coming. "And then I thought he might be dead. It really messed with my head."

"But, honey," interjected General Smith quickly, "we think he's alive now, so there's real hope you'll get him back."

Tamika stood up to pace the small room. "That's why I called you. Sure, we might get him back, but at what cost?"

"Does it matter?" The look he gave her was deep and imploring.

"It would to him, and it does to me. This isn't about some ransom payment or some business deal. This is about America and its future. How do I trade the country I've served loyally for so long for the life of the person I love?"

"You can't," came the quick reply. The general had a determined look in his eyes.

"Daddy, that's exactly what I concluded. We need a plan to short-circuit the blackmail, however it happens." She took a final bite of the pizza crust and washed it down with the last bit of the water.

"Have you received any more emails?"

"Not yet. That's a little surprising, but I don't think they were planning to move Johnny, so they're probably regrouping a bit."

"That's the best time for us to go on the offensive. Do you have anything in mind?"

"What do you think about sacrificing myself?"

She said it with a smile, knowing it was a perfectly reckless idea.

CHAPTER 49

PARTNERS DIVIDED

Ely Basof was a survivor. More than that, he intended to enjoy the fruits of his labor.

When he'd originally suggested this mission to the higher ups in Moscow, he'd assumed his only enemy would ultimately be his business partner, Lee Bowen. He understood that threat well and was not terribly concerned about it. He also had a plan in place to deal with it. But now he was worried about his other partner, code named Maaier.

The Reaper.

Basof had read her entire personnel file before agreeing to have her lead the mission. Maaier's background was interesting and indicated clear motivations for her actions. She was a patriot, both to her country and to the Andropov family name. She was focused on restoring that name to glory. He knew she would fight for country and family and would never betray those loyalties. He'd counted on that to keep her focused on the end objective. And for a while, that had worked.

Intellectually appreciating her motivation was one thing. Internalizing it was another. Basof was driven by completely different goals. Yes, he was Russian and happy to do his employer's bidding. But the FSB was just an employer, and in Basof's increasingly capitalistic world, labor could move seamlessly to other jobs. He found himself in the middle of one of those transitions. Much like the leaders of the new oligarchic order in his motherland, he'd found a way to merge communism and capitalism. He was becoming his cover story: a venture capitalist of the first rank.

Perhaps these differing motivations were why he'd missed what he should have seen in Maaier. Her stubbornness and her inability to deal with the inconveniences of working through the DAO structure made her less than ideal for the role. She was an owner-operator who was used to running her own business. Dealing with a blind entity that was inefficient and slow was not to her liking. He knew she was done with RallyAmerica. He also knew she might be done with him as her handler. The implied traitor commentary had put him on notice. He knew what she was capable of and would take no risks.

Thankfully, the buffoons in Belarus, if that was in fact where they were, had finally broken through. While it hadn't been elegant or efficient, brute force hacking had its advantages, and Ely Basof was now in technical control of the DAO and related projects. Others would only realize that when he was ready. Certainly bad news to come for his other business partner, Lee Bowen, but that wasn't Basof's problem.

Like Maaier, he now realized that RallyAmerica was never going to turn Senator Tamika Smith. She was too stubborn, too principled, and perhaps even too smart. The DAO could deal with the other targets, but he would concentrate Maaier on Smith. That's what his agent wanted to do, in any event. She was still his only real field asset, and her new plan would finally resolve the Smith issue one way or the other. But once that was completed, all bets were off. His loyalty was to his own prosperous future.

If the FSB had to lose an agent in the field in the line of duty, so be it.

• • • • •

Lee Bowen sent a thumbs-up emoji to his partner over the Zoom chat feature. They were on a video call together evaluating a potential investment, each in their own locations. He could see that Basof was in the B^2 offices, while Bowen was in one of his WeWork cubicles using a fake background to camouflage his location. Bowen wanted to make sure his partner knew he liked what he was hearing in the proposal. The smile emoji he received back from Basof was all he needed to see.

Once the meeting was over, he signed in to the Metamask Ethereum portal and to Discord to track progress on the latest Tamika Smith plan.

It looked like the RallyAmerica instructions were about to go out—good progress on the right schedule. But he was concerned that Smith might never come around and his gambit in the Senate would fall short. Successful leaders had backup plans, and Bowen was no exception.

During his initial extortion research and experiments, he'd unearthed damaging information on a number of senior government leaders. Now was the time to monetize that data. He initiated three significant DAO missions that would either support his Senate work or substitute for it, if necessary. Blackmailing the three leaders of America's financial institutions—Treasury, SEC, and the Federal Reserve—would escalate the fiscal instability to crisis proportions. The trick was doing just enough without violating an ethical line he'd drawn in the sand.

Nobody needed to die for his mission to achieve success.

There was still some time to wait before he put his financial strategy into operation, but the building blocks were now in place. After much contemplation, he'd decided to liquidate 75 percent of his assets and make them available for the endgame investments. This was a go-big-or-go-home effort, and he wanted the win to be worth the risk. His outside investors were adding to the fund, so much so that the scale of the operation was becoming a problem.

First, he had to clean his own assets so it would be difficult to trace the investments back to him personally. He began by breaking the resources into smaller amounts and placing them at a variety of different financial institutions. He'd been a longtime user of Cayman Island and Singapore accounts, as well as Ethereum investments, to camouflage the RallyAmerica activities. He used some of the same vehicles in his asset-cleaning process. Then he began circulating the money between locations, a process called layering, that would make it difficult to track the funds. Finally, he would integrate the money back together, now cleansed of his personal financial DNA, and combine it with the RallyAmerica investor money.

The bet was that no forensic accountant could follow the trail. At least before the trail was erased.

The second phase of the scheme was more complicated. He needed to reinvest the assets in a series of stocks, options, commodity assets, and financial instruments that would perform well amid the chaos. This was more art than science, but it also happened to be one of his superpowers. He was slowly adding investments to the portfolio, using another blockchain entity to keep a register of the assets. After all, his investors would expect an accurate accounting in the end.

Some two hours later, he received a notification from Metamask.

And that's when it all started to unravel.

"What the hell?" he said to no one in particular.

"That can't be!" he yelled.

His neighbor in the cubicle next to him slid over on her rolling chair. "Something wrong? You need help?"

Bowen almost shouted again but caught himself. "No thanks," he said with a forced calmness. He tried to smile. "Just looking at my NFL playoff bets. Remind me to never, ever bet on the Jets."

"Will do." And with a smirk that said "you idiot," she disappeared.

He turned his attention back to the Ethereum voting portal. The results were mathematically impossible.

He'd just lost a vote. The details of the Treasury blackmail had been changed.

How the fuck did that happen?

It occurred to him that he might be screwed.

CHAPTER 50

THE WRITING ON THE WALL

"Be careful, my friend." Bryce Roscovitch's alter ego struck a cautionary note.

It was his second day in his backup office location, and he was settling back into the routine.

Indeed, Bryce decided to slow-play his response to Deputy Director Jerry Jessup. How could he really trust the second-in-command at the FBI? Conveniently, he could postpone the decision because he didn't really have any information to share.

The money trail for the WeWork rentals was proving difficult to crack. Between the usual deflections and the additions of cryptocurrency, tracing money had become increasingly complicated. Given that there were four separate office payments involved, all coming from different places, the knots were going to take more time to untie. His frustration led him to an alternative approach that was equally challenging but easier to automate.

For each WeWork location, he identified a series of cameras that could cover the entrance to the building as well as the entrance to any below-ground parking areas. He created a bot that scrapped all the video imagery he could gather and compared it all pairwise, looking for common vehicles, facial recognition matches, and the like. Given enough time, his suspect was bound to enter more than one facility—perhaps more than two—and his AI assistant would find him. With a vehicle or facial identification, Bryce was certain he could trace the subject. This was high-volume computing work that could take weeks depending on the amount of activity at the sites. There was nothing for Bryce to do but allow his machines to hum away.

The Jessup visit to his home on Asher Street had had an unexpected benefit. Bryce rewatched the video several times before it hit him.

"You idiot. What did he write on the whiteboard?" His alter ego was always tough on him.

"Oh shit, right. Let's look." He pulled up the video yet again. He had to enhance it a bit to see the writing.

The first bit was squiggly but still legible.

Afghanistan Source.

This made Bryce feel doubly dumb. "How did I forget to pursue that?"

"Well, to be fair, you ran into a dead end. Remember the reports."

Bryce pulled up the military files and recalled that Tamika's field action report made no mention of the rape or her connection to the pilot. The copilot she'd saved had no recollection of anything that had happened after the initial Taliban attack. He couldn't be the source. There was also no record of Tamika making an official, or unofficial, report of the rape within the military.

"Exactly. A dead end."

"Apparently, the deputy director of the FBI disagrees."

"Yeah . . . there's that." Bryce hated it when his subconscious dogged him. But it usually helped his work.

"So, who else knew about the rape?"

"Her therapist, if she has one," ventured Bryce.

"Doctors take that patient confidentiality thing pretty seriously."

"What about her family?"

"You and I both know she only has her father, and he was a general."

Bryce paused. He knew General Smith would never betray his daughter. But maybe he knew something. The question was how to interview a general without exposing himself.

Stumped for the moment, he went back to the whiteboard to see if Jessup had written anything else.

He focused on a second word and froze.

Mufasa.

CHAPTER 51

DIRECT MESSAGES

When the digital shoe dropped, it landed on Phoenix Humboldt hard.

She found herself wandering through the days since her sojourn in Amsterdam, just getting by in her classes. Her classmates didn't seem to know what to think of her. They all knew she'd been shot. But the rumors about her sudden absence covered the spectrum from "PTSD" to "ran away" to "hero complex." The FBI had asked Phoenix not to discuss what had happened in Amsterdam, so she couldn't explain things to her friends in any event. She found herself avoiding them. All except Vanessa Nathanson.

She and Vanessa met after track practice to walk to a local coffee shop. Vanessa had been with her the day of the shooting—a day neither one of them was ever going to forget—and was the one person who seemed to understand what she was going through. It was Wednesday, January 25, another day neither of them would forget.

They found a table in the corner of the shop and blew on their chai lattes to cool them off just a bit. Phoenix loved that Vanessa was OK with them just sitting in silence but now took the opportunity to open up.

"I know I should feel better now that the FBI thinks my dad is still alive," she said to Vanessa. "After I fucked up in Amsterdam, I thought maybe I'd gotten him killed."

"That's good news, right? Hopefully they can figure something out to get him back." Vanessa put a smile on her face, but to Phoenix it looked doubtful.

"Maybe . . . but my mom says they still don't really know what they want with him. They haven't asked for money. She thinks it might be a political thing."

"Well, your dad does work for Senator Smith. But how would that involve kidnappers?" More doubt in her tone.

"Who the hell knows. But I just feel so helpless going to school, running races, drinking tea." Phoenix swirled her drink as if mixing it could solve her problems.

"I know you miss your dad," Vanessa said. "But he'd want you to be strong. To have faith."

"In my head I know that's true. But my heart is the problem."

Phoenix's phone gave a shudder, indicating a new message. "That's weird. I turned off my social media accounts." She picked up the phone and tapped on the notification to read what was a Twitter DM.

"Holy shit, Vanessa!" she exclaimed as she handed the phone to her friend:

> Tell Smith to play political ball with me. If not, your daddy is gone forever. She'll hear from me. No FBI or police—that is certain death.

When Phoenix took the phone back, a second DM followed quickly:

> You and your mom are in my gunsights. I'm always watching. I won't miss this time.

She looked up at Vanessa, whose face had gone white.

Oh my God, Phoenix thought. *What the hell do I do now?*

• • • • •

"Try to calm down, Phoenix. Take a few deep breaths."

The call came while Tamika was eating an order-in dinner at her Senate office. The hysteria radiating over the line frightened her. She was seriously worried about Phoenix's mental state. Seventeen-year-olds were supposed to be worried about dates to the prom, not dodging terrorist bullets.

"I . . . I . . . I . . . can't."

"Listen to my voice, Phoenix. Listen to each word. You can do this. Take a breath with me." Tamika inhaled slowly and then blew out the air.

"That's it. One breath at a time."

"I'm sorry, Tamika—" Phoenix broke in, still breathing hard. "I just don't know what to do."

"It's OK to be scared, Phoenix. I've told you about my own terrors. Sometimes I can't control them either. It's just . . . being human."

"OK . . . ," came a shaky response.

"Read me the messages—slowly and word for word. Can you do that?"

Phoenix read both DMs in a halting cadence. Tamika wrote them down on a pad of paper on her desk. She paused for a beat. The messages seemed to confirm this was from the woman in Amsterdam. The use of the singular was also interesting. Could this all be one person? She'd been assuming some type of bigger conspiracy.

"But what are we going to do? She'll kill Daddy." Phoenix was settling down a bit, and Tamika thought that she could guide her through the reality of the situation now.

"Have you told your mom or the FBI?"

"No—you were the first person I called. Vanessa's walking me home from the coffee shop. Mom will be home when we get there."

Tamika knew she was once again headed into dangerous territory. But this was important if her plan was to work.

"Listen very carefully to me, Phoenix. I don't think you or your mom are in any danger. They have your dad, so there's no reason to harm you. In fact, they need you alive to put pressure on me." She didn't add that if they'd wanted to hurt the Humboldts, there was little to stop them. "We both know your mom has too much on her plate already, so let's keep this our secret for now."

Jesus, any hope of fixing her relationship with Margaret Humboldt was now gone.

There was another tentative "OK" from Phoenix, followed by an obvious question: "What about the FBI? The agent told me to call him if we heard anything. And we promised to let them find my dad."

"I'm in touch with the FBI, Phoenix. I'll work with them on this. After all, I'm the target, not you."

"So I'm supposed to do nothing?"

"I want you to go on being a high school student and daughter to your mom. I know that's hard, Phoenix. But you're going to have to trust me. Can you do that?"

"Yes . . . you know I can."

"Good. Just give me the Twitter handle—I'll respond to the bitch."

"It's @humboltd_keeper."

Jesus, the bitch has a sick sense of humor.

"OK. You and Vanessa should take a little extra time to get home, Phoenix—try to walk off all the anger and fear so you can face your mom. There may come a time when I need your help, but I've got this for now."

"I love you, Tamika. Bring Daddy home."

As Tamika clicked off the call, she took several deep breaths of her own. She hated the position she'd put Phoenix in. Growing into adulthood was difficult enough without terrorist threats and keeping secrets from your mom. But Tamika also knew this was hers to handle. This time, however, she would do it with the support and help of Jessup and his team at the FBI. That was all built into the plan. But before she brought them into the tent, she wanted to respond to her newfound nemesis.

> Stop playing fucking games. Leave the Humboldts alone. If you touch Johnny, you're dead. I'm the one with the keys to the kingdom. Come and get me. But come prepared. I play for keeps.

The goal was to draw her out into the open while trying to protect Johnny, Phoenix, Nathan, and Margaret. The FBI would get her—or Tamika would go down trying. Either way, Johnny and his family would be safe. And the country would face one less terrorist.

If she had to sacrifice, she was ready.

So be it.

PART IV
WORKING THE PLAN

There's something happening here
But what it is ain't exactly clear
There's a man with a gun over there
Telling me I got to beware
I think it's time we stop
Children, what's that sound?
Everybody look, what's going down?

—Stephen Stills, Buffalo Springfield

CHAPTER 52

A NEW PHASE

To win this fight, Tamika Smith realized she had to sacrifice more than herself.

After the initial Twitter DM interchange with her adversary, she focused on protecting those around her. The FBI had assigned protective details to the Humboldts, the Roscovitches, and her father. While this didn't guarantee anything when facing a talented assassin, it brought some comfort to her extended family and enabled Tamika to get at least a bit more sleep. The FBI also moved Agent Higginbottom from his California assignment to be Tamika's full-time escort. Again, it wasn't foolproof—but comforting, nonetheless.

The more difficult task had been prying back some of the power in the blackmail negotiation with the Dutch bitch. Tamika discussed this problem at great length with her father a week later, again eating leftovers in her apartment.

"Tamika, the only way to deal with blackmailers is from a position of strength. Bullies feed off weakness, so you can't be the pining lover who will do anything for her man." Her father said it with the authority that came from years of military experience.

"But I can't deny Johnny. You know I love him." Tamika felt the tears coming and tried to push them down as best she could.

"And in this case, loving him requires that you let him go."

"What the hell does that mean?"

"You need to call her bluff. You and I both know that's what Johnny would say."

"You want me to sign his death warrant?" Now she felt the sting of tears in the corner of her eyes.

"That's not what I said. We've both agreed that the goal is to force her to come to our turf. We need her on US soil without the comforts of her team and support infrastructure. As long as Johnny is a weapon, she's going to sit near him in Europe and dictate demands to us."

Looking her father in the eye, she realized why only certain people became generals. *Someone has to make the really difficult choices*, she reminded herself. She'd always looked up to her father—and now she understood the burdens he'd borne during his time serving the country.

Tamika wrestled the decision to the ground. "I need to give her an either-or choice. If she wants to stay in Europe, there'll be no deal. She has to come here with Johnny?"

"Exactly." Her father tapped his hand on the table gently and leaned forward intently, driving home his point.

"And the bet is that she won't kill Johnny—because she loses all her leverage."

"Yup." His face went serious.

"And what if we're wrong?"

There was no answer to that.

• • • • •

Deputy Director Jerry Jessup's first instinct was to reject the plan out of hand.

"You've got to be kidding. I know you like playing the tough guy, but I'm not going to put a US senator's life on the line."

They were sitting in Jessup's office, as if Tamika was just another senator getting an update on the FBI's activities. Nothing unusual going on here.

"It won't be the first time you've done it. Don't forget Detroit."

Jessup gave Tamika a cold stare. He considered her reference to the Wilkes affair out of bounds, although he knew there was some truth in her statement. "Not the same thing" was the best he could come up with. "And what about your beau, Johnny?"

Tamika persisted. "What's the alternative?"

Jessup was surprised by the response. He knew Tamika had a hard shell, but he also believed in the power of love—he'd seen her pain before. The implied sacrifice she was proposing threw him a bit off kilter. He defaulted to the official FBI playbook.

"Our best strategy is a delaying action. We continue to go along with her demands, at least on the surface. We have to buy time so that my team can figure out where they have Johnny and how this fits into the broader bullshit that's going on."

"I think my little foray into the Netherlands put an end to that charade."

"Perhaps, but it's still our best option." Jessup knew this was a weak argument, but it was all he had.

"You mentioned broader issues. Have things changed on that front?" He was surprised she'd changed the subject. But her intensity remained.

"Unfortunately, yes. Three more government leaders have received threats. Unfortunately, they are the key figures managing American finances and the economy. Treasury, the Fed, and the SEC. And no, I don't think that's a coincidence."

Now Tamika jumped up, looking excited. "And that's precisely why you have to agree to my plan!"

"And why's that?"

"JJ, this whole set of attacks aren't your typical extortion scheme. They're not about money. They're not about the release of political prisoners. They're not about any of the usual things that blackmailers or terrorists want. This is about the country. It's about democracy. If you attack US leaders, it's about regime change. This isn't a bunch of amateur anarchists or desperate Islamic assholes. It's too well funded and way too well coordinated. It has all the hallmarks of a covert operation. This has to be the FSB or the MSS." Now she was yelling.

JJ yelled right back. "OK, maybe you're right. Maybe it's Russia or China. But even if you're right, that has nothing to do with your crazy-ass plan."

"And that's where you're being your usual pig-headed self. Climb out of the military foxhole with me for a moment. What's the worst thing that can happen to a sniper or assassin?"

That was an easy question for Jessup. "They fail on a mission or miss their target."

"Exactly. She missed me in Amsterdam. Right now she's trying to figure out how to make good on that. She's looking for a way to kill me. Now ask yourself what would our enemy least expect? When would she be most vulnerable? How do you catch a pro?"

JJ watched her, realizing where she was going and hating every bit of it.

"There's only one answer to all those questions, Director," Tamika continued. "We have to surprise her in a way that turns the tables. Something that's not in any playbook. We have to give her exactly what she wants."

The second-in-command at the FBI, the nation's leading law enforcement agency, got up from his chair, turned his back on Tamika, and pulled a Diet Coke from the refrigerator behind his desk. He popped the top, took a big swig, and suppressed the need to burp. He was buying time, assessing the risks, stack-ranking the options, and considering the repercussions. JJ had been down this path all his life, and deep down, he knew he loved it. He also suspected she was right.

He reached a decision. "OK. We'll go your way. What's next?"

Tamika replaced her surprise quickly with a determined, almost angry face.

"I know you'll hate this even more than my plan. But we need to be clear."

Another pause while she looked at him determinedly.

"You, my father, and me are the only ones who need to know."

CHAPTER 53

TECHNICAL PLUMBING

Bryce Roscovitch was a patient man by nature. But there were limits.

He'd been sitting in his cabin in the Appalachians for two weeks with no outside contact. The cabin required a six-mile, mostly uphill hike to reach, and only Bryce understood what passed as trail markings. Like a nuclear survivalist, he'd stocked the hideout with enough preserved food to last him up to six months. He'd dug the well that supplied water and installed the indoor plumbing in the single-room wood building. His elevated energy needs were supplied by a full solar array complete with three battery panels and a propane-fired generator for backup power.

Bryce wasn't the outdoor type, but he was an engineer by training and vocation. He loved working with his hands and building things—something he realized on reflection he'd inherited from his father. As he paused to eat another microwaved meal, he took a moment to survey his new workspace. The main room included everything but the bathroom. The back wall held a galley kitchen and a counter where he ate most of his meals. A couch that doubled as his bed faced the left wall with a fireplace serving as a source of backup heating. The right-hand wall contained all his computing gear with the quad machine setup that matched his original basement workspace. Not luxurious, but efficient, effective, and safe.

Now it was home.

The FBI's offer to protect him—and Jessup's encouragement to "come home and get to work"—were not enough for Bryce. He just couldn't trust anyone that deeply, especially if they were in law enforcement. He chose to stay in his backup location, with access to his own systems in the cloud, and avoid any physical or digital interaction with his Culpeper infrastructure.

But the physical isolation wasn't what was driving Bryce a bit more crazy than usual. He'd used the time to track various digital searches but had met a brick wall. He had all his computing power and considerable talents aimed at unraveling the money trail behind the attacks on Phoenix and Tamika and had almost nothing to show for it. He'd also continued to explore ways to isolate the reporting on Tamika's Afghanistan issues and come up empty handed. To complete the useless work hat trick, he had no new information on the shooter in Amsterdam. In the meantime, Johnny Humboldt had been in captivity for a month.

The only good news was on the Twitter front. Bryce had access to both Phoenix and Tamika's feeds and DM streams and had spent a meaningful amount of time tracing the IP addresses associated with their shared Dutch nemesis. What was most interesting to him was that none of the traces overlapped with the email, video, and money trails he'd been tracking from the original attacks. He was certain the shooter at Aragon High School and at the dock in Amsterdam were the same person. And yet her network address had nothing in common with the rest of the digital record. It was as if there was a black hole in the middle where neither trail met.

More significantly, the original IP trails ultimately reverted to locations in the United States, including the WeWork offices he was investigating. The spiderweb associated with the Twitter trail was more concentrated in Europe. Again, two seemingly separate sets of activity. And yet all the terror and blackmail seemed very orchestrated—well funded and tightly coordinated.

"What the fuck does that all mean?" he said out loud, talking himself through the problem. "Could be the assassin in Europe is a hired gun," he reasoned. "Or if not a hired gun, then just a pawn in a larger conspiracy." That would make sense of much of the information he'd collected. And yet he knew that Tamika was effectively negotiating with the woman in Europe for Johnny's return to US soil. That meant she was a person of influence and importance.

"If she has the authority to barter, she's more than just a hired gun."

Bryce thought about Jessup's written words on the whiteboard. He wondered what Mufasa would make of all this data. Bryce knew Mufasa by reputation only—he was lauded in the hacker world as one of the best, although people suspected he had become a white hat, helping law enforcement when it suited him. It was exactly this profile that worried Bryce. A technical peer who was in contact with the FBI was his worst nightmare. And probably how the FBI had found his Culpeper home.

But in the current circumstances, he found himself looking at it from a different angle. The more he thought about that, the more he realized Tamika Smith was right. Prioritizing the protection and safety of his family was more important than his personal security. To unravel the current riddle, he needed to share information with his cyber nemesis. Perhaps together, they could put the puzzle pieces in place. The problem was figuring out how to do that without risking his own freedom. Bryce considered himself the best, but nobody was infallible in his world.

So now he had two people he needed to communicate with, neither of whom were easy to access. He still wanted to talk with Tamika's father about Afghanistan. He also needed a digitally safe way to exchange information with Mufasa. While he didn't like admitting it, Jessup's offer to help was becoming more necessary, even if it was uninviting.

And then the sweet sound of a *bing* on one of his searches brought him some new data.

Photo kismet: an inside straight on the poker river card. His WeWork video analysis had paid off.

With a bit of facial recognition luck, he had information for the FBI—data he could use to bargain.

"And at least I've got one of the bastards," Bryce said, throwing a triumphant fist into the air.

• • • • •

Ely Basof, the handler known as Mischa, was well satisfied with his work. He enjoyed exercising his somewhat dormant technical skills, and especially enjoyed the fact that his coding prowess far exceeded that of his partner. In communist Russia, his upside would have been limited by the oligarchic power structure. He would have been a cog in someone else's wheel of success. But in capitalist Silicon Valley, he was the one in the driver's seat, and Ely Basof had a plan to reap more than his share of the spoils.

He knew the identity of DAO participants was effectively shielded by the blockchain protocol—at least if the members were careful about their activities. The actual blockchain was there for everyone to peruse, but the identities associated with each owner were masked.

For his plan to succeed, there had to be a fall guy in case the authorities got too close. His underlying assumption was that the FBI, and perhaps others, were pounding away in the digital ether trying to backtrace a variety of activities. Hiding footprints was just as difficult in the digital world as it was in the physical world. By extension, that meant the FBI would eventually achieve a breakthrough. He certainly wasn't going to risk having his fingerprints anywhere near RallyAmerica's activities.

His partner at B^2 Ventures thought of himself as the mastermind behind the scheme. But Lee Bowen knew just enough to be dangerous technically and not enough to really protect himself. With the help of his Belarusian hackers, Basof had cracked into the RallyAmerica infrastructure and was able to leave a few clues in the digital stream that would eventually identify Bowen as the founder of RallyAmerica. A reasonably talented geek would be required to find the trail, and Basof was sure the FBI had a number of those.

The Belarus hack had also enabled Basof to take control of the RallyAmerica voting structure. He allowed Bowen's original plans to blackmail key financial leaders to go ahead, but he didn't believe they were sufficient to drive regime change. At the right time, he would transform those DAO missions to assassinations, which if successful would create an existential crisis. And not coincidentally, send Bowen to prison for a long time once the FBI caught up with him. The only real risk for Basof was that Bowen would panic when he realized what was happening. He would have to keep an eye on his partner.

The final loose end to consider was what to do about Maaier—his reaper FSB asset. He had supplied her with the contacts and logistics necessary to move her operation to the United States for the few weeks leading up to their target date. That date was in fact a range of dates, given that the US government specialized in being unpredictably late meeting deadlines. In any event, his assassin was ready and had her sights set on Tamika Smith. Now the question was whether he trusted Maaier enough to protect her after the fact.

As he thought about that, Basof gave a short laugh.

Not likely.

CHAPTER 54

BE PREPARED

It was go time.

Nastya Andropov would have preferred to stay on her home turf. She had more resources at her disposal in Europe, knew the land and people better, and could escape easier if things went south. She'd originally tilted the scales in her favor by bringing Johnny Humboldt to Europe, but now, just ten days after Andropov's initial Twitter DM, Tamika Smith was forcing the action back to the US.

But Andropov had anticipated this possibility and acted accordingly. Although she was still operating out of her De Cocksdorp house, she was planning to leave for the US the next day. In her final moments in the Netherlands, she was going through her operational checklist.

As part of her preparation, she did more research on her adversary. An interview by a *Washington Post* reporter named Marieke Bergsma was instructive and reminded her that her adversary was more than just a military hero:

BERGSMA: Senator Smith, what's at the heart of the budget negotiations?

SMITH: We have an expanding fiscal crisis—one that has been building for at least twenty-five years—and nobody wants to deal with the financial realities. Colleagues like Senator Stumper are driving us to commit financial suicide. He seems to think that shutting the government down will magically fix everything.

BERGSMA: I think he would point out that the deficit is a huge problem.

SMITH: And he's right about the problem. He just doesn't have a solution. He wants to declare 75 percent of the budget off limits to any constraints and pretend we can solve the problem by cutting the remaining 25 percent.

BERGSMA: What about the proposals to reduce taxes? Some claim that will increase economic growth.

SMITH: That's just a pipe dream. You can't reduce the deficit by cutting federal tax revenue. And the same people want to limit the IRS's ability to enforce the levies we have. No American would ever manage their personal finances that way.

BERGSMA: Senator Stumper is now claiming the deficit is a national security risk.

SMITH: Again, he's right about the problem but exactly wrong about solutions. Driving us into default will escalate the security risks. And it will make the growing social divisions in our country significantly worse. Income inequality has increased by 35 percent over the last thirty years, and that is a recipe for social disaster. Senator Stumper and his Freedom Caucus friends have no answer for that.

With Mischa's help, Andropov was preparing to execute the final elements of their long-game strategy. Relying on the very person she feared was a mole made the final preparations complicated. Rather than turn any element of the plan over to her handler, Andropov used Mischa as a source of contacts. Once she engaged someone's services, she cut her Russian American compatriot out of the loop. With that said, she knew he might have back channels of information, so she was preparing for that eventuality as well.

Andropov was ready for anything Tamika Smith could throw at her. She had been mildly surprised to get the Twitter DM directly from the senator—she'd expected the high school girl to go straight to the FBI. But Smith's response took the middlemen out of the picture, which in most respects was better. Dealing with a mark that had gone rogue from the authorities raised some intriguing possibilities. The real question now was determining exactly what she wanted from the senator.

For months, RallyAmerica had been using deep fake conspiracy theories, pressure tactics, and outright blackmail to drive extremist elements in American politics even further to the left and right. As a prime example, for the first time in at least fifty years, a meaningful percentage of Republicans believed that fighting Russian expansion was bad policy. And these same politicians were now actively blocking financial and military support to Ukraine.

Andropov was shocked by the Republican shift in foreign policy but appreciated how important it was to Mother Russia.

Progressive elements in the Democratic Party had also been pushed to support immigration policies that weakened America's ability to protect its own borders. Beyond the obvious discord it created, an open American border was good for all forms of espionage and terror, to say nothing of the social disaster from the fentanyl drug trade. Nastya couldn't imagine many things more ridiculous than allowing your border to be an open playground, but somehow progressives had convinced themselves this was good for the country.

She had to admire Mischa's work. Andropov cared little about the policy issues themselves. What she craved was the division they created, tearing the US government apart at the seams. It had taken the Speaker of the House fifteen rounds of voting to get elected even though his party controlled the chamber. A sitting president was under investigation without any real evidence to justify it, and the previous president had been indicted on over ninety charges ranging from financial fraud to sexual abuse to election racketeering to violations of national security. Oh yeah . . . elected Democratic and Republican legislators had been charged with a wide variety of criminal and civil crimes and yet somehow were still serving.

Andropov knew that RallyAmerica had not orchestrated all this dysfunction. Americans and their capitalist, egocentric excesses were quite capable of destroying their own democracy. Add the anonymity of social media, the power of AI bots, and a healthy dose of conspiracy theorists spreading fake news and you had a witch's brew of dissent. But she also knew that Russian subversion was accelerating and feeding the flames, pushing the country to the brink. And now she was about to throw gasoline on the fire.

All of which brought her back to Tamika Smith. The senator and other members of her Lincoln Coalition were rallying moderate elements to sound the alarm about the threats to basic democratic principles. Andropov followed a link from the interview to a video of a recent speech from the well of the floor of the Senate:

> **The time has long passed for us to put political expediency and personal egos aside. We've had an insurrection, and somehow managed to ignore it. This body should have convicted Donald Trump and drawn a hard line in the sand on democratic principles. Instead, we've normalized the idea that lies are an appropriate way to respond to inconvenient truths. If you can't face those truths, you just deny them as if that makes their reality go away. Let's be clear that the sedition and crimes remain.**
>
> **I could go on—immigration, infrastructure, energy, the environment, and at least a dozen other major problems are staring us in the face, and we're wasting our time arguing about whether insurrectionists should go to jail. The chaos and self-absorption must end.**
>
> **We were elected to lead this country, and that requires a willingness to do what is right rather than what is convenient. The solutions to our problems are staring us in the face. The difficult work has already been done. What must follow is a commitment to care more about the country than surviving our next extremist primary challenge. We must summon the courage to put party allegiance and electoral calculus aside and work together to approve solutions.**
>
> **Put simply, we have to do our jobs.**

Andropov gave a begrudging nod of approval. Clearly, Smith had balls.

And that was the problem.

CHAPTER 55

TERMS OF THE DEAL

"You have a deal?" Jessup wasn't all that surprised, but he wanted the details.

"To be honest, it was actually a strange . . . discussion, I guess," Tamika responded. "We went back and forth over the course of a few days. She definitely asked me to say and do certain things, but it was still unclear exactly what she wanted."

"Were you right? Was there some legislation or political action she wanted?" Jessup continued to probe.

"At a political level, beyond demanding I disband the Lincoln Coalition, she was all over the map. Wanted me to come out in favor of leniency at the border, more spending on social programs, and defunding law enforcement. At first it sounded very progressive . . . almost socialist. And then a day later she went all MAGA around foreign policy, pushing me to reduce UN funding, cut support to NATO, and back away from support for Taiwan. Just random."

They were meeting away from prying eyes at the FBI or on Capitol Hill, in a secluded area in Rock Creek National Park in northwest DC. Although within a very urban area, Rock Creek was one of the oldest national parks, encompassing over 1,700 acres of public land. A bench overlooking a wooded, rocky ravine seemed appropriate given the circumstances. The clouds had angry, jagged edges, adding to the ambiance.

"Did you get any other personal information or any clues to her identity or affiliation?"

Now Tamika smiled. "I know you're from the wrong generation, but Twitter DM doesn't help you on demographics much. It wasn't like she was using emojis or attaching video for me to see." Jessup saw a hint of a smile in her rebuke.

"OK, I'm not actually that old. But we have to look at every angle."

"I know, I know . . . sorry, I was just yanking your chain. Fun to get a reaction every once in a while."

Jessup was growing impatient. "Come on. Where did you end up?"

"The Lincoln Coalition demand seemed perfunctory. I think she knew that was off the table. I was surprised she didn't bring up the Ukraine or the Middle East—if she's affiliated with Russia, those would certainly be high priorities."

He was surprised at how relaxed Tamika seemed. He was used to a buttoned-up, intense Air Force major dedicated to the cause. Now she looked at peace with what was coming, even though he had great misgivings. "So how did you shift the conversation our way?"

"I told her to look at my original DM. No way I'm going to negotiate my principles away or compromise the Lincoln Coalition."

"You proposed the swap as an alternative?" He couldn't believe he was condoning this.

"Yeah . . . and after some additional random demands, she agreed without much fuss. Almost as if that was her goal all along—or it at least would serve her purposes just as well."

"When and where will you make the exchange?" Jessup knew he had an entire team to deploy and internalize rules of engagement. He needed specifics.

"That's the one hitch. She told me the date, February fourteenth, but she refused to provide a location until the day of the swap. We argued, but it was the best I could do."

"Not knowing the site is a bitch. It will be tough to protect you. You sure you still want to do this?"

"You and I both know we're long past that." Tamika gave him a determined look.

"Well—at least the date means she's got Johnny back in the US . . . or will have him here soon," Jessup mused.

"Well, that's the bet we're making." Again, Tamika seemed far too calm given the stakes.

Jessup plowed ahead. "And we should have a backup plan. She's not stupid."

"Agreed. We can't assume she'll honor the deal. I wouldn't count on that."

"Fair enough. Either way, my team will be there to scoop up whomever shows up. You realize it probably won't be her making the swap."

"Trust me, I'm certain it won't be her. It was just dumb luck she was at the dock in Amsterdam—I had the element of surprise—but that won't happen here. In her line of work, survival is everything. She'll do whatever it takes to shield herself from us. Whomever comes to the swap will be some contract hire."

"Then what's the point?" Jessup was increasingly worried this plan wasn't going to end with him arresting the target.

"She won't be far away—she's not going to let Johnny out of her sight. So we'll have her on US soil and near wherever we make the swap. The rest is up to you."

"And if we can't find her?"

"We'll get Johnny back. And that's a great first step."

• • • • •

Nastya Andropov arrived in DC and went straight to the flat arranged by her handler. Once she'd unpacked her equipment, she composed and hit Send on an encrypted message to Mischa.

> On location. Package ready. Exchange agreed.

His response was immediate.

> Timing and location?

He must have been waiting at his keyboard, she thought. She typed a quick response.

> February 14, 03:00 Zulu, US National Arboretum. Site not disclosed to her yet.

11 p.m. local time on Valentine's Day, among the Roman column remains of the original US Capitol—the perfect venue for Andropov to shoot her arrows at the lovebirds.

> Orders confirmed. Termination approved, if necessary.

She smiled. The FSB brass was on board.

Then she grinned again as she responded.

> Accepted. Capture or terminate with prejudice.

CHAPTER 56

DÉTENTE

Bryce decided to take a step he'd never thought possible. He contacted the FBI for a meeting.

First, he made the difficult journey back to his house on Asher Street in Culpeper. If Jessup wanted to take him, he'd have had the house under surveillance. After thirty minutes in the kitchen with a glass of water waiting for the troops to arrive, Bryce relaxed and realized nobody was coming.

With that, he went down into the comfortable cocoon of his workspace and sent Jessup an encrypted message.

> Urgent conversation needed. In your SCIF. With Senator Smith.

Bryce laughed at what he assumed would be Jessup's displeasure when Bryce called directly into the SCIF. That was supposed to be impossible. But of course in the digital world, nothing was impossible. His only nagging fear was that Mufasa could probably do the same thing. And if somehow he was on the line, he'd be right back in Bryce's face.

His fingers moved across the keyboard as the scheduled time arrived. For some reason, Jessup had suggested a midnight conversation from a mobile SCIF at the FBI field office in Reston. Clearly the deputy director of the FBI didn't trust his own people and suspected that his primary location had been compromised.

But for Bryce, the field office SCIF was even easier to infiltrate. He tapped his mouse to make the connection while masking his background.

No reason to announce that he'd returned home for now. He also activated a sniffer that would check the connection every fifteen seconds to ensure that nobody else was tapped into the conversation. He sat back and waited for Jessup and Smith to enter the SCIF and connect to the video call.

"Bryce—it's good to see you again. I wish we were in person." Tamika looked like she'd fully recovered from her wounds.

"Senator Smith—I feel like I've been with you quite a bit these past few months."

"I should thank you for Amsterdam. Sorry I fucked it up."

Bryce knew better than that and shook his head emphatically. "Actually, that was my fault. I never should have given Phoenix the information. I don't know what I was thinking."

"You were trying to help your family. Believe me, I know all about doing stupid things for people I love."

Bryce adjusted the SCIF's camera to zoom out to see the full room. It held two chairs, a table, and several large screens. Black walls enabled crisp visuals and probably were part of the noise reduction scheme. Bryce confirmed that nobody else was there. Colonel Jerald Jessup was sitting next to Tamika, looking stern.

"I see you can not only break into my secure room, but you can control all of the equipment, Mr. Roscovitch," Jessup said.

"Consider that payback for breaking and entering into my house without a warrant," Bryce replied crisply. No way was he going to let Jessup push him around.

"Boys—I had a brother," Tamika said. "I've seen this before. Put your egos away, please. I'd like to get Johnny back soon." Clearly, she wanted to get down to business.

Bryce resisted the temptation to say "He started it" and went straight to the point.

"Right. Two items for us to cover. First, I need a way to work with Mufasa—I know you've contracted with him." He decided to go with the difficult ask first.

"I don't know what you're talking about," came the predictable reply from Jessup.

"Come on, Director. You wrote his name on my whiteboard. He's the only person who could have traced me to that location. And I know from your files that he's supplied your best intelligence."

Jessup wore an expression that might be frustration that his group was compromised, or perhaps admiration at Bryce's skills. "I'll take that under advisement" was the best response Jessup could muster.

"And I'll take that as a yes," Bryce said, "and leave it up to you to figure out the how. Neither of us really wants to meet or know the other. Competition is competition, after all." He was still wrestling with the idea of declaring a truce with someone as talented as Mufasa.

Tamika cut in. "Bryce, you said you had two items to cover. What's the second one and why am I here?"

"Senator, I wanted you there, both to ensure my own safety and to provide you with some important information."

"OK. Go ahead."

"Well, I know who ordered the shooting at Aragon High School and has been behind most of what's been going on."

"Fuck me," said Jessup, clearly out of reflex. "How the hell do you know that?"

"Does it really matter, Director?" Tamika interjected calmly. "Let's get the information and see where it leads us."

Bryce tried not to laugh as Jessup swallowed his next words.

"Go ahead, Bryce," Tamika continued.

"I started with the digital incursion at the high school. I traced the IP addresses involved around the world about five times. Then I followed the money on a similar trail. And that's where I hit a brick wall. The traces overlapped to a large degree, but I never got to the source. All I had was some common IP address locations."

"Our team did much of the same work," Jessup said with a bit of a defensive tone.

"And I went further." Bryce wasn't done with the pissing match. "I found exactly one person who visited all of the physical locations for those IP addresses."

"And how exactly did you do that?" Jessup sounded determined too.

"I thought you wanted my help, Director? Remember, I can access data you can't legally pursue."

Tamika interrupted again. "Goddamn it, JJ. Shut up and let him finish."

Bryce hid a smirk; Tamika was awesome. "The video was conclusive. As was the facial recognition."

After a long silence, Jessup nearly lost it. "Aaaand?"

"His name is Lee Bowen. He's a venture capitalist in Silicon Valley."

"Wait a second." Jessup was typing on his keyboard frantically. "You're telling us that our terrorist ringleader is the co–managing partner at B^2 Ventures?"

Tamika wore a quizzical expression. "Bryce, are you sure? Kidnapping, extortion, school shootings—those aren't exactly venture-funded activities. We've been thinking more like an FSB operative."

"Well, if he's working for the FSB, he's a first-class Russian capitalist," Bryce said, rubbing the fingers of his right hand together in the gesture for payola.

Then he added, "Wait 'til you hear what he's been doing with his money."

CHAPTER 57

ON THE HOUSE FLOOR

"Michael Gomez is such a patriot. He fights for what he believes in and doesn't give an inch. It's about time someone stood up and said enough is enough."

Lee Bowen sat in his home in Atherton watching three different news services from the comfort of his media room. He had Fox News up on the seventy-five-inch TV that was mounted on the wall. He liked putting them on the big screen since they always seemed to be yelling. The performance art was enjoyable to watch.

His house was a modified California ranch design that rambled across a full acre of land with no lack of space. Five bedrooms, six baths, a swimming pool and hot tub, sport court, and a four-car garage. He'd hired an interior decorator to design and furnish the rooms—he liked to call it "early ostentatious." Several hundred thousand dollars worth of paintings and sculpture pieces were tastefully arranged in the public living spaces. The kitchen was fit for a gourmet, which was useful when he hosted business dinners. After all, he didn't cook.

The irony, of course, was that Bowen was a dedicated bachelor with no children and no plans for that to change. He rarely used most of the rooms in the house, spending the majority of his time in a large office or in the media room. He'd brought a few women home, but those had been well-understood one-night events. He had no time in his life for dating and no desire to distract himself from his financial mission. Sex provided an occasional physical release, but making money was his special pleasure.

In addition to the primary monster TV, his media room featured two extra fifty-five-inch screens. The devices were also projecting to slightly smaller monitors in his adjoining office, since he often went back and forth between the two rooms. He could control all the TVs from an app on his phone. At the moment, the action was focused on activities on the floor of the House of Representatives. He used Fox and MSNBC to track both ends of the political commentary while watching C-SPAN to see the actual work in progress. The Fox commentators were in the middle of a Freedom Caucus lovefest.

"You're so right, Nancy. Gomez is fighting for our financial future and ensuring that the Biden socialists don't ruin our country with their wasteful spending." The Barbie and Ken look-alike anchors smiled at each other.

"And if that means we risk defaulting on our debt, so be it. Maybe that will force everyone to pay attention."

"Indeed, dark times require drastic measures."

This back-and-forth brought a small laugh from Bowen. On the surface, he thought the whole process was ridiculous. Who puts a debt limit in place knowing that they are just going to keep exceeding it? It was a guaranteed nuclear standoff every year. He also enjoyed laughing at Gomez, who he viewed as an ego-driven clown. He was certain Gomez and most of his alt-right crowd had no clue how the economy worked. He also knew that they had no principles other than whatever served their own personal interests. Why did people vote for these turkeys?

At a deeper level, he loved everything he heard from their Freedom Caucus cousins. The more raucous they made things in the House, the better. And the same was true for the leftist Democratic Squad believers who didn't understand the negative impact their do-gooder activities would have in the long term. With both sides caterwauling into the floor of the House, nothing meaningful could get done. And that was the core of the bet Bowen was placing. The animosity had reached a point where only a small push was required to send the system into cardiac arrest.

Satisfied that the debt ceiling debate was going nowhere—which was the goal, after all—Bowen picked up his laptop off the side table and reviewed the RallyAmerica activity. His mood immediately soured as his worst fears were confirmed. The DAO was now converting his blackmail efforts into killings.

Assassinations.

"Fuck," Bowen said. "What the hell is going on?"

• • • • •

Ely Basof knew exactly what was going on. And it was perfect.

He had just made his last move with RallyAmerica—he didn't want to have any possible connections between that group and his final set of activities. He'd replaced Bowen's original extortion plans with something more sinister and dangerous. The best part was that he didn't care if they succeeded or not. Either way, his partner would eventually get caught and have to deal with the consequences on his own.

But casting off RallyAmerica and trapping his partner wasn't enough. In fact, Basof had his own strategic objectives to pursue, safe in the knowledge that his hands were completely clean up until this point. He had just confirmed the talent required and authorized the activities that would ultimately rock the US democracy to its core. The fact that the core was well-rotted already would, of course, help.

The remainder of his plan was simple in concept but involved an endless set of details. Each of the targets was on a different schedule with different vulnerabilities. He'd hired experts who could execute the plan, so to speak, while calling an audible if that was necessary. He'd sourced floor schematics, digital and on-site security, and transportation for a number of private and public facilities that were not bulletproof, but also not easy targets.

The most difficult element of the plan was hiding the preparations. Without the inherent protection of the DAO, he was running some risks that the contracts and finances could be traced. It was a good thing he'd arranged for Maaier's accommodations and technical infrastructure. That had turned out to be very convenient.

Not coincidentally, the plan to deal with Tamika Smith was also well in hand. Maaier was a pro, and while she'd had some stumbles recently, Basof knew she was motivated to finish the job. In fact, her work would blend seamlessly into his own, creating a shock-and-awe morning across America. Except this time, the US would be on the receiving end.

He was in Austin, where he'd just finished several legitimate B^2 meetings with local startups. Now, sitting in a budget hotel he'd reserved under an assumed name, it was time to initiate the final linchpin in his plan. He launched his Tor browser to access the anonymity of the dark web. Using his Proton email account, he sent the missive that would provide the gasoline needed to fuel the fire he was starting. The photos he added would be quite persuasive.

> "I know what you've been doing in your free time. I don't think your constituents would appreciate your inclinations. I'd suggest you follow my instructions exactly to the letter."

The instructions would come at the appropriate time—but Basof also needed to ensure they would be followed.

> "If you ignore me or deviate from my directions, these photos will be everywhere."

Like his Russian oligarch leaders, he was going to take whatever he could get. The opportunities in the AI space were generational in nature, and he could use legitimate B^2 Ventures investments to capture as much wealth as anyone in Putin's Russia. Most importantly, it would be his to keep with no need to share with Bowen.

And if somehow the authorities, or the FSB for that matter, figured out what he'd done, he knew how to disappear.

And he'd take the money with him.

CHAPTER 58

GUT CHECK

Jerald Jessup had a problem. His head and his gut were out of sync.

After Bryce disconnected from the SCIF call, Jessup called Higginbottom in to join him and Tamika. He grabbed some drinks and food he'd DoorDashed from an all-night diner. Eating at 12:30 a.m. seemed ridiculous, but he had a serious case of the munchies. They closed the door and went back into stealth mode. Jessup wondered if Bryce had somehow figured out a way to keep watching—and then realized there wasn't a damn thing he could do about it.

"I love that we have our first tangible lead on this asshole. But I just can't connect all the dots. What does Lee Bowen have to do with the woman in the Netherlands? If she was the shooter and the kidnapper, how are they working together?"

"Did your source find any digital connections?" Higginbottom asked. Jessup hadn't told Higginbottom the origins of the information, but he suspected his senior agent was smart enough to figure it out on his own.

"No . . . in fact, he reported the opposite. The latest digital tracing on the Twitter DMs is completely different from the earlier activity, and the pathways don't intersect. Whatever the Dutch operative is doing, it seems disconnected from the original activity."

Tamika jumped in. "But that makes no sense. She has Johnny. She's blackmailing me, just like other people are being extorted by Bowen . . . or at least that's the way it looks. Has she somehow gone rogue?"

"Perhaps, but that doesn't feel right either. The real problem here is that Bowen is an unlikely terrorist—and equally unlikely to be connected to the FSB. From the banking financial transaction data, he looks like just another money-grubbing Silicon Valley–type with a side hustle in market manipulation."

"Is that what you think this is all about?" Higginbottom interjected.

"Shit, Higgs, I've got no idea. The Bowen evidence says he's trying to leverage some anticipated move in the market. So maybe his motivation is to cause that shift. But everything else points to some political motive—and certainly the Dutch shooter is pushing Tamika that way."

Tamika shifted in her seat. "Maybe those two things aren't so different. What if a political crisis caused an economic collapse? Two masters, but the same result."

That felt right to Jessup. And it hit him hard.

• • • • •

Jessup's job was to connect his gut to the facts his head could confirm.

Over the next three days, his team aggressively pursued the Lee Bowen lead provided by Bryce Roscovitch. The cyber geeks and field agents confirmed much of Bryce's claims, including the IP traces, the physical WeWork locations, and the financial gymnastics Bowen was executing. The problem, of course, was connecting any of these activities to a specific crime and to Bowen personally.

"Look, this is all well and good, but it's not enough for an arrest, and I don't know if we can even get search warrants based on this." Jessup was talking with his field team in California, now under the leadership of Higginbottom's second-in-command Kalen Chen. At almost six feet tall, with dark black hair, broad shoulders, and a track record of success, she was a tough, respected field operative.

"Sir, the intelligence you gave us already identified the problem. There's a giant hole in the middle of the trail. Everything circles around it, but we haven't found a way to penetrate inside."

"I'm an old Air Force guy who flew planes for a living. Explain that to me."

"Well, these WeWork facilities operate like touchdown offices. People come in, use a desk, and then leave. Attaching the use of an IP address to a specific computer at a certain time is damn hard. Even if you could, the computer doesn't stay there any more than the person. And when you have to vector that across four locations, you can't make the dog hunt, so to speak."

That was an expression Jessup could appreciate.

"Should we sit on each facility and wait for him to show up?"

"We can do that—but we still have the problem of connecting him to any of the specific crimes. Maybe we can tie him to the network outage at the high school, but who contracted the shooting? How do you connect him to that?"

"There must be a digital trail somewhere . . ."

Chen's expression across the secure connection lit up a bit. "You know, sir, we've run into something similar in some bank fraud cases."

"What does this have to do with bank fraud?"

"Well . . . when you're trying to follow the money, blockchain and cryptocurrencies are used to obscure what's really going on. Eventually, we can see the transactions, but it's still hard to tie that to an individual."

"You think someone is using blockchain? How would that lead to a shooting?"

"I don't know, sir, but it explains a lot of things. You might push your sources to pursue that angle. See what they can figure out."

"I'll do that, Agent Chen. In the meantime, you should go for a search warrant for Bowen's office and home. If the judge gives you any trouble, let me know."

Jessup knew he might have to bring some DOJ heavyweights in to help. But he also suspected time was running out.

CHAPTER 59

SITE DEVELOPMENT

Andropov got out of the Uber at the New York Avenue gate and walked down the road past the parking lot. It was her first time in DC, much less at the US National Arboretum. It was Friday, February 10, t-minus four days until the agreed-upon meeting with Senator Smith.

The weather was typical for February in the nation's capital, with a stiff breeze, high clouds, and a hint of snow in the future. Nothing like her native land, but cold nonetheless. She was dressed for the elements, including a long black winter coat, gray scarf, and a Commanders football winter hat she'd picked up leaving the hotel. Even though an identification would be tough given her clothing, she'd taken the time to put on a black wig streaked with gray and applied some makeup to age her face. She hoped the effect was a lonely old woman taking a communal walk with nature.

Because she was on foreign soil, she'd done extensive research to pick the site for the proposed swap. The arboretum had been established in 1927 and included almost 450 acres of research labs, forests, exhibits, and open grassy areas. As she strolled down Valley Road she noted that the venue was urban—reminding her of Gorky Park, though it seemed to be focused more on agriculture than entertainment. With nothing in bloom and deteriorating weather, very few people were moving around the immediate area.

That was both good and bad, given her mission.

She needed to verify the information she'd already gathered and confirm the operating plan she would pursue for the prisoner exchange. If the venue was crowded, she'd gain anonymity at the expense of being able to focus closely on her targets. The empty park made it easy to move around, evaluate sight lines, and consider escape routes. But if someone was looking for her, she might stick out like a sore thumb. Given the timing, she didn't have any choice in the matter. Hence the disguise.

Her destination was the National Capitol Columns monument, which she was approaching from a wooded area to its rear. As she entered the long, broad clearing called Ellipse Meadow, she studied the twenty-two Corinthian columns resting on an elevated platform constructed with stone slabs taken from the original US Capitol. The columns had been part of the Capitol from 1828 to 1958 and were installed in the arboretum in 1988. Selecting an exchange site attached to American democracy was a subtle political statement.

Could those columns tip over? she wondered.

She continued her stroll down Ellipse Road moving to the left side of the columns, all the while taking a few photos using her smartphone. No self-respecting tourist could visit the area without shooting some pictures, after all. She had to admit that the venue had a hypnotic, stately ambiance, especially given the lack of people and the dreary weather. Despite their fragile appearance, the columns had stood the test of time—something ageless. It was intimidating.

Don't be an idiot.

She shook her head to eliminate the sentimental cobwebs and focus on the task at hand. The meadow in front of the columns offered multiple open sight lines, making it an ideal location for an FSB-trained agent, and a difficult area to defend. She had no doubt that Tamika Smith would come protected—despite instructions to the contrary; Andropov couldn't imagine her target coming alone. The challenge was finding a spot with good visibility to the platform but shielded sufficiently from prying eyes to allow a clear opportunity.

Andropov turned right on Azalea Road at the bottom of the meadow. She moved casually to the southwest corner of the rectangular-shaped field and found exactly the location she wanted: great visibility to the area in front of the columns, some protection from a small grove of trees, and reasonable egress to the south and the Anacostia River. The wispy meadow grass would also make for good cover. She took another picture to capture the important details. She retraced her tracks back to Ellipse Road and left the park to the south, past the parking lot at the M Street entrance, just as snow began to fall.

Sitting in the back seat of the Prius Uber, she went through the plan in her mind. She only had three more days to put everything in place. No mission was foolproof, and this one carried significant risks. Although the FBI did not know the specific location yet, they would eventually have a target to surround. There was little doubt that they wanted to use the occasion to capture an FSB operative on US soil. In fact, there was a high likelihood that the person being swapped for Johnny Humboldt wasn't Tamika Smith at all, but rather an FBI surrogate.

Nastya Andropov hoped that her psych profile of Smith was accurate. She didn't think the senator would allow someone to take her place. She believed her adversary had a bit of a hero complex and was counting on that to bring the senator center stage on the platform among the columns. She also believed she could make a positive ID of the senator using the high-powered scope on her rifle.

For Andropov, the decision tree was easy. People would die on the platform.

She hoped one of them would be Tamika Smith.

CHAPTER 60

SEARCH AND SEIZURE

"FBI!" The shouts rang out across the B² Ventures office.

Lee Bowen heard the commotion from the reception area and wondered what the hell was going on. Jumping up from his desk with pangs of anxiety, he hurried to the front of the office where he was met by a pack of people in blue coats, all with the FBI logo emblazoned on the front. Some were carrying what looked like computer equipment, several had hand trucks, and he could see a few pistols exposed on people's hips.

"Ellie, what's all the shouting about?"

"These people—they claim they have a search warrant for your office and our files," his flustered assistant managed to get out.

"Are you Lee Bowen?" The agent who was clearly in charge approached him.

"Yes, that's me, and you better explain what the hell you think you're doing." He folded his arms as he positioned himself to block her access to the office.

"Mr. Bowen, I am Special Agent Kalen Chen, and I'm serving a search warrant for your office and B² Ventures' records."

"On whose authority? You have no right to do this. My lawyers will have your asses."

"Well, it's all here in the warrant and perfectly legal. You're welcome to have your lawyer review it. And by the way, a similar warrant was just served at your home. Your cleaning woman was nice enough to let our agents in." The agent was almost as tall as Bowen and physically imposing.

"Ellie, call Annie Petersen and tell her what's going on. I need her here—and now!" It came out as an angry shout, but underneath he felt the motivational fear.

Annie Petersen was Bowen's personal attorney and damn good at her job. He had some hope she could sort this out before things got out of hand. And yet he couldn't push back the sense of panic.

How the fuck did the FBI get to my door?

He tried to return to his office but was restrained by one of the agents.

"Sorry, sir, you'll need to stay out of there until we're done."

At that point, Ely Basof walked in from a meeting with an investor.

"Lee, what the hell is going on?" His partner looked pissed off.

"That's exactly what I asked. Apparently, the FBI has a search warrant for my house and the office here—and all our records."

"Impossible," Basof said. "I assume you called Annie?"

Ellie jumped in. "She's on her way over—should be about fifteen minutes."

"This is not good, Lee. We're right in the middle of fundraising. The FBI will spook our investors." Bowen hated to be talked down to.

"No shit—and oh, there's that thing about me being their target." Bowen was a bit surprised and more than annoyed that this was his partner's first reaction.

"Sorry, Lee—I guess I'm just wound up about finishing the raise. It's not easy out there. We should probably go someplace private to talk."

They adjourned to a conference room that overlooked Sand Hill Road out toward the coastal hills. The sun was turning the brown hills a warm version of amber. On any other day, Bowen would have enjoyed the view as the sun began to set.

Basof jumped in. "What does the warrant say?" He reached as if to grab the document.

Bowen pulled it back, opened it, and scanned through it. "Holy shit. They're looking for evidence related to extortion, kidnapping, and attempted murder—"

"*What?* You've got to be kidding. Do they know what we do around here?"

"Some judge believes there's probable cause that I'm somehow involved in all of this."

"But all of what?" came Basof's response.

Bowen paused.

"Lee?"

Bowen folded the warrant and ran his hands through his hair.

"They think I hired someone to shoot up that high school."

• • • • •

Twenty minutes later, Annie Petersen looked up from the warrant. Bowen had never seen her that worried.

"Ely, I think you should step out," Annie said. "You're not named here, and I don't want anyone else present while Lee and I consult. It could compromise you later."

"OK . . . ," came Basof's tentative response. "Lee, I'm here if you need me . . . for anything."

Once he'd left, Petersen dove straight in. "Lee, you need to understand that as your lawyer, you can and must be totally honest with me. I can't help you if I don't know what's going on."

"I wish I knew, Annie. This is all completely out of the blue." Bowen couldn't bring himself to trust her with the truth.

"They're talking about WeWork offices, security breaches, SEC violations—it's all over the map."

"And then there's the shooting and kidnapping part."

"Well, I know that's ridiculous, but is there anything connecting you to the rest of this?"

Bowen was shocked by the amount of information in the warrant. The FBI had uncovered much more than he thought was possible. Although there was still no mention of RallyAmerica.

He'd always known there was great risk but still believed the DAO would protect him from culpability. After a brief moment, he decided to stick with that theory. What choice did he have?

"I've got no damn clue. There must be a mistake."

Yes . . . and I must have made it.

CHAPTER 61

TEAMWORK

"Jesus, someone give me a sit-rep." Jessup's cry echoed across the task force area they'd established in the FBI's headquarters in DC.

Deputy Director Jessup was standing at the back of the room looking out over an amphitheater of descending rows of desks that faced a phalanx of eighty-inch TV screens on the opposite wall. Analysts were working on their specific workstations while certain sets of data were presented on the wall screens. Outside of Jessup's outburst, the room was relatively quiet, filled with the hum of computers and the tapping of keyboards. The space was brightly lit but had no windows, creating a sense of both urgency and claustrophobia. Special Agent Franklin Higginbottom was standing at Jessup's side holding a tablet as if he'd just received the Ten Commandments on Mount Sinai.

"I'm sorry, Director, but the intel is what it is."

"So you're telling me that we have credible death threats against the secretary of the Treasury, chairman of the SEC, and Federal Reserve chairman?" He shook his head in disbelief, wondering what else could fill their plate.

"I know it's insane, but it's consistent with the trends we've seen. Someone has found vulnerabilities for each of these people and they're trying to exploit them. Not unlike the Senator Smith scenario. The attacks have just moved to a different food chain."

"And now they're focused on the three people who are the leaders of our most important financial institutions." Jessup could feel his stomach muscles tightening. The rest of his digestive system was sure to follow.

"Certainly not a coincidence, sir." Higginbottom said it in a tone that made it clear he knew this was an obvious statement.

Jessup paused, and then he said, "Pull up the financial transaction information on Lee Bowen. Put it on the big board."

Higginbottom called out the request and one of the analysts whacked away at her keyboard for a moment. The financial data followed.

"Jesus—that's hundreds of millions of dollars he's moved over the past month. He's clearly got a plan. Did we find anything in the house and office searches?"

"Not really . . . at least not yet. Nobody does too much on paper anymore. Mufasa and Senator Smith's source are analyzing his digital records now. We should hear back from them soon."

Jessup pondered this. "So what's his play? We can't directly connect him to any of this, but it's not an accident he's moving money around while the financial heartbeat of the country is being threatened."

"Agreed," Higgs replied. "I asked some folks in the securities fraud group what they thought of his money movement. They think he's betting on a meltdown."

"A meltdown of what?"

"The whole thing."

"You mean a market crash."

"Actually, the word they used was *cataclysm*."

Fuck, Jessup thought. "That means this Bowen guy is the greediest son of a bitch on the planet. He's got nearly a billion dollars in assets, and he's going to bet the farm so that he can double his money?"

"This is more like five to ten times," Higginbottom said. The agent raised his eyebrows, emphasizing the scale of the situation.

Jessup whistled. "We gotta nail this asshole."

"I asked the fraud folks how to catch him. Their response was nothing like what I expected."

"Shit, Higgs, out with it."

"They said not to worry about catching him. Focus on preventing the crash. And he'll be ruined."

"Well . . . we gotta do that anyway. Gonna take the entire team, but these folks aren't going to get attacked, much less killed, on my watch.

If that bankrupts our friend Bowen, fine." Jessup said it loudly and with fist-pumping emphasis.

After a few minutes, he finished scanning the data on the board and rubbed his hands through his hair.

"And then I'll figure out a way to put him away for life."

• • • • •

It had taken some negotiation, but ultimately, they'd figured it out. With assurances from both the deputy director and Senator Smith, Bryce had agreed to lower his firewall, both literally and figuratively.

Bryce concluded, despite his high opinion of his own skills, that there was too much on the line to rely solely on his own efforts. He'd been down this path once before and tried to do it all. His father had been killed as a result. He couldn't allow a repeat performance.

Bryce and Mufasa had established an encrypted communication link that enabled them to share information through what was essentially a double-blind drop box. Either of them could have discovered the digital location of the communications hub, but from there it would be a difficult wall to break through. And they'd both agreed that the current effort was too important to waste time trying to track each other.

They'd also decided to concentrate their efforts on finding the source of the threats—a series of traces that had led Bryce on a global chase without a definitive solution.

"Christ, blockchain is the technology I've grown to love and hate." Bryce was back in his trusty cave working from his original equipment. It was early evening, and he was prepared for another long session. This time with help from Mufasa.

He began a round of exchanges. "I use it all the time in my own work—and now it's got me chasing my tail."

"Transparency, my ass" was the response from Mufasa. "The key is to get some specifics on a particular transaction. If we can track just one exchange through to the source, we've got a chance."

Bryce thought about that for a minute. With the senator's permission, he'd finally talked to her father, General Frank Smith. He'd recorded the conversation and pulled it back up on his computer. The general talked about his discovery of Tamika's rape and the subsequent efforts he'd made to expose abuses within the Air Force.

"We never determined who committed the rape," the general intoned, anger showing through. "There were a group of captains under investigation, but the trail went cold when we scrambled after 9/11."

Bryce's voice could be heard on the recording. "So this is all in the Air Force records?"

"Sure . . . I suppose so."

Bryce realized he should have picked up on this at the time. If those records had names and dates, someone could have put the story together—or at least made an educated guess.

Back to his friend Mufasa.

"Want to tag-team to break into the Air Force's disciplinary records?" Bryce waited a few minutes for a response.

Mufasa was all in. "We can tell them the FBI said it was OK."

Bryce didn't plan to get caught.

CHAPTER 62
SETTING THE STAGE

With two days to go, Nastya Andropov was putting her plan into action. And that required a trip to the local Home Depot.

Prisoner exchanges were always messy. The captors always said "No police," and the authorities would show up anyway. Then there was the usual stalemate of who's on first when it comes time to make the exchange. Things would be so much simpler if people weren't involved. To make it slightly more complicated, this wasn't your typical money-for-hostage exchange. This was more like a prisoner swap. Andropov shrugged and realized there was a first time for everything.

A lover for a senator. Whatever. She couldn't worry about Tamika's emotions.

Her priorities were slightly different. She had two overriding objectives. First and foremost, she had to ensure that she was never at any risk personally. Regardless of her loyalty to the Russian cause, she was a survivor and would prioritize that in her planning. She'd delayed notifying Tamika of the site for the exchange so she could have everything in place first. Since she knew the FBI and its three-letter cousins would all be at the arboretum once they knew the location, she had to be anywhere but there. That was why she was at the Home Depot.

Her second priority revolved around her nemesis, Senator Tamika Smith. Her instructions were to neutralize Smith's role in the Senate, either through capture or other means. She had concluded rather quickly that the idea of Smith coming quietly in exchange for Johnny Humboldt seemed far-fetched. Smith would never be that passive, and the FBI was unlikely to sign up for that either. Clearly, they thought they could trap Andropov with Smith as bait.

That meant Smith needed to be terminated.

So be it.

She'd come to the superstore in yet another disguise. This time she had a short blonde wig, a slightly baggy sweatshirt, and Lululemon pants with her phone in the right leg slot. The effort was designed to make her look thirty years younger than the woman in the arboretum, even though the likelihood of a connection was small. She walked up and down the aisles throwing assorted items into her cart.

She accumulated four big traffic safety cones, yellow tape with the words CAUTION and DANGER printed repeatedly on the roll, and two KEEP OFF THE GRASS signs as she moved about. In the garden department she also bought a large bag of loose dried hay.

Andropov paused to consult her list. *Don't forget the reflective worker's vest and hard hat*, she reminded herself. Those were required for the most dangerous part of her mission. She went to the self-checkout area, where she fed cash into the machine to avoid a digital trail. Then she calmly walked out into the blowing wind and cold.

Now she had all the tools on the assassin's checklist.

• • • • •

Jesus, it's all here.

With some fancy keyboard work, Bryce was able to burrow deep into the Air Force's disciplinary records. He found the original evidence associated with the investigation into sexual abuse in the service—and most importantly, he found the records associated with Tamika Smith's rape. True, then Second Lieutenant Tamika Smith had never reported the crime. But she'd written a letter to her brother about it—a letter that General Frank Smith introduced as evidence in a closed-door session of the task force authorized to make recommendations to address the prevalence of abuse. Several captains were named, including one who'd died in Afghanistan. Derrick Tomlinson.

Ordinarily, Bryce would have never gone this far through the firewalls of the military. It was an exceptional risk given the extreme measures the armed forces used to ensure security. Even if Bryce got in and out undetected, his digital presence would have been difficult to erase. But his new détente with Mufasa had its advantages. His dark web compatriot was flying overwatch during the entire incursion, monitoring potential responses and covering Bryce's tracks as he went. As these things go, it was a beautiful operation.

Bryce talked himself through the rest of the exercise.

"OK, at least I know how someone got the information. Mystery one, solved."

He tapped the keyboard furiously as he continued his investigation.

"Now, let's go see who accessed those records recently. It can't be that many people. It was way back in 2001 and 2002."

It took him a full hour, with multiple machines processing in his Culpeper workspace, to find the culprit and trace the IP address.

"Damn," he said. "I guess that makes some kind of sense."

He sent an encrypted message to Mufasa. "Belarus. Likely FSB."

The response didn't surprise him. "Let's get the fuck out of here. No sense pushing our luck."

Bryce terminated his connections, knowing that his partner would clean up any remaining evidence.

He got up from his workstation, washed his hands in the bathroom sink, and splashed some water on his face. If he'd been an athlete, it would have been to wash away the sweat. In Bryce's case, it was to calm his nerves. He was generally rock solid at the keyboard, trusting his own skills. But that was deeper than he'd ever gone in the government's domain, and he was wiped out.

An incoming message from Mufasa brought him back to the table.

"So we have a series of IP traces that revert back to WeWork offices leased by Lee Bowen. He's focused on some financial windfall from a calamity he's trying to cause. We have another set of IP addresses that are connected to some shadowy FSB agent who is into assassination and kidnapping. She's focused on Senator Smith. And now we have a third piece of activity out of Belarus, which might or might not be related to the other two?"

"Exactly," Bryce responded.

What the fuck, he thought.

CHAPTER 63

POISON PILLS

"Time. The ayes appear to have it . . . the ayes do have it, and the bill is passed." The gavel came down with a bang to signify the end of the vote in the US House of Representatives. Tamika could see the tally on the C-SPAN feed: 228 had voted *aye*; 207 had voted *no*. She was sitting in her office the day before Valentine's Day, and she was pissed.

In the middle of her life-and-death negotiations, she was engaged in a complex lobbying effort to shape a piece of legislation that would raise the debt ceiling and prevent a US government default on its obligations. The so-called X date deadline for raising the limit was fast approaching and Congress needed to take action. Without legislation the government would be unable to pay its bills, including interest on Treasury debt. Tamika was certain that defaulting on government obligations would throw the country and the world into a financial crisis.

Her lobbying, and negotiations with the White House and legislative leaders, had shaped a relatively clean bill to raise the debt ceiling in exchange for caps on certain types of discretionary spending. Her conversation with Democratic Congresswoman Valerie Rasmussen from Pennsylvania the previous Friday had been pretty typical.

"Val, the deficit is out of control, and serious action has to be taken to address a long-standing set of issues. An endless stream of continuing resolutions won't work." She'd approached Rasmussen in the Democratic Cloakroom just off the floor of the House. Now they were sitting in Tamika's hideaway office on the second floor of the Capitol. Based on seniority, every senator was assigned an unlisted meeting room where they could escape from the press or other scrutiny to meet, prepare, or relax. Rasmussen was sitting across from Tamika in a leather chair in a wood-paneled room, speaking openly about complex issues.

"I don't disagree with you, Tamika, but cutting childcare resources, SNAP funding, and other social programs isn't right."

"Of course it's not," Tamika said. "We need a multiyear budget plan that addresses health-care costs, retirement security, and defense spending. When those are off the table, safety net spending is what gets sacrificed."

"But fiscal responsibility on retirement funding is an election loser. I won't be here next year if we have that conversation." Like many, Tamika knew that Rasmussen's mind was never far from the next election.

Such was the rock and hard place through which Tamika and the Lincoln Coalition had to lead the country.

In the end, Tamika had convinced enough legislators that the debt ceiling was an artificial deadline that needed to be extended to avoid a full-on default. The euphemistically named Fiscal Responsibility Act of 2023 was fine as far as that went.

The problem had been the poison pills that were introduced into the process.

Amendments were proposed to reduce funding to the IRS, include mandatory cuts to the SNAP food program, end funding for the Ukraine War, and prevent the extension of PEPFAR. Such proposals would have made the entire package controversial in the Senate and untenable for the White House.

Cutbacks at the IRS would help the wealthy and perversely increase the deficit. SNAP was a critically important supplemental food program for those in need. And PEPFAR was one of the most successful foreign health-care programs in US history, saving millions of people suffering from AIDS and other illnesses. Conservatives wanted to kill it because they claimed it was supporting abortions. Ironically it was a Republican, George W. Bush, who had created the program.

Things have certainly changed, Tamika thought. *These days, it's almost impossible to find an issue that can't be spun into a controversial talking point. It just makes finding common ground that much more difficult . . . and necessary.*

Republican members of the Lincoln Coalition were particularly caught in the middle on these proposals. They didn't like the conditions the amendments attached to the debt ceiling increase but knew that voting against them would lead to a backlash from the right wing of their own party. That almost certainly meant a primary opponent who was more conservative—in fact more radical—than they were. That candidate would have national funding from MAGA organizations and might bring out enough primary voters to defeat the incumbent. The choice was a catch-22: Do the right thing and lose their jobs, and with it, the ability to represent people well in their districts. Or hold their noses, vote aye, and hope that the amendments still failed.

With aggressive lobbying by Lincoln Coalition members on both sides of the aisle, the amendments had all failed and the clean legislation had passed. Tamika believed that a similar piece of legislation in the Senate could pass, thus alleviating the threat of a debt apocalypse—at least until they ran up against the ceiling in the future. All of that was good news.

But she was very upset about how the voting in the House had unfolded. It should never have been so difficult.

"Damn it, Johnny," Tamika said out loud. "What are we going to do now?"

She missed Johnny Humboldt's loving touch, his gentle support, and his incredible intuition on how to get the best from her. She was lost without him at every level.

And that was why she would lay it all on the line the next evening.

• • • • •

"I know your secret."

Senator Ronald Stumper's hands were shaking over the keyboard of his computer. The email was from a source he didn't recognize, and he realized that opening it probably wasn't a smart move. But the header about a secret had grabbed his attention.

Stumper was a tough old bird who had been around the Senate block more times than most. He'd been browbeat, cursed, bullied, and shouted down more times than he could count. None of that had ever bothered him—it was just part of the game that was being a US senator. But this email went to the one place he feared.

He glanced over his shoulder reflexively to make sure nobody else could see it, even though he knew nobody was in his office. He wanted to delete the missive and pretend he'd never seen it, but he suspected that wouldn't solve his problem. He'd just have to wait and see what the instructions demanded of him.

Stumper had been married for almost fifty years to his high school sweetheart. They'd raised two children who were now independently successful, and he'd provided for his wife, Gladys. They had three grandchildren. In his speeches, he talked about family values, the role religion played in his work, and the importance of honesty and integrity. All of which played very well with both traditional Republicans as well as the newfangled MAGA crowd.

All of that was about to become a problem. The pictures showed him in compromising positions, which in and of itself was probably survivable in today's political environment. Under normal circumstances he'd have said that Gladys would hate it but would put up a good public face—isn't that what all wives did when their husbands were caught in an affair?

But these weren't normal times. And the problem for Stumper was worse than that.

The pictures were with another man.

• • • • •

"Senator?"

"Come," Tamika said from inside her office. She was happy for the interruption from darker thoughts.

"I assume you saw the vote." Mark Cavanagh's face reflected the same concern Tamika felt.

"Yeah. We squeaked by, but it shouldn't have been that close. Lincolnites on the right nearly passed the poison pill amendments, and not enough of our Democratic members voted for the final bill. That kind of shit can't happen." Tamika never minced words.

"Pardon the expression, but something about 'clowns to the left of me and jokers to the right' comes to mind." Cavanagh was old school. His face bore a crusty, irritated expression, but she knew his usual good humor was just below the surface.

Tamika tried not to laugh. "I know. When push comes to shove, they just can't resist the temptation to grandstand. It would be nice if more of them just wanted to legislate."

Cavanagh nodded. "Total BS. Their job is to do what's right for their voters and for the country. Not to play politics with something as important as the financial future of the nation."

Tamika sighed. "We are where we are. The question is what do we do about it?"

"Well, we're better positioned in the Senate. We have the sixty votes to pass it with a few to spare. The president should be able to sign it in time."

"Nobody knows the precise X date, but I agree we should be able to get it done in time. In the end, that's the most important thing. But we also have to deal with the coalition members like Williams and Lichtman who voted on the wrong side of this. And there is some risk this could set a precedent in the Senate. How do we keep everyone working together?"

"We've never said that the caucus all had to vote the same way," Cavanagh replied. "We may have to chalk it up to individual choice."

"Maybe—but this vote gets right down to core principles. I talked to each of them. They agreed the amendments would never pass the Senate and risked us missing the date. And then they voted for them anyway. And the protest votes against the final bill by some of the Dems is a very bad sign. I don't think we can put up with that kind of behavior."

"I'm sure if you pushed, the caucus would kick them out . . ." Cavanagh said it with some hesitation in his voice.

Tamika thought about what Johnny would say. "Let's take a deep breath and see how this plays out in the Senate. I'd like to consult with some others before we take any action."

"OK. The team and I are prepping your speech for the floor when the bill eventually comes up. We'll have something for you later today."

"Great," she said absentmindedly. All of this was important, sure—but she couldn't help thinking about more immediate events.

Maybe by tomorrow she'd have Johnny back to act as that faithful sounding board.

Or perhaps she'd be dead.

CHAPTER 64

LYING IN WAIT

"OK, Higgs, walk me through the plan." It was early in the morning on the fourteenth of February. The two FBI leaders were sitting in Jessup's office eating bagels as they began what was sure to be a long day.

"Which plan, sir—the Senator Smith Suicide Pact or the Save the Money Men strategy?"

"Ha. Fair enough. Let's start with the Smith craziness." Jessup's relaxed attitude was a cover for the anxiety he felt. He suspected they were touching the elephant's tail while the trunk got ready to swing around and do all the damage. The stakes were immeasurably high, and they had nowhere near enough intelligence to have confidence in their work.

"Smith got the location from our Russian assassin about an hour ago. The exchange is going to be made in front of the Capitol Columns monument in the National Arboretum."

Jessup pondered that nugget over his cup of coffee. "Not exactly what I expected. I thought she'd pick some busy location where it was impossible to manage the situation."

Higginbottom projected a map on the big screen above the conference table. "I agree, but this location has its own challenges. There's a large meadow without much cover. The senator will be exposed, as will whoever brings Humboldt there for the exchange. Not much protection for anyone."

"I assume we're going to have agents in those trees behind the platform and on the other side of the meadow?"

"Well . . . we talked about that with Senator Smith and . . . she rejected it. In fact, she won't let us have anyone in the arboretum."

"When was she put in charge, goddamn it?"

"Sir, you know how she can be. She said she wasn't showing up if we sent any agents anywhere in the park. She's afraid it will spook the bitch."

"For Christ's sake. So how does she expect us to protect her?" Jessup couldn't believe he was having this conversation.

"Drones, sir. It's actually not a bad plan. We'll have four drones in the air above the arboretum, all equipped with night vision and heat detection sensors. We'll monitor the entire area from just off-site with fifteen to twenty agents on each park approach."

Jessup paused in midbite, chewed, then swallowed. "Once our target arrives, we surround and move in?"

"Exactly. We have video of our perp from the Amsterdam dock. We'll try to match that as Humboldt is brought out in the open. If it's her, we move in. If not, we let the exchange play out and take down whoever she's hired."

"How does this help us capture the terrorist herself?"

"It's possible she'll be someplace in the park. She'll run as soon as she sees us take down her man or woman. We'll have her surrounded."

Jessup again paused, this time to take a swig of water. "It's too easy. She's not that dumb. There's no way she'll make the exchange, and she'll know we have the park under surveillance."

"You're probably right, sir, but what are the alternatives?"

"I know—oh hell—it's probably the best we can do. Make it happen."

Jessup hesitated but then dove in. "One last thing, Higgs. I want to be in the field for this one. I'm leaving you in control of the command center."

"Sir? You don't want to be in charge?"

"Look, I'll admit this is personal. Smith and I go way back, and I'm not going to leave her out there on her own. I can be more help to her in the arboretum than in some conference room."

Even as he said this, he knew it was mostly bullshit. From the look on Higginbottom's face, he was sure his lead agent agreed. But it was all part of Smith's unconventional and almost certainly ill-advised plan. The hope was that it would net them a hired gun and maybe get Johnny Humboldt back. That was certainly Smith's first priority. But if the woman was FSB, she'd have something else in mind for Tamika Smith.

God, I hope the senator is ready, Jessup thought.

The plan depended on it.

• • • • •

Ely Basof was set up in an Airbnb. A very specific Airbnb. The apartment itself was nothing fancy. A two-bedroom affair in a multitenant building, decorated with furniture from the Restoration Hardware catalog. The living room featured a futon, two matching chairs, and a coffee table, all organized around a sixty-inch TV mounted on a wall over a gas insert fireplace.

None of that mattered to Basof. What he really cared about was the office nook off the living room and the Cat5 network wiring that had been common in the early 2000s before Wi-Fi was prevalent. He wanted access to maximum performance during the night's activities and appreciated the lack of windows in the nook. He didn't want anyone accidentally seeing him in the window. Fortunately, it was getting dark and many people were out celebrating Valentine's Day.

His equipment had been predelivered, and he'd just completed the wiring to bring everything online. As further protection, he'd made sure that the rental introduction was done electronically, with no personal greeter. He'd also worn a gray wig with short-cropped hair, matched with a worn button-down shirt, old ski coat, loose-fitting pants, and leather gloves. He walked from his van in the basement parking garage to the elevator with a slight limp. He knew there were cameras, which he didn't want to turn off for a number of reasons.

For this evening he'd be acting as both a consultant and conductor. He had no less than six different operations to monitor—seven, if you included Maaier's work—and the phalanx of equipment on the desk in front of him was impressive. He was connected to team leaders for each operation and would monitor their on-site comms to track progress, issues, and success rate. Each leader was also equipped with a bodycam to provide video feeds. All of this required six different laptops and three supplemental monitors. It was a temporary nuclear control room.

The first three teams were associated with RallyAmerica. Their missions had technically been contracted through the DAO, but they were now under Basof's new directive to kill their targets. He couldn't vouch for the quality of the operatives, but the FSB agent wasn't all that concerned about whether they achieved their objectives. With the FBI raiding B^2 Ventures' offices and Lee Bowen's house, Basof suspected they knew what was coming. Certainly there was a high likelihood that the financial leaders targeted had contacted the FBI when they were blackmailed. If the DAO's agents succeeded, that would add to the chaos he so relished. If they failed, the ultimate trail would lead back to Bowen, who would be screwed personally and financially.

Too bad, Basof thought fleetingly. But actually all good. Very, very good.

His second set of teams, code named Optimus, was carefully selected for their professionalism and track record of success. All of them imported from outside the United States so they wouldn't be on anyone's radar screen. The bulk of each team had special forces experience and had worked together before. Discipline and execution were essential, as it was critical they operate on the exact schedule as Maaier's activities in the arboretum. And there could be no mistakes. Basof hired some local talent for very specific activities, but those were low-priority tasks that needed to be accomplished after the fact.

"Control to Optimus 1—sound and video check."

"Camera transmitting, audio is five by five," came the response.

He went on to do sound and video checks with each of his squad leaders and confirmed that everyone was in place and on schedule. He wasn't too concerned about the comms being traced back to his current location. They would eventually find it anyway, and that was part of the plan. Besides, by the time the authorities figured anything out, the unimaginable would have happened.

Titans were about to fall.

• • • • •

Lee Bowen was doing his own monitoring.

The FBI searches had sent him into a temporary tailspin, but Annie

Petersen reported that there was no additional activity based on the warrants.

"I think they were on a fishing expedition," she told him. "Someone strong-armed a judge to approve the warrants, but I don't think they were based on any concrete evidence or data."

"I hope you're right, Annie. I still can't figure out what led them to me."

Bowen had concluded that denial to the end was his best course of action.

As he reflected on the situation, there was still a way for him to win—and win big. He would never have approved the RallyAmerica attacks that were now in motion, but if they went off as planned, his investments would reap the benefit of a dramatic market crash. He would then shift the profits into protected venues with no extradition and leave on a private plane, under a false passport.

It would be close.

If it worked, the juice would be worth the squeeze.

CHAPTER 65

INTO THE NIGHT

"Christ, it's like I'm back in Afghanistan."

As Tamika Smith dressed for the evening, she could almost taste and smell the details of every one of her sorties in the Middle East. In three tours of duty, she'd survived several live-fire extractions, been seriously wounded, and seen others die. She saw their faces—sometimes in her dreams—but often just in moments of quiet if she let her guard down. She'd gone into therapy to deal with PTSD, and that helped her get through. But like many mental illnesses, her troubles would never fully leave her; rather, they were the curse of duty well served.

Most importantly, she knew every step, every comm, every image from that fateful day in Helmand Province. The original radio call: "Bird down, two wounded, in need of evac." The rush as she dashed across the Kandahar helo pad, donning her CSAR rescue gear as she jumped into the back of the Pave Hawk. The crackle of the radio as the downed bird's pilot called for reinforcements when Taliban troops closed in. The surge of adrenaline as she dashed across several hundred yards of open territory, diving for cover behind the wreckage. The desperate choice she'd made to rescue the badly wounded copilot, leaving the pilot to fend for himself. A pilot named Tomlinson who had raped her. The final dash back to the chopper, complete with a gunshot wound to her arm. The horrific sounds of the scene being lit up by an Army Apache, wiping out the Taliban fighters along with the remains of the American pilot.

And then there was the Purple Heart permanently located in a dark drawer.

"Get it together, girl," she told herself. "Now's not the time to rehash history. Focus."

She finished putting on her gear for the hostage exchange and went through a mental checklist. The evening would be cold, so she wore a winter parka over her other clothing, realizing she'd look like the Michelin woman. She had a hat that would keep her head warm as well as hide the comms transmitters in her ears. She checked the connections on a set of clear glasses that contained a camera sending a video feed back to the FBI. It was a bit redundant with the drones overhead, but more eyes were better. She had a Glock wedged in the waistband of her pants, which would be covered by the coat. Not an easy draw, but not visible from the outside and at least a source of comfort.

OK, I'm squared away.

"Comms check."

"Senate 1 is clear," came the reply.

Satisfied with the response from the FBI agents monitoring her comms a few miles away, she moved out of the small FBI truck that was doubling as a dressing room and crossed the street into the arboretum.

In the service, she'd always had a letter prepared that would be delivered to her father if she was killed in action. She hadn't thought about it for a long time but had revisited the discipline as she considered the possible outcomes for the night.

Earlier in the day she'd sat down at the kitchen table in her small apartment, and this time, she opened her heart to the man she knew she loved.

Dear Johnny,

I'm truly sorry that you're reading this letter. I thought I had everything under control and would be there to hold you close again. I was certain I'd thought of every contingency and possibility. Clearly, I was wrong.

I know the last few months must have been hellish for you. I can't imagine the things you've had to endure, and I'm crushed that my work was the cause of your suffering. You did nothing to deserve this treatment, and I hope you realize I've done everything in my power to get you released. I take some comfort knowing that my death may have given you life.

In so many ways, you changed my world. In fact, I think you gave me a second future. I was going through the motions in my first effort, earning a living, keeping my head above water, but just existing. From the time I picked you up in that ditch at Offutt, I knew things would never be the same. You inspired the courage to overcome my past, to let go of the chains shackled around me, to rededicate my life to serving others. I don't know how you did all of that—but I know it was real.

You gave me the opportunity to share your children. Not to be their mother, but to get as close to that as I could. I loved every minute with Phoenix and Nathan, and one of my great regrets in writing this letter is that I will never get to see them grow up. To experience their milestones. To see them put their own mark on the world. I pray that they may have found at least a small amount of fuel for that fight from our time together.

Finally, there is love. I know I was loved by my mom when she was alive, and I know that my dad cares for me deeply, even if he's not always good at showing it. But you gave me an entirely new outlook on love. I learned how to trust someone with my deepest thoughts and fears—how to give in a selfless way that wasn't about duty or honor—how to melt into someone's arms and feel completely at home. That was a gift that truly saved me.

My deepest wish is that you will find someone else who will share a future with you and the kids. We've already sacrificed for each other. You should now be free to share, to grow, and to love someone equally special.

Eternally here for you,
Tamika

She had printed the letter, put it in an envelope, addressed it to Johnny, and given it to Jessup.

As she entered the cold darkness of the arboretum, she felt a shiver run through her body. Was that adrenaline? Was that fear? Foreboding? Or was it just the weather?

She continued her slow walk.

It was time to face the unknown.

• • • • •

Nastya Andropov had no intention of heading out into the cold.

She was warmly ensconced in the Airbnb suggested to her by her handler, Mischa. She wondered where he was and how he was monitoring activities. She knew tonight was a big evening for their cause, even if she didn't know the specifics. Mischa would certainly have his hands on the steering wheel somehow.

She turned her focus to the task at hand. She had a large monitor in front of her that projected a clear view of the platform that supported the Capitol Columns. She could see the stone slab steps that led up a grassy incline from a reflecting pool to the twenty-two columns. The pillars were arranged in a rectangle with two of the columns standing in front, acting as a portico to the monument. The prisoner exchange was set to take place in front of those two columns. The spotlights on each column gave off an eerie effervescence that combined with a light fog to turn the scene into a Cold War spy exchange.

She explored the twenty acres of meadow that fronted the exhibit and scanned from left to right looking for anything out of place. She also zoomed in on the trees behind the monument as well as those on the opposite side of the reflecting pool. She saw no movement and no signs of digital monitoring, either. Just a cold, lonely night at an empty venue.

"Hmmm." Somehow, something didn't feel right.

She'd expected at least some indication of an FBI presence and wasn't sure how to interpret the current situation. Maybe they had nixed the whole operation? Maybe Smith didn't plan to show? Maybe all her preparations were for naught?

And then she saw movement in the trees behind the columns as a lone figure walked out along a stone pathway on the right side of the exhibit. She manipulated the controller to zoom her scope on the person entering the scene. It didn't take much to confirm that it was Tamika Smith. She watched as Smith paused in the shadows to the side of the far-right column, clearly waiting for someone to show.

My enemy in the flesh.

Nastya Andropov's pulse quickened as she continued to focus her scope on Smith. She was clearly being shifty, aware that she was exposed. The fog made visibility a bit worse.

"Go for podium," she said into a headset microphone.

She saw two figures come around the far side of the platform toward the portico. One was blindfolded with hands tied behind his back. The other was brandishing what looked like a Beretta. Smith made her appearance, coming around to meet them.

Andropov took several deep breaths as she considered all the data in front of her. She could go ahead with the exchange—or not.

She took one last, long look through the scope and made her decision.

CHAPTER 66

THE FALLEN

"Stay on your feet, you idiot" was all the communication he received as his guide pulled him along. Johnny Humboldt knew he was back in the United States, but that was about all he knew.

He'd been through a planes, trains, and automobiles journey, beginning with his removal from the shipping container on the dock through his transfer back to his homeland. Much of the time had been spent in a basement location in solitary confinement. Food and water were delivered once a day, with enough to keep him going but nothing more. His confines had again included a toilet but no natural light and four concrete block walls for decor. When they'd finally begun the next leg of his journey, he was grateful that the blindfold blocked out any natural sunlight. He wasn't sure his eyes would ever adjust to sunlight again.

After a long airplane flight, he'd been driven in the back of what he thought was a van for at least three hours. Then back into another cave-like existence for what he estimated was four days. This new location was somehow more peaceful. He heard no city sounds, and occasionally thought he could hear birds chirping. But the darkness and isolation were a constant, consistent with his other stops on the kidnapper's trail. Disorientation had become his new normal.

Several hours earlier he'd been blindfolded, put into what he guessed was an SUV based on the comfort of the seats, and driven to his current location. No light and no conversation. He and the driver had waited for another hour and then gotten out of the vehicle. Now he was being led down a soft, rooted path, still with a blindfold over his eyes and his hands bound behind his back. The footing was uneven, and he stumbled several times. He could feel a strong breeze and some mist on his face—either drizzle or fog.

"We wait here," came the second gruff instruction.

He could hear certain sounds that made him believe he was in the woods someplace, but that was only a guess. No illumination seeped through the fringes of the blindfold, so he assumed it was nighttime.

"Where are we?" Johnny ventured.

"That's why there's a blindfold, asshole."

Johnny smiled in spite of himself. His captor was a real conversationalist with an extensive vocabulary.

He heard a vibrating noise—maybe a text message?

"Walk." More nonconversation.

Johnny noticed some flashes of light around the blindfold as the ground became a concrete pathway. At least now they were someplace—wherever it was.

Then he heard a voice, and his heart sang.

"Johnny . . . is that you?" It was Tamika, her voice a bit uncertain.

"Tamika—yes it's me!" he shouted in excitement.

Then he heard two loud claps of thunder echo across the area—and immediately the *umpff* of something hitting the ground at his feet.

"Tamika? *Tamika*!"

"Holy fuck—" Then there was the sound of shoes hitting the path as his companion dropped the grip on his arm and ran away.

Johnny fell to the ground searching.

All he found was a body, and it wasn't moving.

• • • • •

"Go, go, go!" Jerry Jessup yelled into his headset microphone. He was sitting in a paramedic truck in the south parking lot of the arboretum.

"All teams, move in," he heard Higginbottom shouting from the command center. "Shut the arboretum up tight. Take down the perp who's running from the platform."

"How the hell did someone get in there to take a shot?" Jessup slammed his fist on the counter for emphasis. He turned to his driver. "Let's move out—we need to be there first."

Then to himself he said, *Stay the hell down.*

Bam. Another rifle shot echoed through his headset.

"Where the fuck are those shots coming from?" Higginbottom yelled.

Jessup could hear the commentary as the truck rolled up to a stop off Ellipse Road behind the columns monument.

"One of the drones recorded two flashes from the lower part of the meadow. Only a couple of hundred yards from the platform."

"Team Two, take down the target at the southwest corner of the meadow. Extreme prejudice." Higginbottom was taking charge of the scene. "Team One, secure the podium."

Jessup hopped out of the truck, grabbed a rolling gurney out of the back, and ran up the trail to the scene of the shooting.

"Jessup for Higginbottom." He didn't want to get hit by friendly fire. "I'm almost to the platform. Will take control of the immediate scene."

"Roger that," Higginbottom responded, passing on the information to his field agents.

Rushing up onto the podium, Jessup found Johnny Humboldt hugging what looked like a lifeless body on the ground and screaming for help.

"Jesus, somebody get here!" he yelled.

"Johnny, I've got you. It's Jessup from the FBI. Let me help you with your wrists." He pulled Johnny gently away from the body and cut the ropes away.

He called to the first FBI agent to reach the area. "Get this man to safety. I don't want to lose anyone else." He passed Johnny on to the agent, despite Humboldt's efforts to get back to the body on the ground.

"No, no, no. I'm not leaving her," he cried. The agent seemed to hesitate.

Jessup was insistent. "Get him out of here; that's an order."

Then JJ turned to the body.

Senator Tamika Smith wasn't moving.

• • • • •

Listening to the police scanners, Ely Basof knew shots had been fired at the arboretum and that two victims were down. While he thought there should have been three, the likelihood was that Maaier had reaped as planned. Smith and Humboldt would be dead. Too bad their hired escort had probably escaped, but that would be an easy matter to clean up. His agent hated loose ends and would be sure to take care of that.

While monitoring the arboretum, he'd been more focused on his other teams, coordinating activities over his radio and video connections. As he'd expected, the FBI was well prepared for the RallyAmerica targets, and those teams were all in custody. He was a bit disappointed they hadn't put up a better fight—a good shootout at a prominent Washington, DC, residence would have added to the drama of the moment—but they'd acted as a very effective diversion. The DAO structure provided a great deal of cover, so it would take time for the authorities to figure out who was responsible. At that point, of course, the evidence would point straight at Lee Bowen.

His B^2 partner was done.

So far everything was going perfectly.

• • • • •

Nastya Andropov was almost as happy.

She'd hit her primary target, center mass, with no trouble. Two shots and she was down.

Reaper indeed.

The FSB agent was a bit disappointed that she'd only been able to hit one of her two secondary targets. She'd taken out Humboldt's handler easily enough, but her former ransom prize had fallen on top of his lover too quickly for a shot. Humboldt would live to tell the tale, but she was confident he didn't know anything that could blow back on her.

Fuck, I need to get the hell out of here.

She had no time to consider what might have been. She had already packed and scrubbed down her Airbnb in preparation for a quick departure. Now she disassembled the remaining gear, loaded it into an additional bag, and cleaned up any remaining evidence and DNA. She knew how to dispose of her equipment to eliminate any possible trails. She was headed back to the peace and quiet of a Dutch island that nobody seemed to care about. She'd be shopping at the local bakery and working in the garden within twenty-four hours.

Another mission success to add to her portfolio. And this one would bring redemption to her family, political revenge for Russia, and chaos to America.

United States Senator Tamika Smith was dead.

A fallen democracy was sure to follow.

PART V

THE PLAN EXPOSED

It's amazing what the hard times can reveal
(Have faith that you're not alone)
Like who shows up, who walks away, and who's for real
(Have faith that you're not on your own)
You saved my life, not once but twice
You keep me free from falling
You saved my life, make it all alright
When I don't feel like talking
You make sure I always see the daylight

—Brent Smith, Dave Bassett,
Eric Bass, Zach Myers

CHAPTER 67

PASSINGS

"Jesus, this is so screwed up," she muttered to herself.

Democratic Senator Lillian Kafker was drinking her late-night scotch and soda, reading briefing materials from her staff. She always made a point of preparing for the following day so that she could sleep well knowing she was ready. Dressed in a pink robe with bunny slippers, Kafker loved sitting in her high-back chair in front of a fire at night, even if it was of the fake gas variety. She could hear her husband, James, snoring in their bedroom adjacent to the living room. She picked up her phone and started a classical playlist on her speakers.

The four-term senator from Minnesota was the ranking member of the powerful Senate Finance Committee. The next day the committee would take up consideration of the Fiscal Responsibility Act of 2023, a bill recently passed in the House that would raise the ceiling on the federal government's debt. In the best of times, moving legislation through the Senate was as much art as it was science. Unlike the House of Representatives, where rules strictly governed how legislation moved through the body, the Senate was managed based on tradition, norms, and leadership direction. A good portion of Kafker's job was to navigate that informal process successfully.

Her staff provided a frank assessment of the situation:

The Act passed the House with a bipartisan vote, but the final tally was closer than expected. Leadership recommended and whipped for passage, but there were defectors on both sides. Four amendments were narrowly defeated, and many conservative supporters of those proposals voted against the Act. This group has been increasingly strident in their public opposition,

arguing that they should get more concessions for their support. As a result, we've seen some shifts in the vote count in the Senate. Many of the same amendments will be offered and obviously passage of any changes to the text would require reengagement with the House. Given the X-date estimates from Treasury and the Bipartisan Policy Center, we only have a few days to spare; there is no margin for error to allow for reconsideration.

A cloture vote will be required to end debate on the Act. Our latest whip activity has seen a downward trend in support. We are now just two clear of the three-fifths majority required. Our strong recommendation is that we report the Act out of Committee immediately to head off any continued erosion in support. Failure to reach cloture and approve the measure would be devastating for the financial community and the US economy. The knock-on effects around the world are difficult to forecast, but a global depression cannot be ruled out.

None of this was new news to Senator Kafker. Unlike the House, a filibuster in the Senate could block action on any specific piece of legislation. To avoid the long-ago process of a senator standing up and talking for hours on end, the Senate had established a process where a vote could be taken to end all debate. That cloture vote required "three-fifths of those duly chosen and sworn in" to vote *aye*, meaning sixty votes were required if the full complement of senators was available to vote. Ties could be broken by the vice president if he or she were presiding over the chamber.

Kafker took a sip from her drink. She hated this entire theater of the absurd. It was a terrible process that reflected the worst of governing in Washington. The debt ceiling had been created in 1917 during the elevated spending of World War I and had been raised over ninety times since that era. The issue had become increasingly political over the past twenty years, with both sides making a regular charade of the vehicle but continuing to raise it. The underlying question of spending exceeding revenue could no longer be addressed. Nobody wanted to face the uncomfortable truths—and certainly no senator wanted to explain to their voters that the situation was a flashing red light that could lead to disaster.

A noise to her right made the senator turn from the documents and look up, thinking her husband was there. "We never seem to face the music," she said out loud.

And those were the last words from Senator Lillian Kafker.

• • • • •

"Site clear, stand by."

The stately house in Bethesda, Maryland, had been cased for several weeks. Dealing with a mark that was highly habitual made the assignment easier than they'd originally expected. Bedroom lights out at 9:30 p.m., firelight until 11:00 p.m. Then silence. Military precision provided a road map for the enemy.

The four-man team and their driver waited silently two blocks away in a parked van with black windows and no plates. Each member checked their equipment, seemingly going through the mission mentally. By their standards this was a low-risk operation, but working in the United States raised the stakes significantly.

Few words were spoken, and only in English. Professionals came prepared.

"Move out."

The words from their scout observing the target while on a casual walk sent everyone into action. Night vision goggles were engaged as the van came alive and moved down the street. The rear door was quietly opened, and three members stepped out. Like ninjas of old, they quickly crept bent over across the street, between parked cars, and up the driveway, which was lined with hedges shielding them from prying eyes. They saw the security cameras, but knew they'd been neutralized as soon as the all-clear sign had been given.

Using hand signals, one man knelt down and stood guard at the base of the driveway. The remaining two men moved up the steps to the back door and picked the lock, again knowing that the security system had been deactivated. As they crept into the kitchen, the light from the fireplace required them to turn off their night vision goggles. One of them snuck down a back hall to position himself outside the bedroom.

The remaining man walked catlike into the living room, pulled a syringe from his vest, and quickly administered the shot just as the target saw him. Joined by the guard from the bedroom, they carefully lifted the subject out of the chair and moved to the back door, now held open by the man watching their six. They retraced their tracks to the van, which had backed into the driveway. The doors opened, the package went in, and the team drove away.

No runs, no hits, no errors.

Just another US senator removed from the playing field.

• • • • •

Ely Basof took off his headset with great satisfaction. The Optimus groups had executed their missions as planned, with each event going off on schedule. And while there were some minor hiccups, his trained teams had adapted well. The various field units were transporting their packages to specific locations so that hired locals could orchestrate the rest of the mission.

Killing Senator Kafker had been the riskiest operation, because she was at home in Bethesda in a residential area. Once that mission was complete, Basof turned his attention to the other two targets. Minority leader Senator Dana Golub was taken at a small, private airport in some godforsaken place in North Dakota. He was expecting to hitch a late-night ride back to DC on a donor's private plane. Instead, he got a one-way final trip to the main reception of the state capitol tower in Bismarck. Just like being sent to a gulag in Siberia—except the senator and his sponsor were never coming back.

Golub's Democratic counterpart, Majority Leader Mike Hermansen from California, had gone on an overnight fishing trip in the Chesapeake Bay. The amphibious assault on the boat had caught everyone aboard in their sleep. They weren't expecting a boarding party. The captain and his first mate were killed and dropped overboard, along with a woman who was in bed with Hermansen. Basof knew she wasn't his wife. Unlucky for the mistress, but at least the senator's family would never find out.

Basof's equipment would be picked up by another courier. But he still spent an hour thoroughly cleaning his Airbnb rental to ensure he had removed any trace of his presence. Once he was satisfied, he rode the elevator down two floors to another rental. He punched in the key code number and entered. He'd rented this apartment for Maaier and intentionally put it in the same building, in part so he could keep an eye on his agent and protect her up until the shooting. Now that she'd been successful, having access to her apartment was even more important.

For whatever reason, she suspected him of treason, and he couldn't let that get back to their handlers in Moscow. He knew she was well connected within the FSB and wasn't confident he could survive a challenge from her. He was sure the FBI would trace the communications between the remote sniper rifle and her apartment. So now he entered her Airbnb and left a few breadcrumbs in the rooms she had certainly carefully sanitized.

With the evening complete, four key Senate leaders from both parties had been neutralized and would be found lying at rest in their state capitol buildings. Team Optimus would be out of the country before the sun was up. And that sunrise would bring newspaper, podcast, and social media headlines that would rock the country as never before.

With a bit more encouragement, just maybe the government would take the nation over the brink.

• • • • •

With the help of another FBI agent, Jerry Jessup loaded the gurney carrying Senator Tamika Smith into the back of the paramedic vehicle. It was less than five minutes after the shooting at the Capitol Columns of the arboretum. He climbed into the back of the truck with the body and allowed the agent to close the doors behind him. The two raps on the back panels confirmed the doors were secured.

"Let's move," he called out to the familiar face that looked back at him.

He checked his watch. It was 23:15. His medical examiner would know exactly what to do. "Put the siren on and get us to the FBI morgue. We have to hurry."

Smith getting taken down by the sniper only increased the urgency of the plan.

CHAPTER 68

POSTMORTEM

Johnny Humboldt sat in silence glancing up at a digital clock on the wall. It was 1:30 a.m. He couldn't really focus on anything. None of it seemed to matter. The bright lights hurt his eyes. He closed them tightly and tried to forget.

He'd been quickly evacuated from the arboretum crime scene, given some basic first aid, and driven back to FBI Headquarters in the J. Edgar Hoover Building in downtown DC. Then he was spirited into the tower through a basement entrance and put in what seemed like a service elevator to the eleventh floor. Now he was sitting in a conference room attached to a large office, waiting for something. He wasn't sure what was next and didn't really care.

Tamika was dead.

He'd had several near-death experiences himself and had always assumed he would be the one to go. Somehow, he had survived a near miss on 9/11, recovered from getting thrown from a crashing airplane, and returned from a harrowing kidnapping. His catlike ability to cheat death was poor consolation for the loss of the love of his life. He stared at the sandwiches and drinks they'd left for him on the table, but despite being incredibly hungry, he had no appetite.

How could Tamika be dead?

Since the first time he'd met her from a hospital bed after the plane crash, he'd assumed she was invincible. Tamika had been a tough-as-nails fighter who gave no quarter, whether that was during her track-and-field career, service in the military, or her floor battles in the Senate. The truth was that nobody really wanted to tangle with her. He'd been intimidated to ask her on a date, feeling he should salute on their first outing.

But then he'd discovered Tamika's real secret. For all her tough exterior, her commitment to her country, and her disciplined ethics—beneath all the armor—Tamika was a warm, compassionate, and flawed woman of immense tenderness. That combination of tough exterior and sweet-hearted soul made her seem indomitable. In fact, invincible.

And now she was gone.

The glass doors to the meeting room swung open and two men walked through—Jerry Jessup, who had pulled him away from Tamika on the platform, and another man he recognized but couldn't place.

"Our apologies, Mr. Humboldt, for rushing you off the platform and up here without any explanation. I hope you can appreciate we did it for your own safety. Just to be clear, I'm Jerry Jessup, and I'm the deputy director of the FBI. My colleague is the lead field agent on your kidnapping . . . and Tamika's murder. Agent Franklin Higginbottom."

So that confirmed it. She was dead.

"Why didn't you let me stay with her? I needed to be there for her." Johnny could feel the pain in his own words.

Jessup wiped his hand through his hair. "Look, I'm sorry about that, but it was an active shooting zone, and I couldn't risk anyone else getting hurt."

Johnny didn't know what to say, so he took a deep breath and simply nodded.

Jessup continued, "First, let me express my deep sorrow at your loss. Senator Smith was a personal friend and fellow service member whom I deeply respected. I know from experience that there are no words that will make this easier. Her death is a tragedy for the country and a stain on this agency. This should never have happened."

Johnny had heard Tamika talk about Jessup several times. Usually, she'd been bitching about something he'd said or done, but she always did it in a way that made it clear she respected him.

"Thank you, Director." He paused, feeling the urge to lash out again but realized he just didn't have the energy. "I'm sure your teams did everything they could to protect us."

"Appreciate you saying that, but we're digging in to understand what happened."

"Did you catch the shooter?"

He noticed the two men exchange glances.

"Actually, there wasn't a shooter in the area," Higginbottom began.

What? Johnny had no idea what he meant by that.

"We found an autonomous firing nest across the meadow from the podium. The perp surrounded it with warning tape and traffic cones, as if the arboretum staff had closed off the area for restoration. Unfortunately, nobody searched the area." The regret was all over the agent's face.

"You're telling me the person who shot Tamika did it by remote control?"

"Yes—we have our digital team looking to trace the signals," Jessup jumped in. "Hopefully, we can find the source location and go from there."

"That means I was just the bait." Johnny could feel the combination of anger and shame welling up again. "Shit—all she had to do was stay away and she'd still be alive."

Jessup continued, "You and I both know that wasn't her style. The only thing she wanted was for you to be safe. She gave this to me before she left for the arboretum. She asked me to deliver it to you . . . if that became necessary."

Johnny took the envelope, looking at it like it was infected. How could he open it and read Tamika's last words to him? He'd spent the last six weeks hoping and dreaming for a tear-filled reunion with her. To feel the warmth of her hug and the touch of her lips. Now all he had was an envelope with her final words.

And it's my fault she's dead. A knock on the glass door interrupted his thoughts.

"What?" came Jessup's angry reply to the intrusion.

"Sorry, sir, but this couldn't wait." A young agent stepped partially into the room.

"And?" Johnny could hear the anger of a military leader in his voice.

"There's been three more."

"Three more what?" Now the tone included fatigue.

"Incidents . . . sir."

Jessup looked at Higginbottom. "I thought we stopped those other attacks?"

"I just confirmed it," replied the field agent. "We did. All three financial regulators are safe, and we have suspects in custody."

The agent at the door cut in. "These are different, sir."

Johnny couldn't imagine what that meant, but Jessup took a deep breath and stood up.

"Mr. Humboldt, Agent Higginbottom will have a few more questions. The full debriefing can wait until you've had a chance to eat and rest. Again, my condolences."

And with that, he walked out.

CHAPTER 69
REVELATIONS

"What you're telling me, Agent Higginbottom, is that we went for the head fake."

Jerry Jessup had been up all night. He wasn't in the mood for the usual friendly banter. Not after what had happened.

"Sir, we followed the evidence we had. We're quite certain that Lee Bowen tried to organize a financial collapse by attacking key economic leaders. And we stopped him."

"Great . . . and now the leadership in the Senate is wiped out, including our friend Senator Tamika Smith. Are you trying to tell me that this was some coincidental sneak attack?" He left off the part about them not having enough evidence to charge Bowen.

"Sir, I'm not trying to tell you anything. I'm just pointing out that we had no warning, no chatter, no hints that anyone else was in danger. Without any intel, I don't know how we or the Capitol Police can protect all five hundred thirty-five members of Congress." The frustration showed on his face.

Jessup let out a sigh. "Shit, Higgs, I'm just tired and pissed off. Take me through what we know."

They were sitting in Jessup's office, away from the cacophonous noise of the command center that was tracking every possible lead. It was 8 a.m. DC time, some three hours after Senator Kafker had been found dead in the capitol rotunda in St. Paul, Minnesota. The subsequent reports from North Dakota, California, and Washington made it clear that this was a coordinated attack. A conspiracy of the highest order. And Jessup knew that the FBI, and especially himself, would be held responsible.

Higginbottom pulled up images on the screens that lined the side wall of Jessup's office.

"Sir, I hate to say this, but it's almost like performance art. Four different state capitols, each with a casket in the rotunda or reception area."

"Christ, they're identical."

"Like they were copied from a design on Etsy. Caskets in exactly the same location, flowers arranged in the same way, lighting added to set the mood. Each with a typewritten note. Totally spooky."

"What was on the notes?"

Higginbottom pulled up a crime scene photo. "The same at each location."

THIS IS WHAT HAPPENS TO THOSE

WHO AREN'T TRUE PATRIOTS

Jessup rolled his eyes. "Such BS. How'd they get in?"

"In each case, security alarms and cameras were shut off for precisely twenty minutes, again with an uncanny sense of precision. As a van begins to pull up, the camera goes out before we can see anything or anyone. When the cameras come back on, the van is gone. This was professionally organized and executed. Sick—but efficient and effective."

"Show me Olympia." Jessup really wanted to know how they'd pulled that off.

"This one is only different because of the way they procured the body."

"I delivered her"—Jessup paused with effort—"Senator Smith to the FBI morgue myself from the arboretum."

"Correct. And then they stole the body."

"From the morgue?" *The FBI morgue.*

"Same MO. Cameras and security system go off for eleven minutes and then poof. She's gone from the morgue."

"Then they flew the body to Seattle?" Given the timing and the time zones, this was a precision operation.

"Presumably. Next thing we know, she's lying in state underneath the Olympia rotunda."

Jessup took a long look at the visage under the lights in the Washington State capitol building. The face bore a haunting resemblance to Tamika

Smith's expressions whenever she'd visited him in his office. Defiant, ambitious, committed. She seemed to be smirking at him, telling him she was right all along. Indeed, her worst fears had been vindicated. This wasn't an attack over money. It was about democracy and world hegemony.

Jessup didn't believe in coincidences, but he also didn't see how the attempts on the finance jockeys fit into the operation. The Lee Bowens of the world might be rich, but they were incapable of something this intricate and surgical. The logistics involved in the entire operation were difficult to comprehend. Moreover, someone had tied the Tamika Smith assassination into some broader attack on the US government. There were only a couple of groups with the resources, motivation, and capabilities to do that. Bryce Roscovitch and Mufasa had suspected this all along. Now they all had to deal with the reality.

The FSB had executed four American leaders on US soil.

There would be hell to pay.

CHAPTER 70

JOY, SORROW, FEAR

"Phoenix, Nathan, wake up! Hurry!"

The screaming call from her mom brought Phoenix upright in her bed quickly. A bit disoriented after a strange series of dreams, her first thought was that her mom was in trouble. She threw back the covers, jumped out of bed, and was through the door to the stairs leading below without grabbing a robe or slippers.

"In here," called her mom from her office.

Phoenix rushed around a corner to see her mom crying, looking at her PC. And then she let out a yell as Nathan also rushed into the room.

"Dad!" they cried together. Her father was as big as he could be on a twenty-six-inch screen. Phoenix realized her mom's wet eyes were tears of joy. Her own reaction was a jumble of thoughts and questions.

"Oh my God, Dad, it's so good to see you. Where are you? Are you OK? When can we see you? I love you."

Nathan jumped in, "How'd you get away? We thought you'd been hurt and almost drowned." Phoenix was surprised. Apparently, he knew more about the situation than he'd ever let on.

Her dad gave them a strained smile. "You can't imagine how good it is to see you all. And I can't wait to hold you tight tonight. I was just telling your mom that I'm fine. I've lost some weight but no worse for wear. I'm in an FBI office in Washington, DC."

Phoenix found herself bawling, hugging her mom and Nathan, and wishing she could teleport to DC immediately.

"Ohhh . . . Dad, I've prayed for this day—we've all prayed for this day . . . and now that it's come, I don't know what to say."

"I know, Phoenix. I was thinking about all of you every moment, wishing there was some way I could tell you I was OK. I've been locked up without any way to contact you. This is the first real conversation I've had with anyone in six weeks."

Margaret repeated Nathan's question. "How did you get away? Did you escape or did the FBI free you?"

Phoenix quickly realized her dad had ducked the question the first time and now his face went dark, and he turned away to wipe his eyes.

"I don't know how to tell you this, so I'm just going to be straight." Again, he paused to rub his sleeve across his face.

"Tamika made an agreement with the high school shooter to exchange me for her. But it was a setup. The assassin shot Tamika during the switch." He let it hang there.

"Is she OK?" Phoenix said, feeling the fear well up inside her.

"Honey, I'm sorry. Tamika is dead."

"No, no, no, that can't be!" Phoenix cried. She looked from the screen to Nathan to her mom. "She can't be dead." She got up to run from the room.

But then she felt a giant hug from her mom, heard some sobbing words of comfort from her father, and felt the trembling of Nathan's body as he joined the hug.

As reality began to sink in, another thought rose up and engulfed her. She'd sent the assassin's Twitter DM to Tamika. If she'd just gone to the FBI or told her mother, none of this would have happened. Why had she been so stupid?

Tamika was dead. And it was her fault.

• • • • •

Lee Bowen was happy but very confused.

It was Wednesday evening, a day after RallyAmerica's aborted plan to attack the leaders of the financial system. Bowen was sitting in a cubicle in his WeWork office on Park Boulevard in Palo Alto trying to comprehend what had happened in the last twenty-four hours.

He'd placed his bets in the stock and commodities markets over the previous three weeks. Everything was in place to take advantage of a steep securities sell-off that would make him and his RallyAmerica investors hundreds of millions of dollars. But when he'd logged into the DAO the previous night, there was no feedback from the mission teams. In fact, there was no communication or activity at all.

That silence was not a good thing.

Now a sleepless night and day later, miraculously all was well. While he still had no report on the RallyAmerica missions, four US senators had been murdered. The stock market had reacted predictably with both the Dow and S&P 500 reporting one-day declines of more than 30 percent. It was the single worst day in US stock market history.

Except for Lee Bowen and RallyAmerica.

He was still tabulating the results from various accounts and systems, but the outcome had exceeded his own lofty expectations. This was clearly what it meant to win.

The panic on Wall Street wasn't an isolated financial event. It reflected an explosion of worry and angst across the country. Bowen scanned a few headlines to gauge the situation.

The New York Times led with "4 Senators Dead; National Security at Risk," while *The Wall Street Journal* went with the economic angle, "Murders Send Economy Adrift; Recession Fears Rise."

"Senate Left Leaderless and Adrift as Debt Limit Looms," screamed *The Washington Post.*

Bowen thought the social media headlines were the most extreme, and for him, the best. Twitter was rife with stories blaming the attack on both Antifa and the alt-right movements. The most retweeted post claimed that this was part of an FBI-supported conspiracy to overthrow the government. People were feeding on each other's fears. It was even more chaos than he'd imagined in his original plan.

And yet his stomach was gnawing at him as he scrolled through posts on his PC.

If his RallyAmerica plan had failed—something he now assumed—how could he have succeeded anyway? He didn't believe in coincidences, and this would have been one whopper dose of good luck. His mind shifted to the FBI search warrant, wondering if they'd somehow figured out his plan to attack financial leaders. If they had, they were on the RallyAmerica trail, and his risk profile had escalated.

He leaned back in his office chair and contemplated his options. On reflection, he only had two courses of action. He could close out his positions at the opening bell the next morning and execute his plan to exit stage left. That would maximize his safety but likely reduce his financial gain, as dumping everything at once wasn't a great financial strategy. The alternative was to let things ride for a day or two and slowly exit the market by the end of the week or early on Monday. He brought up the futures data on various market indices—Thursday was going to be another massive down day. Another chance for him to capitalize on the fear and chaos.

He made a decision, shut down his computer, and walked out to his car.

He was in for the big win. He decided to let it all ride.

CHAPTER 71
OPPORTUNITY KNOCKS

Senator Ronald Stumper was ecstatic as he read the papers on Thursday morning. The news was a capstone to an unprecedented week of tragedy and death.

The Senate murders, in particular of Senator Tamika Smith, had sent shock waves through the halls of Congress, and indeed across the country. She had been loved by some and feared by others, but respected by most everyone. Except Stumper. He detested Smith and everything she stood for—and was never very careful about hiding that fact. When he'd been asked in his staff meeting on Wednesday how they should respond to her death, he said, "As far as I'm concerned, good riddance." And he meant it.

The morning before Smith's death, he'd received another blackmail notice giving him specific directives. Legislative instructions. His first reaction had been disbelief. There was no way he could carry out the extortionist's demands. Even if he agreed with the idea—and he wasn't convinced on that point—he just didn't have that type of power or control in the Senate. Whichever alt-right group was driving this train was misguided at best.

But the murders of Senators Hermansen, Golub, and Kafker, along with the unrest spreading across the country, changed the calculus in the Senate in several important ways. First, the leadership on both sides of the aisle was severely weakened. The majority leader, the minority leader, the chair of the Finance Committee, and the leader of the Lincoln Coalition were now all dead. Given his long service in the Senate, Stumper realized he could play an outsized role in how the legislative body ruled.

Second, at least for a short period, the Democrats did not control the Senate majority and had little chance of getting the sixty votes necessary to achieve cloture on any debate. Given the four deaths, other leaders could now drive the chamber. Stumper's challenge was to galvanize them to action—indeed, immediate action—because if they waited, there would be time to replace the murdered senators, elect new leadership, and return balance to the senior body in Congress. Whatever he might feel about the policy implications, Stumper personally could not allow that to happen. He had precise instructions to follow if he hoped to keep his personal proclivities out of the public eye.

Finally, the stock market free fall provided additional opportunity. Investors were taking a bath, and there was no end in sight. The professionals could withstand the pressure, but for the average person with a 401(k) who was retiring—and in Stumper's world that meant most voters—this was a disaster. He could play off that fear.

He pulled out his cell phone and called his chief of staff.

"Dyer, get everyone together in the office." Stumper looked at his watch. "It's 7:30 right now; I want everyone there by 8:15."

"Yes, sir. I'll try. Can I give them an idea on the topic?"

Stumper ignored him. "Get the communications team rolling on social media. I want the message put out that we are shocked by this week's tragic deaths and will begin an immediate investigation into how the FBI and Secret Service failed to protect our leaders."

"Sir, I think you mean the Capitol Police."

"Sure—you can throw them under the bus while we're at it. And I also want a more important message communicated: that while we mourn, we will carry out our duty to govern the country even in this crisis. We will honor our fallen comrades by continuing the work they've begun, especially given the financial crisis we're facing."

"Sir—"

"Shut up and listen, Dyer. It's now our time. A gift from the Almighty. We can finally take action without the bleeding hearts blocking our way. We can do something that will meaningfully change the country."

"I'm confused, sir."

Stumper felt the adrenaline beginning to flow in earnest and stood up to look across the DC landscape. This was now his territory to control.

"Jesus, Dyer, use just a bit of imagination. The Senate leadership is gone, I'm effectively in charge, and we have important legislating to do. Tradition and protocol won't get in the way."

And Stumper was highly motivated to pursue a very specific outcome.

CHAPTER 72

A BLAZED TRAIL

"Dude, you've got to pull your head out of your ass."

Mufasa's message was staring Bryce Roscovitch in the face, but he couldn't see it. He was in mourning for a second time—and again, he felt like he was to blame. His father had been killed at the Lincoln Memorial using explosives Bryce had supplied. Sure, this time he hadn't provided any arms to the killers, but his failure to unravel the scheme in time to save Tamika cut him to the core. He'd seen plenty of signs, walked his fingers through FSB records, and identified the assassin. But all of it had been for naught. He relived the failures over and over in his mind.

Up to and during the most recent attacks, Bryce and Mufasa had continued their deep dive chasing bad guys into cryptoland and across the dark web. Now it was Thursday, some thirty-six hours after Tamika's death, and even together, these two digital savants hadn't found the answers they needed.

Mufasa intervened a second time, perhaps out of concern for Bryce, but certainly out of frustration.

"What's done is done. We can't let someone come into our house, murder our leaders, and then disappear. That's just not our way. There must be some evidence from the attacks—we can still get these bastards if we move quickly."

After walking over to the whiteboard and tracing his hands back and forth across the various lines connecting different elements of the puzzle, Bryce smashed his hand against the board in frustration.

Thwack! The sound echoed across his basement enclave as the board pivoted on its wheels. The noise surprised him but also seemed to pull Bryce back from the dark hole he was facing.

"You're fucking right," he wrote back to Mufasa. "What do we know about the arboretum attack?"

And within two hours, as if Moses had staked his staff into the Red Sea, they broke through to the other side of the problem. Answers began to flow.

With some straightforward hacking, they backtracked the digital signals that had activated the sniper rifle that killed Senator Tamika Smith. What should have been a deeply masked IP address was actually a moderately protected digital signal with several access points. Bryce and Mufasa located a physical address for the shooter's nest without too much trouble. The FBI would know just what to do with that information.

The second part of the breakthrough didn't involve technical skills at all. The leader of the team that tried to kidnap the secretary of the Treasury had slipped up . . . or maybe he was trying to flip . . . or maybe he was just bragging. During FBI interrogation, he claimed that they were all part of a larger movement. Something he called *RallyAmerica*. The FBI team couldn't find any evidence of any organization or group with that moniker in their databases or security information. Nothing official nor anything in what the intelligence community refers to as "chatter." The alt-right and far left had all kinds of formal and informal associations, but none of them were called RallyAmerica.

As Bryce listened to the taped interrogation, he went back to his somewhat wounded whiteboard. They had a series of traces that overlapped. These included the technical work to enable the school shooting as well as the early email threats to Tamika Smith. This all seemed straightforward and had led them to Lee Bowen and his financial plot. Clearly he'd used some cryptocurrency to pay for all this activity. There had to be a parent account for those payments. Bryce had seen the note from Agent Kalen Chen about how they traced these in financial fraud cases. He sent a message to Mufasa.

"What if someone was using blockchain to make it look like nobody is in charge? If there's no leader, who's responsible?"

"Well . . . organizations are formed using blockchain. Maybe an individual could hide behind that."

Bryce was tracking this. "I've been around the DAO block a few times. They have a sordid history as investment vehicles."

Mufasa came back quickly. "What if it was used for more than investing?"

"Could you form an organization to commit crimes?" Bryce was skeptical but considered the possibilities.

"DAOs have anonymous voting for investment activities. People could vote on crimes to commit." Mufasa thought more like a criminal.

"OK, but how would Bowen control what actually was happening?" Bryce was more practical.

"He'd just have to be the largest *investor* in the DAO."

"And then he could approve only the activities that he wanted." Bryce finished the thought.

"That would be genius." Mufasa was clearly impressed. "Now all we have to do is find the DAO."

Bryce was already firing up his system.

Because he knew the name of the organization.

• • • • •

"This is the FBI. We have a warrant for your arrest. Open the door slowly with your hands in plain sight."

Agent Franklin Higginbottom shouted out commands as his team began their raid on an Airbnb rental in northeast DC, just south of the arboretum. He checked the door for triggers—he wasn't going to fuck around anymore.

"Knock it in."

The door splintered with a crash as the FBI SWAT team in full assault gear burst through the doors, yelling out commands and taking up their positions.

The apartment was empty.

"All clear, sir," came the crisp response from the squad leader.

Higginbottom didn't wait for an invitation and stepped inside. Mufasa and his technical partner had traced the digital signals from Tamika Smith's shooting back to the apartment. That part had been relatively easy—at least for them. It had been almost forty-eight hours since the shooting, so Higginbottom was certain that the perp had long left the location, but at this point, he was taking no chances. The assault team was an extra precaution against booby traps or an unexpected encounter.

With the coast clear, he waved the forensics team in. "All right, everyone, let's dig in. I want you to scrub every inch of this place. Nothing is too small. Assume that anything you find is significant." He knew they needed something—anything—to get on the trail of their assassin.

After four hours of a detailed needle-in-the-haystack search of the apartment and a full forensics scrub, Higginbottom was in a much better mood. He dialed Jessup.

"Director, our perp either underestimated us or just got a bit sloppy. The shooter left a pad of paper. Nothing on it, but she left some trace DNA. If we can capture her, we have all the evidence we need." He was assuming this was their Dutch enemy.

"That's great news, Higgs, well done." Jessup didn't give out compliments often. "But any clues on where she might be?" OK . . . he usually wasn't satisfied either. Higginbottom had to laugh to himself—he shouldn't have expected anything less from his boss.

But he'd intentionally buried the lede. "That's the best part," Higginbottom said. "There was a ferry ticket stub buried under the plastic liner of the wastebasket. I've searched the web. That ferry only goes to one place."

And ferries had all kinds of cameras.

CHAPTER 73

REMEMBRANCES

"I know she'll always be there for us."

Johnny thought he heard a hint of grief in General Frank Smith's words. It was Friday morning, and they were together for breakfast in a café close to the Senate offices. The general was formal and stoic, as if he was still in the military informing a family that their son or daughter wasn't coming back. It was more painful given that he was dealing with the loss of his only remaining child. Johnny and the general had never been close—not for any lack of respect, but just because there'd never been a need or an opportunity to develop much of a relationship. Maybe that would change now.

"General, I don't even know what to say. I've never had much of a faith, but I believed in her. I just assumed she would always be there to save me. To save us. To save the country." He'd hoped to keep his emotions in check but could feel the tears forming and heard the cracking in his voice. *Get a grip*, he told himself. *Don't make it any harder on her father.*

He noted that the general seemed to be in complete control—in fact he showed no real signs of any stress at all. Johnny marveled at his composure.

"Your kidnapping and the picture they sent of you was more painful than anything she'd ever experienced. And that is saying something." Frank Smith took a sip of coffee and looked straight at Johnny. "She would have done anything for you."

"But why did she agree to the exchange? There must have been some other way."

"I think you know the answer to that in your heart. She loved you and she loved her country. Nothing was going to get in the way of that."

Her letter had essentially said the same thing. After his FBI debriefing, Johnny had gone back to her apartment in Alexandria. Without turning on any lights or bothering to close the door fully, he went over to the couch where he and Tamika had sat, talked, and loved many times. Looking out over Arlington Cemetery and the Air Force memorial, Johnny finally opened the note. It was classic Tamika—apologizing for her failings, always thinking of others, hopeful for Johnny's future. He read about her love for him three times. Johnny had fixated on the last sentence in the letter.

Eternally here for you.

What the hell was he supposed to do with that? He'd thought he'd have an eternity with Tamika and now there was nothing. His heart was gutted, his spirit broken, and his soul savaged by what had been taken. Anger was there too. Certainly at the assassin who had shot her, but if he was honest, also with Tamika for taking the risk. What good was it to be in love with a martyr?

The general interrupted his thoughts. "How's your family doing? It must have been great to hold them in your arms."

"They got here late Wednesday night. Jessup arranged for special transport. It was great to hug them tight."

"And how are they . . . doing?"

"I don't know what to say, General. I'm barely keeping my head above water, so helping them grieve isn't easy. Phoenix is somehow convinced that the exchange and Tamika's death was her fault. Nathan just seems numb to it all—I know he loved Tamika too, but he's at an age where expressing emotions isn't easy."

"And your ex-wife?" Johnny was surprised to hear him ask.

"Her head and heart are a jumble. I know she's grateful that I'm alive and well—especially given everything the kids need. And despite the complexity, she liked Tamika and is sad that she's gone." Johnny was processing all of this in real time in his head.

The general looked at him gravely. "Johnny, is it OK if I give you some advice? We don't know each other all that well, but I've been through so much loss, both professionally and personally. I will add that you may not like what I have to say."

"Of course, sir—I need all the help I can get."

"See, that's just it. You will need help, but for right now, you have to be the strong one. The courageous one. The rock they can all lean on. Your time to grieve will come, and I'll encourage you to get help then. But in this moment, you have to stand tall, support others, and honor Tamika's memory. What would she want you to do?"

Johnny just nodded. He knew exactly what Tamika would want done.

• • • • •

The first all-hands meeting with Tamika's Senate and Lincoln Coalition teams later that day was equally gut-wrenching. Johnny reserved a large conference room, since he couldn't imagine them gathering in Tamika's office, and the small staff bullpen area just wasn't big enough.

The meeting room was plain vanilla Washington, DC. A large table ran down the center of the space with two entry doors on one side and a wall of windows on the opposite side. There were a few portraits of unremarkable government leaders on the wall. Johnny entered after everyone had assembled and went to the head of the table. People clearly were mourning their leader and Johnny's own personal loss. But they also seemed conflicted, given Johnny's survival. Mostly, he saw a bunch of heads bowed down.

"Good afternoon, everyone." He was going to do everything he could to live up to the general's command.

He received mutters of "Good afternoon" in return.

"Look, there's no easy way to have this conversation. But we need to talk about it to begin healing." He certainly needed that for himself.

Silence.

Well, I knew this would be difficult, he thought.

Johnny continued. "OK. Look—I wish I wasn't here." He paused for effect and to control his emotions. "I wish that Tamika was here with you and that the sniper had hit me instead. I will live with her sacrifice for the rest of my life." Saying it bluntly somehow helped him summon some fortitude.

Murmurs.

"But we all have to recognize that Tamika is . . ." He took a moment to correct himself. "Was wired differently than the rest of us. She believed deeply in service and sacrifice. I know the FBI tried to talk her out of the hostage exchange, and she refused. We all know how stubborn she was about things like that."

Nods around the table, with a few smiles.

"She showed us the way. We must honor her sacrifice. She wouldn't want sympathies and a bunch of moping faces. She'd expect each and every one of us to mourn in our own way—but on our own time. She'd want us to do our jobs. She'd want us to keep the country on course." He opened both hands in front of him, as if inviting them to join him. He saw some people begin to lean in.

After a heartbeat or two, Mark Cavanagh jumped in. "Johnny, first, I'm grateful that you're safe. I can't imagine what the last month was like. It's a miracle you survived."

Johnny just nodded.

"But to everyone else here . . . Johnny's totally right. Tamika would be pissed if she saw us acting this way. She didn't expect anything from her service other than the satisfaction of doing the job right. And that's what we need to do."

Johnny took a moment to scan each of the faces in the room, searching for their inner strength and courage.

Finally he said, "And together, that's exactly what we're all going to do."

CHAPTER 74

GOVERNMENT AT WORK

"What do you think is going to happen?" Johnny asked Cavanagh. They were tuned in to the C-SPAN feed late in the day on Friday, watching activities on the Senate floor with a few other staffers jammed into Johnny's office.

Tamika's replacement had not been appointed—in fact her funeral hadn't even been scheduled yet—so her team was still busy at work, supporting the citizens of Washington State. None of the other senators had been replaced yet either. North Dakota required a special election that would take weeks to organize, and the governors in Minnesota, Washington, and California believed they should wait a few days before making an appointment out of respect to the fallen.

"Great question," Cavanagh responded, shrugging his shoulders in a "who the hell knows" expression. "The Senate doesn't have any written procedures for this circumstance. The Ds control more seats but three of those are now vacant, so the Rs have more sitting senators—and therefore more votes. But the minority leader is also dead, so even they are down one seat and don't have a designated leader."

"Exactly what I feared. A vacuum someone could fill. Someone who might not have the best interests of the country in mind." The pounding of the gavel brought Johnny back to the C-SPAN broadcast.

The camera was set head-on to the elevated president's podium, with a large, marble-faced counter beneath it filled with officials completing various tasks on PCs. Democratic and Republican Party officials were seated at the bottom level with Senate pages located on either side available to act as runners and gophers. The Senate walls were a combination of royal blue and yellow, and there were no windows; skylights provided the only natural light.

The Senate was old school, complete with spittoons still on the floor. A large blue drapery with red fringes hung behind the podium, flanked by two maroon marble columns on each side. A US flag was in its stand to the left of the podium, while the blue Senate flag was on the right. Johnny noted the black drapes on four of the chairs—each with a flower—the traditional way the Senate honored active members who had died.

The flowers brought Johnny another rush of emotion. He turned away, covering the tears with a fake sneeze.

"Bless you," came three responses.

"Mark, turn up the volume. They're doing some procedural wrangling. Normally I wouldn't care, but this makes me nervous." Johnny had heard just enough rumors to be worried about how the Senate was going to adjust to its unprecedented new circumstances.

After turning up the volume, Cavanagh said, "It looks like a pretty intense conversation between the parliamentarian and two senators."

"Oh God, it's that blowhard Stumper. I can't believe he's in a position of power now." Johnny was disgusted—and he knew Tamika would have been too.

Cavanagh looked like he was doing calculus in his head. "The Senate puts a high premium on seniority. With the . . . vacancies . . . he's the leader of the Republican caucus. Since the Republicans have more votes, he's effectively the acting majority leader."

"It's a coup—he's trying to take over the Senate." Which Johnny knew would have horrified Tamika.

"The real problem is if he pushes the debt limit bill," Cavanagh said. "I've done the math. Given the absentees and the lack of leadership, it might not pass. That would be his crowning achievement. And there's not a damn thing we can do about it."

Johnny wasn't going to give in. "Look, the vote can't come up for twenty-four hours, and it's likely they'll wait until Monday. In the meantime, we still own the agenda for the Lincoln Coalition. We need to pull together our talking points and hit the phones and the hallways. I want everyone on notice that this bill *must* pass. It's up to us to make the case."

Because if it didn't pass, Tamika's sacrifice would have been for naught.

• • • • •

Ronald Stumper was totally in his element. If there was one thing he knew, it was the boring but important rules and traditions around the Senate machinery. He'd won the discussion with the parliamentarian. As the Senate was called to order, he was quick to rise.

The Senate's presiding officer, referred to as the president pro tempore, was a Democratic senator from New York who was serving in the role because the US vice president was not in the chamber. "The gentleman from Texas has the floor," Stumper said, nodding to acknowledge the president's invitation to speak.

He intentionally took his time moving to the podium. "Mr. President," he began in a deep, serious voice, facing the podium platform. It was a bit of manufactured drama, since over sixty of his fellow senators weren't even in the chamber given the events of the past few days and the scheduled business on the agenda.

"I'd like my fellow senators and those in the gallery to stand and join me in a moment of silence to honor our fallen comrades." While he had no warm feelings for any of the murdered senators—and in fact hated several of them—he knew he had to begin with some type of memorial note to achieve his objectives.

There was a shuffle of chairs as the small group in attendance stood and bowed their heads, glancing from one of the draped chairs to the next.

Stumper counted to fifteen in his head, which was about five seconds longer than he could stand. Again, appearances were important.

"Mr. President, the tragedy that has befallen our nation is great and grievous. Not since the assassination of John F. Kennedy has our national leadership been attacked so mercilessly. I will join with all of you and the rest of the nation to reflect and pray for the souls of our friends. These were heinous acts of cowardice, and those responsible can and will be brought to justice."

He paused there. He wanted to shift gears, and the pause gave him the opportunity to move beyond the maudlin murders.

"At the same time, we all know we have urgent issues to address, and inaction is unacceptable. We need to demonstrate to the American people, and indeed to the world, that our government is functioning effectively and that our democratic processes will carry us forward. To deliver that message, this body must begin an immediate investigation into the circumstances of these murders and the law enforcement failures that allowed them to happen. Without complete transparency, we can't learn from our shortcomings and mistakes. People must be held accountable."

He stopped again, giving everyone a chance to focus on the hanging chad of accountability. He shifted his notes as if to make sure he got everything just right.

"Secondly, circumstances in this great body have now changed. Until new members can be appointed and new permanent leadership installed, those of us now in the majority must shepherd the ship of state. It is vital that we remain at the helm, guiding the country into calmer waters."

The irony of that statement wasn't lost on him as he continued.

"As a result, and with the president's permission, I'd like to place a motion on the floor for consideration."

"Proceed, Senator." That was the response from the president he'd expected.

"The Finance Committee has reported out H.R. 666, the Fiscal Responsibility Act of 2023, which among other items would suspend the debt limit until March 30, 2024. Given the high likelihood we will hit the current ceiling in the coming days, I move that we entertain debate on this bill at this time with a scheduled cloture vote at 11 a.m. Monday morning."

There: He'd made his gambit. He knew the cloture vote would be close. But the extortion note had been quite clear. He'd become more comfortable with the idea as he considered it overnight. His name would be attached to a seminal moment in US history. Given the Senate absences, it was perhaps the only opportunity he'd get to wield power. Besides, he knew it was high time the country faced its financial vices, to say nothing of keeping his own indiscretions secret.

If chaos was the price, so be it.

Sometimes you had to burn it all down to rebuild it right.

CHAPTER 75

TRAPS SPRUNG

Lee Bowen was staring at the white walls of an enclosed room. He noted the camera in an upper corner, the red light indicating that it was recording everything. He sat at a table facing a mirror, which he was sure was two-way glass.

Welcome to interrogation, he thought. He had no idea what to expect.

The arrest had come on Saturday morning, three days after the murdered senators were discovered on display in the state rotundas. No less than five government SUVs had stormed up to his house in Atherton, bringing neighbors out front doors to view the commotion. He'd been in the backyard watching his dog pee when two agents came around each side of his house yelling, "FBI," and, "Down on the ground."

In the moment he'd frozen—but in the end they'd trussed him up like a common criminal, hauled him out front, pushed his head down, and shoved him into the back of one of the SUVs. Bowen had seen the look on neighbors' faces as the ominous vehicles pulled out of his driveway. He felt some shame . . . but mostly he was just terrified. He knew what he'd done, and he also knew there were things he hadn't done that he might pay for anyway. He'd always thought the DAO would protect him. Now he wasn't so sure.

The door to the conference room flew open, and a tall Asian woman stepped through the door and slapped a folder down on the table. She pulled up a chair and glared at him from across the table.

"Well, Mr. Bowen, we're back together, face-to-face." He could see the anger in her expression.

Damn. Now he remembered. She was the woman who'd led the raid on the B^2 offices.

"As you may recall, my name is Kalen Chen, and I'm wrapping up the FBI investigation into your . . . hmmm, what shall we call them . . . *activities.*" She placed a folder down on the table and spread out some papers.

Bowen managed to regain some composure. "I want to see my lawyer, and I want to see her now. Nothing's changed since our last meeting."

"Oh . . . but it has," Agent Chen said. "And while your lawyer is on her way, you'd be smart to listen to me first. Voluntary cooperation always looks better."

"You're just bluffing. I'll wait for Annie."

"Look, we know about your little investment scheme. We have all the information we need on your autonomous organization thing. The more we dig, the worse it's gonna get for you."

Bowen chose not to reply. The reference to the DAO was a gut punch.

"So far, you're being charged with securities fraud, blackmail, kidnapping, attempted murder, four counts of murder, and twenty-two other felonies. And there's certainly more to follow. I'd say we're going to throw the book at you, but I couldn't find a book big enough." She gave Bowen a shit-eating grin that pissed him off, even in his precarious position.

"There's no way you can pin any of that on me. All I did was form an investment company and place some bets in the market—and now that I've been proven right, you want to take it away from me. It's just another government conspiracy to control my ability to make money." He leaned back in his chair, trying to look confident.

"About that. You should know that the DAO and the rest of your personal assets are now under court supervision. You have no way to control your investment portfolio. Good luck with that. I'm sure your investors will be pleased when the discover they can't access their money."

Fuck.

He'd made the mistake of letting the investments ride rather than getting out of the market when he could. He'd made about $100 million more on paper, but that would do him no good. The raid had caught Bowen off guard, and now he had no access to his accounts. He had no way to take profits and close out his positions. He was worried about his own money, for sure. But he also knew his investors were not the kind of people who would accept a loss easily. He might end up safer in prison.

As a market player, he knew he had two options. Cut his losses and get whatever deal he could. Or double down on his own innocence in the hopes that he could somehow recover control of the DAO's assets. He knew that the latter was the only way he could win.

And he had to win. Now more than ever.

"I have no idea what you mean by securities fraud, and I certainly didn't try to kill anyone, I swear." He knew that was only technically true, given the mistake at the high school. "And I damn sure didn't order anyone to attack any senators. I don't know who it was . . . but it definitely wasn't me."

At that moment Annie Petersen walked through the door.

"Lee, please don't say anything else. Let me do the talking." She walked around to Bowen's side of the room, put her briefcase on the table, and shifted her gaze over to the FBI officer. "Agent Chen, you will not question, talk to, or even look at my client without me being present." Bowen was grateful for her confidence.

Kalen Chen just smiled. "That's OK, Counselor. We already have everything we need."

As she walked out, Bowen felt some pangs of regret.

Sometimes when you went all in, you lost big.

• • • • •

FBI ARRESTS SILICON VALLEY VENTURE CAPITALIST IN SENATE MURDERS

The Sunday home page of *The New York Times* screamed success to Ely Basof. He was sitting on a NetJets Citation X on the way back from DC to San Francisco, looking out the window with a smile on his face. He was on the verge of a major coup, both for himself and for Russia.

And *coup* was an appropriate double entendre.

On the one hand, his accomplishments would certainly destabilize the US government, and that was something worth celebrating. A figurative coup. But depending on how things played out, it could go further. The Senate was poised to take action on a number of pieces of legislation with far from full representation—and that could turn into a more literal coup. His superiors would be ecstatic, which would enable him to continue pursuing his own mission in venture capital. No chance they'd recall such a successful agent.

As he patted himself on the back, he reveled in the knowledge that he'd achieved all of this while avoiding detection and implicating his two partners in crime. To be fair, Bowen had been his own worst enemy. He'd used the DAO without fully understanding its strengths and limitations. That had enabled Basof to take control without Bowen even knowing what had happened. His now disgraced partner had also taken huge risks, both with his own money and the money of foreign investors, demonstrating once again that greed was a dangerous vice. For now, Bowen's investments were paying off, but with him in jail and the markets uncertain, Basof was confident he'd seen the last of Lee Bowen. B^2 Ventures would soon become Basof Ventures.

He had mixed emotions about betraying his agent, Maaier. She was accomplished in her work, had done everything he'd asked, and adapted to some challenging situations in the field. Planting evidence to help the FBI find her left an empty feeling, as if he'd violated some sacred trust. But he also knew that survival was the name of the game, and Maaier wouldn't have hesitated to do the same if their situations were reversed.

As for himself, he had arranged for the senator murders and all Maaier's activities through dark web accounts that would be difficult to trace. Even if someone managed to track them, they would loop back to the IP address for the apartment building where Maaier had controlled the Smith attack. It would all be considered part of the same set of attacks and probably linked back to RallyAmerica and Lee Bowen. After all, Bowen had contracted with Maaier for the original attack at the high school.

The capstone of his achievement was still to be realized. With Bowen out of the way, Basof would take over their venture investments, free to pursue the current AI feeding frenzy. He had the technical chops and contacts to sort the wheat from the chaff and was confident he'd reap a windfall over the next decade. Like many excesses, exploitive capitalism was just fine in his book—as long as you knew when to stop. There really wasn't any such thing as retiring from the FSB, but he hoped they'd leave him alone after his recent success. He'd certainly argue that he couldn't risk further intelligence work.

As his plane entered the airspace over the Rockies, he dreamed about what might happen in the Senate on Monday.

He always enjoyed a good shit show.

CHAPTER 76

FAREWELLS

The weekend had been the longest day of Phoenix's life. She was still trying to process Tamika's death, and watching her father try to soldier through his grief was more than she could handle. She'd gone for several long runs around the mall and monuments area of downtown DC. The physical release was satisfying, but the only time she smiled all weekend was when she realized that some FBI agents were struggling to keep up with her pace.

The head of the FBI—Jessup, the same man that had met her and Tamika at the Air Force base after the Amsterdam mess—had paid his respects to the family at their hotel on Sunday afternoon. Phoenix could see in his eyes tension, stress, anger—and something that almost looked like anticipation. He'd talked privately with her mom and dad, spoken briefly with Nathan, and then asked Phoenix to walk with him.

"Sorry to take you away from your family. I'm not sure how Tamika wanted me to do this, but she clearly had a special place in her heart for you. She left letters for me to give to her father and your dad in case . . ." He let that hang, looking away from Phoenix and fumbling with something in his coat pocket.

"In case she died." Phoenix couldn't help but finish the thought.

"Right." He looked even more uncomfortable, but continued, "She also left a letter for you." He handed over an envelope with her name clearly printed in Tamika's handwriting. "There was a short note for your brother as well, but she asked me to deliver this directly to you."

"Thank you, sir. That was very thoughtful." She took the envelope, which was stationery-sized with Tamika's initials on the back flap.

"Call me JJ."

"OK, JJ."

"I know your mom is a strong person, and your dad will support her as best he can. But you're going to be the one who is there every day. Tamika was so proud of the way you're growing up. She thought of you as an adult. Maybe it's not fair, but I think she was right. Here's my card. If you need anything . . . or you think your mom or brother need anything, make sure you call me. I'll answer the cell phone number, twenty-four hours a day."

"Thank you, JJ. I'm not sure I'm an adult, but my childhood is definitely over." She looked at the letter, put it in her back pocket, and gave him a searching look. "I have no idea how to replace Tamika in my life, but I appreciate everything you've tried to do for us."

And with that she turned and walked away.

She hurried to the end of the hall, into the elevator, and down to the first floor. The lobby of the Marriott was buzzing with activity—people checking out, others hustling to breakfast in the adjacent atrium, and a group of high school students gathering for a tour of the city. Everyone moving in different directions, but each with a sense of certainty and purpose.

Like it was any other day in DC.

Phoenix strode out of the JW Marriott, which was just east of the White House. She turned right, then immediately crossed the street into Freedom Plaza. The concrete public area had the predictable collection of pigeons, along with groups of people eating lunch or relaxing in the spring air. A pack of skateboarders nearly ran her down as she catatonically walked across the concrete. She found a seat on a stone pier amid a scattering of trees that surrounded a reflecting pool of water. She opened the letter and read it twice.

As she wiped away tears, she read the last paragraph a third time, sorting through the emotions as she went:

Remember your name. Phoenix. Whenever you are down, rise up like your namesake and tackle whatever challenges you face. Perseverance is the elixir of life. It overcomes obstacles and finds positive opportunities on the other side.

Even with my death, I pray that you may keep the faith, find a way to use it as positive motivation, and help others around you in their grief.

Know that I will find a way to be there.

Always.

With love,
Tamika

Phoenix looked at the buzz of people in the plaza, each moving with a mission in mind. Their lives looked normal. She wished hers could feel that way again.

Tamika wrote about perseverance as if it were an easy thing to do. Phoenix wanted to follow her example. She just wasn't sure how to do it. Looking off toward the White House and the monuments didn't seem to help.

How had Tamika found the courage to sacrifice it all?

• • • • •

Margaret Humboldt bowed her head to see if her tea could bring some absolution. She had asked Shea Roscovitch to come down to DC when Johnny was freed. She needed to talk to someone. Shea was her funder, advisor, and confidant. And now confessor.

"Shea, I called her a *bitch*," Margaret said.

"We all say things we regret, dear. I'm sure Tamika understood your point of view. She was always good that way." They were sitting in Margaret's hotel room for a drink—Margaret with her tea and Shea with a black coffee. Shea's soft voice reflected the love she had for her friend.

"Even after she brought Phoenix home from Amsterdam, I was so cold to her. Never thanked her for saving my daughter's life. And then she sacrificed herself for the best friend I've ever known."

"It's a blessing that Johnny survived. Phoenix and Nathan will still have their father. Fathers are so important. Tamika certainly knew that."

Margaret was painfully aware that Shea's son and father had never had a chance to reconcile. Maybe that was her own problem. She wanted to reconcile herself with Tamika.

"She left notes for Phoenix and Nathan," Margaret said. "She knew she might die. How does someone do that?"

"It takes courage and conviction . . . and mostly it takes love. She loved Johnny—and she obviously loved Phoenix and Nathan." Shea paused. "And real love is unconditional."

Margaret looked up from her tea with tears rolling down her face. "I keep asking myself if I could have done what she did."

"You will always do whatever it takes to save your children. That's what mothers and fathers do." Shea reached out with her hand and covered Margaret's.

Margaret just nodded, still numb. She knew that Shea was trying to help, and what she said made sense in her head. Her heart wasn't so sure.

The doubt remained.

CHAPTER 77

PRESENT AND ACCOUNTED

On Monday, Johnny had never seen so much activity, such a buzz, so much tension and excitement. The Senate chamber had become a living, breathing organism.

"Can you believe this?" he said to Mark Cavanagh. They were sitting next to each other in the front row of the gallery overlooking the floor of the upper chamber of Congress. After family members had surrendered their electronic devices to security guards, they'd come to the chamber via underground train from Tamika's office. Several stairways delivered them to the visitor seating.

"One way or another, it's going to be an historic day," Cavanagh responded.

It was only six days after Tamika's murder and Johnny was still engulfed with grief—but for a brief moment, he was able to focus on what he was witnessing from the gallery of the Senate. With four assassinated senators, most pundits had assumed the Senate would pause its work on legislation, both to mourn and honor the dead and to allow governors and legislators to replace their fallen representatives. But Senator Ronald Stumper and his acolytes had other ideas. The debt ceiling cloture vote would begin in minutes, and the future of the US economy and the world financial system hung in the balance.

Johnny looked down the row of the balcony, which was overflowing beyond capacity. He'd managed to squeeze Margaret, Phoenix, Nathan, and General Smith in with him. He had told them what was about to happen and why it could be significant. Their faces reflected the nervousness of someone who sees a punch coming but isn't sure how much it will hurt. Margaret squeezed his hand without any hesitation, and the general gave him a brief nod. Nathan's gaze wandered around the chamber, trying to absorb what he saw. Phoenix was locked in, face forward, ready to explode. Johnny knew that Tamika's death had hit her the hardest—perhaps as hard as it had hit him.

Below him, the Senate floor staff was moving back and forth between the marble platform, the president's dais, and the senators' desks. The Senate stenographer was arranging his equipment in preparation to record what was sure to be some chaotic action. The bustle itself was not unusual, but the quantity of people and the noise associated with it was exceptional in a body that was usually relatively tranquil and dignified. He also noticed a squadron of Capitol Police guarding the semicircle of doors on the chamber floor and the top of the gallery. Important to see that . . . but way too late in Johnny's mind.

He glanced down at the desk that Tamika usually occupied. The black drape and flower were still there. His sadness over her absence was replaced by a sense of outrage and anger that the Senate was going to proceed with business as usual. It was a sign of the times that there was no sensibility or civil respect being shown to those who had died in the service of their country.

Recognizing the significance of the day's vote, the vice president of the United States was in attendance and would preside over the session. She could cast deciding votes in certain circumstances, underscoring the gravity of the situation. She consulted with several officials at the marble table below her and then nodded in agreement with something that was said. Apparently, it was time to begin.

"Will the chamber please come to order." She paused to give people a chance to respond. When they moved too slowly or continued talking, she got a bit more insistent and rapped her gavel. "Order. Order in the Senate. I remind the gallery that you are here as observers and should remain quiet throughout today's important proceedings."

Johnny saw that Stumper was again the first to rise.

"Madam President?"

And with that the shit show began.

• • • • •

"Don't worry, Sonny," Andropov whispered. "The main threat has been eliminated." She sat at her desk looking out toward the small canal that led to the beach and water beyond, her cat purring in her lap. "And maybe Mischa wasn't the mole."

She'd had a few days to reflect on the possibilities. Killing the other senators spoke for itself. Mischa had executed what might be the FSB's crowning mission. The spy agency's leaders in Moscow would be ecstatic. "We might even have some time off to take care of the garden." She smiled down at Sonny, wondering if that could be true.

In addition to enjoying the relaxing view out the window, she was watching the Senate proceedings with mild interest. She had a passing understanding of the byzantine budget and financial machinations of the US government, and she'd read enough to know that if the debt limit bill was rejected, the significance and impact of the FSB missions would be magnified tenfold. This was what the Americans called an icing-on-the-cake moment. She put her headphones on so she could hear the audio without broadcasting it to the homes sandwiched next to hers. Nobody else in De Cocksdorp on the isle of Texel would expect to hear an American government broadcast.

Andropov was used to the tightly controlled activity that masqueraded as legislative action in Russia. She'd adjusted to the intricacies of parliamentary governance in her adopted homeland of the Netherlands, accustomed to the back-and-forth of the discussion, but she knew that the coalition in control would always get their way. The debate on the floor of the US Senate, however, was like nothing she'd ever seen before.

"Why do they keep having these votes?" she asked Sonny. "What are all of these amendments?"

She watched and listened as no fewer than ten amendments were proposed to the debit limit bill. She couldn't track who was proposing the changes or why, but she realized that none of them were passing.

Was that good or bad? Get on with it.

Finally, it seemed they had reached the critical vote. She'd read enough to know that 60 percent of those present needed to vote aye for the bill to proceed. She quickly realized that each senator was coming forward to cast their vote by talking to someone at the front of the chamber.

This was really old school. You'd think they'd just push a button.

In spite of herself, she couldn't help but tick off the votes, *aye* and *no*, on the pad of paper in front of her. As the voting continued, hope began to well up inside her as she counted the results. With the last vote cast, she realized that the tally was 56 *aye* and 38 *no* with two voting *present*, whatever that meant. She had to get out her calculator to figure out the 60 percent threshold of ninety-four voting members.

Holy shit. It failed by one vote!

She celebrated by tossing Sonny up in the air. The cat landed perfectly on all four feet and ran away.

Then she looked at the TV and stopped dead, mid-celebration. She couldn't believe what she was seeing.

"*Ni za chto, blyad!* No fucking way!"

• • • • •

"Got her!" Bryce yelled in triumph. It had taken fifty-three hours of tedious work, but they'd found the sniper.

Bryce had taken the FBI's ferry clue and started a search for Tamika's Dutch assassin. Tracking her from the ferry terminal to a specific address on the island was no easy feat. First, he had images from his earlier work of her with three different hair colors, and none of the pictures were crystal clear to begin with. And once she left the ferry terminal area on Texel, video coverage was damn scarce. The island had some small towns but was mostly farmland and undeveloped woods. Even when houses had security cameras, the distance to the road made them useless.

After some reflection and a brief chat session with Mufasa, Bryce decided to focus his efforts on retail locations. Presumably she had to shop, get food, maybe take some cash from an ATM. Each camera had to be hacked—not difficult, but time-consuming. Once he had access, the large volume of video yielded a substantial number of false positives that had to be reviewed individually, with Bryce making the final judgment. Grunt work at best.

In the end, it was a security camera in a bakery in the hamlet of De Cocksdorp that yielded success. He saw her walk in to a grocery store at 9:05 a.m. and then exit the shop at 9:45 carrying two large canvas bags of groceries. She walked so close to the camera by the front door that it was easy to confirm the identity.

Bryce felt some sense of redemption. His information would enable the FBI to capture Johnny's tormentor and the murderer of his friend Tamika. *They* were the family he was supposed to protect. He knew it wasn't right, but deep down he wanted the Reaper to put up a fight.

"I hope they kill her."

• • • • •

Johnny sat stone-still as the recorded Senate vote proceeded.

Tamika's team had counted heads during their weekend lobbying of those who were on the fence. Those opposed on the right were focused on the need to instill discipline in the government. In their view, the threat of default was the only way to force congressional leaders to face the financial music. Some on the far left were still incensed that the bill included what was effectively a spending freeze on any programs not already tied to inflation. They might vote against the bill to register their displeasure. A few who were facing reelection didn't want to be on the record either way.

Mark Cavanagh had predicted the vote for cloture would fail—barely. Johnny knew they had more than the fifty votes necessary to approve the Act. But they needed fifty-eight votes to end the filibuster so that the full bill could even be considered. Neither he nor Cavanagh could see how they were going to get there. He glanced nervously over at General Smith, noting with some surprise that he seemed as calm as the proverbial cucumber. Perhaps that reflected years of watching and waiting for action reports from the field. Or maybe just a belief that the ball could bounce their way. Or maybe he, too, was hiding the grief he felt. He certainly knew the importance Tamika had placed on this and understood she would have voted *aye*.

The general smiled as a second senator voted *present*. Johnny knew that could be significant. But why was he smiling?

When every senator had voted, Johnny's head fell. They were one vote short. General Smith still had a smile on his face. By Senate rule, the voting had to remain open for a full fifteen minutes. Johnny realized that some senators had cast their votes reluctantly on one side or the other and might reconsider given the reality of a failed vote. He also knew that the *present* votes had lowered their threshold to get to 60 percent. All they needed was one of those senators to flip.

They needed just one more vote.

With fifteen seconds left in the vote, the doors at the back of the chamber flew open. Johnny jumped up. He saw the smile on the general's face.

"Senator Tamika Smith from the great state of Washington votes *aye*."

Chaos ensued.

CHAPTER 78
MISSIONS

Tamika looked up at the gallery to find her family. She saw a huge smile on her dad's face as he shook his fist in triumph at her. Over the tumult, she thought she heard a scream from Phoenix. *Where was Johnny?* She couldn't find him.

She heard the vice president in the background. "Order, order—the Senate will come to order!"

And then she saw him. Johnny had moved down the row of the balcony to the other aisle, apparently trying to get closer to her. She rushed up the side aisle of the Senate floor and shouted her love up to him in the balcony. She could see joy on his face—but also a mixture of surprise and confusion.

Given the depth of their relationship, Tamika was strangely anxious about finally reuniting with Johnny. She'd hoped and prayed for this day for weeks, but now that the moment was upon her, she was nervous. After all, she'd withheld a secret from him and put the most important person in her life through almost a week of hell.

"It'll be fine, Tamika. He loves you." She felt Jerry Jessup's surprisingly gentle touch as he escorted her out of the Senate chamber. She knew JJ had been married for thirty years—surely he'd had more than a few reunions like this during his military career.

Would Johnny forgive her? Could she forgive herself?

"I'm shaking." Tamika could barely turn the knob when they got to a conference room in the bowels of the Senate wing.

"Go to him." Jessup opened the door for her.

Tamika looked across the room where Johnny was staring out the window. He turned toward her with a searching expression and moved slowly across the floor. Then he flashed a smile, and she knew it would be OK. Their embrace and kisses seemed to last forever.

"Oh my God, how can you ever forgive me?"

"You're right—what the hell were you thinking? You knew that bitch wasn't going to make the exchange." She saw pure energy in his eyes—or was that anger?

Tamika paused. "You're mad at me for trying to save you? How could I not risk my life for you? Isn't that what our love means?"

Johnny seemed to consider that for a moment, as if he'd never thought about it that way. "How'd you survive? I thought you were hit twice in the chest."

"I was. But the Army's latest Kevlar is amazing. If she'd taken a head shot, I'd have been in the ground, but I was shifting around enough to make that difficult. My guess is she went for an easier, more secure shot."

"What about the body in the Olympia rotunda?"

"Jessup and my dad took me to the FBI morgue. They made a swap there for a medical cadaver. I've been at JJ's house ever since. We didn't even trust an FBI safe house."

Johnny shook his head. "Damn, you are one crazy woman."

"I made Jessup swear that he wouldn't tell you." Tamika wanted him to know everything.

She felt his arms tense up around her, and when he looked at her again, the electric stare was back.

"Don't you see it, love? I wanted to save you. And I was the bait to draw her out. Nobody could know . . . before or after. She had to believe I was dead." She could tell he wasn't so sure.

Jessup opened the door. "Sorry to interrupt. But Tamika, we need you."

"Come on in, Director. No more secrets from Johnny."

Jessup, her father, and Agent Higginbottom entered the room.

"Tell everyone what you know, Higgs." Jessup was energized.

"Your tech friend was able to track her. Once she thought you were dead, she must have let down her guard a bit—your game of possum worked. We found some trace evidence at the scene. A bit careless, honestly. With some IP tracing, security cameras, and final confirmation from some military satellite images I'm not supposed to know about, we have her location." Higginbottom spread out some images on the conference table.

Jessup continued, "The Dutch government is cooperating. But they want both of us there. We need to move quickly now that she knows you're still alive. Our jet leaves in forty-five minutes."

Tamika smiled, realizing her risky plan was coming to fruition. She turned to Johnny. The coldness was gone, replaced by wonder.

"You're going to go no matter what I say, right?"

She nodded.

"Can I come with you?" His question sounded resigned to its fate.

"Not a chance."

"I didn't think so." He reached out to give her a fierce hug.

Tamika held him tight and then turned to Jessup and Higginbottom. "Where are we going?"

"De Cocksdorp."

The hell you say?

• • • • •

Andropov realized she was now at risk.

Between the wind, the fog, and Smith moving around so much on the platform, she'd had to forgo the certain head shot. But she was positive she'd hit the target twice in the chest. If Smith was alive, they'd somehow protected her from high-velocity ordnance. Now it looked like the trap had sprung back on the FSB agent. She'd left herself exposed to get the kill shot. Unlikely they had any real way to track her, but they would put every resource they had on the problem. That was the whole point of pulling her to the United States for the exchange. And there was still the unresolved question of the FSB. Even if it wasn't Mischa, there was a leak somewhere.

Feeling compromised, her initial instinct was to follow procedure. That meant contacting her handler for instructions.

"That's not going to work," she said to Sonny, her cat advisor. She wasn't going to put her life in Mischa's hands.

Her next option was to contact Moscow directly—there were exceptional procedures she could invoke—but she wasn't clear how many people there even knew about her mission. How could they possibly support her? That left her with immediate evacuation—technically an emergency extraction—which maximized her safety but also sacrificed everything she had built in De Cocksdorp and in the Netherlands. She needed something with more optionality.

She decided to prepare for the worst. To be ready to move at a moment's notice. But she wouldn't take any definitive action. The next twenty-four hours would reveal if they were on to her location.

Once the decision was made, she knew exactly what to do. She carefully went through every room cleaning up any possible evidence. She only had a few important papers and shredded those immediately. Her laptop was mirrored on a secure FSB cloud share. She wiped the local drive clean and ran an FSB reformatting protocol. The laptop would be useless. She cleaned the bathroom with bleach, wiped down the rest of the cottage, and ran the remaining dishes through a cycle in the washer. There was probably some DNA somewhere, but she'd made the job difficult for them. Even if they found something, they didn't have anything to compare it to as far as she knew.

She pulled her go bag out from a closet and checked the contents. The backpack had multiple passports, US dollars and euros, two burner phones, a change of clothes, foul-weather gear, a flashlight, a garden trowel, and her Glock 17. She'd never had to execute an evacuation, and it was unnerving. She sat down with Sonny and stroked her companion.

"I've filled up your feeder and water, boy. But if I have to leave, I can't take you with me." She felt the tears coming and tried to wipe them away. She knew he was just a cat, but she didn't have any other friends. She had a neighbor, Nicolette, who would check in on Sonny. Andropov would leave a note for her. At least he'd have a new home.

Sentimentality will get you killed, she reminded herself.

She returned her thoughts to what her superiors at the FSB would say. As valuable an asset as she'd been over the years, Andropov knew she was a dangling loose end on an operation that otherwise had gone well. If Mischa didn't back her up, there was a good chance they'd have her terminated.

And she wasn't about to let that happen.

• • • • •

Commissaris Pieter Snijders met them at De Kooy Airfield outside Den Helder. It was 4:30 a.m. local time.

"Welcome back to the Netherlands, Senator Smith."

"Good to see you again, Commissaris." Tamika felt a rush of Air Force adrenaline she hadn't experienced in some time. This was all a bit déjà vu for her.

"You must be Deputy Director Jessup. Good to meet you, sir."

"Thank you for the invitation. I hope we can help bring this asshole down." Jessup shook his hand several times.

They went into a low building just off the tarmac. The Dutch National Police had taken over the room, which was well-equipped with maps, charts, and a collection of video screens.

"This building is usually used for search and rescue, Senator—I think that's actually more your area of expertise." Snijders was tall, sturdy, and blond, with a commanding voice speaking nearly perfect English. He projected a professionalism that inspired confidence in Tamika.

"Please, it's Tamika. I'm assuming the oil rigs, turbines, and boaters keep your coast guard busy."

"They do. But they've given us the run of the place given the circumstances. And the Dutch Air Force is providing staffing and support." He waved his hands at the people and equipment.

"What's your plan, Commissaris?" Jessup appeared antsy for the chase.

"If she's an FSB agent, as your people hypothesize, she's almost certainly well connected here. De Cocksdorp is an unusual place to hide, but then again, it's not an easy place to sneak up on."

"We can't just take the ferry and drive in, I suppose," Tamika added. "This woman plans carefully. She'll have some emergency plan."

"That's our assumption, and there's a storm moving in, so we're going in with a quick strike force. Choppers."

"I hope we can join you." Tamika could tell that Jessup really was itching for a fight, and she felt the same way. She smiled. They'd never really left the Air Force culture.

"Of course; we wouldn't have had you come for the view. Here's your gear. The Pave Hawks are ready."

Tamika took a deep breath. The Pave Hawk mission in Kandahar came rushing back.

This was going to be a bit too close for comfort.

CHAPTER 79

MOVING ON

Whoop, whoop, whoop, whoop!

Andropov jolted awake at the pounding sound of helicopters. Shit—they were coming for her . . . and sooner than she'd expected. She glanced at her watch. It was 5:15 a.m. The darkness would provide some cover.

She jumped out of bed where she'd been resting fitfully. She quickly put on her travel clothes and hoisted the backpack over her shoulder after pulling out one of the burner phones and turning it on. She gave Sonny one last chin scratch and placed the note for Nicolette on the table. "Love you, my friend."

Then she walked through the shadows by a fence to a small shed that bordered the waterfront in her backyard. She spun the combination lock, ripped it off the buckle hinge, and entered. She closed the double doors and reattached the lock to the clasp on the other side. That wouldn't stop them, but it might slow them down. She pulled up a recessed handle and lifted a section of the flooring, revealing a dark hole.

The hidden opening and the tunnel that ran from it had been dug during World War II. The Dutch resistance had used her house as an exit point for the evacuation of downed Allied pilots and crew members. They were escorted down the tunnel to a dike at the edge of town that bordered the open sea. From there, they could escape by boat. She climbed down the ladder, pulling the trap door shut and locked it behind her. Again, they would find it. But by then it would be too late.

She ran down the low-ceilinged tunnel knowing that each second would be valuable later. After a five-minute jog, stumbling into old wooden beams several times, she reached another locked double door. She paused to listen to the helicopter drumbeat. As she'd expected, they'd gone a bit farther south, probably landing on the polder area above the canal behind her house. Her pulse quickened as she realized how close this was going to be.

She had to risk using her flashlight to dial the lock combination. With the task done, she extinguished the light, pushed open the double doors, and pulled out the bicycle that she had stored at the end of the tunnel. With her transportation out of the passageway, she closed the doors that were covered with fake grasses blending into the embankment of the dike that protected the north end of Texel from the ravages of the North Sea.

Andropov pulled out the burner phone and sent a short text message. Then she cautiously pushed the bike up the small path to the top of the dike. The helicopter noise had eased with their landing. She could see the lights in the distance rushing down the streets of De Cocksdorp to her former home. Sonny would be waiting for them.

Give 'em hell, pal.

De Cocksdorp was technically on the Wadden Sea, on the inside of the border islands. She needed to cross part of the island of Texel to get access to the North Sea itself. She made her way down the dike path to Stenweg. Mounting her bicycle, she turned on the small headlamp so she could see through the morning dark and increasing mist. She couldn't afford to run into anything. She pedaled to Langveldstraat, turned right, and headed southwest, only one block away from where the police were undoubtedly raiding her home. It was a risk she had to take. And in a few blocks, she would be in the clear.

Just forty-five minutes to freedom.

• • • • •

The Pave Hawks flew up the west coast of Texel over the North Sea. At the northern tip of the island they banked to the right around a lighthouse, then headed southeast to the tiny village of De Cocksdorp.

Tamika scanned the grassy area to where a series of houses were arranged along a single road. The noise of their arrival was quickly bringing the town to life as lights turned on and people stumbled into the main street. She followed Commissaris Snijders and his two teams. They quickly surrounded the house and breached the front door. Tamika and JJ kept a safe distance, not knowing whether their terrorist would stand and fight or run.

"*Politie! Politie!*" rang the shouts in Dutch, followed shortly by, "*Alles duidelijk*," which Tamika quickly concluded meant *all clear*.

Snijders jogged out of the front door. "She's not here, and it looks like she just left. The helos are hard to disguise."

"How'd she get out? I thought you had people on the ground watching the house?" Jessup sounded incensed, although Tamika knew he'd had his own challenges with house searches in the past.

"There's a shed in the back," Snijders explained. "Complete with an escape tunnel. Our team is working down the passage, but it's going to be slow. She could be waiting." He ran back into the house.

Tamika looked around at the small crowd that had gathered, their peaceful existence upended. Her eye caught a brief glimpse of light and someone riding a bicycle hard and fast a block over from the main street. Who the hell was out riding a bike that hard at 5:30 a.m.?

"JJ—" she started, turning to her former boss.

"*Go*," he said, understanding her perfectly. "I'll be right behind." With a quick, intense look, he squeezed her arm, handed her his gun, and then went toward the house to find the commissaris.

Tamika stepped away quietly and moved beyond the thin line of gawkers. Someone had put their bike up against a street sign as they rushed to the scene of the activity. Tamika grabbed the bike, put JJ's gun in her waistband, and took off.

She raced down the block and turned left where she'd seen the cyclist. The bike seat was the wrong height, and she was riding blind. All she could see was a bobbing light in the distance and knew she had to pick up speed. The bike had one gear, so her only hope was to pedal faster. The light weaved a bit to the left, which Tamika realized was the entry to a bike trail that ran parallel to the road. She followed suit and pedaled more urgently.

This was proving to be more difficult than the bike trip through Amsterdam.

Come on, you used to be an athlete . . .

The path took a bend to the left and entered a long straightaway. As the dawn began to break, she could just make out the open spaces of farmland to her left and a steep mound to her right that seemed to run forever into the distance. She realized it was a very large earthen dike. She also realized that the wind was picking up and low clouds were descending almost to fog level. The North Sea storm was apparently arriving. All she could do was keep churning.

After another five minutes, a building suddenly came into view through the mist. The sign said "Café Restaurant De Slufter." She saw a lone bike thrown in a rack across the street next to a sign. Tamika couldn't read Dutch, but peering up a steep staircase, the translation was obvious. It was Dunes National Park.

"Jesus, I'm in the flattest place on earth, and I find the only hill in a hundred miles."

She dumped the bike and sprinted up the thirty steps to the top of the dike. Catching her breath for an instant, she felt the wind whipping across the peak at what seemed like thirty miles an hour. She also was pelted with fine grains of sand, stirred up by the gale from the dunes beyond. She looked out through the low clouds and could just make out an estuary. High dunes marked the left side of the inlet with a broad, wet plain laid out before her. It was a complex mix of sand, strips of water, and areas that looked like marshland—a real mess to navigate in the early dawn.

Then in the distance, she saw it. A light moving up and down.

She began to run.

CHAPTER 80

THE DUNES

Nastya Andropov was moving as quickly as she could. She'd run down from the huge dike area and was now marching through the sand and wetlands of the small estuary. It was the dead of winter in the Netherlands with temperatures just above zero degrees Celsius, so the route was slippery in places. The mist, wind, and tricky landscape slowed her progress. And she couldn't afford to lose the trail.

She paused briefly to shift the bag she was carrying and glanced back at the dike. Silhouetted against the dawn light was a lone figure who took off down the hill in a run. Even in the terrible conditions and poor visibility, Andropov knew instinctively who was on her tail.

"Fucking hell, how did she get here?" The curse came as she unzipped her backpack and pulled out the Glock 17. No suppressor this time.

She needed to pick up the pace.

Part of being an FSB agent was a regular regimen of physical training. Andropov ran the myriad of trails on Texel and worked out at a gym in the slightly larger town of Den Burg. She took what looked like the long way around going to the left, but she knew from hiking and running in the area that this was the only predictable way to avoid water and the incoming tide.

Twenty minutes later, she reached the dunes that bordered the entrance from the North Sea just as full dawn was breaking. Although the wind and mist continued, she could now see partway back to the dike. She didn't like the view. She moved down the beach fifty yards and then climbed up in between the high dunes. Just before the peak was a small, flat area surrounded by dune grass and marked by a large rock. She set her backpack down, pulled out the garden trowel, and began to dig.

After five minutes of determined effort, she'd moved enough sand away to reveal a wooden box. She dialed the combination, opened the box, and pulled the package that was going to save her life. With some determined effort, she dragged it down to the bottom of the dune at the edge of the beach, which was slowly giving way to the incoming tide. She pulled the handle, waited for a moment, and threw her backpack inside. Her burner phone buzzed with a message.

Everything was ready.

She hesitated but couldn't resist. She ran back up to the top of the dune.

The wind was now blowing so hard she had trouble standing steady. She had to crawl along the ridge of the dune until she could see the open approach from the estuary and the dike beyond. Visibility came and went, brief glimpses into a white soup of swirling mist and sand. For just an instant, she saw her quarry. She shifted her body into a full prone position so that she was well braced.

Then she pulled the trigger.

• • • • •

Tamika knew she could cover more ground than the terrorist she was chasing—she was born to run. The problem was moving in the right direction. Twice she ran headlong into mud, and once she went ankle deep in a small side stream of water she couldn't see. For all her speed, she wasn't closing ground quickly enough.

She shifted left and ran along the line of dunes that began near the dike and extended in various shapes and sizes out to the main beach. She was wet and now chilled to the bone from her accidental detour into the water. Still she forged ahead, burning with the desire to finish off the Dutch bitch that had gone after her entire family. The sniper who had already shot and hit Tamika twice.

She paused as she got within two hundred yards of the outer beach. The surf pounded the shore, even as the wind howled around her. She ducked into the relative shelter of a large dune and caught her breath. She pulled out Jessup's Glock and chambered a round into the magazine. The last time she'd fired a gun, Ford Wilkes had been a stationary target at thirty yards under ideal conditions. And since she and JJ had both fired, it was unclear whether she'd hit the mark. Now she was on the move in shitty conditions, trying to kill a professional shooter at long distance.

It's go time, girl.

She jumped out from cover and sprinted into the wind across a wide sandy stretch, hoping to burst around the final dune and catch her prey by surprise. Instead she was met with two sprays of sand at her feet and the echoing sound of shots fired. She dove to the ground, instinctively looking up at the dune to try and spot the shooter. She fired off several rounds in the general direction of the top of the dune.

No reaction. Just the sound of the wind and increased pelting from what was now a driving rain. She didn't move, betting the visibility would make it tough on her adversary.

But then another shot rang out, and she felt a searing pain in her calf. Stunned at first by the realization that she'd been hit and swearing in anger, she rolled over several times to avoid being an easy target.

I gotta keep moving.

She crawled on her elbows as best she could to get closer to the dune and out of the shooter's field of view. Three more shots rang out, but they whistled overhead before thudding into the sand behind her. She sat up, ripped away the bottom of her shirt, and tied a makeshift tourniquet above the wound. From her search-and-rescue training she knew she was at risk of slipping into shock, but she pulled herself to her feet and half hopped, half limped down the dune line until she could see the shore.

She reached round the dune with her right hand and fired off several shots up the beach, trying to clear the way for her to take the final steps out into the open. But the beach was empty. Just the dunes, blowing sand, and even more rain. She glanced up the dunes to see if the shooter might be laying a trap but didn't see anything.

Thwap, thwap, thwap. Three puffs of sand flew up between her and the ocean.

She turned quickly to her right and searched into the gloom—and then she did a double take. There, in the pounding surf, was an inflatable raft with her target frantically pulling the paddles into the surf.

Tamika whipped up her gun, emptying the remaining magazine. She knew that hitting the target was a long shot. For a moment the raft teetered at the top of a wave, and the former Air Force major thought she might have gotten off a lucky shot or a rogue wave might have swamped the boat.

But then the raft steadied itself, and her target was off into the mist.

And there wasn't a damn thing Tamika could do about it.

CHAPTER 81
CONSEQUENCES

Senator Tamika Smith and Johnny Humboldt walked into the deputy director of the FBI's office for their final debriefing. Jerald Jessup had called them in to clarify any last details before he made his report to the director of the FBI and the Department of Justice. It had been a full week since the climactic vote in the Senate and the failed mission in the Netherlands. Jessup also wanted them to know what the FBI had uncovered in the aftermath of the killings.

He came around his desk and helped Tamika into a chair.

"How's your leg, Senator?"

She glanced at the crutches. "I'll be fine. The walking is way more painful than the wound, that's for sure."

He smiled. "I'd give you a medal, but I'm informed Congress doesn't have the equivalent of a Purple Heart."

"Well . . . I'm working on making sure the heart is still beating in Congress."

He smiled. "I know you have a big speech to get to, so I'll get this rolling. First off, let me answer the big question of the day: Unfortunately we don't know what happened to your shooter. As you know, the weather was horrible, and we don't exactly have great satellite or submarine reconnaissance pointed at the Dutch coast. We do know there were several fishing trawlers in that area—which, by the way, isn't that uncommon. But we did trace some cell activity, and it could be that one of those boats was her contact."

"I'm sure she survived," responded Tamika. "I know it."

"I agree with you," JJ said, "but until we have confirmation, she'll be treated as an asset in play."

"Have we confirmed her identity? Is she FSB? What's her connection to Bowen?"

"We're working with Interpol and other intelligence agencies, but you know how the CIA is—they only share when they want something from you. You'd think that three murdered senators would motivate them, but they claim to have no information on her. They've promised to 'keep us advised,' whatever that means."

"They know more than they're telling. Maybe we should have a Senate hearing?" Tamika said it with a laugh.

Johnny jumped in. "What about RallyAmerica and Lee Bowen?"

"He's going to jail for a long time would be my guess, but there are many things still up in the air. I have no idea how the judicial system is going to deal with the DAO structure. That's new legal territory."

Agent Higginbottom, who was sitting quietly in the background, chimed in. "Bryce Roscovitch and our intelligence consultant have discovered a great deal. Turns out Lee Bowen was adopted by Chinese parents. His given name was Bo Wen Li, which they changed when he entered public school. They used the Chinese convention of last name first to get Lee Bowen. We're trying to identify the investors in RallyAmerica, but blockchain makes that difficult. We think the parents may be a link to others. Bowen claims that his parents know nothing about his work, and the rest of his money came from accredited financial investors. He's refused to identify any of them."

"And of course, he's also denied any involvement in the senator murders and claims to know nothing about an FSB agent," Jessup said dismissively.

"All of which raises the question of Chinese MSS involvement," interjected Johnny. "Hard to imagine them working in concert with an FSB agent, but who knows?"

"What does Bryce think?" Tamika asked.

"Surprisingly, both of our dark web gurus are on the fence. At a technical level, the IP sources for RallyAmerica directives changed midstream, which matches Bowen's claim that he was no longer in charge of the DAO.

They can't identify—at least not yet—where the new directions were coming from, but they've found no clear evidence that the Chinese intelligence service or the FSB were involved."

"Truth is, we may never know," Higginbottom said.

"And the Supreme Court will probably end up deciding if RallyAmerica investors can be held liable for the illegal activities. After all, it's a blind investment. Who's the owner when nobody's officially in charge?" Jessup hoped the court would throw the book at all of them.

"We gotta go, Tamika." Johnny was back to playing his role as chief of staff, Jessup observed.

But he wasn't quite done. "Senator, one last thing. You and I both know that we've had our differences—and I'm sure you understand that I think you're a bit reckless sometimes. But I want you to know that I deeply respect what you did, both in the arboretum and on Texel. I suspect I'll feel the same after I watch your speech."

He paused, recalling his first impressions of Major Tamika Smith at Offutt Air Force Base years earlier. She'd changed in important ways, but the warrior was still there.

"Courage doesn't come cheap. And moral courage is the most important of all."

EPILOGUE

BEACON ON THE HILL

"Madam President." Tamika rose quickly as the Senate was called to order. She was going to be first up one way or the other. Given the state of the current leadership, she wasn't going to stand on tradition and allow someone else to be recognized.

"The president recognizes the junior member from the state of Washington." The vice president of the United States had once again joined the session to be the presiding officer. And she knew that recognizing Senator Tamika Smith first was her only real job for the day.

"Thank you, Madam President." She'd dressed in a dark blue pant suit, with a white blouse underneath and a red scarf around her neck. She used the crutches to make her way up into the well of the chamber and then gave them to a Senate page to free her hands and project the strength she knew everyone needed. She took a moment to gather herself. Sharing her emotions was not something that came easily.

"Usually when I'm on the floor, I'm here to talk policy." She took another breath. "Not today."

She looked up to see Johnny, Phoenix, Nathan, Margaret, Shea, and her father in the gallery. She drew strength from the ones she loved—her new family. She turned back toward the main podium, following Senate tradition to address comments to the presiding officer.

"During my service as an Air Force combat search and rescue leader, I experienced the best, the worst, and the ugliest of humanity. I've seen more wounded and dead than I care to count. And they revisit me in nightmares at night. I've been shot three times, twice wounded, once murdered. I was raped in the Air Force." The entire chamber seemed to inhale on that last comment, as if all the oxygen was sucked out of the room.

Tamika held back the tears with great effort.

"So I begin today with a deep empathy for the families who lost their loved ones last week. I grieve the loss of my colleagues Senator Lillian Kafker, Senator Dana Golub, and Senator Mike Hermansen. They never signed up to be harassed and abused for their commitment to our country, nor did their families. And they certainly didn't enlist to be victims in a war that seems to know no limits. Instead, they should be here today leading the Senate to a better place.

"In the aftermath of their murders, this body committed a grievous and horrible offense. We allowed raw ambition, political agendas, and conspiratorial logic to overwhelm our humanity, our good sense, and our responsibility to the American people. The vote on the debt limit should never have taken place—and in fact, no votes should have taken place—until we fully honored those that gave the ultimate sacrifice for their country. And until the people of the United States were fully represented and led by duly designated leaders." She turned from the speaker's dais and gave Senator Ronald Stumper a cold stare.

She limped uncomfortably in front of the marble counter filled with Senate clerks. Then she committed a sin and turned her attention from the dais and the president's seat to face the full Senate. This was not something senators generally did. But the time had come to address her friends and enemies directly. This was going to be deeply personal, and they all needed to see and feel that.

"In any room of one hundred people there are bound to be friends you love, acquaintances you respect, and people you dislike. That's just the way human nature works. In truth, I'm sure the Senate has always been that way and probably always will be. But I do expect more from this body. We may not like each other, we may disagree with each other, but we have to work together. Because we should have the same goal. The same purpose. The same North Star. To make America a better place for people to grow, prosper, and achieve their highest hopes. Indeed, our job is to make the American dream possible."

The chamber was unusually quiet. The typical background hum and hubbub had come to a halt. The gallery was silent, leaning on the edge of their seats. Even the podium officials who were usually shuffling papers and preparing for the next agenda item had stopped to listen.

Tamika used the railing to gimp over to her left to get a bit more personal. “But we all know that this chamber hasn’t really been acting that way for a long time. We’ve perfected the art of avoiding difficult issues to let someone else clean up the mess in the future. The financial sword of Damocles that nearly lanced us last week is a direct result of our unwillingness to face our challenges head-on. We came within one vote of pushing our country into default and financial chaos. The implications of that action are as dangerous and damaging as they are obvious. How could we have thought that was even an option?”

Tamika shifted her attention to the right half of the chamber, again limping across the face of the body as if she was talking to a jury.

“To be clear, this isn’t about Republicans or Democrats. We’ve all been party to this charade. One side wants to lower taxes while the other just wants to spend. The math of that equation does not work, especially when health-care costs, Medicare, Medicaid, Social Security, and a host of other topics are *off limits*. One side wants to build a wall, while the other isn’t capable of excluding anyone. We have members who are willing to say anything about anybody at any time. We have others who are so worried about political correctness that they won’t speak the truth. And nobody wants to stand up to the lobbyists and special interest groups that object whenever we try to make progress.”

She took a deep breath, gauging whether she should take the next step. She looked around the room and up to the gallery. Seeing her family reminded her why she was here. Why she put so much of herself into her work. This wasn’t just about patriotism—this was about the people she loved.

“And when the president of the United States incites an insurrection, conspires to obstruct the peaceful transfer of power, and pretends that the rules of law don’t apply to him, we sit on the sidelines and refuse to judge the behavior. There are some actions that require consequences, regardless of your political beliefs.”

Several senators got up as if to leave the chamber.

"Sit down and listen." She said it as a military command.

"I've served my country. I've paid the price. I've earned your attention. And I will get it." She was angry, and the time for niceties was over.

"Nobody in this senior chamber is without accountability, me included. Let's be clear and honest with each other. Enough is more than too much." She eased her way back to the center and faced the vice president.

"I've had enough of the social media pandering. Enough of the buckling under to special interests. Enough of the kicking the can down the road. Enough of the name-calling and incivility. Enough of the negative narratives. Enough of the finger-pointing and ducking accountability. Enough of the self-indulgence and self-interest. I've had more than enough.

"As leader of the Lincoln Coalition, I've met with most of you. You know where I stand. America is a great country, with boundless resources, incredible human capital, and an indomitable spirit. It's time we applied those assets to change our direction. We need to flip the script and prove to those who elected us, and indeed the rest of the world, that we can, in fact, govern."

She looked up into the gallery again. She saw the faces of her future.

"Our democracy has responded to every crisis and obstacle for almost two hundred fifty years. We're at another of those critical pivot points. And as we have before, we must come together to shape a new direction for the country. We must rise together like a phoenix from the ashes of our infamy. If not for our generation, then as a gift to those who will inherit our work."

One last step, she told herself.

"Ask yourselves the simple question I asked myself as I walked out onto that platform in the National Arboretum, knowing someone would shoot me.

"Ask yourself: How much would you give for someone you love?"

She didn't hear the applause. She didn't see those standing behind her recognizing her courage. She didn't acknowledge either the smiles or the scowls of her fellow senators. Instead, she thought of Winston Churchill and his belief that while this might not be the end or the beginning of the end, perhaps this was the end of the beginning.

But deep in her heart, she feared things might need to get worse before they got better.

ACKNOWLEDGMENTS

When I published my first novel, *The Wilkes Insurrection*, in November of 2021, there were several things I didn't fully understand. I had no idea how much time, effort, and commitment it would take to market and promote a book. I misunderstood the impact of the COVID pandemic on the bookselling process. And I didn't comprehend the energy required to go back to square one to continue the story, no matter how much I enjoy writing.

Thankfully, I also failed to appreciate how much I loved Tamika Smith and her journey. She was never intended to be the heroine in *The Wilkes Insurrection*, but as the writing progressed, it became clear that she was the centerpiece of the novel and of the book's underlying message. She's not modeled after any one person and consequently has her own story arc to explore. And I needed to act as her scribe and creative team. So in November of 2022, I set aside the marketing of *The Wilkes Insurrection* and turned the page to the next phase of Tamika's life, without having any idea where the adventure would take me.

The Blockchain Syndicate is certainly grounded in the challenging events and unprecedented circumstances facing our country today. The technology elements in the story are real, as are the basic government processes that rule Congress. In particular, the details surrounding Senate votes, the national debt data, and the budget dynamics at play are factual and very current. With all of that said, the characters and scenes in the story are of my own invention and any similarities or likenesses to actual people or events are purely coincidental.

My wife, Pauline, and I celebrated our fortieth anniversary this year, and she has remained supportive and steadfast through all my business, civic, and literary efforts. Her love for her homeland inspired me to explore the Netherlands in more detail, including the final scene on Texel. Likewise, my children have provided important feedback throughout the writing process and challenged me to think about aspects of the story and characters that I could easily have missed. I'm so proud of our family, which has added a son-in-law and two grandchildren since my last novel. The Bach family is at the heart of my support group, and I'm exceptionally grateful for their love.

One of my goals when I begin a new manuscript is to challenge myself to explore areas where I have great curiosity but little personal knowledge. In doing that, I endeavor to be as accurate as possible in my writing, and consequently, have consulted a number of people to provide background information, personal insights, and factual data in the many areas where I have less expertise. Before I thank them, I should make it clear that any remaining errors are of my own making or involve some amount of literary license.

I lived in San Mateo when I was very young, and while I don't remember much from that time, my siblings went to middle school and high school there. When I was envisioning the shooting at Aragon High School, I turned to Assistant Chief (Retired) Patrick Arpin of the Bellevue, Washington, police department for the proper active shooter protocols. He reviewed manuscript drafts and corrected many inaccuracies and misconceptions I had about police response procedures. His attention to detail and thoughtful commentary was much appreciated.

The DAO concept began with an informative discussion I had with James Seely, a family friend who worked for a company in that sector. Chris Williams did the heavy lifting, helping me create an experimental DAO, including all the related crypto and blockchain appendages. He was incredibly patient, recorded the entire process so I could play it back as I wrote, and even loaned me a bit of Ethereum currency to start the work. Pete Higgins, Mat Mathews, Moshe Lichtman, and Will Poole also volunteered their services for this effort. I'm fortunate to have such good friends who love and understand technology.

While I travel extensively and worked for a summer at Pan American Airlines, my practical knowledge of flying is very limited. The original draft of Bryce Roscovitch's tracking of the private jet flight to the Netherlands was hopelessly inaccurate. Thankfully, Moshe Lichtman and José Tomás Andreu Cooper, with military, private, and commercial flying experience, provided extensive information on ATC procedures, radar tracking, and emergency response protocols. The resulting scene may still have a bit of author's prerogative, but their information was invaluable.

I've served on the board of directors at the Bipartisan Policy Center since 2016. It is an incredible organization focused on practical policy solutions to complex issues, including the difficult financial challenges our country faces. Bill Hoagland and Michael Thorning, experts on fiscal and economic policy and the workings of Congress, provided excellent feedback on specific, technical issues as well as the atmosphere and operations of the Senate. They patiently answered my detailed (and often hypothetical) questions and brought a level of authenticity to the scenes. They also introduced me to Audrey, who gave me an incredible personal tour of the Senate and clarified various aspects of the somewhat arcane voting process on specific pieces of legislation. Tamika Smith would love to meet and thank all three of them.

While I visit the Netherlands for almost a month every year and can speak a bit of Dutch, I needed significant assistance from some native Nederlanders. Rik van der Kooi and Paul Pruijmboom were very generous with their feedback on Dutch history, language and grammar, and local customs. Rik grew up on the island of Texel, so his local knowledge was especially useful. He also speaks Russian, which informed some of Nastya Andropov's occasional lapses into her native tongue. I hope their passion for the Netherlands shines through.

As a writer, it's never easy to evaluate your own work. I'm fortunate to have many friends who are either writers themselves or voracious readers, and they provided significant feedback (and encouragement) as they reviewed various working drafts. My heartfelt thanks to Justina Chen, Kim Seely, Kalen Holmes, and Alex Mazer for their effort and honesty. I also want to thank Paul Schmidt who helped with some important details and Leslie Higgins for making me look good in photos. Appreciation also goes out to many of my friends who unwittingly supplied first or last names for some of my characters.

This is my second time working with Greenleaf Publishing, and I continue to be impressed with their high-quality team and their focus on producing a polished, successful novel. My great thanks to Justin, Erin, Brian, Anne, Pam, Dayna, Adrian, and the rest of the team for their dedication, feedback, and support on my behalf. And with gratitude to Matt Brown and Fauzia Burke for their guidance, creativity, and commitment to promote *The Blockchain Syndicate* to the only audience that matters—my readers.

Each of my books has a song soundtrack that embodies the plot, characters, and ideas in the novel. I develop my most creative ideas and write my best scenes when I'm listening to music. Most of the time, I'm a straight pop fan with Ed Sheeran, Taylor Swift, OneRepublic, Train, and Rachel Platten at the top of my playlist, but I throw in some John Mellencamp, Eagles, and Simon & Garfunkel just to prove I'm old. If you are interested in playlists for the novels and main characters, you can find them at www.theblockchainsyndicate.com. I will just say, "Long Live."

The Blockchain Syndicate is first and foremost a techno-thriller, and I hope Tamika's journey kept readers on the edge of their seats. Plot twists, interesting characters, dramatic venues, and unexpected outcomes are all part of the craft. But I've always intended my writing to carry a deeper message. Leaving aside the question of political affiliation (and I don't feel like I have a natural home anymore), I am gravely concerned about the direction of our great nation. The leadership vacuum, both at a policy and at a morality level, is frightening and creates significant risks for all of us.

As someone who cares deeply about our country and our communities, we need Tamika Smith and the Lincoln Coalition now more than ever.

My best,
—Robbie Bach
Medina, Washington

ABOUT THE AUTHOR

ROBBIE BACH joined Microsoft in 1988. Over the next twenty-two years, he worked in various marketing, general management, and business leadership roles, including supporting the successful launch and expansion of Microsoft Office. As Chief Xbox Officer, he led the creation and development of the Xbox business, including the launch of the Xbox and the highly popular successor product, Xbox 360. He retired from Microsoft as the president of the Entertainment and Devices Division in 2010.

In his new role as a civic engineer, Robbie works with corporate, philanthropic, and civic organizations who are driving positive change in our communities. He guest lectures extensively at a variety of colleges and universities and speaks to corporate, civic, and trade association audiences across the country. In 2015, he published his first book, *Xbox Revisited: A Game Plan for Corporate and Civic Renewal*. His debut novel featuring Tamika Smith, *The Wilkes Insurrection*, was published in 2021.

He is the previous past chairman and current board member at the Bipartisan Policy Center. He serves on the national board of governors for Boys and Girls Clubs of America and was the chairman of that board from 2009 to 2011. He is also a board member for Habitat for Humanity International and Genius Sports. He previously served as a board member of the United States Olympic Committee, Sonos Inc., Brooks Running Company, the Space Needle Inc., Magic Leap, and Year Up Puget Sound. He is the co-owner of Manini's Inc., a gluten-free food company.

He was an Arjay Miller Scholar at the Stanford Graduate School of Business, where he earned his MBA, and a Morehead Scholar at the University of North Carolina, where he earned his degree in economics and was also named an Academic All-American on the Tar Heels' tennis team.

He and his wife, Pauline, reside in Medina, Washington, with their yellow lab, Roscoe. They have three grown children and two grandchildren.

ON SOCIAL MEDIA:

LinkedIn: robbiebach
Instagram: @robbiejbach
Facebook: @robbiebach61
X: @Robbie_Bach
For more information, go to www.robbiebach.com

Grateful acknowledgment is made to the following sources for permission to reproduce copyrighted materials.

THE CLIMB

Words and Music by JESSI ALEXANDER and JON MABE

© 2008 HOPELESS ROSE MUSIC (ASCAP)

All rights on behalf of HOPELESS ROSE MUSIC administered by WC MUSIC CORP.

All Rights Reserved Used by Permission of ALFRED MUSIC

JACK AND DIANE

Words and Music by John Mellencamp

Copyright © 1982 Belmont Mall Publishing

All Rights Administered by Sony Music Publishing (US) LLC, 424 Church Street, Suite 1200, Nashville, TN 37219

International Copyright Secured All Rights Reserved

Reprinted by Permission of Hal Leonard LLC

THE CLIMB

from HANNAH MONTANA: THE MOVIE

Words and Music by Jon Mabe and Jessi Alexander

Copyright © 2009 Music Of Stage Three, Mabe It Big, Vistaville Music and Hopeless Rose Music

All Rights for Music Of Stage Three and Mabe It Big Administered by BMG Rights Management (US) LLC

All Rights for Hopeless Rose Music Administered by WC Music Corp

All Rights Reserved Used by Permission

Reprinted by Permission of Hal Leonard LLC

FOR WHAT IT'S WORTH

Words and Music by Stephen Stills

Copyright © 1966 ICONIC STILLS SONGS

Copyright Renewed

All Rights Administered by UNIVERSAL MUSIC WORKS

All Rights Reserved Used by Permission

Reprinted by Permission of Hal Leonard LLC

DAYLIGHT

Words and Music by Dave Bassett, Brent Smith, Eric Bass and Zach Myers